The Road into the Open

The Road into the Open

(Der Weg ins Freie)

Arthur Schnitzler

Translated by Roger Byers

Introduction by Russell A. Berman

UNIVERSITY OF CALIFORNIA PRESS
Berkeley · Los Angeles · Oxford

The publisher gratefully acknowledges the contribution provided by the Literature in Translation endowment, which is supported by a generous grant from Joan Palevsky.

University of California Press
Berkeley and Los Angeles, California

University of California Press
Oxford, England

Library of Congress Cataloging-in-Publication Data

Schnitzler, Arthur, 1862–1931.
    [Weg ins Freie. English]
    The road into the open / Arthur Schnitzler; translated by Roger Byers; introduction by Russell A. Berman.
        p.   cm.
    Translation of: Der Weg ins Freie.
    ISBN 0–520–07575–7 (cloth); 0–520–07774–1 (paper)
    I. Title
PT2638.N5W413   1992
833'.8—dc20   91–31559
                                                                     CIP

Printed in the United States of America

1   2   3   4   5   6   7   8   9

Translator's Preface

When I first picked up the German edition of this novel, I did not do so with the intent of translating it. But from the first page I found myself reading and rereading individual sentences with the same pleasure with which one listens to a finely crafted and expressive melody, and I became intrigued with the challenge of recreating this verbal art in my own native language. It was the music in Schnitzler that captured me. I have, therefore, tried to preserve the style of the original, and I have made little attempt to modernize or streamline the German, except where necessary to keep a comparable degree of naturalness.

I soon realized that to create an English rendering that sounded the same as the original meant two things. First, I wanted to preserve the *literal sound* as much as possible: to reproduce a similar rhythm, lyricism, or percussiveness; to begin and end sentences with the same up- or down-beat structure; and to maintain a comparable degree of melodic momentum. This involved reading the German and then the English versions aloud many times to achieve a satisfactory consonance. Second, I wanted to convey the naturalness (or perhaps deliberate awkwardness) of the original. This occasionally involved trade-offs. German sentence structure, given the advantage of grammatical gender (among other things), seems to support a somewhat higher degree of complexity than is natural in English, especially in narrative passages, so sentences can become quite long. In most cases I have preserved this structure and hope the reader will be glad to have as faithful a rendering as possible. I only compromised to avoid creating an awkwardness in English that did not exist in the German.

I wish to offer my heartfelt thanks to the people who helped me in the long process of producing this translation.

First, let me thank my friend and colleague, Frau Marianne Paape Hoffman, who generously devoted countless hours proofing my original draft and coaching me in the use of German colloquialisms. Without her efforts, this translation would have been impossible for me.

Next, I wish to thank Mr. Richard Heier for reading the revised pages and correcting the remaining errors, as well as for offering his many valuable insights into German literature and geography.

Finally, I want to thank my dear wife Elaine, who provided invaluable support and encouragement, forced me to make those last, long-postponed decisions, and tirelessly proofed the many revisions and the final translation.

R.E.B.

Introduction

The Road into the Open

RUSSELL A. BERMAN

Arthur Schnitzler called *The Road into the Open* his "most personal" work; it is, to be sure, also his most political one, and it is precisely this unexpected combination that makes the text such a compelling and vexing document of turn-of-the-century Vienna. It is a personal novel not only in the sense that many of the fictional figures are modeled closely on various acquaintances of Schnitzler's or that, for example, both Georg von Wergenthin and Heinrich Bermann are caught up in love affairs reminiscent of Schnitzler's own biographical experiences. It is, rather, a highly personal novel in its focus on the private, emotional life of the central figure, Georg, whose perspective dominates most of the descriptions and whose smallest shifts in mood can redirect the stream of consciousness of the narration. Yet this emphasis on Georg's private world is not at all a sort of psychological escapism. On the contrary, Georg, an outsider in a society of outsiders—he is the Christian aristocrat who socializes largely with upper middle-class Jews against the backdrop of rising anti-Semitism—functions as the vehicle for Schnitzler to unfold a sweeping description of the crisis of the middle classes and, especially, the assimilationist Jewry of Hapsburg Vienna. The personal (Georg's privacy) and the political (the social panorama) are, if not identical, then at the very least, backed up against each other, pushing on each other, transforming each other, and it is precisely this tense coexistence of psyche and society, private desire and social change, that epitomizes the Vienna of Schnitzler's time.

The Personal and the Political: if we take the first term to point toward the psychoanalysis of Sigmund Freud and the latter as an indication of modern mass movements like the Austro-Marxist socialism of Viktor Adler, then the unique complexity of *The Road into the Open* is an indication of the specific cultural-historical moment of turn-of-the-century Vienna. Not only were psychoanalysis and socialism contemporaries in Vienna, Freud and Adler knew each other (Freud took over

the apartment in the Berggasse from Adler who lived there before him).
The point is, of course, not to suggest that psychoanalysis and socialism
are identical or even compatible. Many proponents of each rejected the
other adamantly—for socialists, psychoanalysis could appear to be es-
capist, ignoring objective, social ills while focusing on merely personal
experience; for psychoanalysts, socialism could seem embarrassingly
naive, ignoring deep instinctual or unconscious desires of much greater
significance than the superficially rational behavior of economic actors.
The two conflicting paradigms meet however in the suggestion that individual consciousness is always undercut by some more profound
structure: economic organization (for socialism) or the unconscious (for
psychoanalysis). Both, therefore, might be treated as expressions of a
dissatisfaction with the sort of liberal individualism that had prevailed
in Europe through the 1870s and that had implied that individual happiness and social progress might be achieved simultaneously through a
process of capitalist modernization. By the end of the century, after the
stockmarket crash of 1873, decades of economic depression, and the
increasingly obvious social difficulties associated with industrialization,
liberal optimism lost ground to various more pessimistic theories and
ideologies.

   The Road into the Open does not ask us to choose sides between
psychoanalysis and socialism, between private desire and social transformation. The novel does, however, in its formal composition, display
the coexistence of the two agendas and the improbability of their con-
fluence. While it is Georg who guides the reader through most of the
text, he is himself split into a private and a public persona, almost as
if the text combined two fully distinct narratives, linked arbitrarily and
unconvincingly through the single figure: on the one hand, the story of
Georg in love with Anna Rosner and struggling with his identity as a
composer, and, on the other, the story of Georg observing the world
of Jewish Vienna, the wealthy industrialists, the intellectual elite, the
political activists. The novel is perhaps so perplexing because it never
lets us fully determine which material is central and which is merely
background—private desire or public life—on the contrary, the perspective constantly shifts, neither realm is entirely stable, each contami-
nates the other. Political anxieties regarding the rise of anti-Semitism
and, as the Jewish response, Zionism, reach into the private rumina-
tions, just as private wishes distort the public debate.

   Literary critics have sometimes regarded this ambiguity as a failing
of Schnitzler, unable to decide what sort of novel he intended to write:

a Bildungsroman (or novel of development) in which Georg's growth from a still immature and youthful stage toward an adult command of his destiny might be traced or, alternatively, a novel of society, a description of many interconnected figures, engrossed in the politics and passions of their time. *The Road into the Open* certainly plays with conventions inherited from the traditions of both sorts of narratives; yet it sets these distinct conventions in a new relationship to each other and thereby becomes a penetrating investigation into turn-of-the-century Viennese culture, a seismographic register of deep-seated conflicts and contradictions.

Attempting to read it as a novel of development—measuring it against, say, *David Copperfield* or, in the German tradition, Goethe's *Wilhelm Meister*—one is quickly disappointed to learn that very little development actually ensues. Georg is not much farther along at the end of the book than he was at the beginning and, despite all the hopes and aspirations, little new has occurred, and nothing is likely to change (this lack of creativity is symbolized most powerfully by the stillborn child). A novel of development without development: it is also, however, a novel of society without social interconnectedness. Neither does a shared historical experience hold the many fictional figures together (as do, for example, the Napoleonic Wars in *War and Peace*) nor does even the shared location in the same city afford an illusion of cohesion. Unlike Dickens's novels of London or Balzac's of Paris, *The Road into the Open* is less a novel of Vienna, the metropolis, than an account of the collapse of the metropolis, where centrifugal forces catapult the Zionists to Palestine, the nationalists to Germany, and everyone onto excursions. Hence the remarkable constellation of generic conventions in the work: the Bildungsroman material, which one would normally expect to entail change and growth, turns out to be the locus of permanence and a nearly deadening stability, while the social description encompasses explosion rather than cohesion. Only a figure as immobile as Georg could record the mercurial evanescence of his environment (although his own immobility is disastrous for his artistic aspirations). Conversely, the overheated illusions regarding social change—socialist, zionist, or anti-Semitic—all seem to be ultimately compatible with a deep-seated cynicism that nothing will ever really change at all. Radicalism and pessimism, extremism and desperation: opposite positions that end up agreeing that no road into the open is likely to lead anywhere at all. Meanwhile everything continues to collapse and nothing really happens, as Privy Councillor Wilt remarks to Georg: "one sometimes has a dark foreboding that in Austria nothing in the slightest would change, even if one didn't go to one's office for a whole year" (141).

If it is the precise form of the conflict between the private and the public, the subjective and the objective material that makes *The Road into the Open* characteristic of fin-de-siècle Vienna, it is important to scrutinize each aspect, for each is representative of elements of modern culture as crucial at the end of the twentieth century as they were at the beginning. One road into the open leads inwardly, into the psychoanalytic realms of desire, dream, and fantasy. It is perhaps surprising that Schnitzler and his Viennese contemporary Freud had next to nothing to do with each other, despite their shared medical background and their shared literary interests. Eventually Freud would concede that Schnitzler had apparently discovered through literature what he, Freud, had attempted to prove through scientific observation: the fundamental tenets of psychoanalysis. Indeed various features of *The Road into the Open* seem to testify to the validity of central categories of Freudian theory, such as the importance of Georg's dream in the seventh chapter or, more generally, the desultory, day-dreamlike organization of the course of the narrative. Instead of attempting to pursue a clear agenda in an organized fashion, Georg drifts, from encounter to encounter, from thought to thought; whatever it is that is directing his path, it is not always the conscious intention of his ego but, rather, an underlying unconscious beyond the control of his purposive will.

Schnitzler's recognition of the importance of depth psychology beneath the surface of rational consciousness gives his writing its characteristically rich and subtle ability to describe complex human behavior. Yet the psychological wealth of the writing is, strangely perhaps, an indication of a certain weakness of the fictional personalities themselves. For these are figures whose rational identities are so overpowered by unarticulated wishes that they are stymied and prevented from making choices or actively pursuing their own plans. The nearly universal immobility of the figures—no one can make decisions, no one can act definitively—is the psychological corollary to the decline of liberal individualism: the richer interior life of the Viennese fin-de-siècle corresponds to a decline in external activity. Georg is, so to speak, highly sensitive and for just that reason incapacitated, so that the title of the novel tends to take on an oxymoronic character—the more open the realm of psychic interiority has become, the less likely anyone is to set

out on any road, although everyone speaks constantly, and neuroti-
cally, about grandiose schemes. This specifically postliberal personality
form is, furthermore, historicized by the novel through the generational
contrast of fathers and sons, an additional connection to the central
categories of psychoanalysis.

Psychoanalysis is nothing if not a theory of generational conflict.
Freud's first major work, *The Interpretation of Dreams,* was written
soon after the death of his father, and central passages, in which Freud
analyzes his own dreams, involve the ambivalence of love and hate that
children feel toward their parents. It is there too that Freud first presents
the paradigm that became central to his theory and, especially, to psychoanalytic literary criticism: the Oedipus complex. The son who loves
his mother becomes the rival of his father and is forced to challenge
paternal authority. In order for the child to assert its own identity, it
must come into conflict with the restrictiveness of the older generation,
and a struggle ensues which is the only viable path into the open of
freedom, knowledge, and desire. Yet even the most successful outcome
will always be bitter, since the relationship to the parent was certainly
always mixed: overcoming the father—or, in the terms of the oedipal
narrative, killing the father—calls for mourning as much as it does for
celebration.

Freud's invocation of the Oedipus material has often been misun-
derstood as a suggestion that a fundamental pattern is inescapable and
must always be repeated. Such a distortion misses the extremely subtle
and variegated analytic potential in psychoanalysis, which employs the
hypothesis of the oedipal complex as a flexible description in many per-
mutations and not as a rigid directive. Indeed Freud himself juxtaposes
his reading of Sophocles' *Oedipus* with a literary-critical commentary
on *Hamlet.* In both cases, psychoanalysis recognizes shared material:
intergenerational tension, the death of the father, the desire for the
mother, the son wavering between pride and remorse. Yet how very different the two outcomes! Oedipus truly does carry out the deed, no matter how unknowingly, while Hamlet cannot act. Freud takes issue with
commentators, like Goethe, who attribute Hamlet's passivity to his excessively reflective personality. Instead Freud insists that Hamlet's inability to avenge his father's death betrays a deeper emotional complexity, a reluctance to punish the culprit for a crime he himself would have
liked to carry out. It is then again the oedipal scenario, but in a more
modern—and more repressive—setting where basic instinctual desires

for parricide and incest are less likely to be carried out, but precisely therefore all the more likely to influence personality structures and social relations.

Many of the personalities and relations in *The Road into the Open* depend on the conflicts, repressed or open, between fathers and sons. The problem is announced at the outset:

> Involuntarily [Georg's] gaze came to rest on the empty armchair at the upper end of the table over which the September sun flowed in through the open middle window; and it seemed to him as though he could have seen his father, who had been dead for two months, sitting there only an hour ago, so clearly did even the smallest gesture of the departed stand before his eyes, from his way of pushing back his coffee cup, or putting on his glasses, to leafing through a brochure. (3)

As in Freud's *Interpretation of Dreams,* Schnitzler's novel explores the death of the father; as in *Hamlet,* the ghost—or memory—of the father beckons to the central figure and challenges him to overcome his lassitude, his lack of will, his inactivity. Thus Georg recalls his own earlier failures, in love and art, his refusal to make choices, his reluctance even to write down the melodies he had composed.

> He had played the theme for his father, in a fantasy of such excessive harmonic richness that the simple melody was almost engulfed; and as he began a new wildly modulating variation, his father had asked, smiling from the other end of the grand piano: "Where, where?" Georg, as if embarrassed, let the flood of tones die away, and then, warmly as always, but not in so light a tone as before, the father started a conversation with the son about his future, a matter which had in fact been on Georg's mind that day and become heavy with presentiment. (4)

Whether Georg has a future, as a lover, a father, or an artist, is one of the questions the novel explores, an exemplary inquiry into the vicissitudes of the fin-de-siècle generation, eager to set out in new and unconventional directions but hampered by an epigonic sense of inadequacy, an inability to meet the standards set by the fathers.

The problem pervades the novel, but the solutions vary widely. Felician chooses a very different path than does his brother Georg, just as the other sons, facing similar paternal challenges, opt for individual solutions: Dr. Stauber, Heinrich Bermann, and, especially interesting, Oskar Ehrenberg. For the conflict within the Ehrenberg household links the psychological material to the social thematics of the novel. Father Ehrenberg, the industrial magnate, insists on flaunting his Jewish background and loyalties, to the chagrin of his social-climbing family, especially his son, who is eager to imitate the feudal charades of the Catholic aristocracy. Read as social document, the case presents the Jewish variant of the conflict between an older generation with its virtues of liberalism, industriousness and productivity and a younger generation of consumption, status, and conservatism. Read more complexly as a commentary on the origins of anti-Semitism—the son's distaste for his father's Jewishness—the case anticipates an insight of psychoanalysis (especially from Freud's late work, *Moses and Monotheism*): that anti-Semitism is itself a version of Oedipus, the hatred by the adherents of the religion of the son for the proponents of the religion of the father. *The Road into the Open* therefore explores the oedipal conflict, both as a shared experience of the modernist generation of 1900 and as a central feature in the relationship between Christianity and Judaism. In this light, Georg's reflection at Anna's bed begins to sound like a prayer for reconciliation:

> And it occurred to him: just as Anna is lying today, so my own mother was lying before I was born. Did my father walk around worried like this? What if he were here today, if he were still alive? Would I have told him all about it? Would all this have happened if he were still alive? (220)

If *The Road into the Open* offers little reconciliation, it does undertake the attempt to represent the totality of Viennese society that is rapidly collapsing, like the Austro-Hungarian Empire in general, into a collection of fragmented and antagonistic classes, parties, and ethnic groups. The three focal points are the Ehrenberg salon of the haute-bourgeoisie, where the economically most successful segment of the Jewish population tries to assimilate into the hegemonic Catholicism of the Empire by jettisoning as much as possible of its own heritage; the world of writers and intellectuals—which Schnitzler knew best—where a heady critical intelligence appeared to offer a different road to assimilation; and the more conservative middle-class setting of the Rosner's, shading into the political anti-Semitism of the younger generation. Of course, major segments of society are excluded from this description; the power center of the court is not treated, nor are the lower classes. Yet the focus on the upper middle class is legitimate insofar as the novel's central agenda entails an exploration of the demise of political liberalism. As elsewhere in Europe, liberalism in Austria was most viable in the early part of the second half of the century. Its program, deeply indebted to elements of the eighteenth-century enlightenment, called for a rationalization of politics, economy, and culture (i.e., civic equality, capitalism, and religious tolerance) in order to break down the entrenched privileges of the aristocracy and to bring Austria into the modern world. Yet Austrian liberalism had a peculiar history as well, if measured against similar developments in other countries. For mid-century liberalism, for example in Germany, tended to be compatible with nationalism and calls for national unification (which were implicitly opposed to the particularist basis of aristocratic power), while in Austria the liberal agenda for modernization always quickly came into conflict with the competing nationalisms of the various ethnic components of the multinational Empire.

This conflict was especially tragic for the liberalism of the German-speaking Austrians. In 1848 they looked forward to unification with Germany on modern, democratic terms. The defeat of the revolution and, subsequently, the conservative form that German unification took under Bismarck's leadership—the exclusion of the ethnic German provinces of Austria from the new German state—dashed those hopes. After the crisis of 1873, the German nationalist undercurrent returned to haunt Austrian liberalism and tear it apart: nationalism—once a vision of a citizenry of equals united against feudal privilege—took on a racial and religiously intolerant character and became the underpinning of political anti-Semitism. The erstwhile call for equal rights turned into an animosity to the Jews as the group that represented difference. Theodor Adorno and Max Horkheimer later described this sort of inversion as a "dialectic of enlightenment," a slide from a principled tolerance, to an assertion of equality, into a hostility to any real assertion of concrete difference. Certainly, one of the most prominent points of comparison between turn-of-the-century Austria and the contemporary United States has to do with the urgency of understanding the status of minority groups within multicultural societies.

Liberalism buckled under another pressure as well, the rise of a working-class movement that resisted the capitalist organization of economic modernization and which, by the end of the century, had largely adopted moderately Marxist positions. This Social Democracy insisted on its loyalty to central aspects of liberalism—the goal of a modern, rational society—but it played out the program for civic equality (universal suffrage and equal treatment by the law) against the unequal structure of capitalist relations. Consequently, both nationalism on the right and Social Democracy on the left forced liberalism to retreat into an increasing elitism that ran absolutely counter to its own universalist ideology. Meanwhile, the social democrats could attack both the liberals and the nationalists as defenders of the capitalist order, with all of its attending social ills, and the nationalists eagerly mobilized anti-Semitism to denounce liberals and socialists alike in nativist terms. The attack on the minority group served to deflect attention away from structural issues and toward a vulnerable scapegoat.

The Road into the Open explores Austrian political culture in the wake of liberalism: the socialism of Therese Golowski, the political anti-Semitism of Josef Rosner, the Zionism of numerous Jewish figures. While the novel describes each of these positions, it is less concerned with a precise and extensive elaboration of each ideology than with a suggestion of their interrelation—each road into the open is blocked by another—and with their historical situation between the liberalism of the fathers that once, long ago, seemed credible and the aestheticism of the new generation. Consider Georg's report of Heinrich Bermann's account of his father's political career:

> Georg found the tone of mixed tenderness and animosity, feelings of attachment and alienation in which Heinrich spoke of his family, especially of his sick father, who had been an attorney in that little town, and a long time deputy of Parliament, strange and sometimes almost painful. Yes, he even seemed to be a little proud that as a twenty-year-old, he had already predicted the destiny of his all-too-trusting father exactly as it would later be fulfilled: after a brief period of popularity and success, the growth of the anti-Semitic movement had driven him out of the German Liberal Party, most of his friends had abandoned and betrayed him, and a dissolute art student, who portrayed the associations of Czechs and Jews as the most dangerous enemies of German culture and breeding, who beat his wife at home, and got his maids pregnant, had been his successor in the trust of the electorate and in Parliament. Heinrich, grated by his father's phrases of Germanity, Freedom, and Progress, in all their reverence, had greeted the downfall of the old man initially with malicious glee; gradually though, as the once sought-after attorney also began to lose his clients, and the material situation of the family declined day by day, there emerged in the son a belated sympathy. He had abandoned his legal studies early enough, and was forced to come to the aid of his family through regular journalistic work. His first artistic successes met with no further response in the darkened house of his homeland. (69–70)

Here again the two components of the novel, the personal and the political, the generation conflict and the collapse of liberalism, are brought together. Bermann senior's fate is symptomatic of the tidal change on the Austrian political landscape. Once upon a time, in a fairy-tale world where liberalism was still convincing, the Jewish lawyer and politician could assert a loyalty to "Germanity" and assume that it was identical with "Freedom and Progress." Now, however, the era of liberal nationalism has come to an irrevocable conclusion, "freedom"—in the mouths of nationalist politicians—only means freedom from minorities, and "progress" has been occupied by socialism. This transformation is viewed, moreover, through the eyes of the son, with all the affective ambiguity of his relationship to the father. The point however is that precisely here, for Heinrich Bermann, another option begins to open up, neither psychoanalysis nor politics, neither personal escapism nor political radicalism: the world of literature and art. If the aesthetic culture of turn-of-the-century Austria is rarely political—the art is not tendentious or driven largely by social engagement—the very fact that aestheticism flourished so voluptuously is itself symptomatic of the political crisis. In other words: the father's failure in liberal politics is the precondition of the son's adamance as a writer.

Is art the only viable road into the open? Or is it an escape from the exigencies of reality, perhaps precisely the sort of escape that became endemic in fin-de-siècle Vienna? The text provides no conclusive answer, although one can certainly point to one work of art, *The Road into the Open* itself, as evidence of Schnitzler's effort to overcome the ruptures between private and public life. Furthermore, the novel describes how the younger generation opts for art, as an alternative to the disappointments their elders had encountered in politics. Perhaps however it makes less sense to ask whether the aesthetic path is necessarily an improvement than to note that problems similar to those in contemporary society and politics return within the work of art. Georg's inability to concentrate, his reluctance to grow up, are mirrored in his lack of compositional control and the constant threat of dilettantism. In a society that is disintegrating, aesthetic culture is, at best, fragmentary and dissatisfying, and—this may be Schnitzler's verdict—if art is the only remaining path, it is hardly an easy one. It is, on the contrary, extremely difficult, especially for modern art which attempts to thrive in a context where the conventions of the past have ceased to be binding, where qualitatively new forms are needed, but an effective source of inspiration and innovation is lacking. The old no longer holds; the new is not yet apparent; or one has to struggle to invent the new oneself. That would mean living without authorities and without guarantees, with the likelihood of error but with the greater potential of freedom. These insights that Schnitzler gives us into the Viennese culture of his day are insights into the fundamental structures of modern culture, which is why fin-de-siècle Vienna and its most penetrating commentary, *The Road into the Open*, retain their relevance for us today.

The Road into the Open

First Chapter

Georg von Wergenthin sat all alone at the table today. Felician, his older brother, had preferred, after a long time, to dine once again with friends. But Georg still felt no particular inclination to again see Ralph Skelton, Count Schoenstein, or any of the other young people with whom he was otherwise glad to chat; for the moment, he still wasn't feeling sociable.

The servant cleaned up and vanished. Georg lit a cigarette and walked, as was his custom, back and forth in the large, three-windowed, and somewhat low-ceilinged room wondering how this space, which for many weeks had seemed to him as if darkened by a cloud, had gradually begun to regain its former friendly appearance. Involuntarily his gaze came to rest on the empty armchair at the upper end of the table over which the September sun flowed in through the open middle window; and it seemed to him as though he could have seen his father, who had been dead for two months, sitting there only an hour ago, so clearly did even the smallest gesture of the departed stand before his eyes, from his way of pushing back his coffee cup, or putting on his glasses, to leafing through a brochure.

Georg thought of one of his last conversations with his father, which had taken place in late spring shortly before the move to the villa on the Veldeser See. Georg had just returned from Sicily where he had spent April with Grace, on a melancholy and somewhat boring farewell journey before the final return of the beloved to America. He had not really worked again for a half year or longer; not even the melancholy Adagio that he had heard in the roaring of the waves on an agitated morning in Palermo as he walked along the shore had been written down. He had played the theme for his father, in a fantasy of such excessive harmonic richness that the simple melody was almost engulfed; and as he began a new wildly modulating variation, his father had asked, smiling from the other end of the grand piano: "Where, where?" Georg, as if embarrassed, let the flood of tones die away, and then, warmly as always, but not in so light a tone as before, the father started a conversation with the son about his future, a matter which had in fact been on Georg's mind that day and become heavy with presentiment.

He stood at the window and looked out. Outside, the park was rather empty. On a bench sat an old woman wearing an outmoded coat with black glass pearls. A governess walked by, a little boy on her hand, and another person, much smaller and in a hussar's uniform, with his sabre buckled on and a pistol at his side, walked ahead, looked proudly around himself, and saluted an invalid who came down the path smoking. Deeper in the garden, around the kiosk, a few people sat drinking coffee and reading newspapers. The foliage was still rather thick, and the park seemed oppressed, dusty, and on the whole more summer-like than usual in late September. Georg braced his arms on the window sill, bent forward, and contemplated the sky. Since the death of his father he had not left Vienna, despite many opportunities that had been open to him. He could have gone with Felician to the Schoenstein estate; Frau Ehrenberg had invited him to the Auhof[1] in a kindly letter; and he could easily have found a companion for the bicycle tour through Carinthia and the Tyrol that he had planned for a long time but could not decide on alone. But he preferred to stay in Vienna, and passed the time leafing through and ordering old family papers. He found remembrances going back to his great-grandfather Anastasius von Wergenthin, who had come from the Rhine region, and who had, through marriage with a certain Fraulein Recco, come into the possession of an old, long uninhabitable little castle near Bozen. There were also documents concerning Georg's grandfather, an artillery officer who had fallen at Chlum in 1866. His son, Felician and Georg's father, had devoted himself to scientific, primarily botanical, studies and had taken his doctorate at Innsbruck. At the age of twenty-four he met a young

1. The name of the Ehrenbergs' country estate.

lady from an old Austrian official family who had trained herself to be a singer, perhaps more to escape the narrow, almost poverty stricken condition of her house, than from any inner calling. Baron von Wergenthin saw and heard her for the first time in winter in a concert performance of the *Missa Solemnis*, and the following May she became his wife. In the second year of the marriage Felician was born, in the third, Georg. Three years later the baroness's health began to decline, and she was sent to the south by her doctors. As they awaited her recovery the household in Vienna was disbanded, and so it happened that the baron and his family came to live a sort of hotel- and wander-life. Though business and studies often took the baron to Vienna, the sons almost never left their mother. They lived in Sicily, in Rome, in Tunis, in Corfu, in Athens, in Malta, in Meran, on the Riviera, and finally in Florence; by no means extravagantly, but in accordance with their rank; and not economically enough to keep a good part of the baronial fortune from being gradually used up.

Georg was eighteen years old when his mother died. Nine years had passed since then, but undimmed was the memory of that spring evening when his father and brother were by chance not at home, and he had stood alone and helpless at the bed of his dying mother while the clamor and laughter of strollers poured in offensively loud with the air of spring through the hastily opened window.

The survivors took the body of the mother back to Vienna. The baron devoted himself to his studies with a new, almost desperate fervor. Whereas earlier he had been regarded only as a distinguished amateur, he now began to be taken seriously even in academic circles, and when he was elected honorary president of the Botanical Society, he had more to thank for this distinction than the accident of noble birth. Felician and Georg registered as auditors with the legal faculty. But it was the father himself who, after a time, gave his son the choice to quit his university studies and to give his musical inclinations more suitable development, an offer that was accepted with gratitude and relief. But perseverance even in this self-chosen field eluded him, and often for weeks he could fritter away his time with all sorts of things that lay in his path. It was also this frivolous tendency that set him leafing through those old family papers with such seriousness, as if they contained important mysteries from the past to be penetrated. He passed many hours pondering with emotion over letters that his parents had exchanged with one another in earlier years, over yearnings, fancies, melancholies, and consolations from which not only the departed them-

selves but also other half-forgotten people became newly vivid. The
German teacher with the sad, pale forehead, who was in the habit of
quoting Horace on their long walks together appeared to him again;
the brown, wild young face of Prince Alexander of Macedonia, in
whose company Georg had taken his first riding lessons in Rome
emerged; and in a dreamlike manner, as if drawn with black lines on
a pale blue horizon, the pyramid of Cestius[2] rose up, just as Georg
had seen it in the sunset, returning home from his first ride on the
Campagna. And as he continued dreaming there appeared seashores,
gardens, and streets, about which he hardly knew anything of the landscape or city from which his memory had preserved them. Forms floated
by, many perfectly clear, which he had known only once in moments
of indifference, while others, with which he must have spent many days
at a time, appeared shadowy and distant. As Georg brought his own
papers in order while sifting through those old letters, he found, in an
old green portfolio, musical sketches from his boyhood that, until their
rediscovery, had so completely vanished that one could without further
explanation have put them forward as the writings of someone else. By
some he was pleasantly but painfully surprised, for they appeared to
him to contain promises that he perhaps might never fulfill. And yet
he felt lately that something was preparing itself within him. He saw a
mysterious but sure line pointing from those first hopeful writings in
the green portfolio, to new inspirations. And this he knew: the two
songs from the *West-oestlichen Divan*[3] that he had composed this summer, on a humid evening while Felician lay in the hammock and his
father sat in a lounge chair on the cool terrace, could not have been
done by just anyone.

Georg stepped back from the window as though suddenly surprised
by a completely unexpected thought. He had never before realized with
such clarity that since the death of his father until now his existence
had been, as it were, interrupted. He had not thought during that whole
time of Anna Rosner, to whom he had sent those two songs in manuscript. And as it now occurred to him that he could hear her full dark
voice again, and could accompany her singing at that musty old piano
as soon as he wished, he was pleasantly stirred. And he remembered

2. An 88-foot-high pyramid of Carrara marble finished in 11 B.C. as the tomb of
Caius Cestius, a Praetor of the Roman Republic. It lies on the south leg of the Aurelian
Wall of Rome.
3. *West-eastern Collection,* by Goethe.

the old house on Paulanergasse,[4] the low gate and the badly lit path which until now he had walked only three or four times, like something dear and long familiar.

Outside in the park a gentle breeze was blowing through the leaves. Thin clouds appeared over the tower of St. Stephen's, which could be seen through the window, across the park and a considerable part of the city. A long afternoon, completely without obligations, stretched out before Georg. In the course of the last two months of mourning, it seemed that all his former relationships had weakened or broken. He thought of the past winter and spring, with their complex entanglements and confused motives, and a multitude of memories appeared vividly before him: the ride with Frau Marianne through the snow-covered forest in the closed *fiaker*;[5] the masquerade at the Ehrenbergs, with Else's pensive, childish remark about Hedda Gabler, to whom she felt related, and with Sissy's fleeting kiss under the black lace of her mask. A mountain tour in the snow from Edlach up to the Rax[6] with Count Schoenstein and Oskar Ehrenberg, who, without any innate Alpine inclinations, gladly seized the opportunity to accompany the two high-born gentlemen. The evening at Ronacher's with Grace and the young Labinski who shot himself four days later; one had never quite found out why—because of Grace, or debts, from boredom with life, or purely out of affectation. The peculiar coldly-glowing conversation with Grace at the cemetery in the melting February snow two days after Labinski's burial. The evening in the hot, high-vaulted fencing hall, where Felician's sword crossed the dangerous weapon of the Italian master. The late night walk after the Paderewski concert during which his father confided in him as never before about that distant evening when their departed mother had sung in the *Missa Solemnis* in that very hall from which they had just come. And finally Anna Rosner's tall, relaxed figure, leaning against the piano, the music in her hand, and her smiling blue eyes watching the keyboard; and he could even hear her voice ringing in his soul.

As he was standing at the window looking down at the park, which was gradually becoming more lively, he felt reassured by the fact that

4. *Gasse* is the word for the narrower, often quaintly winding streets in the older parts of the city; compound words such as "Paulanergasse" are proper names like Paulaner Street. *Strasse* is the more general word for "street."

5. The one-horse carriages still seen all around Vienna and often used as taxicabs or for sightseeing.

6. Rax Alpe, a picturesque mountain southwest of Vienna, elevation 6,584 feet.

he had no close relationship with a single human being, though there were many with whom he could pick up again, in whose circle he would be welcome, as soon as he wished. At the same time he felt wonderfully rested, prepared for work and happiness as never before. He was filled with lofty and bold intentions, and rejoiced in his youth and independence. Indeed, he felt a certain embarrassment that, at this moment at least, his sorrow over his departed father was much diminished; but he found a consolation within himself for this indifference as he thought of the painless end the dear man was granted. In the garden, walking up and down in animated conversation with his two sons, he suddenly looked around as if he heard distant voices, looked up into the sky, and fell dead on the grass, without a cry, without even a twitch of the lips.

Georg walked back into the room, got ready to go out, and left the house. He planned to spend a couple of hours walking around, wherever chance would take him, and in the evening finally to begin work again on his quintet, for which the right mood had finally come to him. He crossed the street and went into the park. The humidity had let up. As before, the old woman with the coat sat on the bench staring at the ground. Children played in the sandy ring around the trees. At the kiosk all seats were taken. In the pavilion sat a clean-shaven man whom Georg knew from sight, and who had caught his attention through his resemblance to the old Grillparzer. At the pond Georg encountered a governess with two beautifully dressed children who regarded him with bright eyes. As he came out of the park and onto the Ringstrasse,[7] he met Willy Eissler in a dark striped autumn coat who greeted him:

"Good afternoon, Baron. Back in Vienna again?"

"I've been back for a long time," Georg replied. "I haven't left Vienna since my father's funeral."

"Yes, yes, naturally. . . . Permit me to once again offer my . . ." and Willy squeezed Georg's hand.

"And what did you do with yourself this summer?" asked Georg.

"All sorts of things. Played tennis, painted, wasted time, spent a few amusing, but more boring, hours." Willy spoke extremely fast, with a deliberate light hoarseness, elegantly, with Hungarian, French, and Viennese Jewish accents. "By the way," he continued, "I've just come back this morning from Przemysl."[8]

7. The name of the wide boulevard that replaced the old city walls during Schnitzler's lifetime and now surrounds the old town with the most important government and cultural buildings.

8. A small city in the extreme southeast of present-day Poland, in Schnitzler's time the northeast of Austria-Hungary.

"Weapons practice?"

"Yes, the last, I'm sad to say. It's still been fun for me, even though I'm getting so much older, to walk around in the yellow lapels, spurs jingling, sabre clanking, a feeling of impending danger in the air, to be regarded as some higher noble by the lower ranks." They walked on along the grating of the Stadtpark.[9]

"Were you on your way to the Ehrenbergs?" asked Willy.

"No, I don't even think about going there."

"I just thought because it's on the way. By the way, have you heard that Fraulein Else is supposed to be engaged?"

"Really?" asked Georg slowly. "To whom?"

"Guess, Herr Baron."

"It must be Privy Councillor Wilt."

"Good grief!" cried Willy. "He'd never consider it. Ties to S. Ehrenberg could complicate his government career, nowadays."

"Captain Ladisc?" Georg continued.

"Ah, Fraulein Else is too smart to get tangled up with him."

Now Georg remembered that Willy had quarreled with Ladisc a couple of years ago. Willy felt Georg's gaze, twisted his blond, drooping, Polish-styled moustache with somewhat nervous fingers, and responded quickly and casually: "The fact that I once had differences with Captain Ladisc cannot keep me from observing that he's always been a drunken pig. I have an insurmountable revulsion, irredeemable even by blood, against people who associate with Jews when it's to their advantage, but who begin to revile them as soon as they're outside on the steps. One could at least wait until one got to the coffeehouse. But don't strain yourself further with your guessing; Heinrich Bermann's the lucky man."

"Not possible!" cried Georg.

"Why?" asked Willy. "In the end it has to be someone. Bermann is no Adonis, to be sure, but he's on his way to fame; and the mixture of master horseman and perfect athlete that Else's been dreaming of will be hard to find. She's twenty-four years old now, and has been more than sufficiently terrorized by Salomon's tactlessness and wit . . . so. . . ."

"Salomon? . . . oh yes . . . Ehrenberg."

"You know him only by the 'S'? . . . S. stands, naturally, for Salomon, and the simple S. on the plaque on the door is a concession he made to his family. If it was up to him, he'd rather appear at Madame

9. The name of Vienna's principal park.

Ehrenberg's social gatherings in his caftan and wearing that certain little curl." [10]

"Do you think? . . . Is he really that pious?"

"Pious . . . Good heavens! Piety has nothing to do with it. It's only malice, mainly against his son Oskar, with the feudal aspirations."

"Oh yes," said Georg smiling. "Isn't Oskar baptized? He's a reserve officer in the Dragoons."

"Oh, that. . . . Well, I'm not baptized either, but in spite of that . . . there are always a few exceptions . . . with good intentions. . . ." He laughed and went on: "As far as Oskar is concerned, he really would rather be Catholic. But the cost of the pleasure of going to confession would be, for the moment, a little too high to bear. It's been anticipated in the will that he mustn't convert."

They had arrived at the Cafe Imperial. Willy stopped. "I'm meeting Demeter Stanzides."

"Give him my greetings."

"Of course. But won't you come in and join us for an ice cream?"

"Thank you, but I think I'll stroll around a bit."

"You love the solitude?"

"Such a general question is hard to answer," replied Georg.

"To be sure," replied Willy, who became suddenly serious and lifted his hat. "It's been an honor, Herr Baron."

Georg extended his hand. He felt that Willy was a man who unremittingly defended a position even when there was no urgent necessity. "Good-bye," he said with sudden warmth. He found it almost strange, as he often had before, that Willy was Jewish. The older Eissler, Willy's father, composer of charming Viennese waltzes and songs, distinguished art and antique collector and sometime dealer, with his giant's physique, had been known in his time as the foremost boxer in Vienna, and with his long, full, grey beard and monocle, resembled more a Hungarian magnate than a Jewish patriarch. But talent, dilettantism, and an iron will had given Willy the affected image of a born cavalier. But what really distinguished him from other young people of his background and aspirations was the fact that he was content not to renounce his heritage, to pursue an explanation or reconciliation for every ambiguous smile, and in the face of pettiness or prejudice, by which he often appeared to be affected, to make light of it whenever possible.

10. The ear lock or *pais,* worn by highly religious Jews like the Hasidim in observance of the Biblical injunction against cutting the hair at the sides of the head or trimming the edges of the beard (Leviticus 19:27 and 21:5).

Georg continued walking. Willy's last question came back to him. Did he love solitude? . . . He remembered how in Palermo he spent whole mornings walking by himself, while Grace, in accordance with her own custom, lay in bed until noon. Grace. . . . Where might she be now? . . . Since they said farewell in Naples she had not been heard from, which, by the way, had been agreed on. He thought about that deep blue night that floated over the water as he went back to Genoa alone after their farewell, and about the strange, soft, fairy-tale-like song of two children clasping each other tightly, wrapped in a quilt beside their sleeping mother on the deck.

He continued walking with growing contentment among the people who passed by in Sunday lassitude. Many friendly feminine glances met his own, and appeared to wish to console him for being alone on this lovely holiday afternoon and, to all outward appearances, carrying a burden of sadness. And once again an image arose in him. He saw himself lying on a hilly field, late in the evening, after a hot June day. Darkness all around. Far below him a confusion of people, laughter and noise, glittering lanterns. Quite near in the darkness the voices of young girls. He lights the small pipe which he only liked to smoke when in the country. By the light of the match he can see two pretty, young peasant girls, barely more than children. He speaks to them. They are afraid because it is so dark; they creep close to him. Suddenly crackling, rockets in the air. From below a loud "Ah!" Bengal light, violet and red over the invisible lake below. The girls vanish down the hill. Then it becomes dark again, and he lies alone staring into the sky with the damp air weighing down on him. It had been the night before the day when his father was to die. And he thought of this too today for the first time.

He had left the Ringstrasse and took the way toward Wieden.[11] Would the Rosners be at home on this lovely day? Nevertheless it made sense to take the shorter route, and in any case he was drawn that way more than to the Ehrenbergs. He didn't long to see Else at all, and whether or not she really might become Heinrich Bermann's bride was almost a matter of indifference to him. He had known her for a long time. She had been eleven, he fourteen years old, when they had played tennis together on the Riviera. She looked like a gypsy girl then. Blue-black curls encircled her forehead and cheeks, and she was wild and exuberant like a boy. Her brother was already playing the nobleman then, and Georg still had to chuckle as he remembered how the fifteen-

11. The name of one of the city's districts, which lies just south of the city center.

year-old, in a light grey button coat, with white, black-embroidered gloves and a monocle in his eye appeared one day on the promenade. Frau Ehrenberg was thirty-four years old then, noble, of large figure, but still attractive, with clouded eyes and was usually very tired. It remained unforgettable for Georg how one day her husband, the wealthy munitions manufacturer, astonished his family and, simply through his appearance, had brought a hasty end to the distinguished image of the house of Ehrenberg. Georg could see him now, just as he appeared for breakfast on the hotel terrace, an emaciated little man with a grey streaked beard and Japanese eyes, in a white, poorly ironed flannel suit and a dark straw hat with a red and white striped band on his round head, and with dusty black shoes. He spoke very slowly, always cynically, even over the most trivial matters. And whenever he opened his mouth, a mysterious dread lay on his wife's face, concealed behind an appearance of calm. She tried to avenge herself by always treating him with derision, but she was no match for his sheer inconsiderateness. Oskar behaved, whenever possible, as though he were not a part of it. An uncertain contempt for his not altogether worthy progenitor[12] played on his features, and he would smile in the direction of the young baron, seeking understanding. Only Else was nice to the father at that time. On the promenade she would happily walk arm-in-arm with him, and sometimes even embrace him in public.

Georg had seen Else again in Florence a year before his mother's death. She was taking drawing lessons then from a grey- and wild-haired old German, about whom it was said that he had once been famous. It was he himself who spread the rumor that he had renounced his formerly celebrated name and left the city of his work, which he never mentioned, when he felt his genius had left him. The blame for his demise, if one can believe his account, was born by a demonic female whom he had married and who destroyed his most significant painting in a fit of jealous rage and ended her own life with a leap from a window. This man, who even the seventeen-year-old Georg recognized as a sort of swindling clown, was the object of Else's first infatuation. She was fourteen years old at the time, with the wildness and naiveté of youth behind her. In front of Titian's *Venus* in the Uffizi her cheeks glowed with curiosity, yearning, and wonder, and dark dreams of future experiences shown in her eyes. She often came with her mother to the house the Wergenthins had rented in Lugano; and while Frau

12. *Erzeuger*. A judicious choice of noun which may also mean "producer" or "manufacturer."

Ehrenberg tried in her world-weary way to engage the ailing baroness in conversation, Else stood with Georg at the window having precocious conversations about the art of the Pre-Raphaelites and smiling over their past childish play. Felician sometimes also appeared, slim and handsome, and would look past things and people alike with his cold grey eyes, mumble a few courteous words, almost contemptuously, and sit down on his mother's bed, tenderly caressing and kissing her hand. He usually left again soon, but not before leaving, for Else, an acrid air of ancient nobility, heartless seduction, and an elegant contempt for death. She always had the impression that he was on his way to a gaming table on which a hundred-thousand was riding, to a duel of life and death, or to a princess with red hair and a dagger on her night stand. Georg remembered that he had been a little jealous of both the swindling drawing teacher and his brother. The teacher, for reasons that never became known, was suddenly dismissed, and shortly after that Felician and Baron von Wergenthin returned to Vienna. Georg played the piano for the ladies now more than ever, others' music and his own, and Else sang the lighter songs of Schubert and Schumann from the score, with her small, rather shrill voice. She and her mother visited the galleries and churches with Georg, and as spring came again, they would ride together out into the hilly countryside, or to Fiesole, where smiling glances would pass between Georg and Else, which spoke of a deeper understanding than was actually present. Their relationship continued to develop in this somewhat insincere manner when they met again in Vienna. Else always seemed touched by the gallant way in which Georg approached her whenever they had been apart for some months. She herself however, grew from year to year outwardly more assured but inwardly more restless. She had given up her artistic aspirations early, and in the course of time she appeared to be destined to move in the most contradictory directions. Sometimes she saw herself in the future as a grande dame, organizer of flower festivals, patroness of grand balls, collaborator for aristocratic charities; more often though, she saw herself enthroned among painters, musicians, and poets, at artistic salons, as a great cognoscente. Other times she would dream of a more adventurous life: sensational marriage to an American millionaire; elopement with a violin virtuoso or Spanish officer; demonic destruction of all men who came near her. Sometimes a quiet life in the country at the side of some capable estate owner seemed the most desirable to her; and then she would envision herself in a circle of many children, if possible with prematurely grey hair, a mild, resigned smile on her lips, sitting at a simply set table, and stroking the furrowed brow of her devoted husband. Georg, however, felt that her tendency toward indolence, which was deeper than she realized, would protect her from any rash step. She confided various things to Georg, without thereby ever being really honest with him, for she most often earnestly cherished the wish to be his wife. Georg knew that perfectly well, but it was not only for this reason that this newest rumor about her engagement to Heinrich Bermann seemed dubious to him. This Bermann was a haggard looking, beardless man with gloomy eyes and plain, somewhat too-long hair, who had recently become known as a writer, and whose demeanor and appearance reminded Georg, he didn't himself know why, of some fanatical Jewish teacher from the provinces. All this was nothing which could attract Else, or that she would find touching. To be sure, when one spoke longer with him one's impression changed. One evening this past spring, Georg had left the Ehrenbergs with him and had gotten into such an animated conversation about musical matters that they continued their discussion on a Ringstrasse bench until three in the morning.

It's strange, thought Georg, how much is going through my head today that I scarcely thought about any more. And it seemed to him that he would, on this fall afternoon, gradually emerge from many weeks of numbing preoccupation into the light of day.

He was standing in front of the house on Paulanergasse where the Rosners lived. He looked up to the second floor. A window was open, and white curtains, pulled together in the middle, moved gently in the breeze.

The Rosners were at home. The chambermaid let Georg in. Anna sat opposite the door, her coffee cup in her hand and her eyes directed at the new arrival. The father, to her right, was reading a newspaper and smoking a pipe. He was clean shaven except for two narrow sideburns on his cheeks. His thin hair, of an unusual grey-green color, was combed forward from the temples, and looked like a poorly made wig. His eyes were light blue and red-ringed.

The full-figured mother, with her brow still encircled by memories of lovelier years, looked down in front of herself; her hands, clasped contemplatively together, rested on the table.

Anna sat her cup down slowly, nodded, and smiled quietly. The two elders moved to stand up as Georg entered.

"Oh no, please don't disturb yourselves, please," said Georg.

There was a creak off to one side. Josef, the son, got up from the divan on which he had been reclining.

"It's an honor, Herr Baron," he said in a very deep voice as he straightened the yellow, somewhat spattered sports jacket that he had turned up around his neck.

"So how have you been, Herr Baron?" asked the old man, who stood thin and somewhat bent over and would not sit down again until Georg had found a seat. Josef pushed a chair between his father and sister. Anna gave the visitor her hand.

"We haven't seen each other for a long time," she said and took another sip from her cup.

"You've gone through a sad time, Herr Baron," remarked Frau Rosner sympathetically.

"Indeed," continued Herr Rosner. "We read of your loss with the deepest regret. . . . And your Herr father always enjoyed the best of health, as far as we knew." He always spoke very slowly, as if something else was coming to mind, rubbing his head with his left hand and nodding when he was listening.

"Yes, it came quite unexpectedly," Georg said softly and looked down on the faded, dark red carpet at his feet.

"So, a sudden death, so to speak," remarked Herr Rosner, and all around were silent.

Georg took a cigarette out of his case, and offered one to Josef.

"I kiss your hand," said Josef, who took the cigarette, bowed, and for no apparent reason clicked his heals together. As he was giving the baron a light, he thought he felt Georg staring at his jacket and remarked apologetically and with an even deeper voice than usual, "Office jacket."

"Office jackets come from an office," said Anna simply, without looking at her brother.

"The lady likes to play the same ironic tune over and over," replied Josef cheerfully; but it could be observed from his restrained tone that under different circumstances he would have expressed himself less agreeably.

"The sympathetic feelings were quite general," began the old Herr Rosner again. "I read the notice in the *New Free Press*[13] about your Herr father . . . by Herr Privy Councillor Kerner, if I remember correctly; it was highly respectful. Science has suffered a bitter loss as well."

Georg nodded self-consciously and looked down at his hands.

Anna told about their past summer holiday. "It was wonderful in

13. The *Neue Freie Presse,* the most prestigious Viennese newspaper and at that time a leading candidate for the greatest newspaper in Europe.

Weissenfeld," she said. "The forest was right behind our house, with beautiful level paths, isn't that right, Papa? One could go walking out there for hours without seeing another single human being."

"And did you have a piano out there?" asked Georg.

"That too."

"A wretched little tinkle-box," remarked Herr Rosner. "The sort of thing that can make stones cringe and send men raving."

"It wasn't that bad," said Anna.

"Good enough for little Graubinger, anyway," added Frau Rosner.

"Little Graubinger, by the way, is the daughter of a merchant from there," explained Anna. "I taught her the fundamentals of piano playing. A pretty little girl with long, blond pigtails."

"It was a favor to the gentleman," said Frau Rosner.

"But it must also be said," Anna appended, "that I gave a regular paid lesson as well."

"There in Weissenfeld?" asked Georg.

"To some children, on a summer trip. It's really sad, Herr Baron, that you didn't once visit us out there. You'd certainly have liked it."

Georg then remembered that he had mentioned casually to Anna that he might visit her during the summer on a bicycle tour.

"The Herr Baron wouldn't have found everything in this resort to his satisfaction," began Herr Rosner.

"Why not?" asked Georg.

"The needs of our pampered city folk are not taken into account out there."

"Oh, I'm not pampered," said Georg.

". . . Weren't you out at the Auhof?" said Anna, turning to Georg.

"Oh, no," he responded quickly. "No, I wasn't there," he added less hastily. "They had invited me. . . . Frau Ehrenberg was very kind. . . . I had various invitations for the summer. But I preferred to stay by myself in Vienna."

"I really feel bad that I hardly ever see Else any more," said Anna. "You know we went to the same school together. Of course that was a long time ago. I really liked her. Sad how we grow apart in the course of time."

"How did that happen?" asked Georg.

"Well, it's primarily the fact that the whole circle is not really congenial to me."

"Me neither," said Josef, who was blowing smoke rings in the air. "I haven't been there for years. Frankly . . . I don't know how

the Herr Baron feels about these things . . . I'm not much attracted to
the Israelites."

Herr Rosner looked up at his son. "The Herr Baron is often a guest
in that house, dear Josef, and it will appear rather strange to him . . . "

"Me?" said Georg politely. "I don't have any particularly close relationship with the Ehrenbergs, though I do enjoy talking to the two
ladies." And he continued by asking, "But didn't you give Else singing
lessons last year, Fraulein Anna?"

"Yes, in a way. I just accompanied her."

"Would you like to do that again this year?"

"I don't know. I haven't heard from her since then. Maybe she's
given it all up."

"You think so?"

"It would almost be for the best," Anna responded softly, "since she
really chirped more than sang. By the way," she said, casting Georg a
glance that seemed to greet him anew, "the songs you sent me are
lovely. Shall I sing them for you?"

"So you've looked at them? That's nice."

Anna had gotten up. She raised both her hands to her temples and
lightly straightened her wavy hair. She wore it done up rather high,
which made her look even taller than she was. A small gold watch chain
was wound twice around her open neck, hung down across her breast,
and disappeared in a grey leather waist band. She beckoned Georg to
follow her with an almost imperceptible motion of her head.

He stood up and said, "If I may? . . ."

"Please, please, of course," said Herr Rosner. "Herr Baron will be
so kind as to make a little music with my daughter. Lovely, lovely."
Anna had gone into the next room. Georg followed her and left the
door standing open. The white lace curtains of the open window were
pulled together and moved gently.

Georg sat down at the upright piano and struck a few chords. Meanwhile Anna knelt down in front of an old, black, partially gilded étagère and removed the music. Georg modulated into the opening key
of his song. Anna joined him, and sang Georg's melody to Goethe's
lines:

> Your glance to comfort me,
> Your mouth, your breast,
> To hear your voice,
> My joy, first and best.

She stood behind him and read the notes over his shoulder. Sometimes she would bend forward a little, and he would feel the breath of her lips on his temples. Her voice was even more beautiful than he had remembered.

There was loud conversation in the next room. Without interrupting the song, Anna pushed the door shut.

It was Josef who hadn't been able to restrain his voice any longer. "I need to stop in over at the coffeehouse now," he said.

No one replied. Herr Rosner drummed lightly on the table and his wife nodded with apparent indifference.

"So, *adieu*." At the door Josef turned around again and said with controlled firmness, "Mama, if you perhaps have a moment . . . "

"I can hear you," said Frau Rosner. "There aren't any secrets here."

"No. It's only that I'm in debt to you already."

"Does one have to go to the coffeehouse?" asked the older Rosner plainly, without looking up.

"It's not really a matter of the coffeehouse. It's only that . . . You can believe me, I would certainly prefer not to have to sponge off of you. But what can a person do?"

"A person can work," said the old Herr Rosner softly and painfully, and his eyes grew redder. His wife cast a sad and reproachful look at her son.

"So," said Josef, unbuttoning and rebuttoning his jacket, "it really is . . . because of every little florin note. . . ."

"Psst," said Frau Rosner, with a look toward the partially-closed door through which, after Anna's song had ended, only Georg's muffled piano playing could be heard.

Josef answered his mother's look with a contemptuous wave of his hand. "So, Father says I should work. As if I hadn't already proved that I can." He saw two pairs of questioning eyes directed at him. "Oh yes, I certainly have proved it, and if it were only a matter of my good will, I'd have had my own income all along. It's only because I won't simply take everything that's thrown at me. I won't allow myself to be screamed at by my bosses because I come to work quarter-of-an-hour too late once . . . or something."

"We know the story," interrupted Herr Rosner wearily. "But as long as we're talking about it, you're finally going to have to look around for something again."

"Look around . . . fine. . . ." replied Josef. "But I will not work for another Jew. It would make me the laughing stock of my acquaintances . . . of my entire circle."

"Your circle!" said Frau Rosner. "Who's that? Coffeehouse companions!"

"All right, please, since we're discussing it," said Josef, "this is a matter of money too. I have an appointment now at the coffeehouse with the young Jalaudeck. I'd have preferred to wait to tell you about this until it had all been worked out, but I see now that I have to show my colors sooner. So, this Jalaudeck is the son of Alderman Jalaudeck, the famous publisher. And the older Jalaudeck is known to be a very influential person with the Party . . . very close to the editor of the *Christian Daily Messenger*, Zelltinkel his name is. And they're looking for young people of good manners at the *Messenger*—Christian naturally—for the advertising business. And that's why I'm meeting Jalaudeck at the coffeehouse, because he has promised me that his father will recommend me to Zelltinkel. That would be great. . . . I'd be out of the woods then. In a short time I could earn a hundred or even a hundred and fifty florins a month there."

"Oh, God," sighed the older Rosner. Outside, the doorbell rang. Rosner looked up.

"That must be young Doctor Stauber," Frau Rosner said and cast a worried glance at the door through which Georg's piano playing was still coming, though more softly than before.

"So mother, what do you think?" said Josef.

Frau Rosner took her change purse and, sighing, handed her son a silver florin.

"I kiss your hand," said Josef, and turned to go.

"Josef!" said Herr Rosner. "It's somewhat discourteous to leave just at the moment when a visitor arrives."

"Oh, thanks anyway, but I don't have to be included in everything."

There was a knock. Doctor Berthold Stauber walked in.

"Excuse me, Herr Doctor," said Josef. "I was just on my way out."

"Certainly," responded Doctor Stauber coolly, and Josef disappeared.

Frau Rosner invited the young doctor to take a seat. He sat down on the divan and listened toward the side of the room from which the piano playing was coming.

"The Baron Wergenthin," explained Frau Rosner, somewhat embarrassed. "The composer. Anna has just finished singing." And she made a motion to call her daughter.

Doctor Berthold lightly took hold of her arm and said courteously, "No. There's no need to disturb Fraulein Anna, absolutely not. I'm not in the slightest hurry. It's a farewell visit, by the way." This last sentence

came as though forced out of his throat, though Berthold smiled politely, leaned back comfortably in the corner, and stroked his short full
beard with his right hand.

Frau Rosner looked at him absolutely astonished.

Herr Rosner asked, "A farewell visit? Is Herr Doctor taking a leave
of absence? I understood from the newspapers that the Parliament only
recently convened."

"I have resigned my mandate," said Berthold.

"What?" cried Herr Rosner.

"Yes, resigned," Berthold repeated and smiled distractedly.

The piano playing had suddenly ended and the door opened. Georg
and Anna appeared.

"Oh, Doctor Berthold," Anna said, extending her hand as he quickly
stood up. "Have you been here long? Did you perhaps hear me sing?"

"No Fraulein Anna, unfortunately I missed it. I only caught a few
tones from the piano."

"Baron Wergenthin," said Anna, wishing to introduce them. "The
gentlemen are acquainted?"

"Certainly," replied Georg, and extended Berthold his hand.

"The Doctor is paying us a farewell visit," said Frau Rosner.

"What?" cried Anna in astonishment.

"I'm leaving shortly," said Berthold, looking Anna earnestly and impenetrably in the eyes. "I'm giving up my political career," he then
added somewhat derisively. . . . "Better said, I'm interrupting it for a
while."

Georg leaned back in the window, his arms folded across his chest,
and contemplated Anna from the side. She had sat down and looked
up calmly at Berthold, who was still standing, one hand propped on
the back of the divan, as though he were about to give a speech.

"And where are you going?" asked Anna.

"To Paris. I want to work at the Pasteur Institute. I'm returning to
my old love, to bacteriology. It's a purer occupation than politics."

It had become darker. The faces grew dim; only Berthold's forehead,
which was directly opposite the window, was still bathed in light. His
brows were twitching. He really does have his own particular sort of
handsomeness, thought Georg, who leaned motionlessly in the corner
of the window, and felt an agreeable peace flowing through him.

The chambermaid brought in a burning lamp and hung it over the
table.

"But the press carried no announcement that Herr Doctor had resigned his mandate," said Herr Rosner.

"That would be premature," replied Berthold. "My party colleagues understand my intentions, but the matter has not yet been made official."

"This news," said Herr Rosner, "will not fail to create quite a sensation in the concerned circles. Especially after the recent tumultuous debate in which the Herr Doctor took part with such determination. Herr Baron has surely read about it," he said turning toward Georg.

"I must confess," replied Georg, "that I don't follow the parliamentary reports as regularly as one really must."

"Must," repeated Berthold indulgently. "One certainly doesn't have to, although the recent session has not been uninteresting. If only as proof of how low the standards of a public assembly can sink."

"It has grown very heated," said Herr Rosner.

"Heated? . . . Well yes, what one in Austria calls heated. One is inwardly indifferent and outwardly crass."

"What was it all about?" asked Georg.

"It was the debate stemming from the interpellation over the Golowski case . . . Therese Golowski."

"Therese Golowski . . . ," repeated Georg. "I should know that name."

"Of course you know it," said Anna. "You know Therese herself. She was just leaving the last time you visited us."

"Oh yes," said Georg, "a friend of yours."

"I wouldn't call her a friend; that implies a certain inner agreement which really isn't present any longer."

"You wouldn't disavow Therese," said Doctor Berthold smiling but sternly.

"Oh no," responded Anna quickly, "that had truly never occurred to me. I even admire her. I admire all people in general who are willing to risk so much for something that is really none of their concern. And when it happens to be a young lady, a beautiful young lady like Therese . . . ," she continued, directing this last remark at Georg who was listening intently, "I am only all the more impressed. You must know that Therese is one of the leaders of the Social Democratic Party."

"And do you know what I took her for?" said Georg. "An aspiring actress!"

"You're a great judge of character, Herr Baron," said Berthold.

"She really did want to go on the stage once," Frau Rosner confirmed coolly.

"I ask you, dear lady," said Berthold, "what young woman with some imagination, who lives in such tight circumstances, has not at some point in her life at least played with this sort of intention?"

"It's charming that you forgive her," said Anna smiling.

It occurred too late to Berthold that his remark might have struck a delicate point in Anna's sensibilities. But he continued on with even more certainty: "I assure you Fraulein Anna, it could have gone even worse for Therese. And it cannot be foreseen how much she may still accomplish for the Party if she is not somehow deterred from her course."

"Do you really believe that?" asked Anna.

"Certainly," responded Berthold. "For Therese there are really two dangers: either she'll talk herself out of her head . . ."

"Or?" asked Georg, who had become curious.

"Or she'll marry a baron," concluded Berthold tersely.

"I don't quite understand," said Georg somewhat distant.

"That I just said baron was naturally a joke. If we put *prince* in place of *baron* my meaning will be clearer."

"All right, I think I understand what you're getting at, Herr Doctor. . . . But why has the parliament become involved in this?"

"Oh, yes. This past year—at the time of the big coal strike—Therese Golowski gave a speech in some wretched Bohemian village that allegedly contained an offensive remark about a member of the royal family. She was charged and acquitted. One could perhaps conclude from this that the charge might not have been particularly tenable. In spite of this the public prosecutor appealed, a different verdict was issued, and Therese was sentenced to two months in prison, which, by the way, she is now serving. And if this is not enough, the judge who acquitted her the first time, has been transferred . . . someplace on the Russian border, from which there is no return. Well, we have brought an interpellation over all of this, very timidly in my opinion. The minister replied, rather hypocritically, to the rejoicing of the so-called conservative parties. I have permitted myself to respond perhaps somewhat more energetically than is otherwise my custom; and since the opposing benches have nothing objective with which to respond, they have tried to murder me with screaming and insults. And what the most powerful argument of a certain type of conservative against my position was, you can well imagine, Herr Baron."

"Well?" asked Georg.

"Shut your trap Jew!" replied Berthold with pressed lips.

"Oh," said Georg embarrassed, and shook his head.

"Quiet, Jew! Shut your trap. Jew! Jew! Sit!" Berthold continued, and seemed to revel in the memory.

Anna looked down. Georg felt that was enough. A short, painful silence ensued.

"So, because of that?" asked Anna slowly.

"What do you mean?" asked Berthold.

"Is that why you resigned your mandate?"

Berthold shook his head and smiled. "No, not for that."

"Herr Doctor is surely above these crass insults," said Herr Rosner.

"I'm not sure I could say that. But one must nevertheless keep one's composure in the face of such things. The cause of my resignation lies elsewhere."

"And may one know? . . ." asked Georg.

Berthold looked at him penetratingly, though distractedly. Then he replied obligingly: "Certainly one may. After my speech I went to a buffet. There I encountered, among others, one of the most idiotic and insolent of our free-elected representatives who had been during my speech, as was usual for him, altogether the most obnoxious . . . the publisher Jalaudek. I naturally don't associate with him. He had just set down an empty glass. When he saw me, he nodded at me and greeted me cordially, as though nothing had happened: 'May I have the pleasure of your company for a little refreshment, Herr Doctor?'"

"Incredible!" said Georg.

"Incredible? . . . No, Austrian. With us indignation is just as insincere as enthusiasm. Only envy and hatred of real talent are genuine here."

"Well, what did you say to the man?" asked Anna.

"What did I say? Nothing, of course."

"And you resigned your mandate," continued Anna with mild scorn.

Berthold smiled. At the same time his brows twitched as was usual when he felt uncomfortable or hurt. It was too late to tell her that he had actually come to ask her advice, as he did in former times. And yet he felt he had been clever to cut off his own retreat right from the outset, to present his resignation as an accomplished fact, and his departure for Paris as imminent. For he could see that Anna had once again slipped away from him, perhaps for a long time. That another person could really take her from him for good he could never believe, and to be jealous of this elegant young artist who stood so calmly with crossed arms at the window would never even occur to him. It had happened before that Anna would drift for a time, as if enchanted, into what was for him a foreign element. And two years ago, when she was seriously thinking of preparing herself for the stage and had begun to study her roles, he had for a short time completely given her up for lost. Later, as she was forced by the unreliability of her voice to give up her artistic plans, she seemed to return to him; but he had deliberately let this opportunity pass by unused. For, before making her his wife, he wanted to have achieved some measure of success in either the scientific or the political field so she would truly admire him. He had been on his way to that. In that same place where she now sat looking him in the face with clear though strange eyes, she had had lying before her the proof sheets of his last medical-philosophical work, which bore the title: *Preliminary Remarks Toward a Physiognomic of Illness*. And then, as he completed his conversion to politics, to the time when he began to give speeches in the electoral assembly, and while he prepared for his new profession with earnest historical and national-economic studies, she had rejoiced in his many-sidedness and energy. All that was over now. Gradually she began clearly to see his shortcomings, which were not altogether invisible even to himself, particularly his tendency to become intoxicated by his own words, to cast a sharper look than before, and he began thereby gradually to lose his confidence with her. He was no longer himself when he spoke to her or in her presence. Today too, he was not satisfied with himself. He became aware, with an anger which he had difficulty overcoming, that he had not explained his encounter at the buffet with Jalaudek effectively enough, and that he should have explained his disgust with politics more convincingly. "You may be right, Fraulein Anna," he said, "to smile over the fact that I have resigned my mandate over this foolish incident. A parliamentary life without theatricality is impossible anyway. I should have considered the possibility of going ahead and having a drink with this lout who had publicly insulted me. That would have been convenient, Austrian, and perhaps the most appropriate response." He felt he was rolling again and went on with animation: "There are, in the end, only two methods for achieving something practical in politics; either through a grand frivolity, which regards the entirety of public life as an amusing play, which in truth is inspired by nothing, enraged by nothing, and which remains completely indifferent to the people whose happiness or misery is being decided. So far, I'm not that way, and I don't know if I ever will be. Truthfully, I've sometimes wished I was. The other method is: for the cause of what one believes in, to be prepared at every moment, one's entire existence, one's life in the truest sense of the word—"

Berthold suddenly stopped. His father, the elder Doctor Stauber, had entered and was warmly greeted. He offered Georg, who had been introduced by Frau Rosner, his hand, and looked so warmly at him that Georg felt immediately attracted to him. He looked decidedly younger than he actually was. His long reddish-blond beard was only shot through by a few individual grey threads, and his smoothly combed, long hair fell in thick locks to his broad neck. His forehead, of striking height, gave his slightly stocky, high-shouldered appearance a certain dignity. His eyes, when not deliberately looking friendly or clever, seemed to rest themselves under weary lids in preparation for their next encounter.

"I knew your mother, Herr Baron," he said rather softly to Georg.

"My mother, Herr Doctor? . . ."

"You will scarcely remember. You were only a little boy of three or four years then."

"You were her doctor?" asked Georg.

"I visited her sometimes representing Professor Duchegg, whose assistant I was. You lived on Habsburgergasse at that time, in an old house that has long been torn down. I could still describe to you the furnishings of the room in which your Herr father, who has left us all too soon, received me. There was a bronze figure on the writing table, a knight in armor with a standard, to be precise. And a copy of a Van Dyck from the Liechtenstein Gallery hung on the wall."

"Yes," said Georg, amazed by the Doctor's good memory, "absolutely correct."

"But I have just interrupted a conversation," continued Doctor Stauber in that somewhat melancholy, lyrical, if superior, tone which was his own, and sat down in the corner of the divan.

"Doctor Berthold had just informed us to our astonishment," said Herr Rosner, "that he has decided to resign his mandate."

The older Stauber directed a calm glance at his son, which was returned just as calmly. Georg, who had observed this play of eyes, had the impression that a silent harmony, which required no words, governed their relationship.

"Yes," said Doctor Stauber, "in any case it didn't surprise me. I always had the impression that Berthold was more of a guest in parliament, and I am glad that he felt a sort of homesickness for his true calling. Yes, yes, your true calling, Berthold," he repeated as though in response to a frown from his son. "That is not to prejudice anything for the future. Nothing complicates our existence so much as that we so frequently believe in definitives, and thereby lose time being ashamed of a mistake instead of admitting it and simply starting our lives over."

Berthold explained that he wanted to leave in a week at the latest. Any further postponement would serve no purpose. It was also possible that he would not remain in Paris. His studies could make further travel necessary. He had also decided to forgo any further good-byes; as he explained, he had abandoned the associations of former years with the middle-class circles in which his father had an extensive practice.

"Didn't we meet once this past winter at the Ehrenbergs?" asked Georg with some satisfaction.

"That's true," replied Berthold. "We are distantly related to the Ehrenbergs, by the way. The connecting link between us is, strange to say, the Golowski family. Any attempt to explain it more clearly than that, Herr Baron, would be futile. I would have to undertake a walking tour with you through the records offices and cultural associations of Timisoara, Ternopol, and other such agreeable places, and I couldn't expect that of you."

"And anyway," continued the older Doctor Stauber with resignation, "the Herr Baron certainly knows that all Jews are related to one another."

Georg smiled pleasantly. But in reality he was a little disconcerted. He felt that there had been absolutely no reason for the older Doctor Stauber to give him official notice of his relation to Jewry. He knew it quite well anyway and didn't hold it against him. He didn't take it ill in general; but why did they always start talking about it themselves? Wherever he went, he encountered only Jews who were ashamed of being Jewish, or those who were proud of it and were worried that someone might think they were ashamed.

"By the way, I talked to Frau Golowski yesterday," continued Doctor Stauber.

"That poor woman," said Herr Rosner.

"How is she doing?" asked Anna.

"How she is doing you can well imagine . . . her daughter in custody, her son a volunteer living in the barracks at the state's expense. . . . Imagine it, Leo Golowski as patriot! And the old man sits in the coffeehouse and watches while the others play chess, without ten kreuzer to play a game himself."

"Therese's sentence must be nearly over," said Berthold.

"It will be another twelve or fourteen days yet," his father responded. "Now, Annerl," he said turning to the young lady, "it would be really nice of you if you would drop in again on Rembrandtstrasse; the old lady has an almost touching affection for you. I really don't understand why," he added, smiling as he contemplated Anna almost tenderly. She, however, looked down and said nothing.

The wall clock struck seven. Georg got up, as though he had only been waiting for this signal.

"Herr Baron is leaving us already?" said Herr Rosner standing up.

Georg asked everyone present not to disturb themselves and shook hands all around.

"It's strange," said the older Stauber, "how your voice reminds one of your late Herr father."

"Yes, I've often been told that," responded Georg. "I can hardly understand it myself."

"There is no one in the world who knows the sound of his own voice," remarked the older Stauber, and it sounded like the beginning of a popular lecture.

But Georg took his leave. Anna accompanied him to the hallway, despite his mild objections, and left the door—somewhat deliberately as Georg noticed—standing half open. "It's too bad that we couldn't continue with our music," she said.

"I'm sorry too, Fraulein Anna."

"I liked the song better today than the first time when I had to accompany myself. Only it seems to drift a little at the end. . . . I don't quite know how I should put it."

"I know what you mean. The conclusion is conventional; I felt it myself. Hopefully I can bring you something better soon, Fraulein Anna."

"But don't keep me waiting for it too long."

"Certainly not. So, *adieu*, Fraulein Anna."

They shook hands and both smiled.

"Why didn't you come to Weissenfeld?" asked Anna gently.

"I'm really sorry, but you see, Fraulein Anna, I truly wouldn't have been very good company at that time, as you can well imagine.

Anna looked at him seriously. "Don't you believe," she said, "that we might have been able to help you get through it?"

"It's drafty, Anna!" shouted Frau Rosner from the other room.

"I'm coming!" replied Anna, somewhat impatiently. But Frau Rosner had already closed the door.

"When may I come again?" asked Georg.

"Whenever you would like. Of course, I should give you a written appointment, so you'll know I'm home and won't be busy. I go walking a lot, or have business in the city, or go to galleries or exhibitions . . ."

"We could do that together sometime," said Georg.

"Oh, yes," replied Anna, taking her purse from her pocket and producing a tiny notebook.

"What do you have there?" asked Georg.

Anna smiled and leafed through the little book. "Just wait a minute. . . . Thursday at eleven I want to see the miniature exhibit at the Imperial Library. We could go there if you're interested."

"That would be lovely."

"Very good. There we can discuss when you can accompany my singing again."

"Agreed," said Georg, and gave her his hand. It occurred to him that surely while Anna was out here talking to him the young Doctor Stauber must be getting quite irritated back in the living room. And he wondered how it could be that he evidently found this situation more uncomfortable than Anna, who on the whole appeared to be a courteous person. He released his hand from hers, said good-bye, and left.

By the time Georg came out onto the street, it had grown completely dark. He slowly strolled over the Elisabeth bridge,[14] past the opera, toward the inner city, unperturbed by the noise and activity all around, listening to his song in his mind. He found it strange that Anna's voice, so pure and strong in a small room, would break down whenever she stepped out onto the stage or entered a concert hall, and stranger still that Anna appeared to suffer very little from this fate. Of course it was not clear that this composure genuinely represented Anna's true feelings.

He had known her only superficially for a few years; but one evening this past spring they got to know each other a little better. There had been a big gathering at the Waldstein Garden. They ate outdoors under tall chestnut trees. Everyone was happy, excited, and enchanted by the first warm May evening of the year. Georg saw everyone who had come again. Frau Ehrenberg, the organizer of the affair, deliberately matronly with a loose-fitting, dark foulard dress; Privy Councillor Wilt, as if in the mask of an English statesman, with his pompous gestures and that same cheap tone of superiority over all things and persons; Frau Oberberger, with her grey powdered hair, her flashing eyes, and paste-on

14. This bridge no longer exists since this section of the Wien river, which the bridge crossed at this point, was covered over in the course of the city's urban development.

beauty spot on her chin looking like a rococo marquise; Demeter Stanzides, with his shining white teeth and the weariness of an old heroic
family on his pale forehead; Oskar Ehrenberg, with an elegance that
owed much to the top clerk at a fashion house, some to a once youthful
theater singer, and a little to a young man from high society; Sissy
Wyner, who sent her dark, laughing eyes darting from one guest to
another as though she were bound to each individual through some
unique and amusing secret; Willy Eissler, hoarse and jovial, relating all
manner of Jewish anecdotes and tales from his military years; Else
Ehrenberg, overflowing with tender spring melancholy, in white English
lace, with the comportment of a grande dame which made her child's
face and delicate figure look charming, almost touching; Felician, cool
and polite, with proud eyes that looked between the guests toward
other tables, and then past these into the distance; Sissy's mother,
young, rosy-cheeked and chattering, wanting to speak to everyone and
hear everything at once; Edmund Nuernberger, in whose piercing eyes
and narrow mouth could be read an almost masklike smile of contempt
for the business of the world, which he saw through from the ground
up, and in which, however, he sometimes found himself an active par-
ticipant, much to his own surprise; finally, Heinrich Bermann, in a suit
that was too loose, a straw hat that was too cheap, and a tie that was
too light, who now spoke more loudly, and now fell into a deeper silence than anyone else. Later, without an escort and looking confident,
Anna Rosner appeared, greeted the crowd with a light nod of her head,
and unassumingly took a seat between Frau Ehrenberg and Georg. "I
invited her for you," remarked Frau Ehrenberg softly to Georg, who
until this evening had scarcely given a thought to Anna. Those words,
perhaps nothing more than a passing comment from Frau Ehrenberg,
proved true in the course of the evening. From the moment the gathering broke up and began its merry journey through the Volksprater,[15]
everywhere, at the booths, on the merry-go-round, by the clowns, and
even later as the party, for fun, returned to town on foot, Georg and
Anna stayed together; and finally, their heads buzzing from hours of
joking and clowning, they fell into a completely serious conversation.
A few days later he visited her and brought her, as promised, the piano
edition of *Eugene Onegin* and a few of his own songs. At his next visit

15. The Prater park extends for a considerable distance along the south bank of the
Danube. It begins at the northwest end with the Volksprater, which contains the actual
amusement park, and extends southeast into wooded walking-gardens and parks, with
Freudenau at the far end.

she sang these songs as well as some by Schubert, and her voice pleased him very much. Soon after that they took leave of each other for the summer, without a trace of sorrow or tenderness; Anna's invitation to Weissenfeld had struck Georg as only a courtesy, just as he believed his acceptance was; and in comparison to the innocence of their relations up to the present, the tone of today's visit seemed quite peculiar to Georg.

At St. Stephen's Square Georg noticed that he was being hailed by someone standing on the omnibus platform. Georg, who was slightly nearsighted, did not recognize who it was right away.

"It's me," said the man from the platform.

"Oh, Herr Bermann! Good evening," said Georg, reaching his hand up. "Where are you off to?"

"I'm going to the Prater. I want to have supper there. Do you have other plans, Herr Baron?"

"Nothing in the slightest."

"So, why don't you join me?"

Georg swung himself up onto the omnibus, which had already begun to rumble on. They casually related to one another how they had spent their summer. Heinrich had been in Salzkammergut, later in Germany, from where he had returned only a few days ago.

"And in Berlin too," added Georg.

"No."

"I thought that perhaps in regard to a new play . . ."

"I haven't written a new play," Heinrich interrupted, somewhat rudely. "I was in the Taunus[16] and on the Rhine, and some other places."

What did he have to do on the Rhine, thought Georg, though he really wasn't that interested. It struck him that Bermann was staring in front of himself rather distractedly, almost depressed.

"And how is it going with your work, dear Baron?" Heinrich asked, suddenly more alert, as he pulled his dark grey overcoat, which was hanging over his shoulders, tighter around himself. "Is your quintet finished?"

"My quintet?" repeated Georg with surprise. "Have I spoken to you about my quintet?"

"No, not you; Fraulein Else told me you were working on a quintet."

16. A mountain range north of Frankfurt.

"Oh yes, Fraulein Else. No, I haven't gotten much further. I wasn't really in the mood, as you can well imagine."

"Oh, yes," Heinrich said and fell silent for a while. "And your Herr father was still so young," he added slowly.

Georg nodded silently.

"How's your brother?" asked Heinrich suddenly.

"Quite well thanks," responded Georg, somewhat surprised. Heinrich threw his cigar over the railing and immediately lit another. Then he said: "You may wonder that I would inquire after your brother, to whom I have hardly ever spoken. But he interests me. In his way he represents for me a perfect archetype, and I regard him as one of the most fortunate people there could be."

"That may well be," replied Georg. "But how have you arrived at this opinion, since you hardly know him?"

"First, his name is Felician Freiherr von Wergenthin-Recco," said Heinrich very seriously, and blew smoke into the air.

Georg listened with surprise.

"You are also named Wergenthin-Recco," continued Heinrich, "but just Georg—and that's not quite the same, is it? More, your brother is very handsome. You're not bad looking yourself. But people whose primary attribute is to be handsome are, in reality, better off than those whose primary attribute is to be gifted. When one is handsome, one is so all the time, while the gifted spend at least nine-tenths of their existence without a trace of inspiration. Yes, it is certainly true. The line of one's life is, so to speak, truer when one is handsome than when one is a genius. Of course that could be better expressed."

What was with him then, thought Georg, a little perturbed. Could he possibly be jealous of Felician . . . on account of Else Ehrenberg?

They got off at the Prater intersection. The great stream of Sunday crowds flowed toward them. They took the way to the main avenue, which was not so busy anymore, and went ahead slowly. It had become cool. Georg commented on the autumn mood of the evening, about the people sitting in the inns, about the military bands that were playing in the kiosks. Heinrich commented at first perfunctorily, then not at all, and finally appeared to be scarcely listening, which Georg found rude. He almost regretted having joined Heinrich, all the more as it was not otherwise his custom to accept such chance invitations without further consideration, and he made the excuse for himself that he had only done it this time out of distraction. Heinrich walked beside him, or a few steps ahead, as though he had completely forgotten Georg's presence. He still held the overcoat he had thrown over his shoulders tightly with both hands, wore his soft, dark-grey hat pulled down on his forehead, and looked, as Georg suddenly began to notice with consternation, most inelegant. Heinrich Bermann's earlier remarks about Felician impressed him now as being in poor taste as well as tactless, and as time passed, it occurred to him that pretty much everything he knew of Heinrich's literary accomplishments had gone against his grain. He had seen two plays by him: one that took place in lower-class settings among manual laborers and factory workers, and which ended with murder and death; the other, a sort of satirical society comedy, which had aroused a scandal after opening and quickly vanished from the repertoire. At the time Georg was not yet personally acquainted with the author and took no further interest in the matter. He only remembered that Felician had found the play ridiculous, and that Count Schoenstein had expressed the view that, if it were up to him, plays by Jews would only be permitted performance at the Budapest Orpheum Society. In particular, Doctor von Breitner, baptized and objective, had expressed indignation that this upstart young man had presumed to bring to the stage a world that was obviously closed to him, and of which he naturally could understand nothing. While all this was going through Georg's mind, his irritation with the mannerless behavior and persistent silence of his companion began to intensify into a real animosity, and half unconsciously he began to give credence to all the slander that had been directed at Bermann at that time. He now also remembered that Heinrich had been personally unsympathetic to him from the very beginning, and that he had expressed himself ironically to Frau Ehrenberg about the cleverness she had shown in capturing this young celebrity for her salon. Else had, of course, immediately taken Heinrich's side, described him as an interesting and sometimes even pleasant person and prophesied to Georg that sooner or later he would become good friends with him. And as a matter of fact, Georg had retained a certain sympathy for Bermann, which had lasted until this evening, ever since that conversation they had had on the Ringstrasse bench this past spring night.

They had long passed the last inns. Next to them the lonely white road ran straight between the trees and off into the night, and the sound of distant music came to them only in detached broken tones.

"Where now?" said Heinrich suddenly, as though someone had dragged him here against his will, and stood still.

"I really can't help it," replied Georg simply.

"Forgive me," said Heinrich.

"You were so deep in thought," responded Georg, coolly.

"Deep I really can't say. But it sometimes happens that one gets lost in oneself."

"I know that," said Georg, a little reconciled.

"By the way, you were expected in August out at the Auhof," said Heinrich suddenly.

"Expected? Well, Frau Ehrenberg was kind enough to invite me once, but I hadn't accepted by any means. Have you spent a lot of time out there, Herr Bermann?"

"A lot, no. I've been up there occasionally, but only for a few hours."

"I thought you stayed up there."

"Not at all. I lodged down below at an inn. I've only been up there a few times. It's too noisy and chaotic for me. . . . The house is swarming with guests, and I can't stand most of the people who go there anyway."

An open *fiaker* with a lady and a gentleman sitting in it rolled by.

"That was Oskar Ehrenberg," said Heinrich.

"And the lady?" asked Georg, looking at something bright that was shining through the darkness.

"Don't know."

They took the way through a dark side street. Again the conversation faltered. Finally Heinrich began: "Fraulein Else sang some of your songs for me at the Auhof. I had heard a few of them done before, by Bellini if I remember correctly."

"Yes, Bellini sang them in a concert last winter."

"Well, Fraulein Else sang those and a few other songs of yours."

"Who accompanied her?"

"I did, as well as I could. I must tell you, dear Baron, the songs made a stronger impression on me than they did the first time at the concert, despite the fact that Fraulein Else has considerably less voice and artistry than Fraulein Bellini. On the other hand, one must take into account that it was a glorious summer afternoon when Fraulein Else sang your songs. The window was open and one could see the mountains and deep blue sky outside . . . but there was enough left over for you."

"Very flattering," said Georg, stung by Heinrich's sarcastic tone.

"You know," continued Heinrich, speaking, as he sometimes did, with teeth clenched together and an unnecessarily heavy emphasis, "You know, in general it's not my custom to invite people I see by

chance on the street onto the bus, and I readily confess to you that I
regarded it . . . how should I put it . . . as a sign of fate when I suddenly
caught sight of you in St. Stephen's Square."

Georg listened to him, puzzled.

"Perhaps you don't remember as clearly as I do," continued Heinrich, "our last conversation on the Ringstrasse bench."

Now it occurred to Georg that at the time Heinrich had cursorily
spoken of an opera libretto he was working on, for which Georg had
offered himself, just as casually and half-jokingly, as composer. And
deliberately cool, he responded: "Oh yes, I remember."

"Of course you were not obligated," replied Heinrich, even cooler
still, "all the more since, to tell the truth, I had not even thought about
my libretto since then, until that lovely summer afternoon when Fraulein Else sang your songs. How would it be if we stopped here?"

The wine garden they entered was rather empty. Heinrich and Georg
sat down in a small arbor next to a green picket fence, and ordered
their supper.

Heinrich leaned back, stretched out his legs, and contemplated
Georg, who was persistently silent, with probing, almost scornful eyes,
and suddenly said: "I believe I would not be mistaken if I were to assume that the things I have written up to now have not really appealed
to you."

"Oh," replied Georg, turning a little red. "How did you arrive at
that opinion?"

"Well, I know my plays . . . and I know you."

"Me?" asked Georg, nearly offended.

"Certainly," said Heinrich with superiority. "At least, I have this
feeling about most men, and even consider this ability my own particular absolute, without a doubt. The rest I find a little problematic. In
particular, my so-called artistry is quite modest, and there is a lot to
object to in my own character. The only thing which gives me a certain
confidence is the consciousness that I am able to see into the human
soul . . . deep inside, in everyone, honest or dishonest, men, women, or
children, heathens, Jews, Protestants, even Catholics, nobles, and Germans, although I have heard that precisely this is what should be so
endlessly difficult or even impossible for one of us."

Georg gave a light shrug. He knew that Heinrich had been severely
personally attacked by the conservative and clerical press, particularly
on the occasion of his last play. But what's that to me, thought Georg.
Just another fellow who someone has insulted! It was absolutely impos-

sible to deal with these people without any risk to oneself. Courteously but distant, in a scarcely conscious recollection of the older Herr Rosner's reply to the young Doctor Stauber, he said: "Actually I thought people like you were above attacks of the sort to which you were obviously alluding."

"So . . . is that what you thought?" asked Heinrich in that cold, almost offensive tone he sometimes used. "Well," he continued more gently, "sometimes it's true. But unfortunately not always. It doesn't take much to awaken the self-contempt which is constantly lurking in us; and once that happens there is hardly a fool or scoundrel with whom we are not ready to take sides against ourselves. Pardon me if I say 'we.' . . ."

"Oh, I have often felt quite the same. Of course, I still haven't had occasion to face publicity as often and as openly as you."

"Well if ever . . . You will never have to go through exactly the same thing as I have."

"Why is that?" asked Georg, a little annoyed.

Heinrich looked him squarely in the eyes. "You are the Baron von Wergenthin-Recco."

"Oh, that! Pardon me, but nowadays there is a whole mob of people who are prejudiced against one for precisely that reason—and who really know how to throw in one's face the fact that one is a baron."

"Yes, yes, but you will grant that there is a different tone in it, and also a different meaning when one throws in your face that you are a baron than that you are a Jew, although the latter . . . you will forgive me . . . may sometimes be the more noble. Well, you needn't look at me so sympathetically," he suddenly added roughly. "I'm not always so sensitive. There are other moods in which nothing and no one can hurt me. Then I have only this one feeling: what do you all know, what do you know about me?"

He fell silent, proud, with a scornful look that bored through the lattice work of the arbor into the darkness. Then he turned his head, looked around, and said plainly, in a new tone to Georg, "Look, we are nearly the only ones."

"It's also becoming quite cool," said Georg.

"I think we should walk a little through the Prater."

"Gladly."

They got up and left. On a meadow, which they came upon, lay a fine, grey fog.

"The illusion of summer does not last into the evening. Soon it will finally be over," said Heinrich with exaggerated oppressiveness, adding, as if to console himself, "So, one will work."

They arrived at the Wurstelprater.[17] Music was coming from the inns and Georg fell in at once with the festive mood, emerging suddenly from the autumnal sadness of the wine garden and a somewhat disturbing conversation.

In front of a carousel, from which a gigantic barrel-organ was pouring a fantastic organ-like potpourri of melodies from *Il Trovatore* out into the open, and at whose entrance a hawker was inviting the crowd on trips to London, Atzgersdorf, and Australia, Georg again remembered the spring party with the Ehrenberg circle. On this narrow bench, on the inside of the circle, Frau Oberberger had been seated with the cavalier of the evening, Demeter Stanzides, at her side, to whom she had evidently just related one of her incredible stories: that her mother had been the mistress of a Russian archduke; that she herself had spent a night with an admirer at the Hallstaedter cemetery, without anything happening, naturally; or that her husband, the famous traveler, had conquered seventeen women in a single week in a harem in Smyrna. In this red velvet-upholstered wagon Else had reclined across from Privy Councillor Wilt, ladylike, charming, rather like in a *fiaker* on Derby day, and had understood how to project, through her demeanor and expression, that she, when it came down to it, could be just as childlike as other simpler, more happy people. Anna Rosner, the reigns held lightly in her hands, respectable, but with a rather sly look on her face, rode on a white Arabian; Sissy rode on a black horse, which not only moved in a circle with the other animals and wagons, but also rocked back and forth. Under a flamboyant hairdo, with an enormous black feather hat, her mischievous eyes flashed and laughed, and her white skirt fluttered and flew above the low dress shoes and filigreed stockings. Sissy's appearance made such an impression on two strange men that they called out an unmistakable invitation to her, whereupon a short, mysterious conversation took place between Willy, who was right on the spot, and the two rather disconcerted men, who at first tried to rescue their position by casually lighting new cigarettes, but quickly vanished into the crowd.

Even the booths with the "illusions" and lantern slides had their own special memories for Georg. Here, as Daphne transformed herself into

17. The children's carnival within the Prater, which featured a puppet theater among other children's attractions.

a tree, Sissy whispered a soft "remember" in his ear to remind him of
that masked ball at the Ehrenbergs when she had lifted her lace veil to
give him, but not him alone, a fleeting kiss. Then came the booth where
the whole group had itself photographed: the three young ladies, Anna,
Else, and Sissy, in a genial pose, the gentlemen at their feet with uplifted
eyes, so the whole had something of the appearance of an apotheosis
from a magic farce. And as Georg recalled that little experience, today's
farewell from Anna hovered before his memory and seemed filled with
the most delightful promises.

A conspicuously large crowd was standing in front of an open shooting gallery. Soon the drummer was struck in the heart and beat with
rapid whirling movements on the drum skin; then a glass ball which
was dancing up and down on a stream of water burst with a light tinkle;
now a camp sutler hurriedly raised the trumpet to her mouth and blew
the alarm; then a door sprung open and out thundered a tiny train
which dashed over a suspension bridge and was swallowed up by
another door. As a few of the onlookers gradually moved along, Georg
and Heinrich pushed their way forward and recognized the sure shot
of Oskar Ehrenberg and his girlfriend. Oskar leveled the gun at an
eagle, which was swaying back and forth near the ceiling with out-
spread wings, and missed for the first time. He laid the weapon down
indignantly, looked around, caught sight of the two men behind him,
and greeted them.

The young lady, the weapon at her cheek, cast a quick glance at
the new arrivals, took deliberate aim, and fired. The eagle dropped his
stricken wing and moved no more.

"Bravo!" cried Oskar.

The lady laid the rifle down on the table in front of her.

"That's enough," she said to the boy, who wanted to load up again,
"I won anyway."

"How many shots was that?" asked Oskar.

"Forty," answered the boy. "Comes to eighty kreuzer." Oskar
reached into his vest pocket, tossed a silver gulden on the counter and
accepted the attendant's thanks with condescension. "Permit me," he
said, putting his hands in his side pockets, bowing slightly from the
waist and putting his left foot forward, "permit me, Amy, to introduce
the gentlemen who were witnesses of your triumph. Baron Wergenthin,
Herr von Bermann . . . Fraulein Amelie Reiter."

The gentlemen lifted their hats and Amelie nodded her head a couple of times in return. She wore a plain, white-patterned, foulard dress with a light, bright yellow coat hemmed in lace over it, and a black, but very cheerful hat.

"I am acquainted with Herr von Bermann," she said. She turned to him: "I saw you last winter at the premiere of your play when you came out for your bow. I thoroughly enjoyed myself, and I'm not just saying that out of courtesy."

Heinrich thanked her warmly.

They walked along between the booths, which were becoming quieter, and past the wine gardens, which were gradually emptying.

Oskar hung his right arm in the left of his companion, and then turned to Georg: "Why didn't you come up to the Auhof this year? We were all very disappointed."

"Unfortunately I wasn't in much of a social mood."

"Naturally, I can imagine," said Oskar, with the appropriate seriousness. "I was only there a few weeks myself. In August I strengthened my tired limbs in the waves of the North Sea; and I was on the Isle of Wight, of course."

"It's supposed to be very nice there," said Georg. "Who is it that always goes there?"

"The Wyners, you mean," replied Oskar. "At least while they still lived in London, they went there regularly. Now only every two or three years."

"So they brought the 'y' back to Austria with them," said Georg, smiling.[18]

Oskar remained serious. "The old Herr Wyner," he replied "has won his right to the 'y' honorably. He went to England in his thirteenth year, was naturalized, and as quite a young man became a partner in the great steel mill which is still called Black and Wyner."

"But he got his wife from Vienna?"

"Yes. And since he died seven or eight years ago, she has resettled here with the two children. But James was never at home here. . . . You know that Frau Oberberger calls him The Lord Antinous.[19] He's back in Cambridge now, where he's studying Greek philology, of all things. By the way, Demeter was in Ventnor for a couple of days."

18. The original Austrian spelling of the name would have been "Wiener." There are almost no uses for the letter 'y' in unadulterated German.

19. A notably handsome youth from Claudiopolis in Bythnia, and a favorite of the Roman emperor Hadrian, with whom he traveled. His likeness is often depicted on ancient statues, busts, and coins as the ideal of youthful beauty.

"Stanzides?" asked Georg.

"Do you know Herr von Stanzides, Herr Baron?" asked Amy.

"Yes indeed."

"So, he really exists!" she cried.

"Yes, but now listen," said Oskar. "This spring she bet on him at Freudenau and won a heap of money, and now she wonders whether or not he exists."

"Why do you doubt the existence of Stanzides, Fraulein?" asked Georg.

"Well, you know, whenever I don't know where Oskar is, it's always: 'I had a meeting with Stanzides,' or: 'I was riding with Stanzides in the Prater.' Stanzides here, Stanzides there, it sounds more like an excuse than a name."

"Now please be still for a moment," said Oskar gently.

"Not only does Stanzides exist, but he has the most marvelous black moustache and the shiniest black eyes that there could possibly be."

"That's possible, but when I saw him, he looked like a clown. Yellow jacket, green lapels, violet bow tie."

"And you won forty gulden on him," continued Oskar with humor.

"Where are the forty gulden?" sighed Fraulein Amelie. . . . Suddenly she stood still and cried, "I've never ridden on it!"

"That can be fixed," said Oskar plainly.

It was the Riesenrad[20] with its lighted cars, which was turning slowly and majestically before them. The young people passed through the turnstile, climbed into an empty compartment, and vanished upward.

"Do you know who I got to know this summer, Georg?" said Oskar. "Prince von Guastalla."

"Which one?" asked Georg.

"The youngest one, of course, Karl Friedrich. He was there incognito. He gets along very well with Stanzides, a remarkable man. I can assure you," he added softly, "if people like us were to say a hundredth part of the things the prince does we'd spend our whole lives in the dungeon."

"Look Oskar," cried Amy, "the tables and the people down there! Like little toys, aren't they? And that mass of lights way over there is surely Prague, don't you think, Herr Bermann?"

"Possibly," Heinrich replied and stared through the glass pane with wrinkled forehead into the night.

20. The immense and famous ferris wheel in the Prater amusement park.

As they left the compartment and walked out into the open, the Sunday bustle was fading.

"The little one," said Oskar Ehrenberg to Georg while Amy walked up ahead with Heinrich, "doesn't suspect that we're walking together in the Prater today for the last time."

"Why for the last time," asked Georg, without any deep interest.

"It has to be," replied Oskar. "Such things shouldn't last longer than a year at most. By the way, after December you can buy your gloves from her," he continued cheerfully, but not without a tinge of melancholy. "I'm setting her up with a small business. I owe it to her to a certain extent, since I pulled her away from a more or less secure situation."

"A secure situation?"

"Yes, she was engaged, to an etui maker. Did you know there was such a thing?"

Meanwhile Amy and Heinrich had stopped in front of a narrow circular staircase which led boldly up to a platform, and were waiting for the others. All were in agreement that they couldn't leave the Prater without having ridden on the roller coaster.

They rushed through the dark, down and then up again in the rumbling wagon, under black tree tops; and the low rhythmic racket gradually intoned for Georg a grotesque motive in three-quarter time. As he came down the circular staircase with the others, he already knew that the melody was for oboe and clarinet, with cello and double bass accompaniment. It was obviously a scherzo, possibly for a symphony.

"If I were a contractor," declared Heinrich with determination, "I'd build a roller coaster many miles long, that went over meadows, hills, through forests, dance halls, and had lots of surprises along the way." In any case, he went on, the time had come to bring the fantastic element of the Wurstelprater to a higher culmination. He himself had a tentative idea for a carousel that would rise up, and would, through a unique mechanism, spiraling ever higher above the ground, finally arrive at the top of some sort of tower. Unfortunately he lacked the necessary technical expertise for a more precise explanation. As they went on he conceived of burlesque figures and groups for the shooting galleries, and finally spoke of the pressing need for a really grand puppet theater, for which original writers should write profound and entertaining plays.

So they finally arrived at the exit of the Prater, where Oskar's coach was waiting. Packed in, but in good spirits, they rode to a wine restaurant in the city. Oskar served champagne in a private room. Georg sat down at the piano and improvised on the theme which had come to him on the roller coaster. Amy reclined in the corner of the divan, and Oskar whispered all sorts of things in her ear, which made her laugh. Heinrich had become quiet again and turned his glass slowly back and forth between his fingers. Suddenly Georg stopped his playing and left his hands lying on the keys. A feeling of the dreamlike quality and purposelessness of existence came over him, as it sometimes did when he had been drinking wine. It seemed many days since he had come down that poorly lit stairway on the Paulanergasse, and the walk with Heinrich through the dark autumn avenue lay in the distant past. On the other hand, he suddenly remembered as vividly as if it had been yesterday, a very young and very wicked creature with whom he had spent a few weeks in cheerful meaningless dalliance many years ago, rather like Oskar now with Amy. One evening she had kept him waiting too long on the street; impatiently he had left, and he never saw or heard from her again. How easily life sometimes goes by. . . . He heard Amy's gentle laugh, turned, and his glance encountered Oskar's eyes which were looking for his over Amy's blond head. The look seemed angry to him and he deliberately turned away and played a few more tones in a melancholy folk song style. He felt a need to write down everything that he had experienced today, and looked up at the clock which hung over the door. It was past one. He and Heinrich came to an agreement through a glance, and the two stood up. Oskar indicated toward Amy, who slumbered on his shoulder, and made it known through a smiling shrug that he couldn't think of leaving yet under the circumstances. The two others gave him their hands, whispered good night, and left.

"Do you know what I did," said Heinrich, "while you were improvising so beautifully on that horrid piano? I tried to work out that material I spoke to you about in the spring."

"Oh, the libretto! That's interesting. Would you care to tell me about it again?"

Heinrich shook his head. "I'd like to, but the problem is, as it turns out, it really isn't there. Just like most of the rest of my so-called material."

Georg looked at him questioningly. "In the spring, when we last saw each other, you had a whole mass of things in mind."

"Sure, there are plenty of notes. But there's nothing more there than sentences. . . . No, words! No, letters on white paper. It's just as if a death's hand had touched it all. I'm afraid that the next time I pick up the thread again, it will fall apart like tinder. I'm having a hard time, and who knows if a better one is coming?"

Georg was silent. Then, suddenly remembering a newspaper article he had read somewhere about Heinrich's father, Dr. Bermann, the former deputy of parliament, and suspecting a connection, he asked, "Your Herr father isn't well, is he?"

Without looking at him, Heinrich answered: "Yes, my father is in an asylum for the depressed, since June."

Georg shook his head sympathetically.

Heinrich continued, "It's a terrible thing. And even though I haven't had very close relations with him lately, it's still worse than one can describe."

"Under the circumstances," said Georg, "it's quite understandable that your work isn't going well."

"Yes," answered Heinrich, somewhat hesitantly. "But it isn't only that. To tell the truth, in my present state of mind this matter plays a relatively unimportant role. I won't make myself out to be better than I am. Better . . . ! Would I be better?" He gave a short laugh, and then went on. "You see, yesterday I still thought it was that everything possible was happening all at once that was oppressing me so much. But today I again received irrefutable proof that completely trivial, even foolish things have a deeper effect on me than really important ones, like, for example, the illness of my father. Disgusting, isn't it?"

Georg looked down. What am I doing here with him, he thought, and yet why did he find it entirely obvious?

Heinrich continued speaking with teeth clenched together and an excessively forceful tone: "This afternoon, to be specific, I received two letters. Two letters, yes . . . one from my mother, who visited my father in the asylum yesterday. This letter contained the news that he's doing poorly, very poorly; short and sweet, it will not last much longer." He took a deep breath. "And naturally, all sorts of things are contingent on that, as you can imagine. Difficulties of various sorts, grief for my mother and sister, for myself. And now just think; at the same time as this letter, another one came that contained nothing of significance, so to speak. A letter from a person I was close to for two years. And there was a passage in this letter that seemed a little suspicious to me. One single passage. Otherwise this letter was, like every other letter from this person, very sweet, very nice. . . . And now imagine, the memory of this one suspicious passage, which someone else would not have noticed at all, pursued me, tormented me the entire day. I don't think about my father, who is in an asylum, or about my mother, or my sister, who are in despair, only about this insignificant passage in that stupid letter from a by-no-means-important female. It devours everything else in me, makes me incapable of feeling like a son, like a man. . . . Isn't it awful?"

Georg listened with shock. It seemed strange to him how this sullen and gloomy man suddenly opened up to a casual acquaintance like himself, and he couldn't fend off a painful embarrassment over this unexpected candor. In addition, he did not have the impression that he owed this confession to a particular sympathy of Heinrich's, but instead he sensed a lack of tact, a certain inability to control himself, something for which the words 'poor upbringing' that he had once heard applied to Heinrich—wasn't it by Privy Councillor Wilt?—seemed very descriptive. They passed by the Burgtor.[21] A starless sky lay over the silent city. There was a light rustling through the trees of the Volksgarten,[22] and from somewhere could be heard the noise of a rolling wagon moving off into the distance.

As Heinrich fell silent again, Georg stood still and said, in the friendliest tone possible, "Now, I must bid you good night, dear Herr Bermann."

"Oh!" said Heinrich. "It's just occurred to me that you have accompanied me all this time—while I've related to you, or better, to myself in your presence, these tactlessly unvarnished stories that you couldn't have the slightest interest in. . . . Forgive me."

"What is there to forgive," replied Georg gently, finding himself a little surprised by Heinrich's self-criticism, and gave him his hand. Heinrich shook it, said "*Auf Wiedersehen*, dear Baron," and, as if he suddenly regarded any further word as an importunity, walked off hurriedly.

Georg watched him with sympathy and revulsion at the same time, and a sudden, free, almost jubilant mood came over him in which he saw himself as young, carefree, and destined for the happiest future. He anticipated the coming winter with joy. Everything possible was in prospect; work, pleasure, tenderness, and it hardly mattered where all this happiness would come from. He lingered a moment at the opera. It wouldn't be much of a detour if he went home by way of Paulanergasse. He smiled at the memory of window-watching in former years.

21. A monumental arch at the southwest end of the Heldenplatz courtyard, next to the Imperial Palace, or Hofburg.
22. A section of park along the west leg of the Ring which contains a model Greek temple known as the Theseus Temple since it was originally built to hold Canova's sculpture group *Theseus Slaying the Minotaur*, now in the Kunsthistorisches Museum.

Not far from here was the street where he had on many evenings looked up to a window behind whose draperies Marianne would show herself if her husband was asleep. This woman, who was always playing with danger, the seriousness of which she herself didn't realize, had never been really good enough for Georg. . . . Another memory, more distant than this one, was much more dear to him. In Florence, as an inexperienced seventeen-year-old youth, he had spent many a night walking back and forth before the window of a beautiful young girl who had been the first woman to surrender her innocence to him. And he thought of the hour in which he had seen the beloved walk, on the arm of her groom, to the altar where the priest would consecrate their marriage, and of the glance of eternal farewell she had sent him under the white veil. . . . He was at his destination. Only the two lamps at the ends of the short street were still burning, so he stood across from the house in complete darkness. The window of Anna's room was open, and the lace curtains pulled together in the middle still moved gently in the breeze just as they had in the afternoon. Behind them it was completely dark. A gentle tenderness welled up in Georg. Of all beings who had not concealed their attraction to him, Anna appeared the best and the purest. Also, she was the first who contributed a real sympathy toward his artistic aspirations; a more genuine one in any case than Marianne, who would send tears rolling down her cheeks no matter what he played for her on the piano; a deeper one than Else Ehrenberg, who only wanted to protect her pride in being the first to recognize his talent. And Anna was better suited than anyone else to counteract his tendency toward frivolousness and carelessness and to spur him on to purposeful and productive activity. Already last winter he had thought of looking for a position with a German opera company as conductor or rehearsal accompanist; at the Ehrenbergs he had spoken casually of his intentions, which were not taken very seriously, and Frau Ehrenberg, motherly and prudent, had advised him that it would be better to go on a tour through the United States as a composer and conductor, whereupon Else had boldly added: "And an American heiress should not be scoffed at." While he was remembering this conversation, he was very attracted to the idea of venturing out into the world a little, wanting to acquaint himself with foreign cities and people, to win fame and love in a far off place; and he felt in the end that his present existence was, on the whole, far too bland and monotonous.

Finally, without ever having taken leave of Anna inwardly, he had left Paulanergasse and soon was home. As he entered the dining room he noticed that light was coming from Felician's room.

"Good evening, Felician!" he called loudly.

The door opened, and Felician, still fully dressed, came out.

The brothers shook hands.

"Did you just get home too?" said Felician. "I thought you were long asleep." As he spoke, he looked past him, as was his manner, and tilted his head to the right side. "What were you doing?"

"I went to the Prater," replied Georg.

"Alone?"

"No, I met some people. Oskar Ehrenberg and his girlfriend, and the writer Bermann. We were shooting and rode the roller coaster. It was very enjoyable. . . . What's that in your hand?" he interrupted himself. "Did you go walking like that?" he added jokingly.

Felician let the sword he was holding in his right hand shine in the light of the lamp. "I just took it down from the wall. I'm beginning in earnest again tomorrow. The tournament is coming up in mid-November. And this year I want to challenge Forestier."

"Oh, my!" cried Georg.

"An impudence you think? But it's still a long time until November. And what's strange, I have the feeling that I learned something during the six weeks this summer when I hardly had the thing in my hand. It's as if my arm got some new ideas in the meantime. I can't really explain it to you."

"I understand what you mean."

Felician held the sword stretched out in front of him, and contemplated it with tenderness. Then he said, "Ralph asked about you, Guido too. . . . Too bad you weren't along."

"Did you spend the whole afternoon with them?"

"Oh, no. After dinner I stayed home. You must have already gone out. I studied."

"Studied?"

"Yes. I really have to get going. I want to pass the diplomatic examination by May at the latest."

"So, you've definitely decided?"

"Absolutely. It makes no sense for me to stay in the Governor's office. The longer I sit there, the clearer it is to me. But the time hasn't been lost. It's taken into account if one has spent a couple of years in civil service."

"Then you might be leaving Vienna already in the fall."

"That's to be assumed."

"Where do you think they'll send you?"

"If one only knew."

Georg looked down. So the farewell was near! But why did that suddenly bother him so much? . . . He had decided to leave himself, and he had only recently talked with his brother about his plans for next year. Was he still not taking him seriously? If only one could talk to him openly again, like a brother, like on the evening after their father's funeral. Truthfully, they only really found each other when life revealed its sadness to them. Otherwise there always remained this strange reserve between the two. Evidently it couldn't be otherwise. One had to be satisfied to talk in the manner of good acquaintances. And, as if resigned, Georg asked, "What did you do this evening?"

"I ate with Guido and an interesting young lady."

"Well?"

"He's in love again."

"Who is she?"

"Conservatory student, Jewish girl, violin. But she didn't have it with her. Not especially pretty, but bright. She cultivates him, and he respects her. He wants her to get baptized. A strange relationship, I tell you. You'd really have enjoyed yourself."

Georg was looking at the sword that Felician still held in his hand. "Would you care to fence a little?" he asked.

"Why not?" replied Felician, and brought a second foil from his room. Meanwhile Georg had moved the large table out of the middle of the room against the wall.

"I haven't had one of these things in my hand since May," he said as he grasped the sword. They laid their jackets down and crossed swords. In the next second Georg was touched.

"Again!" cried Georg, who found it a joy to be able to stand opposite his brother, in bold posture, the flashing, slender weapon in his hand.

Felician could score as often as he wished, without being touched himself a single time. Then he lowered his sword and said, "You're too tired today, there's no point. But you should start working out at the club again. I assure you, it's too bad, with your talent."

Georg rejoiced in the brotherly praise. He laid the sword on the table, took a deep breath, and went to the open, wide, middle window. "Wonderful air!" he said. A single lantern was shining from the park; it was completely still.

Felician walked up behind Georg, and while Georg leaned with both hands on the railing, the older brother stood upright and swept the street, park, and city with one of his proud, self-assured looks. They were silent for a long time. And they knew that each was thinking of the same thing: of a May evening this past spring when they were coming home together through the park, and their father had greeted them with a silent nod of his head from the same window where they were now standing. And both shuddered a little at the thought that they had spent the day so happily, without remembering with pain the dear man who now lay buried in the ground.

"So, good night," said Felician, softer than usual, and gave Georg his hand. He squeezed it silently, and each went to his room.

Georg switched on the writing table lamp, took out some music paper, and began to write. It was not the scherzo which had come to him three hours ago as he had rushed under the black tree tops through the night with the others; nor was it the melancholy folk tune from the restaurant; but an entirely new theme that emerged from a mysterious depth, slowly and irresistibly. It seemed to Georg that he had only to let something incomprehensible go its own way. He wrote down the melody, which he imagined sung by an alto voice or played on a viola; and he heard a strange accompaniment with it, which he knew could never fade from his memory.

It was four in the morning when he went to bed; at peace like one whom nothing harmful in life could ever touch, and for whom neither loneliness, poverty, nor death held the slightest fear.

Second Chapter

Frau Ehrenberg sat on the green velvet sofa in the raised alcove with her embroidery; Else was across from her, reading a book. From the dark depths of the room, behind the piano, shone the white head of the marble Isis, and a bright stripe flowed across the grey carpet from the open door of the next room. Else looked up from her book through the window at the tall trees of the Schwarzenberg Park, which were blowing in the autumn wind, and said casually: "We could telephone Georg Wergenthin and see if he could come this evening."

Frau Ehrenberg let her embroidery down in her lap. "I don't know," she said. "You remember what a really cordial letter of condolence I sent him, and how I implored him to visit us at the Auhof. He didn't come, and his reply was strikingly cool. I wouldn't telephone him."

"One can't treat him like the others," replied Else. "He's the kind of person one has to remind occasionally that one is still around. Once you've reminded him, he's glad for it."

Frau Ehrenberg continued sewing. "Nothing will come of it," she said calmly.

"Nothing should come of it," responded Else, "don't you know that yet, Mama? He's my good friend, nothing more—and even that only with interruptions. Or do you really believe that I'm in love with him, Mama? Sure, as a little girl I was, in Nice, when we used to play tennis together. But that was a long time ago."

"Well—and in Florence?"

"In Florence I was in love with Felician."

"And now?" asked Frau Ehrenberg slowly.

"Now? . . . You think perhaps with Heinrich Bermann. . . . But you're wrong, Mama."

"I'd be glad if I were wrong. But this past summer I really had the impression that . . ."

"I'll tell you right now," interrupted Else, a little impatiently. "It's nothing, and never was. One single time, on that humid afternoon while we were boating—you were watching us from the balcony with your opera glasses—it got a little precarious. Even if we had embraced once, which, by the way never happened, it wouldn't have meant anything. It was just one of those summer things."

"And he's supposed to have a very serious relationship," said Frau Ehrenberg.

"You mean . . . with that actress, Mama?"

Frau Ehrenberg looked up. "Did he tell you about her?"

"Tell me? . . . Not directly. But when we were walking together in the park, or in the evening by the lake, he hardly spoke of anything but her. Naturally without mentioning her name. . . . And the more he liked me, men are the strangest people, the more jealous he was of her . . . if that's all it was. And what young man doesn't have a serious relationship anyway? Do you think, Mama, that Georg Wergenthin doesn't?"

"A serious one? . . . No. It'll never happen. He's too cool, too aloof, too bland."

"Precisely for that reason," explained Else knowingly. "He'll slip into something that will close over him before he's even noticed it. And one fine day he'll be married . . . out of sheer indolence . . . to some person who might be completely indifferent to him."

"You must have a definite suspicion," said Frau Ehrenberg.

"I certainly do."

"Marianne?"

"Marianne! But that was over a long time ago, Mama. And it was never particularly serious."

"So, who is it then?"

"Well, who do you think, Mama?"

"I have no idea."

"It's Anna," said Else tersely.

"Which Anna?"

"Anna Rosner, of course."

"But!"

"You can say 'but' all you want—it's true."

"Else, you can't really believe that Anna, with her modest nature, could really forget herself to that extent . . . !"

"Forget herself . . . ! No Mama; you sometimes have such a way of putting things!—Anyway, in my opinion, one doesn't have to be so forgetful for that."

Frau Ehrenberg smiled, not without a certain pride.

Outside the doorbell rang. "I'll bet it's him," said Else.

"It could also be Demeter Stanzides," remarked Frau Ehrenberg.

"Stanzides should bring the Prince sometime," Else added casually.

"Do you think he would?" asked Frau Ehrenberg, letting her embroidery down into her lap.

"Why shouldn't he?" said Else. "They're so close."

The door opened, but none of the expected came in; rather it was Edmund Nuernberger. He was dressed, as always, with the greatest carefulness, though not in the latest fashion. His coat was somewhat too short, and an emerald pin was stuck in the bulging dark satin tie. He bowed while still at the door, not without expressing in his manner a certain scorn for his own courteousness. "Am I the first?" he asked. "No one else yet? Neither a privy councillor, nor a count, nor a poet, nor a demonic female?"

"Only one who unfortunately never has been," replied Frau Ehrenberg as she gave him her hand, "and one . . . who may be some day."

"Oh, I'm convinced," said Nuernberger, "that Fraulein Else will make it, if she's really determined to." And he rubbed his left hand slowly over his black, smooth, rather shiny hair.

Frau Ehrenberg expressed her regrets that they had waited for him in vain at the Auhof. Had he really been in Vienna the whole summer?

"Why do you wonder about that, dear lady? If I go walking here and there in some mountain landscape, or on the sea shore, or within my four walls, in the end it's pretty much the same."

"But you must have felt quite lonely," said Frau Ehrenberg.

"Being alone comes, to be sure, more naturally to a person when one finds no one in the vicinity who indicates the need to want to speak with one. . . . But let's talk about more interesting and optimistic people than I am. How are the many friends of your beloved house?"

"Friends!" repeated Else. "First one must know who you are including in that."

"Well, anyone who speaks pleasantly to you on any occasion, and whom you believe."

The bedroom door opened; Herr Ehrenberg appeared, and greeted Nuernberger.

"Have you finished packing?" asked Else.

"All set," answered Ehrenberg, who had on a much too loose grey suit, and held a large cigar in his teeth. He turned to Nuernberger with an explanation. "As you see me, I'm on my way to Corfu . . . for the present. The season begins before times become intolerable for me at the Ehrenberg house."

"No one is demanding," replied Frau Ehrenberg gently, "that you honor them with your presence."

"Very kind of them," said Ehrenberg, steaming. "I'd gladly give up your time. But when I would simply like to come home on a Thursday night to have a quiet supper, and in the corner sits an attaché, in another a hussar, over there someone is performing one of his own compositions, on the divan someone is having a cordial, and at the window, Frau Oberberger is waiting for a rendezvous with whomever she's meeting, it makes me nervous. Sometimes one can tolerate it, sometimes not."

"Are you planning to stay away all winter?" asked Nuernberger.

"It would be possible. I intend to continue on to Egypt, Syria, and possibly to Palestine. Yes, maybe it's just because I'm getting older, maybe because one reads so much about Zionism and such, but I can't help it that I want to have seen Jerusalem before I die."

Frau Ehrenberg shrugged her shoulders.

"These are things," said Ehrenberg, "that my wife doesn't understand—and my children even less. What is it to you, Else, even you. But when one reads what goes on in the world, one sometimes could believe that there is no other way out for us."

"For us?" repeated Nuernberger. "I haven't observed until now you've suffered much from anti-Semitism."

"You mean because I've become a rich man? If I tried to tell you that the money doesn't matter to me, you wouldn't believe me, and you'd be right. But as surely as you're looking at me, I swear to you, I'd give half of my fortune to see the worst of our enemies at the gallows."

"I'm just afraid," remarked Nuernberger, "you'd have the wrong man hanged."

"The danger isn't great," replied Ehrenberg. "Grab the next fellow, you'll catch one."

"I observe, not for the first time, dear Herr Ehrenberg, that you do not approach this question with the desirable objectivity."

Ehrenberg suddenly bit off his cigar and laid it on the ash tray, fingers trembling with rage. "When someone gives me that business . . . and quite . . . excuse me . . . or are you perhaps baptized? . . . One never knows these days."

"I am not baptized," replied Nuernberger calmly. But, to be sure, I am not Jewish either. I have long been without a creed; for the simple reason that I have never felt like a Jew."

"If someone knocks your hat off once on the Ringstrasse because you have, with your permission, a rather Jewish nose, you will feel hit like a Jew, you can rely on it."

"But Papa, why are you exciting yourself like this?" Else said, and stroked him across his bald, shining red head.

The old Ehrenberg took her hand, stroked it, and asked, for no apparent reason, "Will I still have the pleasure of seeing my Herr Son before I leave?"

Frau Ehrenberg answered, "Oskar will be home any time now."

"You will surely be pleased to learn," said Ehrenberg, turning to Nuernberger, "that my son Oskar is also an anti-Semite."

Frau Ehrenberg sighed softly. "It is an *idée fixe* with him," she said to Nuernberger. "He sees anti-Semites everywhere, even in his own family."

"It's the latest national illness of the Jews," said Nuernberger. "I have only succeeded in meeting one single genuine anti-Semite myself. I can't conceal from you, dear Herr Ehrenberg, that he was a well-known Zionist leader."

Ehrenberg made only an expressive wave of the hand.

Demeter Stanzides and Willy Eissler walked in, spreading at once a vivacious lustre about themselves. Bright and resplendent, Demeter wore his outfit more like a costume than a military uniform. Willy, in a smoking jacket, standing tall, pale, and weary, had the conversation in hand at once, and his pleasantly hoarse voice floated authoritatively and amiably through the air. He talked about the preparations for an aristocrats' production for which, like last year, he had been enlisted as adviser, stage manager, and collaborator. He described a meeting of the young worthies which had resembled, if one could believe him, a convention of imbeciles, and related, as the best part, a humorous conversation between two countesses of whose manner of speaking he knew how to give a priceless imitation. Ehrenberg was always very amused by Willy Eissler. The vague perception that this Hungarian Jew in some way outwitted, and regarded as fools, the whole feudal clan which he personally so detested, filled him with admiration for the young man.

Else sat at the small table in the corner with Demeter and listened about the Isle of Wight.

"You were there with your friend, weren't you," she asked, "with Prince Karl Friedrich?"

"My friend the Prince? . . . that's not quite right, Fraulein Else. The Prince has no friends, and neither do I. We're not the type."

"From all we've heard, he must be an interesting person."

"I don't know about interesting. In any case, he has thought about a lot of things that people in his position don't usually care to think about. He might have been able to do all sorts of things if they had let him go his own way. Well, who knows, maybe it's better for him that they kept a tight rein on him,—for him and for the country. One can't do anything alone. There's no way. It's best if one just lets go and withdraws the way he did."

Else looked at him somewhat annoyed. "You're so philosophical today, why is that? It seems to me that Willy Eissler has ruined you."

"Willy, me?"

"Well you know, you shouldn't associate with these clever people."

"Why not?"

"You should just be young, shine, live, and then, if something doesn't work out, do what you like . . . but without thinking about yourself or the world."

"You should have told me that before, Fraulein Else. When I first started to become clever."

Else shook her head. "But with you, all that might have been avoided," she said quite earnestly. And then they both had to laugh.

The chandeliers were turned up. Georg von Wergenthin and Heinrich Bermann had come in. Invited over by a smile from Else, Georg sat down beside her.

"I knew that you would come," she said insincerely, but warmly, and squeezed his hand. That he sat next to her again after so long a time, that she saw his charming, proud face, and heard his soft, warm voice, pleased her more than she had expected.

Frau Wyner appeared; small, bright red, cheerful, and ill at ease. Her daughter Sissy was with her. The groups broke up in the giving and taking of greetings.

"Well, have you composed the song for me yet?" Sissy asked Georg with laughing eyes and laughing lips, while playing with one of her gloves and wriggling in her dark, varied-green dress like a snake.

"A song?" asked Georg. He really didn't remember.

"Or a waltz or something. But you promised that you would dedicate something to me." While she spoke, her eyes wandered all around. They stared into Willy's eyes, flirted in passing with Demeter, asked Heinrich Bermann a mysterious question. It was as if a will-o'-the-wisp was dancing through the salon.

Frau Wyner stood suddenly next to her daughter, deep red. "Sissy is so dumb. . . . What do you think, Sissy, Baron Georg has had more important things to do this year than to compose for you."

"Oh, certainly not," said Georg politely.

"You buried your father, that's no triviality."

Georg looked down. Frau Wyner continued on unperturbed: "Your father was not very old, was he? And such a handsome man. . . . Isn't it true that he had been a chemist?"

"No," replied Georg with composure. "He was president of the Botanical Society."

Heinrich, an arm on the closed piano lid, spoke with Else.

"So you were in Germany?" she asked.

"Yes," answered Heinrich, "though it was a while ago, four or five weeks."

"And when are you going back?"

"That I don't know; perhaps never."

"Oh, you don't believe that yourself.—What are you working on?" she added quickly.

"All sorts of things," he responded. "I'm in a rather restless period. I sketch out a lot, but I haven't finished anything. Completion in general rarely interests me. Obviously I finish too quickly with things in my own mind."

"And with people," added Else.

"Could be. It's unfortunate that we sometimes still have feelings for people after our understanding can get nothing more out of them. A poet—if you will permit me the word—has to withdraw from everyone who holds no more mystery for him . . . particularly from those he loves."

"It happens however," objected Else, "that we least understand precisely the ones we love."

"That's what Nuernberger says, but it's not entirely true. If it were, dear Else, life would probably be more pleasant than it is. No, we know the ones we love even better than we know the others,—only we know them with shame, with bitterness, and with the fear that others know them just as well as we do. Love means: to be afraid that the weaknesses we have discovered in the beloved will be as obvious to others. Love means: to be able to see into the future, and to curse the gift. . . . Love means: to know someone so well that it is one's downfall."

Else leaned on the piano in her adolescent, girlish way, with curiosity, and listened to him. How well he pleased her at such moments. She would have liked to stroke him consolingly across his hair as she did before on the lake, when he was as if torn from his love for that other woman. But when he suddenly pulled back, cool, dry, looking as if quenched, then she felt that she could never live with him, that she would have to run away from him after a few weeks . . . with a Spanish officer or a violin virtuoso.

"It's good," she said, somewhat patronizingly, "that you're socializing with Georg Wergenthin. He'll have a beneficial effect on you. He's calmer than you are. But I don't believe that he's as talented and certainly not as smart as you are."

"What do you know about his talent?" Heinrich interrupted her almost rudely.

Georg walked up and asked Else if they were to have the pleasure of hearing a song from her today. She wasn't in the mood. In any case, she had recently been studying primarily opera parts. They interested her more. She wasn't really of lyrical temperament. Georg asked her as a joke if she didn't perhaps have the secret intention of going on the stage.

"With this little voice!" said Else.

Nuernberger stood next to them. "That would be no hindrance," he remarked. "I am even convinced that there would very soon be found a modern critic who would declare you a great singer for precisely that reason, Fraulein Else, because you possess no voice; who will discover, for example, some other gift instead that he finds characteristic of you. Just as there are today famous painters who have no sense of color, but have 'spirit'; and poets of reputation, to whom nothing of significance ever occurs, but who succeed in finding the falsest possible adjective for every noun."

Else noticed that Nuernberger's manner of speaking made Georg nervous, and turned to him. "I want to show you something," she said, and took a few steps over to the music étagère.

Georg followed her.

"Here's the collection of old Italian folk songs. I'd like for you to point out the most important ones for me. I don't really know enough about it myself."

"I really don't understand," Georg said softly, "why you tolerate people like this Nuernberger around you. He spreads an atmosphere of mistrust and ill will around him."

"I've often told you, Georg, a great judge of character you are not. What do you really know about him? He's different than you think. Ask your friend Heinrich Bermann once."

"Oh, I know he's wild about him too," Georg replied.

"You're talking about Nuernberger?" asked Frau Ehrenberg, who had just walked up.

"Georg can't stand him," said Else in her off-hand manner.

"You do him an injustice; have you ever read anything of his?"

Georg shook his head.

"Not even his novel, which made such an enormous sensation fifteen or sixteen years ago? That's almost a disgrace! We just loaned it to Privy Councillor Wilt. I tell you, he was astounded by the way the whole of present day Austria is foreseen in that book."

"Yes, well," said Georg without conviction.

"You can't imagine," continued Frau Ehrenberg, "with what celebrity Nuernberger was received at that time. One could say that all doors were thrown open to him."

"Maybe that was enough for him," remarked Else, reflectively precocious.

Heinrich stood by the piano in conversation with Nuernberger and tried, as he often did, to interest him in starting a new work, or in republishing his older ones.

Nuernberger declined. The thought of seeing his name dragged into the public eye again, of being drawn into the literary whirlpool of the time, which seemed to him both repulsive and ridiculous, filled him with horror. He had no desire to contend with that. For what? Cliques which scarcely bothered to disguise themselves were everywhere at work. Was there still a capable, sincerely struggling talent who did not have to be prepared at every moment to be dragged through the muck; was there a dunce yet to be found who could not succeed in getting himself declared a genius in some literary rag? Does reputation in our time still have the slightest relationship to integrity? And to be overlooked, forgotten, is that worth a shrug of regret? And in the end, who can know which view would turn out to be right in the future? Were not the fools really the geniuses and the geniuses the fools? It was ridiculous to put one's peace of mind, even one's self-respect, into a game in which the highest gain possible promised no satisfaction.

"None at all?" asked Heinrich. "I will grant you this of all sorts of things—fame, wealth, far-reaching influence;—but that one should, because all these prizes are dubious, also renounce something so unquestionable, as are the moments of the inner feeling of power . . ."

"Inner feeling of power! Why don't you say instead the blessedness of creation?"

"All right, Nuernberger!"

"Could be. I believe I can even remember a long time ago having occasionally felt something of the sort. . . . It's only that, as you know, in the course of the years, I have completely lost the capacity for self-deception."

"Maybe you only believe that," replied Heinrich. "Who knows if it's not precisely this capacity for self-deception which has, in the course of time, become the strongest in you!"

Nuernberger laughed. "Do you know how it feels to me, when I hear you talk like that? About like a fencing master who has just received a stab in the heart from one of his own students."

"And not even from your best," said Heinrich.

Suddenly Herr Ehrenberg appeared in the door, to the amazement of his wife, who had thought him already on the way to the train station. He led by the hand a young lady who was dressed in simple black and wore her hair quite high in an outmoded style. Her lips were full and red; the eyes in the lively, pale face looked clear and hard.

"Come along now," Ehrenberg said with a certain malice in his small eyes, and led the guest directly to Else who was still speaking with Stanzides. "I am bringing you a visitor."

Else extended her hand to her. "How nice." She introduced her: "Herr Demeter Stanzides.—Fraulein Therese Golowski."

Therese gave a short nod and let her gaze rest on him for a moment, unaffectedly, as though contemplating a beautiful animal. Then she turned to Else: "If I had known that you had such important company . . ."

"You know what she looks like?" said Stanzides softly to Georg, "Like a Russian student, don't you think?"

Georg nodded. "A little. I know her. She's a school friend of Fraulein

Else, and yet, think of it, she plays a leading role with the Socialists. She was even in prison recently, for lese majesty I think."

"Yes, it seems to me that I read something about that," replied Demeter. "One should really get to know such a creature better. She's lovely. A face like ivory."

"And there's a lot of energy in her expressions," continued Georg. "Her brother, by the way, is also a remarkable person. Pianist and mathematician. I recently got to know him. And the father is supposed to be a ruined Jewish fur trader."

"It's a strange race," remarked Demeter.

Meanwhile Frau Ehrenberg had walked up to Therese and regarded it as proper to show no surprise. "Have a seat, Therese," she said. "How have you been? Since you embarked on the political life you don't seem to care for your former acquaintances any more."

"Yes, unfortunately my calling leaves me little time to care for my family relationships," Therese replied, and thrust her chin forward, which made her appearance suddenly masculine and almost ugly.

Frau Ehrenberg wavered about whether or not to mention Therese's completed prison term. Nevertheless, it had to be considered that there was scarcely another house in Vienna where ladies who had recently been in jail visited.

"How is your brother?" asked Else.

"This is his year of service," answered Therese. "You can roughly imagine how it's going for him there. . . ." and she cast an ironic look at Demeter's hussar uniform.

"He surely doesn't play the piano much there," said Frau Ehrenberg.

"Oh, he doesn't even think about becoming a pianist any more," answered Therese. "He's completely immersed in politics." And with a smile she turned to Demeter and added, "You won't inform on him, will you, Herr Lieutenant?"

Stanzides smiled, somewhat embarrassed.

"What does that mean, politics?" asked Herr Ehrenberg. "Does he want to become a minister?"

"Certainly not in Austria," replied Therese. "He's a Zionist, of course."

"What!?" cried Herr Ehrenberg, and his face was beaming.

"Of course, this is a matter that we cannot completely understand," added Therese.

"Dear Therese . . . ," began Ehrenberg.

"You'll miss the train," his wife interrupted him.

"I won't miss the train, and there's another one tomorrow. Dear

Therese, I will only say: each should become happy in his own way. But in this case, your brother is the wiser, and not you. Forgive me, I am perhaps only a layman in political matters, but I assure you Therese, it will go the same for you Jewish Social Democrats as it has gone for the Jewish Liberals and German Nationalists."

"In what way," asked Therese, haughtily. "In what way will it go the same for us?"

"In what way? I'll tell you right now. Who created the Liberal movement in Austria? . . . The Jews! . . . By whom have the Jews been betrayed and abandoned? By the Liberals. Who created the German Nationalist movement in Austria? The Jews. By whom have the Jews been left in the lurch . . . why do I say left in the lurch . . . spit on like a dog? By the Germans! And it will be just the same for you with Socialism and Communism. When the soup is finally served, you will be driven from the table. It has always been that way, and always will be."

"We'll wait and see," replied Therese calmly.

Georg and Demeter looked at each other like two friends who had been washed-up on an island together. Oskar, who had come in right in the middle of his father's oration, had narrow lips and was very embarrassed. Everyone saw it as a form of deliverance when Ehrenberg looked at the clock and excused himself.

"We won't come to an agreement today," he said to Therese.

Therese smiled. "Hardly. Have a good trip, and once again, in the name . . . "

"Pst," said Ehrenberg, and vanished.

"Why actually were you thanking Papa?" Else asked her softly.

"For a contribution I shamelessly came to ask him for. But there's no other wealthy man in my circle of acquaintances. I'm not authorized to discuss the purpose."

Frau Ehrenberg walked over to Bermann and Nuernberger, who were talking to each other across the piano lid, and said softly: "You of course know that she . . ." motioning toward Therese with her eyes, "has just gotten out of prison?"

"I read about it," replied Heinrich.

Nuernberger squinted and cast a glance at the group in the corner where the three ladies were talking with Stanzides and Willy Eissler, and shook his head.

"What sort of wickedness are you suppressing?" asked Frau Ehrenberg.

"I was just thinking how easily it could have happened that Fraulein

Else might have had to languish for two months in prison and that Fraulein Therese had given parties in an elegant salon as daughter of the
house."

"Easily happened? . . ."

"Herr Ehrenberg had good luck, Herr Golowski bad. . . . Perhaps
that's the only difference."

"Well listen, Nuernberger," said Heinrich, "you can't completely
deny the role of the individual in the world. . . . Else and Therese are
of quite different natures."

"I think so too," remarked Frau Ehrenberg.

Nuernberger shrugged his shoulders. "Both are young ladies, quite
gifted, quite pretty. . . . Everything else is like with most other young
ladies—and with most other people—more or less circumstantial."

Heinrich shook his head vigorously. "No, no," he said, "life is just
not that simple."

"It's not simpler because of that, dear Heinrich."

Frau Ehrenberg's look was directed at the door and brightened. Felician had just come in. With the assurance of a sleepwalker he walked
up to the woman of the house and kissed her hand. "I just had the
pleasure of encountering Herr Ehrenberg on the stairway. . . . He told
me he was leaving for Corfu. It must be beautiful there now."

"You're familiar with Corfu?"

"Yes, dear lady, a childhood memory." He greeted Nuernberger and
Bermann, and they all talked about the south, for which Bermann was
yearning, and by which Nuernberger was not impressed.

Georg shook his brother's hand in greeting and good-bye at the same
time. As he inconspicuously vanished through the open door to the dining room and looked around again, he noticed Marianne, who was sitting in the most distant corner of the salon regarding him scornfully
through a lorgnette. It had always been the mysterious gift of this
woman suddenly to appear without one's knowing were she came from.
Then on the steps he encountered a veiled woman in his way. "Don't
be in such a hurry. She can wait a moment yet," she said. "In general,
one should not pamper the ladies that way. . . . Would you have hurried
so much if you were on your way to a rendezvous with me? . . . But
you wouldn't want to know about that. Perhaps because you are afraid
that my husband would shoot you down when he returns from Stock-
holm, although today he is already in Copenhagen. But he has complete trust in me. Justifiably, by the way. For I can swear to you, more
than a kiss on the hand . . . no, not to tell a lie, on this neck, no one

has been permitted. You surely also believe that I have had a relationship with Stanzides? No, he wouldn't be for me! Handsome men in general are a horror to me. I can find nothing in your brother Felician as
well . . ."

It was not to be seen when the veiled lady would stop talking, for it
was Frau Oberberger. With other women this same behavior would
have indicated a certain willingness to be approached, but not with her,
about whom, however dubious her manner might seem, there had never
been a word of scandal. She lived in a strange, but apparently happy,
childless marriage. Her handsome and brilliant husband, a geologist by
profession, had in earlier years undertaken expeditions concerning
which, as Privy Councillor Wilt asserted, he placed less importance on
the unexplored nature of the region in question than on good travel ac-
commodations and the quality of the food. For the last few years, however, he only traveled to give lectures and conquer women. When he
was back at home again, he lived with his wife in the best of cama-
raderie. Sometimes, but only fleetingly, Georg had weighed the possibility of having an affair with Frau Oberberger. He had even been one of
those who had kissed her neck, which she apparently no longer remembered. And as she now threw back her veil, Georg once again felt with
pleasure the attraction of this no longer young but charmingly animated
face. He wanted to strike up a conversation with her, but she continued
talking: "Do you know that you are very pale? You must live a fine
life. What sort of woman is it, by the way, for whom you must tear
yourself away from me this time?"

Privy Councillor Wilt, inaudible as usual, suddenly stood beside
them. Casual, superior, and gallant, he remarked: "I kiss your hand,
dear lady; my greetings, Baron . . ." and was about to continue.

Frau Oberberger, however, found it suitable to first inform him that
Baron Georg was just on his way to some orgy, as was his way,—then
she followed the Privy Councillor up to the second floor, where there
would be the danger, as she herself remarked, that someone seeing him
together with her at the Ehrenbergs would believe him to be her ninety-
fifth lover.

It was seven o'clock before Georg could finally sit down in the wagon
and ride to Mariahilf.[1] He felt totally exhausted by the two hours at
the Ehrenbergs, and now more than usual he looked forward to the
meeting with Anna, which stood before him. Since that morning at the

1. The name of another of the city's districts.

miniature exhibition they had seen each other almost daily; in gardens, in picture galleries, at her home. They talked mostly about the little details of their existence, or discussed books and music. They did not speak about the past very often, and when they did, it was without mistrust or doubt. And besides, the adventures which Georg had had were not surrounded for Anna with the disturbing atmosphere of mystery; and as she herself had already had several romantic experiences, Georg took her jesting intimations lightly, unconcerned, and without further inquiry. He had kissed her for the first time a week ago in an empty hall in the Liechtenstein Gallery, and from this moment on, Anna addressed him as *du*, as though the more formal address would have appeared a deception.[2]

The wagon stopped at a street corner. Georg got out, lit a cigarette, and walked back and forth in front of the house from which Anna would appear.

After a few minutes she came out of the door. He hurried across the street to her and happily kissed her hand. As usual, because she often liked to read while they rode, she had a book with her, in a cover of pressed leather.

"It's a little cool, Anna," said Georg, who took the book from her hand and helped her into her jacket, which she had carried over her arm.

"I was running a little late," she said, "and was very anxious to see you. Yes," she said smiling, "I even had a temper tantrum. Well, what do you think of my new outfit?" she asked as they continued walking.

"It looks very good on you."

"At the lesson, they thought I looked like a lady of the court."

"Who thought that?"

"Frau Bittner herself, and both the daughters I'm teaching."

"I would rather say, like an archduchess."

Anna nodded, satisfied.

"So Anna, tell me everything you have done since yesterday."

She began seriously. "At twelve, after we parted at the house door, lunch with the family. In the afternoon I rested a little and thought about you. From four until six-thirty I had students, then read, *Gruener*

---

2. German has two subject pronouns for the second person singular: *du*, used for familiar address, and *Sie*, for formal address. It is customary to reserve *du* for more intimate relationships. In a relationship between a man and a woman, this switch would signal a significant change in attitude.

Heinrich[3] and the evening paper. Too lazy to go back out, puttered around the house. Supper. The usual domestic scene.

"Brother?" asked Georg.

She answered with a "Yes," which precluded further questions. "After supper, I played a little music. . . . Even tried to sing."

"Were you satisfied?"

"It's always good enough for me," she said, and Georg thought he perceived a gentle sadness in the sound of her words. Quickly she continued reporting: "At ten-thirty went to bed, slept well, up at eight in the morning. . . . One can't sleep past that at our house. . . . Fixed myself up until nine-thirty, and then till eleven just . . ."

"Puttered around," Georg completed.

"Right. Then went to the Weil's and taught the little boy for a while."

"How old is he really?" asked Georg.

"Thirteen," replied Anna, with an amusingly thoughtful face.

"Well, that's not really so young."

"Certainly not," said Anna. "But you may learn to your reassurance that he is in love with his aunt Adele, a delicate blond of thirty-three years, and for the moment cannot think of breaking faith with her. . . . So, to continue the chronicle. Got home at one-thirty, ate alone, thank God, Papa already at the office, Mama sleeping. Rested again from three to four, thought about you again, more seriously than yesterday, then had some business in town, gloves, safety pins, and something for Mama, and finally read on the tram out to Mariahilf to teach the two little Bittner brats. So now you know everything. All satisfactory?"

"Except for the thirteen-year-old boy."

"So I will grant you that that may be disturbing, but now we will hear whether or not you have even darker confessions to make to me."

They were in a narrow, quiet street that seemed completely strange to Georg, and Anna took his arm.

"I just came from the Ehrenbergs," he began.

"Well," asked Anna, "did they try very hard to trap you?"

"I can't really say.—They even seemed a little offended that I wasn't out at the Auhof this summer," he added.

"Did dear little Else show something off?"

"No. Of course, I don't know what might have happened after I left."

3. A partially autobiographical novel about the life of an artist, in four volumes by Gottfried Keller, the second version of which is the best known and was published in 1880.

"It wouldn't have been worth the trouble, then," said Anna, over-flowing with derision.

"You're wrong, Anna. There are people there for whom it is very worthwhile to sing."

"Like who?"

"Heinrich Bermann, Willy Eissler, Demeter Stanzides . . ."

"Oh, Stanzides!" cried Anna. "Now I'm really sorry I wasn't there."

"It seems to me," said Georg, "that wasn't as jokingly meant as said."

"Certainly not," replied Anna. "I think Demeter is absolutely dev-astating."

Georg fell silent for a few seconds, then, suddenly more agitated than was usual for him, he asked: "Could it be him? . . ."

"Who do you mean, 'him'?"

"Him, whom you . . . loved more than me!"

She smiled, gripped him more tightly, and answered plainly, but with mild scorn, "Am I really supposed to have loved someone more than you?"

"You confessed it to me yourself," replied Georg.

"But I have also 'confessed' that with time I will love you more than I ever have loved anyone, or ever could."

"Are you really sure of that, Anna?"

"Yes, Georg, I'm really sure."

They were once again in a busier street, and unconsciously loosened their arms. They lingered in front of various shop windows, discovered the display window of a photographer in a house doorway, and were much amused by the laborious and unaffected postures in which some celebrating couples, deputy cadet officers, cooks in their Sunday best, and ladies decked out for a masked ball had been photographed.

Georg, in a lighter tone, continued asking: "So, was it Stanzides?"

"But what are you thinking of. In my whole life I've barely spoken a hundred words to him."

They continued walking.

"What about Leo Golowski?" asked Georg.

She shook her head and smiled. "That was my childhood love," she replied. "That doesn't count. Anyway, I'd like to meet the sixteen-year-old girl who wouldn't have fallen in love out in the country with a hand-some boy who had just fought a duel with a real count and then walked around for a week with his arm in a sling."

"But he didn't do it on your account, but for the honor of his sister, so to speak."

"For Therese's honor? Where did you get that idea?"

"You explained to me yourself that the young man had accosted Therese in the woods, while she was studying *Emilia Galotti*."[4]

"Yes, that's true. But she let herself be accosted quite willingly. Leo was only against it because the young count belonged to a group of young people who really behaved rather insolently, and were even a little anti-Semitic. And once, while Therese was walking on the shore with her brother, the count came over to her and spoke to Therese like a good acquaintance, and mumbled his name so carelessly to Leo, that Leo hunched over and introduced himself with the words: 'Leo Golowski, Jew from Cracow.' What happened next, I don't know exactly. It came to an exchange of words, and the duel was fought the next day in the cavalry barracks in Klagenfurt."

"So I had it right," persisted Georg scornfully. "He fought a duel for the honor of his sister."

"No, I tell you. I was there once when he spoke later with Therese about the story and told her: 'As far as I'm concerned, you can do whatever you want, be courted by whomever you want' . . ."

"Only he has to be a Jew," Georg completed the thought.

Anna shook her head. "He's really not like that."

"I know," Georg replied softly. "We've recently become good friends, your Leo and I. We met again at a coffeehouse just last night, and he was really very cordial. I think he even forgives me my birth. By the way, I didn't tell you yet that Therese had been up at the Ehrenbergs today." And he reported about the appearance of the young lady at the Ehrenberg salon, and on the impression she made on Demeter.

Anna smiled with pleasure at this.

Later, while they were walking arm-in-arm on another quiet street, Georg began again: "But I still don't know who your great love was."

Anna was silent and looked down.

"Now, Anna, you promised me, didn't you?"

Without looking at him, she replied, "If only you knew how strange the story seems to me today."

"Why strange?"

4. A tragic play in five acts by Gotthold E. Lessing which first appeared in 1772, with a demanding lead role for a beautiful young woman. In Goethe's *The Sorrows of Young Werther*, it lies open on Werther's desk when he shoots himself.

"Because the one you are asking about was really an old man."

"Thirty-five," Georg joked, "right?"

She shook her head earnestly. "He was fifty-eight or sixty."

"And you," Georg asked slowly.

"This summer it will be two years. I was twenty-one at the time."

Georg stood suddenly still. "Now I know, it was your singing teacher, wasn't it?"

Anna didn't answer.

"So, really," said Georg, without actually being surprised, for it was not unknown to him that, despite his grey hair, all his students fell in love with the famous master.

"And you loved him," asked Georg, "more than anyone else you ever met?"

"Strange, isn't it? But it's true. . . ."

"Did he know it?"

"I think so."

They had come to a widened plaza with a small garden plot that was only sparingly lit. Behind it rose a red, shimmering church. There, as if drawn to a quiet spot, they strolled under the dark, gently swaying branches.

"And what really happened between you, if one may ask?"

Anna fell silent, and at this moment, Georg thought anything was possible. Even that Anna had been this man's lover. But along with the anxiety he experienced at this thought, there also grew in him, gently and scarcely conscious, the wish to hear his fears confirmed. For how easy and free of responsibility this adventure would seem, if Anna had already belonged to someone else, before she was his.

"I'll explain the whole story to you," said Anna finally. "It's really not so terrible."

"So?" asked Georg, unusually anxious.

"Once, after a lesson," Anna began hesitantly, "he gallantly helped me into my jacket. And suddenly he pulled me to him, put his arms around me, and kissed me."

"And you? . . ."

"I . . . I was completely enraptured."

"Enraptured . . ."

"Yes. It was something indescribable. He kissed me on the forehead, and on the mouth, and on the hair. . . . And then he took my hand and murmured all sorts of things that I didn't really hear properly. . . ."

"And . . . "

"And then . . . then there were voices next door . . . he let go of my hand . . . and it was over."

"Over?"

"Yes, over. Obviously, it was over."

"I really don't find it so obvious. Did you ever see him again?"

"Of course, I continued to study with him."

"And . . . "

"I told you, it was over . . . completely, as though nothing had ever happened."

Georg was surprised that he felt reassured. "And he never tried again?" he asked.

"Never again. It would have been ridiculous. And because he was very smart, he knew it quite well himself. Before that, it is true, I loved him deeply. But after this incident, he was nothing more to me than my old teacher. To a certain extent, even older than he actually was. I don't know if you can completely understand it. It was as if he had expended his last remaining youth in that moment."

"I understand it quite well," said Georg. He believed her, and loved her even more than before. They went into the church. It was almost dark in the wide space. Only before a side altar were dim candles burning, and on the other side, behind a small religious statue, shimmered a feeble light. A wide cloud of incense floated toward them between the vaulting and stonework. The sexton walked by, softly jingling his keys. Dim figures could be seen from the back, motionless in the pews. Slowly Georg stepped forward with Anna, and he felt like a young groom on a trip, who was sightseeing in a church with his young wife. He told Anna this. She only nodded. "It would be even more beautiful," whispered Georg, as they stood at the chancel, holding each other tightly, "if we were really away together in a strange place. . . ."

She looked at him as though filled with happiness, yet questioningly; and he was startled by his own words. Would Anna have understood it as a serious proposal or only as a kind of courtship? Was he not obligated to clarify that it was not intended that way? . . . A recent conversation occurred to him which they had had while hanging on to an umbrella on a windy and rainy day walking along the way to Schoenbrunn.[5] He had made the suggestion to her that she come to town with him to have supper in a private room at an inn;—she had replied, in that iciness in which her whole being sometimes seemed to solidify: "I

5. The famous baroque summer palace of the royal family, on the southwest edge of town.

am not for such things." He hadn't pressed it further. But, a quarter of an hour later, to be sure, in the course of a conversation about Georg's style of living, but with an ambiguous smile, she had spoken the words to him: "You have no initiative, Georg." And in this moment he suddenly felt that unsuspected and dangerous depths of her soul were opening up, in which it was wise to be very cautious. He had to think about this again. What was going on in her? . . . What did she want, and what were her plans? . . . And what did he want and expect himself? Life was so unpredictable. Was it not quite possible that he really might go traveling in the world with her, to share a period of happiness with her . . . and finally to part from her as he had parted from many others? But when he thought of the end, which must come in any case, whether brought by death or by life itself, he felt a tender sadness in his heart. . . . She was still silent. Did she feel him lacking in initiative again? . . . Or did she perhaps think: I will succeed; I will be his wife . . . ?

Then he felt her hand gently caressing his with, for him, a new and most comforting tenderness. "Georg," she said.

"What is it?" he asked.

"If I were pious," she replied, "I would want to pray for something."

"For what?" asked Georg, almost frightened.

"For what you will become, Georg. Something really meaningful! A true, a great artist."

Involuntarily he looked at the floor, in shame that her thoughts had followed so much purer a road than his own.

A beggar held the thick green curtain back, and Georg gave the man a coin; they were in the open. Streetlights were lit up, the noise of wagons and roll shutters was nearby, and Georg felt that a delicate veil had torn, which the church in twilight had woven around them, and in a liberated tone suggested a short pleasure ride. Anna was happily in agreement. In an open *fiaker*, whose cover they put up over themselves, they rode along the streets, around the Ring, seeing little of the buildings and gardens, not speaking a word, and snuggling ever closer together. Each felt their own and the other's impatience, and they knew there was no turning back.

As they neared Anna's house, Georg said, "How sad that you have to go home already."

She shrugged her shoulders and smiled strangely. The depths, thought Georg again, but without dread, almost cheerfully. Before the wagon stopped at the corner, they made a date for the next morning in the Schwarzenberg Garden, and then got out. Anna hurried home, and Georg strolled slowly toward the city.

He considered whether or not to go to the coffeehouse. He wasn't particularly in the mood. Bermann probably stayed at the Ehrenbergs for dinner, one couldn't count on Leo Golowski's coming, and the other young people, mostly Jewish literati that Georg had recently come to know casually, didn't really attract him that much, even though he had found some of them not uninteresting. On the whole he found the tone of the young people among themselves sometimes too intimate, sometimes too strange, sometimes too witty, sometimes too solemn; none seemed to behave toward the others, scarcely toward themselves, without affectation. Heinrich had recently explained that he wanted nothing more to do with the whole circle, which had been spitefully disposed toward him ever since his successes. Georg regarded it as possible, to be sure, that Heinrich, in his vain and hypochondriac manner, sensed animosity and persecution there also, where perhaps only indifference or dislike were present. He, for his part, knew that it was not so much friendship that attracted him to the young writer, as curiosity to get to know an unusual man better; perhaps also an interest in peering into a world that until now had remained rather foreign to him. For while he, as before, remained rather reserved, and in particular avoided any reference to his relations with women, Heinrich had not only told him about his distant love, for whom he claimed to suffer torments of jealousy, but also about a pretty blond person with whom he had recently begun to spend his evenings,—just for distraction, as he added with self irony; not only of his Viennese student and journalistic years, which were not yet so far behind, but also of his childhood and boyhood in the tiny Bohemian provincial town where he had been born thirty years ago. Georg found the tone of mixed tenderness and animosity, feelings of attachment and alienation in which Heinrich spoke of his family, especially of his sick father, who had been an attorney in that little town, and a long-time deputy of Parliament, strange and sometimes almost painful. Yes, he even seemed to be a little proud that as a twenty-year-old, he had already predicted the destiny of his all-too-trusting father exactly as it would later be fulfilled: after a brief period of popularity and success, the growth of the anti-Semitic movement had driven him out of the German Liberal Party, most of his friends had abandoned and betrayed him, and a dissolute art student, who portrayed the associations of Czechs and Jews as the most dangerous enemies of German culture and breeding, who beat his wife at home, and got his maids pregnant, had been his successor in the trust of the electorate and in Parliament. Heinrich, grated by his father's phrases of Germany, Freedom, and Progress, in all their reverence, had greeted the downfall of the old man initially with malicious glee; gradually though, as the once sought-after attorney also began to lose his clients, and the material situation of the family declined day by day, there emerged in the son a belated sympathy. He had abandoned his legal studies early enough, and was forced to come to the aid of his family through regular journalistic work. His first artistic successes met with no further response in the darkened house of his homeland. There were dark signs that his father was nearing madness, and the mother, for whom, as it were, State and Fatherland had ceased to exist as her husband was no longer elected to Parliament, withdrew now from the whole world as he sank into spiritual night. Heinrich's only sister, at first a blooming and capable creature, had fallen into depression after an unhappy passion for a sort of provincial Don Juan, and with morbid stubbornness blamed her brother, with whom in her youth she had had an excellent understanding, for the unhappiness of the parental home. Heinrich also spoke about other relatives which he remembered from years past, and a partially ridiculous, partially touching stream of pious, narrow-minded old Jews and Jewesses passed before Georg, like ghosts from another world. He came to understand in the end that Heinrich did not feel drawn by any sort of homesickness back to that small, lamentably strife-torn town, or to the stuffy narrowness of the crumbling parental household, and realized that Heinrich's egoism meant both deliverance and liberation to him.

It struck nine from the tower of St. Michael's as Georg stood in front of the coffeehouse. He saw the critic Rapp sitting in front of a window which was not covered by the curtains, a pile of newspapers in front of him on the table. He had just taken his glasses from his nose to clean them, and the pale, otherwise maliciously clever face, with those dull eyes, looked as if dead. Across from him, gesturing into the emptiness, sat the poet Gleissner, with the polish of his false elegance, and an enormous black cravat in which a red stone sparkled. As Georg could not hear their voices, but only observe the movement of their lips and their exchange of glances, he could hardly comprehend how they could stand to sit across from each other for a quarter of an hour in this cloud of hate. He felt in an instant that this was the atmosphere in which the life of this entire circle took place, and through which flashed, only occasionally, escaping sparks of spirit and self-understanding. What did he have to do with these people? A sort of dread seized him, he turned away, and decided, instead of going to the coffeehouse, finally to visit the club again, whose rooms he had not entered for months. It was only a few steps away. Soon Georg climbed the broad marble staircase and proceeded to the small dining room with the light green draperies, and was greeted with dignified warmth, like one who had been missed for a long time, by Ralph Skelton, the attaché of the British Embassy, and Doctor von Breitner, who sat having dinner in a corner. They spoke of the coming tournament, about the banquet that was being arranged in the honor of the foreign fencing master; they discussed the new operetta at the Wieden Theater, in which Fraulein Lovan, as Bajadere, appeared almost naked, and the duel between the industrialist Heidenfeld and Lieutenant Novotny in which the offended husband had fallen. After dinner Georg played a game of billiards with Skelton and won. He gradually felt more comfortable, and decided to come more often again to these airy and well-appointed rooms, which were frequented by pleasant and well-dressed young people with whom one could converse in a proper and lighthearted manner. Felician appeared and explained to his brother that things had become quite amusing at the Ehrenbergs, and brought him greetings from Frau Marianne. Breitner, one of his famous giant cigars in his mouth, joined the brothers and explained that the pictures of a few deserving club members would be hung in the neighboring dining room, especially some by the young Labinski, who had ended his life the past year through suicide. And Georg thought back about Grace, about that strange, coldly glowing conversation with her at the cemetery in the melting February snow, and about that marvelous night on the moon-blanched deck of the steamer that had brought them from Palermo to Naples. He hardly knew which woman he longed for most at this moment: for Marianne, the forsaken, for Grace, the departed, or for the delightful young creature with whom he had been walking a few hours before in a church at twilight, as if on a wedding trip in a strange city, and who wanted to pray to heaven that he would become a great artist. In this memory he felt a subtle emotion. Did it not almost seem that she was more interested in his artistic future than in himself? . . . No, . . . not any more. She had only expressed what was slumbering deep in his own soul. He just forgot sometimes, so to speak, that he was an artist. But that had to change. So much was begun and prepared. Only a little ambition, and it could not fail to succeed. And in the next year, he would go out into the world. A position as *Kapellmeister*[6] would soon be found, and with one mighty leap he would stand in the middle of a career which would bring wealth and respect. He would get to know new people, a new sky would shine above him; and mysteriously, as from distant fog, unknown white arms stretched out to him. And while the young people next to him seriously weighed the chances of the competitors in the coming tournament, Georg dreamed in his corner of a future full of work, fame, and love.

At the same hour Anna lay in her dark room, without sleeping, her wide-open eyes directed at the ceiling; for the first time in her life with the unerring feeling that there was a person in the world who could make of her what he wished; with the firm resolution to accept all happiness and all sorrow that lay in store for her; and with a tender hope, lovelier than all which had ever appeared to her, for a lasting and serene happiness.

---

6. A position roughly equivalent to the modern music director and including the duties of principal conductor.

Third Chapter

Georg and Heinrich got down from their bicycles. The last villas lay behind them, and the broad road, gradually rising, led into the forest. The foliage still hung rather thick on the trees, but every light breeze took leaves with it and dropped them slowly to the ground. The orange hills were in autumn splendor. The road continued upward past a stately inn garden, to which stone steps led. Only a few people were sitting in the open; most were sitting in the glass veranda, as if they didn't completely trust the warmth of this gratifying late October day, through which every now and then a threatening coldness blew. Georg thought with dreary reminiscence of the winter evening on which he and Frau Marianne were the only guests staying here. Bored, he sat beside her, had listened impatiently to her murmuring conversation about the previous evening's concert in which Fraulein Bellini had sung his songs; and on the return trip, as he had to get out of the wagon in a suburban street on account of Marianne's anxiousness, he had breathed a sigh of relief. A similar feeling of liberation came over him almost every time he took leave from a lover, even after a pleasant time together. Even as he had left Anna at her door three days ago, after the first evening of complete fulfillment, he had become aware, before any other feeling, of the pleasure of being alone again. And immediately after that, even before the feeling of gratitude and the anticipation of a genuine sense of belonging with this gentle creature whom his whole being had embraced with such fervor had arisen in his soul, there flowed through him a dream of yearning for voyages across a shimmering sea, of coasts that approached alluringly, of walks along shores that vanished again the next day, of blue horizons, freedom, and solitude. On a later morning, as the air of the past evening's memories and obligations flowed through the awakened lovers, the trip was naturally postponed until a later, perhaps not so distant, but more opportune time. For that this adventure too, however earnestly and propitiously it had begun, was also destined to come to an end, Georg knew even at that moment, only without any dread. Anna had given herself to him without indicating by a word, a look, or a gesture, that now for her, in some way, a new chapter in her life had begun. And so Georg felt deep inside that the farewell also must be without gloominess or melancholy: a handshake, a smile, and a soft "it was nice." And it appeared all the easier to him at their next meeting, when she approached him with a simple, intimate greeting, without that affected tone of compliant melancholy, or fulfilled destiny that he had heard trembling in the words of many another who had awakened, not for the first time, to such a morning.

A faintly drawn line of mountains appeared in the distance, and vanished again, as the road led up through a thick tract of forest. Deciduous and coniferous trees grew peacefully together, and through the subdued color of the pines shone the autumn-colored leaves of beeches and birches. Hikers appeared, some with backpacks, climbing staffs, and studded boots as though fitted out for serious mountain climbing; sometimes, in an exuberant rush, bicyclers would speed down the road.

Heinrich spoke to his companion about a bicycle tour along the Rhine that he had undertaken at the beginning of September.

"Isn't it strange," said Georg, "I've traveled around so much in the world, and still don't know the region where my ancestors came from at all."

"Really?" asked Heinrich. "Doesn't something stir in you when you hear the word 'Rhine' spoken?"

Georg smiled. "It's been nearly a hundred years since my great-grandparents left Biebrich."

"Why do you smile, Georg? It's been a lot longer than that since my forefathers came from Palestine, and yet plenty of otherwise quite logical people assert that my heart trembles with longing for that country."

Georg shook his head angrily. "Why do you constantly worry about these people? It's really becoming an *idée fixe* with you."

"Oh, you believe I'm thinking of the anti-Semites? Absolutely not. I don't take it seriously from them any more, at least usually. But ask our friend Leo what he thinks about this matter sometime."

"Oh, you mean him. Well, but he doesn't understand it so verbally, but more symbolically—or politically," he added hesitantly.

Heinrich nodded. "These two emotions lie right beside one another in the minds of this type." He sank for a moment in reflection, pushed his bicycle ahead with easy, impatient strides, and was soon a few paces ahead again. Then he began to speak of his September trip again. He thought back about it almost with emotion. Solitude, foreign lands, travel, was this not a three-fold happiness that he enjoyed? "Such a feeling of inner freedom flowed through me then," he said, "that I can hardly describe it to you. Do you ever have this feeling, in which all memories, near and distant, lose their reality, so to speak; all people to whom one is otherwise attached, through pain, care, tenderness, float like mere shadows, or better said, like spirits that we have ourselves imagined? And imagined spirits naturally appear too, and are at least as vivid as the people one really does remember. The most peculiar relationships develop between the real and the imagined characters. I could tell you about a conversation that took place between my late great-uncle, who was a rabbi, and Duke Heliodor, you know, the one who appears in my libretto—a conversation too amusing, too profound, ever to happen in life or a libretto. . . . Yes, trips like that are wonderful! And so one goes through cities that one has never seen before and perhaps will never see again, past mere, unfamiliar faces which vanish again immediately for all eternity . . . and then one hurries along on bright streets between river and wine country. Such moods are truly purifying. It's too bad we get them so rarely."

Georg always felt a certain embarrassment when Heinrich got lofty. "I suppose we could go on riding now," he said, and they swung back onto their bicycles. A narrow, rather rough side road took them between the forest and a meadow to an unedifying, plain, two-story house that made itself known as an inn through a morose, brown signboard. A large group of tables stood in the meadow, which was separated from the house by the road, some covered with what once were white, others with floral-patterned, cloths. Right by the road, at some tables that had been pushed together, sat ten or twelve young people, members of a bicycle club. Some had taken off their jackets, others had them smartly pulled on; on the sky-blue, yellow-trimmed sweaters were displayed emblems in vivid red and green embroidery. Strong voices, though not with the purest intonation, raised the choral song: "The Lord, Who Makes Iron, Wants No Bondsmen." [1]

Heinrich examined the group with a quick glance, squinted his eyes, and said to Georg with clenched teeth and heavy tone: "I don't know if these young people really are honest, true, and brave, as they in any case regard themselves; but that they smell like wool and sweat is certain, so I'd be in favor of finding a seat relatively far from them."

What does he really want, Georg thought to himself. Would he be more sympathetic if a group of Polish Jews were sitting there singing psalms?

The two pushed their bicycles to a distant table and sat down. A waiter appeared in a black, grease-and-vegetable-spattered dress coat, wiped off the table with a dirty napkin, took their order, and vanished.

"Isn't it a shame," said Heinrich, "the way these run-down inns are everywhere around Vienna? It makes a person depressed."

Georg found this excessive gloom uncalled for. "Oh God, in the country," he said, "one expects it. It almost goes with it."

Heinrich didn't accept this view, and began to discuss the plan to establish seven hotels on the edge of the Vienna Woods, and even estimated that one would need at most three to four million, when suddenly Leo Golowski was standing there. He was in civilian clothes, which, as often with him, were not without a certain bizarre element. Today he wore a light grey sport coat with a blue velvet vest and a yellow silk tie in a smooth steel ring. The two others greeted him with joy, and expressed their surprise.

Leo took a seat with them: "I heard," he said, "that you decided on an outing last night, and when we were released from the barracks early this morning at nine, I thought immediately that it would be nice to spend an hour in the country with two intelligent, agreeable gentlemen. So I went home, threw on my civilian clothes, and was on my way." He spoke in his customary congenial, almost naive-sounding tone, which Georg always found engaging, but which carried with it in his memory a ring of irony, even duplicity. But this, as it were, ambiguous tone in Leo's words only occurred in casual conversation; he carried on serious discussions with a clarity which quite impressed Georg. Recently he had had a few occasions to listen in on discussions at the coffeehouse between Leo and Heinrich about aesthetic questions, in

1. The first line of a popular patriotic song from the Napoleonic period. It also became current again for a time during the Third Reich.

particular about the relationship between the laws of music and mathematics. Leo believed the foundation to lie in the way the major and minor tonalities moved the human soul in such diverse ways. Georg followed the clear and incisive repartee with enjoyment, though something in him also resisted hearing the bold attempt to explain all the magic and all the mystery of the sounds through the rule of laws, which stemmed just as inexorably from the same eternal root as those by which the earth and stars turned. Georg only became impatient when Heinrich tried to develop Leo's theories further and occasionally to apply them to a literary work, and he immediately felt himself a silent ally of Leo's, who would gently smile at Heinrich's fantastic and confused elaborations.

The food was served, and the young people ate with relish; Heinrich no less than the others, despite the fact that he expressed great disapproval over the inferiority of the cooking, and was inclined to interpret the proceedings at the inn not only as an expression of an individually low character, but as characteristic of the decline of Austria in many other fields. The conversation turned to the military situation of the country, and Leo related stories making fun of comrades and officers which greatly amused the two others. In particular, a first lieutenant gave cause for merriment who had introduced himself to the volunteer regiment with the words of warning: "Wit' me you'll have notin' to laugh at, a'am a beast in human form."

While they were still eating, a man walked up to the table, clicked his heals together, raised his hand, saluting, to his bicycler's cap, greeted them with a jovial "*All Heil,*" added for Leo a comradely "*servus,*" and introduced himself to Heinrich: "Josef Rosner is my name." Then he began a conversation cheerfully with the words: "The gentlemen are also on a bicycle party. . . ." As no one replied, he continued: "One must make use of these last fine days; this splendor will not last much longer."

"Would you like to have a seat, Herr Rosner?" Georg asked courteously.

"I kiss your hand, but . . . ," he indicated toward his group . . . "we were just about to leave; we have a long way to go yet, riding to Tulln, and then through Stockerau to Vienna. The gentlemen will permit me . . ." He took a match from the table and elegantly lit a cigarette.

"What sort of club is this you're with, actually?" asked Leo, and Georg wondered about the familiar address, until it struck him that the two had been boyhood friends.

"That's the Sechshauser Bicycle Club," replied Josef. Although no one had expressed surprise, he added: "The gentlemen will wonder why, as a child from Margareten,[2] I belong to this suburban club; it's only because a good friend of mine is the chairman there. You see that fat fellow who has just pulled on his jacket? That's the young Jalaudek, the son of the alderman and deputy of Parliament."

"Jalaudek . . ." Heinrich repeated with evident contempt in his voice, and said nothing further.

"Ah," said Leo, "he's the one who recently gave that splendid definition of science in a debate about the Public Education Association. Didn't you read about it?" he turned to the others.

They did not remember.

"Science," quoted Leo, "Science is what a Jew plagiarizes from others."

Everyone laughed. Josef too, although he immediately explained: "Actually he's not like that, I know him. He's only so crass in his political life . . . because that's the way opponents blast each other in our dear Austria. But in general, he's a very likeable gentleman. The young one is the more radical."

"Is your club Christian-Social, or German-National?" Leo asked obligingly.

"Oh, we don't make distinctions like that, only naturally as long as . . ." he interrupted himself, suddenly embarrassed.

"Well, yes," Leo encouraged him, "that your club is non-Jewish is self-evident. One can see that from a distance."

Josef considered it best to laugh. Then he said: "Oh please, no politics in the mountains; besides, the gentlemen will get the wrong impression if we talk about this matter. In our club we have, for example, one who is engaged to an Israelite. But they're signaling me. It's been an honor, gentlemen, *servus* Leo, *all Heil.*" He saluted again and left with swaggering stride. The others, involuntarily smiling, watched after him.

Then, turning to Georg, Leo suddenly asked: "How is his sister really doing with her singing?"

"What?" said Georg, startled and a little red.

"Therese told me," Leo continued, "that you sometimes make music with Anna. Is her voice in order now?"

"Yes," Georg replied hesitantly, "I think so; in any case I find it very

2. The district bordering the old city center to the south and slightly west.

agreeable, very full, especially in the lower ranges. Too bad that it doesn't suffice, for larger spaces, I mean."

"Doesn't suffice," Leo repeated reflectively. "That's an odd way of putting it."

"How else would you describe it?"

Leo shrugged his shoulders and looked calmly at Georg. "You see," he said, "I've always found her voice very agreeable too, but right from the time when Anna got the idea to go on the stage . . . I honestly confess that I never believed anything would come of it."

"Then you apparently knew," Georg replied with deliberate casualness, "that Fraulein Anna suffers from this peculiar weakness of the vocal chords."

"Yes, of course I knew; but had she been committed to an artistic career, inwardly committed I mean, she would have overcome even this weakness."

"You think so?"

"Yes I think so, I definitely think so. I also think that words like 'peculiar weakness,' or 'the voice does not suffice,' indicate in some way substitutes for something deeper, psychological. It's obviously not in the line of her destiny to become an artist, that's it. She was, so to speak, destined from the outset to end up middle class."

Heinrich was highly in agreement with the theory of the line of destiny, and carried the thought in his confused way further and further, from insight, to distortion, to nonsense. Then he suggested that they should lie down in the meadow for a half-hour in the sun, which would not often shine so warmly again this year. The others agreed.

A hundred paces from the inn Georg and Leo stretched out on their coats. Heinrich sat down on the grass, folded his arms around his knees, and looked down. At his feet the meadow led down toward the forest. Further below, buried in dense foliage, rested the cottages of Neuwaldegg. The steeple crosses and sun-dazzled windows of the town shimmered forth out of a blue-grey fog, and far off, as though carried up by a moving mist, the plains floated and grew dusky.

Strollers walked across the meadow toward the inn. Some gave greetings in passing, and one, still a young man, who had a child by the hand, remarked to Heinrich: "Such a lovely day, just like in May."

Heinrich felt his heart open up at first, against his will, as it sometimes did in response to such casual, but unexpected friendliness. But he remembered himself at once, for he well knew that this young man

too was only enchanted by the mildness of the day, the peacefulness of
the countryside; in the depths of his soul this fellow was just as full of
hostility as all the others who walked by him so innocently. And once
again he couldn't quite understand why the appearance of these gently
rolling hills, this twilight town, moved him with such painful sweetness,
while the people who lived here meant so little to him, and rarely anything good.

The bicycle club sped along the nearby road, their jackets blowing,
emblems beaming, and a raw laughter resounded over the meadow.

"Horrible people," remarked Leo casually, without changing position.

Heinrich indicated below with a vague nod of the head. "And such
fellows," he said, with teeth clenched together, "still imagine that they
can sooner call this home than people like us."

"Well, yes," responded Leo calmly, "and they're not so wrong about
that, these fellows."

Heinrich turned scornfully to him: "Excuse me, Leo. I forgot for
a moment that you yourself cherish the desire to pass as only being
tolerated."

"I wish no such thing," answered Leo, smiling, "and you don't need
to misunderstand me so spitefully right away. But that these people regard themselves as the natives and you and I as the foreigners can't be
held against them. That's only an expression of their healthy instinct
for an anthropological and historical matter of firm fact. Against that,
and therefore against everything which follows from it, nothing is to
be done with either Jewish or Christian sentimentality." And turning
to Georg, he asked in an all too obliging tone: "Don't you agree?"

Georg turned red, cleared his throat, and had no chance to reply, as
Heinrich, on whose forehead two deep furrows appeared, immediately
angered, picked up the discussion: "My instinct is at least as authorita-
tive for me as that of Herrs Jalaudek, junior and senior; and this instinct
tells me indubitably that here, precisely here, is my homeland, and not
in some place that I don't know, which, from the descriptions, promises
me nothing in the slightest, and which certain people now try to persuade me is my fatherland, for the reason that my ancient ancestors had
been scattered into the world from there several thousand years ago.
Whereupon it could be observed that the ancestors of Herrs Jalaudek,
and even those of our friend Baron von Wergenthin, had been just as
little native here as mine and yours."

"You don't need to be angry with me," replied Leo, "but your view in these matters is a little restricted. You always think of yourself and of the incidental circumstance . . . pardon in this question the 'incidental circumstance,' that you are a writer who, by chance, because he was born in a German country, with the German language, and because he lives in Austria, writes about Austrian people and circumstances. In the first place, it isn't a matter at all of you or of me, nor of a few Jewish officials who are not promoted, a few Jewish volunteers who are not made officers, or of Jewish docents who are never or only late made professors,—those are mere inconveniences of secondary importance so to speak; it is a matter here of entirely different people, whom you know little or not at all, and of destiny, about which you, I assure you dear Heinrich, about which you certainly, despite the obligation that you actually should feel, have not yet considered thoroughly enough. Certainly not. . . . Otherwise you couldn't speak of these things in such a shallow and . . . egotistical manner, the way you do." He then related his experiences at the Basel Zionist Congress, in which he had taken part last year, and where he had been granted a deeper insight into the character and state of mind of the Jewish people than ever before. In these people, whom he saw close up for the first time, the yearning for Palestine was not, he knew this now, artificially induced; a genuine, and now necessary, newly kindled and inextinguishable feeling was at work in them. No one could doubt it, who, like him, had seen the holy wrath flash in their eyes, when a speaker explained that one should, for the time being, give up hopes for Palestine, and must be content with colonies in Africa and Argentina. Yes, he had seen old men, not just uneducated ones, no, scholarly, wise men, cry, because they feared that the land of their forefathers, which they could not themselves have entered again by any means, even by the realization of the boldest Zionist plans, might not be made accessible even by their children or grandchildren.

Georg had listened amazed, even a little moved. But Heinrich, who had paced back and forth in the meadow with short steps during Leo's story, explained that Zionism appeared to him to be the worst affliction that had yet infected the Jews, and precisely Leo's words had convinced him more deeply of this than any other consideration or experience before. *Patriotism* and *Religion*, those were words which, from the very beginning, had angered him by their thoughtless, even malicious ambiguity. *Fatherland* . . . that was, in general, a fiction, a political concept, undefined, changeable, unintelligible. Only *Homeland* indicated something real, not *Fatherland*. And so the feeling of *Homeland* was one's right of settlement. And as concerns religion, he could tolerate equally the Christian and Jewish legends, as well as the Hellenistic or Indian; but all were equally intolerable and revolting to him when they sought to force their dogmas on him. And he felt a sense of community with no one, no, not any one in the world. With the sobbing Jews in Basel just as little as with the howling Pan-Germans in the Austrian Parliament; with Jewish money lenders as little as with the high-born robber knights; with a Zionist brandy merchant as little as an old Christian Socialist. And least of all would the consciousness of a commonly suffered persecution, a jointly endured hatred, bind him to other men from whom he felt inwardly distant. He would accept Zionism as a moral principle and as a welfare scheme if it would honestly make itself known as such; but the idea of the establishment of a Jewish state on religious and national grounds appeared to him an insane revolt against the spirit of all historical development. "And in the depths of your soul," he cried standing still in front of Leo, "even you don't believe that this goal will ever be achieved, you don't even wish it, as long as you enjoy yourself for this or that reason along the way. What does your 'Homeland Palestine' mean to you? A geographical concept. What does 'the Faith of your Fathers' mean to you? A collection of customs that you have long ceased to practice, most of which you find as ridiculous and tasteless as I do."

They continued arguing for a long time, now forcefully, almost with animosity, then calmly again and in a sincere effort to win the other over; sometimes they found themselves, to their amazement, of a common view, only to lose the other the next moment in a new dispute. Georg, stretched out on his coat, listened to them. Sometimes his feelings were inclined toward Leo, in whose words a glowing compassion for his suffering clansmen seemed to tremble, and who proudly turned from people who were not willing to accept him as their equal. At other times he felt closer to Heinrich, who angrily rejected an undertaking which, fantastic and short-sighted at the same time, called together the members of a race, whose best had everywhere flourished in the culture of their homelands, or at least contributed to it, from the far ends of the earth, only to send them out to a common destination, for which they felt no homesickness. And Georg began to understand how difficult the best among them, of whom Heinrich spoke and in whose souls the future of humanity was preparing itself, must find it to decide, tossed back and forth as they were between the reluctance to appear obtrusive and their resentment of the imputation to cower before an insolent majority—between their innate sense of belonging where they lived and worked, and their rebellion at seeing themselves insulted and reviled, even there; how the sense of their existence, their worth, their rights, must vacillate between defiance and exhaustion. For the first time the name Jew, which had so often frivolously, derisively, and contemptuously crossed his lips, began to appear to him in a completely new, as it were darker sense. A presentiment of this people's mysterious destiny, that somehow expressed itself in everyone who sprang from this origin, began to dawn in him; not less in those who tried to escape from it like a disgrace, an injury or a legend that didn't concern them, than in those who stubbornly referred back to it, as to a fate, an honor, or a fact of history which stood fast and immovable.

And as he forgot himself watching the two speakers and contemplated their figures, which delineated themselves with sharply drawn and vigorously moving lines against the violet-red sky, it occurred to him, not for the first time, that Heinrich, who insisted that he belonged here, resembled in form and gesture some fanatical Jewish preacher, while Leo, who wanted to move to Palestine with his people, reminded him in profile and demeanor of the busts of Greek youths he had once seen in the Vatican, or the museum in Naples. And once again, as his eyes followed Leo's lively and noble gestures with pleasure, he well understood how Anna had felt an infatuated attraction to the brother of her friend years ago during that summer by the lake.

Heinrich and Leo still stood facing each other in the meadow, and their exchange became lost in entanglement. The sentences stormed into one another, cramped each other, and, missing their mark, flew out into empty space;—and at some point Georg realized that he could hear only the noise of their argument, without being able to follow the content.

A cool wind blew in from the plain, and Georg rose, shivering slightly, from the grass. The others, who had almost forgotten he was there, were called back into the present, and decided to get going. The light of the ending day still shown on the landscape, though the sun rested, dark red and faint, on a long, stretched out evening cloud.

While he was hanging his coat on his bicycle, Heinrich said: "After conversations like this I always have a feeling of dissatisfaction which usually leads to a bad sensation in my stomach. Yes, really. They never lead anywhere. And what do political opinions mean anyway among men for whom politics is neither a calling nor a profession? Do they have the slightest influence on the course of our lives, the structure of our existence? You Leo, just as well as I, neither of us will ever do anything, will ever be able to do anything, other than precisely that which is given to us to do within our character and abilities. You will not emigrate to Palestine in your lifetime, even if the Jewish state were founded and they immediately offered you a post as Prime Minister—or at least as official pianist."

"Oh, you can't know that," Leo interrupted him.

"I know it for certain," said Heinrich. "Although I'll also confess to you that, despite my complete indifference toward every form of religion, I will never, ever be baptized, even if it were possible through such a subterfuge to escape the anti-Semitic narrow-mindedness and villainy once and for all, which is less possible now than before."

"Hmm," said Leo, "but if the stake is fired up again . . . ?"

"In this case," responded Heinrich, "I hereby solemnly commit myself to devote myself completely to your cause."

"Oh," Georg interjected, "those times will never come again."

The others had to laugh that Georg was so kind as to reassure them about their future with these words, as Heinrich noted, in the name of all Christianity.

In the meantime they had crossed the meadow. Georg and Heinrich pushed their bicycles forward up the rough cart path; Leo, in flowing coat, came along beside them on the grass. All were silent for quite a while, as though exhausted. At the point where the rough path met the wide road Leo stood still and said; "Here, unfortunately, we must part." He extended his hand to Georg and smiled. "You must have been awfully bored today," he said.

Georg turned red. "Now listen, you regard me as something . . ."

Leo held on to Georg's hand. "I regard you as a very bright and also as a very good person. Do you believe me?"

Georg was silent.

"I want to know," continued Leo, "if you believe me, Georg, it concerns me." His tone became more genuinely sincere.

"Yes, of course I believe you," replied Georg, still a little impatient.

"I'm glad," said Leo, "because I really care about you, Georg." He looked deep in his eyes, then once more extended his hand to him and Heinrich in leaving, and turned to go.

Georg however, suddenly had the feeling that this young man, who was walking there down the middle of the road, in flowing mantle, his head slightly lowered, was not going to a "home", but to some foreign land where one could not follow him. This feeling seemed all the more incomprehensible, as he had recently not only spent a number of hours at the coffeehouse in conversation with Leo, but also had learned many enlightening things about him, his family, and their situation, through Anna. He knew that that summer by the lake, which now lay, along with Anna's youthful infatuation, six years in the past, represented the last carefree time for the Golowski family, and that the father's business had completely collapsed the following winter. It must have been quite remarkable how, according to Anna's explanation, every member of the family adapted so easily to the changed circumstances, as though they had been prepared for this turn of events for a long time. They moved from the comfortable residence in the Rathaus[3] district to a gloomy street near the Augarten.[4] Herr Golowski undertook all sorts of trading ventures and Frau Golowski made handicrafts for sale. Therese gave lessons in French and English, and at first continued to take her lessons at the drama school. It was a young violinist from an impoverished Russian noble family who awakened her interest in political questions.[5] She soon renounced her art, for which, by the way, she always showed more enthusiasm than talent, and within a short time stood right in the middle of the Social Democratic Movement, as a speaker and agitator. Leo enjoyed her fresh and audacious character, but without sharing her views. Sometimes he would even attend meetings with her; but as he was not easily impressed by big words, nor by oaths which would never be kept, nor by threats made into the empty air, he enjoyed, usually already on the way home, demonstrating with irrefutable acuteness the contradictions in her speeches and those of her party comrades. In particular he repeatedly tried to make clear to her that she could not so completely forget her great task for days and weeks at a time if her compassion for the poor and suffering was really as deep as she imagined. However, Leo's life was not moving toward any clear goal either. He attended lectures at the technical school, gave piano lessons, even planned a virtuoso career for a time, and then would practice five to six hours a day. But it still could not be foreseen how he would decide in the end. As it was his way unconsciously to wait for a miracle which could spare him the inconvenience, he had long put off his year of military service until the final period approached, and only now was serving

3. The imposing neo-Gothic city hall of the Ringstrasse period, finished in 1883 and located on the west leg of the Ring. It is modeled after the townhall of Brussels and features a 325-foot-tall central steepled tower with a clock.
4. A sizeable garden park outside the old town center, but within walking distance to the north.
5. It is noteworthy to recall that when Demeter Stanzides first met Therese, he remarked that she reminded him of a Russian student. Could Schnitzler be implying that when Therese engages in political activity she is acting out a role that was first suggested to her by a young Russian radical?

his time, at the age of twenty-five. The parents let Leo and Therese go their own way, and so there appeared to be many differences of opinion, but few serious arguments, in the Golowski home. The mother mostly sat at home, sewing, embroidering, and crocheting, the father went later and later to work, and preferred to watch the chess players in the coffeehouse, a diversion through which he was able to forget the decline of his existence. Since the ruin of his business he had not been able to overcome a certain embarrassment with respect to his children, so he was almost proud when Therese occasionally gave him an article that she had written to read, or Leo would condescend on a Sunday afternoon to play a game with him on the beloved board.

It sometimes seemed to Georg that there might be some deep connection between his own attraction to Leo, and Anna's long passed infatuation with him. For this was not the first time he felt drawn in a quite singular way to a man to whom a soul had once been attracted that now belonged to him.

Georg and Heinrich had mounted their bicycles and followed a narrow road through thick, dark forest. Later, as the forest pulled back from both sides of the road, they had the setting sun at their backs, and the elongated shadows of their own bodies on their bicycles ran on ahead of them. The road slanted steeply downward and soon led between low houses which were overhung with red foliage. An old man sat by a house door on a bench; a pale child looked out of an open window. Otherwise there was not a soul to be seen.

"Like an enchanted village," said Georg.

Heinrich nodded. He knew the place. He had also been here with his sweetheart, on a marvelous summer day this year. As he thought about it, a burning longing pulled at his heart. And he remembered the last hours that he had spent together with her in Vienna in his cool room with the lowered blinds through the slits of which the hot August morning had glimmered; the last walk through stone-cool streets in Sunday silence, and through old empty courtyards,—and his complete lack of suspicion that all this was for the last time. For it was not until the next day that the letter came, the terrible letter in which it was written that she had wanted to spare him the pain of a farewell, and that she would be long across the border when he would read these words, on the way to the new and foreign city.

The road became more animated. Friendly villas appeared, pleasantly surrounded by little gardens; behind the houses, forested hills rose gently upward. Once more the valley spread out before them, and the departing day rested on the meadows and fields. In a large, empty inn garden, the lamps were lit up. A hastening nightfall seemed to creep in from all sides. Now they were at the crossroads. Georg and Heinrich got down and lit cigarettes.

"Right or left," asked Heinrich.

Georg looked at his watch: "Six . . . and I have to be in the city by eight."

"So we can't have supper together then?" said Heinrich.

"Unfortunately not."

"Too bad. So we'll take the short way, through Sievering."

They lit their head lamps and pushed their bicycles along the serpentine road through the forest. One tree after another sprang out of line from the darkness in the beam of the headlights, and then fell back again into the night. The wind was blowing stronger through the trees, and leaves rustled downward. Heinrich felt a mild dread which sometimes came upon him in darkness when in open nature. He felt a disappointment that he would have to spend the evening alone. He was annoyed with Georg about it and also became angry over Georg's reserve toward him. He decided, not for the first time, not to speak to Georg any more about his own personal affairs. It was better that way. He needed no one's trust, no one's sympathy. It had always seemed best to him when he went his own way alone. He had done that often enough. So why should he open his soul to anyone? Yes, acquaintances for walks together and trips, for cool, intelligent discussions about various aspects of life and art,—women to embrace fleetingly; but he needed no friend or lover. This way life would be more dignified and tranquil. He was delighted with these resolutions, and felt himself grow hard and superior. The forest darkness lost its dread, and he walked through the softly rustling night as through a native element.

They soon arrived at the hilltop. The dark sky lay starless over the grey road and over the misty meadows which stretched on both sides in deceptive distance to the forest hills. A light shone from a nearby customs booth. They mounted their bicycles again and road downward as fast as the darkness permitted. Georg wanted to get back soon. It seemed strangely impossible to him that in an hour-and-a-half he would see the quiet room again, of which no one knew except Anna and him; that dim room with the oleographs on the wall, the blue velvet sofa, and the piano on which stood the photographs of unknown people and a white plaster bust of Schiller; with its high, narrow windows across from which rose the old, dark grey church.

Lamps were burning along the road. Once more the road opened up and a last glance back toward the hills presented itself. From then on things went more quickly, at first still between well-kept country houses, and finally through a noisy main street full of people, deeper in the city. They got down at the Votivkirche.[6]

"*Adieu*," said Georg, "and *auf Wiedersehen* until tomorrow in the coffeehouse."

"I don't know . . . ," replied Heinrich; and as Georg looked at him questioningly, he added, "It's possible that I'll be leaving town."

"Oh, such a sudden decision!"

"Yes, sometimes it just seizes one. . . ."

"The yearning," added Georg smiling.

"Or anxiety," said Heinrich, and gave a short laugh.

"You have no cause for that," replied Georg.

"Do you know that for sure," asked Heinrich scornfully.

"You told me yourself . . ."

"What?"

"That you get news every day."

"Yes, that's true, every day. I get tender, fervent letters. Every day at the same hour. But what does that prove? I write even more fervent and tender ones but . . ."

"Well, yes," said Georg, who understood him. And he ventured the question: "Really, why don't you stay there with her?"

Heinrich shrugged his shoulders. "Tell me yourself, Georg, wouldn't it seem a little strange to you if one were to break camp on account of such an affair, to be dragged around in the world by a little actress. . . ."

"Personally I'd regret it very much . . . but strange . . . what would be strange about it?"

"No, I have no desire to," concluded Heinrich firmly.

"But if you . . . if you really insisted on it . . . if you demanded it straight out . . . might not the young lady give her career up?"

"Maybe. But I don't demand it. I won't demand it. No. Better pain than responsibility."

"Would it really be such a great responsibility?" Georg asked. "I mean . . . is the young lady's talent so outstanding, is she so committed to her art, that it would really be a sacrifice if she gave the thing up?"[7]

6. The neo-Gothic Votive Church on the northwest corner of the Ringstrasse, and the official church of the city garrison.

7. This discussion is highly autobiographical. Schnitzler's own marriage ended in divorce in 1921, largely over precisely this problem.

"If she has talent?" said Heinrich. "Yes, I don't know that myself. I even believe that she's the only creature in the whole world about whose talent I'm not able to make a judgment. Every time I've seen her on the stage, her voice sounded like a stranger's, and as it were, more distant than all other voices. It's really quite remarkable. . . . But you've seen her act too, Georg. What sort of impression do you have? Tell me completely honestly."

"Well, frankly . . . I don't really remember her very well. Forgive me, I didn't know at the time. . . . When you speak of her I always see a reddish-blond lock of hair that falls down her forehead a little,—and a small, pale face with very large, black, wandering eyes."

"Yes, wandering eyes," Heinrich repeated, bit his lip, and fell silent for a while. "Take care of yourself," he then said suddenly.

"But you'll write to me?" asked Georg.

"Yes, of course. And in any case I'll be back," he added, and smiled stiffly.

"Have a good trip," said Georg, who gave him his hand and squeezed it with special warmth. That was good for Heinrich. This warm hand-shake suddenly reassured him not only that Georg did not find him ridiculous, but strangely also that his distant love had been true to him, and that he was a person to whom more was permitted than many others.

Georg watched him as he sped away on his bicycle. Again, just as a few hours ago when they had said good-bye to Leo, he felt as though someone were leaving for a strange land; and at this moment he knew that he would never achieve, through any amount of sympathy, a truly natural intimacy with these two, like when they had introduced him to Guido Schoenstein last year, and before that, to poor Labinski. He wondered if that might be grounded in the racial difference between him and them, and asked himself if, without the conversation of the two others, he would have been so clearly aware of it through his own feelings of strangeness. He doubted it. Didn't he feel closer, even more related, to these two and many others of their race, than to many people who were from a similar stock as his? Yes, didn't he sense quite clearly sometimes that somewhere in the depths, stronger threads ran between him and these two than between him and Guido, and possibly his own brother? But if this were so, shouldn't he have said this to the two men at some moment this afternoon? To have said to them: trust me, don't shut me out. Try accepting me as a friend! . . . And as he asked himself why he hadn't done this, and had scarcely taken part in their conversation, he became aware with amazement that during that whole time he had not been free of a kind of guilty feeling, exactly as though he had not been free himself his whole life long of a certain, personally completely unjustified thoughtlessness and animosity toward the "Strangers," as Leo himself called them, and so contributed his own part to the mistrust and obstinacy with which so many had closed up in his presence, those whom he himself had had occasion and inclination to accommodate. This thought stirred a growing uneasiness in him that he couldn't quite explain, and that was nothing other than the dark insight that genuine relationships, even between individually genuine people, cannot develop in an atmosphere of folly, injustice and insincerity.

He rode back, faster and faster, as though to run from this uneasiness. Arriving home he dressed hastily so Anna would not have to wait too long. He longed for her as never before. It seemed to him as though he were coming home from a long journey, to the only being who completely belonged to him.

Fourth Chapter

Georg stood at the window. Directly below arched the stony backs of the bearded giants who carried the weathered crest of a long vanished noble family in their powerful arms. Across the way, the stairs crept forward from the darkness of the ancient houses to the gate of the grey church, which shimmered in the snowfall as though from behind a fluttering curtain. The light of a street lamp in the square shone pale through the last light of day. The snowy street below, which led from the middle of town, but away from all the activity, was even quieter than usual on this holiday afternoon. And once again, as he always did when he had climbed the broad staircase of this old palace-turned-apartment-house, and had entered the spacious, low-vaulted room, Georg felt he had escaped his familiar world, as though he had entered the other part of a wonderful double existence.

He heard a key squeaking in the door and turned around. Anna came in. Georg took her happily in his arms and kissed her on the forehead and mouth. Her dark blue jacket, broad-brimmed hat, and fur boa were all covered with snow.

"You've been working," said Anna, as she took off her coat, indicating toward the table where sheets of handwritten music paper lay next to the green-shaded lamp.

"I looked through the quintet, the first movement. But there's still a lot to do."

"But then it will be marvelous."

"Let's hope so. Did you come from home, Anna?"

"No, from the Bittners."

"On a holiday?"

"Yes. The two girls missed a lot, which has to be made up, because of the measles. Which is fine with me, for financial reasons."

"A giant sum!"

"And then one can escape at least for a few hours from one's 'happy home.'"

"Well yes," said Georg, as he laid Anna's boa across the back of an armchair and smoothed the fur distractedly with his fingers. Anna's remark, which sounded to him, and not for the first time, like a mild reproach, had affected him unpleasantly. She sat down on the divan, raised her hands to her temples, gently smoothed her wavy dark blond hair back, and looked at Georg smilingly. He stood with both hands in his coat pockets, leaning against the chest of drawers, and began to tell about last night, which he spent with Guido and the violinist. For the last few weeks, by wish of the count, the young lady had been taking catechism from the confessor of an archduchess; for her part, she had started Guido reading Nietzsche and Ibsen. However, as a result of these studies there was, by Georg's account, so far nothing more to report than that the young count had jokingly begun to call his girlfriend Rattenmamsell, after the odd character from *Little Eyolf*.[1]

Anna had little cheerful to report about last night. They had had visitors. "First," explained Anna, "Mama's two cousins, then a friend of Papa's from the office to play tarok. Even Josef resigned himself to stay home, laid on the divan from three until five when his new pal came, Herr Jalaudek, who made a serious pass at me."

"Well?"

"He was enchanted. I only say: a violet tie with yellow dots; you should hide yourself. Anyway, he brought me an honorable request, to collaborate in a production of the Wilder Mann[2] with a so-called academy for the benefit of the Waehringer church building fund."

"You naturally agreed."

"I excused myself, for lack of voice and piety."

"Well, as for the voice . . ."

She interrupted him. "No Georg," she said gently, "*that* hope I have given up forever."

1. A late play (1894) by Ibsen, dealing primarily with erotic themes, including incest.
2. Wilder Mann was a priest at Cologne and author of several poems on moral themes, including one written around the year 1170 on the life of Saint Veronica.

He looked at her and searched her eyes, which remained clear and open. Soft and muffled, the sound of the organ could be heard coming from the church.

"Yes, right," said Georg, "I brought you the ticket for *Carmen* for tomorrow."

"Thank you," she replied, and took the ticket. "Are you going too?"

"Yes. I have a box on the fourth level and invited Bermann. I'm taking the score with me like I did last time with *Lohengrin*, to practice my conducting again. In the back, of course. You can hardly imagine how much one learns by it. By the way, I'd like to suggest something to you," he added hesitantly. "Would you like to go to dinner with Bermann and me after the theater?"

She was silent.

He continued. "It would really please me if you would get to know him better. For all his faults, he's an interesting person, and . . ."

"I'm no Rattenmamsell," she interrupted him sharply, and put on her stern, bourgeois face. Georg pulled in the corner of his mouth. "That has nothing to do with me, dear child, I differ in many respects from Guido. But, as you wish." He walked back and forth in the room; she remained sitting on the divan. "So you're going to the Ehrenbergs this evening?" she then asked.

"Yes, you knew that. I've turned them down twice lately. This time I couldn't really . . ."

"You don't need to make excuses, Georg. I have an invitation too."

"Oh, where?"

"To the Ehrenbergs."

"Really!" cried Georg, involuntarily.

"Why are you so surprised?" she asked sharply. "Obviously they don't know yet that they can't have any more to do with me."

"But Anna, what is it with you today? Why are you so sensitive? Even if they knew . . . do you think that would stop them from inviting you? On the contrary. I'm sure that Frau Ehrenberg would have nothing but respect for you."

"And little Else might be quite envious. Don't you think? By the way, she has written me a very nice letter. Here it is. Do you want to read it?" Georg scanned through it, found it of somewhat deliberate cordiality, said nothing further, and returned it to Anna.

"By the way, there's another one," said Anna, "if it interests you."

"From Doctor Stauber? So? Would it be all right with him if he knew that I read it?"

"Why are you suddenly so considerate?" And she continued, almost reproachfully: "There would probably be a lot of things he wouldn't like."

Georg read the letter quickly for himself. In a dry, sometimes rather humorously colored way, Berthold reported on the progress of his work at the Pasteur Institute, on walks, day trips, and theatergoing, and included many general observations of all sorts; however the letter contained no allusion, in its eight pages, to the past or future. Georg asked casually, "How long is he staying in Paris?"

"As you can see, he doesn't say a word about coming home."

"Your friend Therese recently told me that his party colleagues would really like to have him back again."

"Oh, has she been to the coffeehouse again?"

"Yes. I spoke to her there two or three days ago. She really amuses me."

"How?"

"In the beginning she was very haughty, even with me. Obviously because I waste my life with art and other such trivialities, while there are so many more important things to be done in the world. But after she loosens up a little, it comes out that she's just as interested in all these trivialities as the rest of us ordinary people."

"She warms up easily," Anna said rigidly.

Georg walked back and forth, and continued talking. "She was just precious at the last fencing tournament in the Musikvereinsaal.[3] By the way, who was the fellow she was sitting with up in the gallery?"

Anna shrugged her shoulders. "I didn't have a chance to see the tournament. And I don't know all of Therese's companions anyway."

"I assume," said Georg, "he was a colleague, in every respect. In any case, he was very gloomy and rather poorly dressed. When Therese applauded Felician's win, he nearly curled up with envy."

"What actually did Therese tell you about Doctor Berthold?" asked Anna.

"Oh," Georg joked, "there's still some active interest, it would seem."

Anna did not answer.

"So," Georg reported, "I can tell you that they want him to be the candidate for the legislature in the fall, which I find quite logical in view of his brilliant speaking gifts."

3. The hall of the Music Association. Classical concerts are still given there.

"What do you know about that! Have you ever heard him speak?"

"Of course, don't you remember? At your apartment!"

"It's really not necessary for you to make fun of him."

"But that never occurred to me."

"I definitely noticed that at the time he struck you as a little strange. He and his father as well. You certainly seized the first opportunity to get away from them."

"That's absolutely untrue, Anna. It's quite unfair of you to insinuate such a thing of me."

"They may have their weaknesses, both of them, but at least they're the kind of people one can rely on. That's something too."

"Have I ever denied that, Anna? Really, I've never heard you talk so illogically. What is it you really want from me? Should I have been jealous on account of this letter?"

"Jealous? Not a chance, not with your background."

Georg shrugged his shoulders. Memories arose in him of similar verbal disputes in the course of earlier relationships, of those sudden, mysterious disagreements and estrangements that usually meant nothing other than the beginning of the end. Could he really be so far from his kind and intelligent Anna already? Upset, almost sad, he walked back and forth in the room. Sometimes he cast a fleeting glance at his beloved, who sat silently in her corner of the divan and rubbed her hands together as though they were cold. In the silence of the suddenly saddened room, the organ sounded louder than before, singing voices could also be heard, and the windowpane rattled lightly. Georg's glance fell on the little Christmas tree which stood on the chest, whose candles had burned for him and Anna two nights ago. Half bored, half distracted, he took matches out of his pocket and began to light the little candles, one after another. Then the sound of Anna's voice came to him: "In an important matter," she said slowly, "I'd trust old Doctor Stauber more than anyone else."

Surprised, Georg turned around to her and blew out the burning match he was still holding in his hand. He knew at once what Anna was thinking, was surprised that since the last time they had been together he had not thought any more about it himself, went over to her and took her hand. Only now did she look up, impenetrably, with motionless expression.

"Anna dear, tell me . . ." He sat down beside her on the divan, her two hands in his own.

She said nothing.

"Why don't you talk?"

She shrugged her shoulders. "It's just that there's nothing new to tell about," she explained simply.

"So," he said slowly. He wondered if her strange irritability today could not be explained as an indication of the situation to which she had alluded, and an uneasiness arose in him. "But it won't be certain for a while," he said in a somewhat cooler tone than he actually wanted. "And . . . and even if—," he added with forced cheerfulness.

"So, you'll forgive me?" she asked smiling.

He pressed her to him, and was suddenly completely relieved. A strong and moving tenderness flamed up in him for the sweet, gentle creature that he held in his arms, and from whom, he deeply believed, a serious injury could never come to him. "It really wouldn't be so bad," he said cheerfully. "You'd just be leaving Vienna for a little while, that's all."

"Well, it certainly wouldn't be as simple as you suddenly seem to be suggesting."

"Why not? We'll easily find an excuse. And anyway, whose business is it? The two of us. No one else. And as far as I'm concerned, as you know, I can leave any time. And can stay as long as I wish. I haven't even signed a contract for next year yet," he added smiling. Then he got up to blow out the candles, whose tiny flames had almost burned completely down; and, even more cheerfully, he continued talking. "It would be wonderful. Just think, Anna! At the end of February or the beginning of March we would leave, for the south naturally, to Italy, maybe by the sea. We'd live in some quiet place, where not a soul would know us, in a lovely hotel with an immense park. And one could work there; it'd be great!"

"So that's it!" she said, as if suddenly understanding. He laughed, squeezed her tighter in his arms, and she pressed herself against his chest. The noise was no longer coming from outside. The organ and voices had died away. The curtain of snow hung down in front of the window. . . . Georg and Anna were happy as never before.

As they rested in the dark, he spoke of his upcoming musical plans, and explained Heinrich's opera libretto to her, as far as he could. The room was filled with flickering shadows. A fairy-tale-like royal chamber with a wedding festival. A vehement youth steals in and draws his dagger on the prince. A dark oath, more mysterious than death, is pronounced. On the evening tide, a slow ship sets out for unknown lands.

At the feet of the youth rests a princess, who had been the bride of a prince. An unknown person approached in a bright boat with strange news; jesters, astrologers, dancers, courtiers floated by. Anna listened quietly. At the end Georg was curious to know what sort of impression she had gotten from the fleeting images.

"I can't really say," she replied. "In any case I'm puzzled at the moment as to how anything convincing can ever be made from this rather confused train of thought."

"Of course you can't imagine it yet today—especially after my explanation. . . . But the musical breath that blows from the story—you can sense that, can't you? I've even written down a few themes already,—and I'd like very much for Bermann to really get going with it soon."

"In your position, Georg . . . may I say something?"

"Of course, what is it?"

"If I were in your position, I'd finish the quintet first. There can't be all that much left to do."

"Not that much, and yet . . . Anyway you mustn't forget, that I've recently started all sorts of other things. The two piano pieces, then the orchestral scherzo—that's already pretty far along. But it undoubtedly belongs in a symphony."

Anna did not answer. Georg remarked that her thoughts had strayed, and asked her where they had wandered to.

"Not really so far," she replied. "It was just going through my mind, all that can happen before the opera can actually be finished."

"Yes," Georg said slowly, almost a little self-consciously, "if only one could see into the future."

She sighed softly, and he snuggled up closer to her, almost sympathetically. "It's all right, darling," he said, "I'm here . . . and I'll always be here." He thought he could feel what she was thinking: Can't he say anything better? . . . anything stronger? . . . something that will remove all fear forever? And insincerely, as though to expose himself to danger by the thought, he asked her: "What are you thinking about?" And once again, as she still didn't answer: "Anna, what are you thinking about?"

"About something very strange," she replied softly.

"What's that?"

"That the house already exists, where it will be born—and we have no idea where. . . . Something made me think about that."

"About that," he said, strangely touched. And with newly waxing tenderness he said, pressing her to his heart: "I will never leave you, either of you. . . ."

As it grew lighter in the room again, they became quite cheerful, and picked the last forgotten sweets from the branches of the little Christmas tree, enjoyed the thought of the coming reunion with their casual acquaintances, and, like on some merry adventure, laughed, and talked jovial nonsense.

As soon as Anna had gone, Georg locked the music paper in the desk drawer, blew the lamp out, and opened a window. The snow was falling light and thin. An old man came up the path out of the dark, and his weary breathing could be heard coming through the motionless air. The silent church rose grey across the way. . . . Georg stood for a while at the window. He was at this moment almost convinced that Anna had deceived herself with her acceptance. With consolation, Leo Golowski's statement that Anna was destined to end up middle class occurred to him. Surely it couldn't be in the "line of her destiny" to have a child by a lover. And it couldn't be in his own line to carry obligations of a serious kind, and already today to be bound to a woman, perhaps forever; to be a father at his young age! Father! . . . Heavily, almost darkly, the word sank into his soul.

He entered the Ehrenberg salon at eight in the evening. He was met by the sound of waltz music. At the piano sat the elder Eissler, whose long, grey, full beard fell almost down to the keys. Georg, who stood still in the entrance so as not to disturb him, was greeted on all sides by glances. The old Eissler played his famous Viennese dances and songs with light touch and strong rhythm, and Georg much enjoyed, as he always did, the sweet, swaying melodies.

"Magnificent," said Frau Ehrenberg, as the old man got up.

"Save the grand words for grander occasions, Leonie," replied Eissler, whose ancient prerogative it was to call all women and girls by their first name. And it seemed to do them good, to hear it spoken by this handsome old gentleman with the deep, resonant voice, in which it sometimes trembled like a sentimental echo from the touching days of youth. Georg asked him if all his compositions had appeared in print.

"Only a very few, dear Baron; unfortunately I myself cannot write a note."

"It would really be terribly sad if these charming melodies were to become completely lost."

"Yes, I have often told him that too," added Frau Ehrenberg. "But unfortunately he's one of those people who have never taken themselves completely seriously."

"Oh, that's not true, Leonie. Do you know how I began my musical career? I wanted to write a grand opera. To be sure, I was seventeen years old at the time, and madly in love with a singer."

The voice of Frau Oberberger came over from the table in the corner: "I'll bet it was a chorus girl."

"You're wrong, Katerina," replied Eissler. "Chorus girls were never my problem. It was even a Platonic love, like most of the great passions of my life."

"Were you that awkward?" asked Frau Oberberger.

"Sometimes that too," Eissler answered sonorously and with propriety, "for I apparently could have had just as much luck as a hussar captain. But I don't regret having been awkward. We cherish untroubled memories only of missed opportunities."

Frau Ehrenberg nodded in agreement.

"One may therefore not go wrong, Herr Eissler," remarked Nuernberger, "if one attributed the greater role in your life story to the troubled memories." Frau Ehrenberg nodded again. She was delighted when people were clever in her salon.

"Why did you say," asked Frau Oberberger, "that you could have had as much luck as a hussar captain? It's not at all true that officers have particularly good luck with women. When my sister-in-law once had a relationship with a first lieutenant . . ."

"I don't believe in Platonic love," Sissy said and beamed through the hall.

Frau Wyner gave a low moan.

"Fraulein Sissy is probably right," said Nuernberger. "At least I am convinced that most women interpret Platonic love either as an insult or as an excuse."

"There are young ladies here," Frau Ehrenberg gently reminded him.

"One can't help noticing," said Nuernberger, "that they're participating in the conversation."

"Despite that, I might allow myself to add a little anecdote to the chapter on Platonic love," said Heinrich.

"Just no Jewish ones," Else tossed in.

"Of course not. Just listen. A small, blond girl . . ."

"That doesn't prove anything," Else interrupted.

"Let him finish," Frau Ehrenberg admonished.

"So, a small, blond girl," Heinrich began again, "once expressed to me, in contrast to Fraulein Sissy, the conviction that Platonic love in fact exists. And do you know what she conveyed to me as proof of it . . . ? One personal experience. She had once spent, as she explained to me, one hour completely alone in a room with a lieutenant, and . . ."

"That's enough," Frau Ehrenberg cried anxiously.

"And," Heinrich concluded, unperturbed and unmoved, "in this hour, nothing in the slightest happened."

"Says the blond girl," Else appended.

The door opened, and Georg saw a strange lady enter, in a light blue, four-cornered, and low-necked dress, pale, simple, and noble. Only when she smiled did he realize that the lady was Anna Rosner, and he felt something like pride in her. As he reached his hand to the beloved, he felt Else's glance directed at him.

They all went into the next room, where the table was set out with unpretentious festivity. The son of the house was absent. He was away at Neuhaus, at his father's factory. However, Herr Ehrenberg himself was suddenly sitting at the table as supper was being served. He had only recently returned home from his trip, which in fact had taken him to Palestine. When he was asked by Privy Councillor Wilt about his experiences, he wouldn't talk about them at first. Finally he confessed that the scenery disappointed him, the exertions of the trip had been vexing, and that he had seen as good as nothing of the Jewish settlements which, from what had been heard from reliable sources, were being established. "So we have well-founded hopes," remarked Nuernberger, "of keeping you here, even in case the Jewish state should be founded in the course of the next few years?"

Ehrenberg replied sullenly: "Have I ever told you that it was my intention to emigrate? I'm too old for that."

"Oh, I see," said Nuernberger. "I didn't know that you had toured the region just to please Fraulein Else and Herr Oskar."

"Dear Nuernberger, I don't want to fight with you about it. And Zionism is too good for table talk."

"If too good," said Privy Councillor Wilt, "we may leave undecided; in any case too complex, especially since everyone understands something different by it."

"Or wants to understand," added Nuernberger, "as is the case, by the way, with most catchwords, and not only in politics. That's why there's so much babble in the world."

Heinrich explained that of all human creatures, politicians represented for him, to a certain extent, the most enigmatic phenomenon.

"I understand pickpockets," he said, "acrobats, bank directors, hoteliers, kings . . . which means that I can transfer myself into the souls of all these people without any special effort. From this it obviously follows that it's only a rather quantitative matter, even if enormous changes in my character would be required, to make it possible for me to play in the world the role of an acrobat, a king, or a bank director. I feel quite certain about that: I could expand my character immeasurably, but I could never be what people call a politician, a party leader, a colleague, a minister."

Nuernberger smiled over Heinrich's concept that a politician represented a special sort of human being, while, however, it only belonged to the external, and not even indispensable, exigencies of his profession to pose as a special human being, to hide his greatness or his mediocrity, his actions or his indolence, behind titles, abstracts, and symbols. What the insignificant or the corrupt among them represent is obvious: they were just common business people, or swindlers, or sweet-talkers. But the significant ones, the doers, the genuinely gifted, they were, in the depths of their souls, nothing except artists. They too tried to create a work, and one which, in the idea, raised claim to immortality and finality just the same as any other work of art. Only that the material from which they built was nothing fixed, nothing relatively enduring, like tones or words are, but rather it was of a more dynamic human form, uninterrupted in flow and motion.

Willy Eissler appeared, excused himself to the lady of the house for being late, took a seat between Sissy and Frau Oberberger, and greeted his father like a dear old friend after a long separation. It appeared that the two hadn't seen each other for many days, despite the fact that they lived together. Willy received compliments on his success at the aristocrats' production where he had played a marquis in a French proverb, with the countess Liebenberg-Rathony. Frau Oberberger asked him, quite loud enough for the neighboring sitters to hear, where he had his rendezvous with the countess, and if he received her in the same lodgings where he met his middle-class flames. The conversation grew more lively, with exchanges darting all around and intermingling here and there. Georg caught detached words, including some from a conversation between Anna and Heinrich in which the subject was Therese Golowski. During the conversation he noticed that Anna sometimes would cast a curious, dark look toward Demeter Stanzides, who appeared today in a frock coat with a gardenia in the buttonhole; and without experiencing actual jealousy, felt oddly bothered. Could she be thinking at this moment that she might be carrying his child beneath her heart? "The Depths" occurred to him again. Suddenly she looked over to him with a smile as though she were coming home from a trip. He felt inwardly relieved, and sensed with a certain fear how much he loved her. Then he raised his glass to his lips and drank to her. Else, who until this time had been talking with her other neighbor, Demeter, turned to Georg; in her deliberately casual manner, with a glance at Anna, she remarked: "She looks pretty. So feminine. She's always been that way. Do you still make music with her?"

"Sometimes," answered Georg coolly.

"Maybe I'll ask her to play with me again after the New Year. I don't know why I haven't until now."

Georg was silent.

"And how are things going," she said with a look toward Heinrich, "with your opera?"

"With our opera? Nothing yet. Who knows if anything will ever come of it."

"Naturally nothing will come of it."

Georg smiled. "So why are you so hard on me today?"

"I'm quite angry with you."

"With me? Why?"

"Because you're always giving people reason to regard you as a dilettante."

Georg was struck in the heart, and even felt a little resentment toward Else; but he got a grip on himself quickly and replied: "Maybe that's all I am. And if one is not a genius, then it's better to be an honest dilettante than an inflated artist."

"Who demands that you achieve greatness immediately? But that's no reason to let yourself go like you do, inwardly and outwardly."

"I really don't understand you Else. How can you say . . . Don't you know that I'm going to Germany in the fall, as *Kapellmeister?*"

"Your career will go to ruin because you won't be able to make it to your 10 A.M. rehearsal."

Georg was still fuming inside. "By the way, who called me a dilettante, if I may ask?"

"Who? God, it was in the newspaper."

"Oh, I see," said Georg, reassured, as he now remembered that a critic had described him as "aristocratic dilettante" after the concert in which Fraulein Bellini sang his songs. At that time, Georg's friends had explained that this hostile review had as its cause the fact that he hadn't paid a call to the gentleman in question, who was known to be very envious.

So that's how it was. There were always extraneous reasons to blame when these people made a negative judgment about one. Even Else's present irritability, what else was it at bottom but jealousy. . . .

They all got up from the table and went back into the salon. Georg went over to Anna, who was leaning against the piano, and said softly to her: "You look lovely."

She nodded with satisfaction.

Then he asked her: "Did you have a nice conversation with Heinrich? What did you talk about? Therese, wasn't it?"

She didn't answer, and Georg noted with consternation how her eyelids suddenly fell, and she began to waiver.

"What . . . what's wrong with you?" he asked, startled.

She didn't hear him, and would have gone down if he hadn't quickly grabbed her wrist. Frau Ehrenberg and Else were on the spot immediately.

Had they been watching us? Georg thought.

Anna soon had her eyes open again, forced herself to smile, and whispered: "Oh, it's nothing; sometimes I don't handle the heat very well."

"Come along," said Frau Ehrenberg, motherly. "Perhaps you should lie down for a minute."

Anna appeared confused, did not reply, and the ladies of the house accompanied her into the next room.

Georg looked around him. The guests appeared to have noticed nothing. Coffee was handed out. Georg took a cup and stirred around distractedly with the spoon. In the end, she won't end up middle class, he thought. But at the same time he inwardly felt so removed from her, as though it all had nothing to do with him personally. Frau Oberberger stood next to him. "So, what do you really think about Platonic love? You're an expert." He answered distractedly; she continued talking in her own way, without caring if he was listening or if he answered. Suddenly Else was back again. Georg inquired sympathetically and courteously about Anna's condition.

"I'm sure it's nothing serious," said Else, and looked him oddly in the face.

Demeter Stanzides walked up and asked her to sing. "Would you care to accompany me?" she said turning to Georg. He bowed and sat down at the piano.

"What shall it be then?" asked Else.

"Whatever you like," replied Wilt, "Only nothing modern." After dinner he liked to play the reactionary, at least in artistic matters.

"Very well," Else said, and handed Georg a folder. She sang "The Old Picture" by Hugo Wolf, with her small, well-trained, and rather touching voice. Georg accompanied with taste, though rather distractedly. He was a little annoyed about Anna, however much he tried to resist it. In any case, no one appeared to have noticed the incident, except Frau Ehrenberg and Else. Oh, what did it matter anyway . . . even if they knew everything? . . . Who did it concern? . . . Who would even care? . . . Now they are all listening to Else, he thought further, and are feeling the beauty of the song. Even Frau Oberberger, who is completely unmusical, has forgotten for a few minutes that she is a woman, and has a still, sexless face. And Heinrich too is listening spellbound, and perhaps for a moment isn't thinking about his work, or the fate of the Jews, or the distant beloved, or the one who is near, the little blond, whom to please he had of late become altogether elegant. Truthfully, the frock doesn't look bad on him, and the cravat isn't one of those bought-ready-made ones that he usually wears, but carefully tied. . . . Who's standing so close behind me, Georg thought, that I can feel their breath on my hair? . . . Sissy perhaps? . . . If the world were coming to an end tomorrow morning, it would be Sissy I'd choose to spend the night with me. That's for sure. Ah, here comes Anna with Frau Ehrenberg. . . . It seems like I'm the only one who noticed, but I'd better pay attention to my playing and Else's song. I'll greet her with my eyes . . . Yes, I greet you, mother of my child. . . . How strange life is. . . .

The song was finished. Everyone applauded and asked for more. Georg accompanied Else in some other songs, by Schumann, by Brahms, and to close, by general wish, in two of his own, which he had come personally to dislike since someone said they reminded one of Mendelssohn. While he was accompanying, he felt all attachment with Else lost, and tried through his playing to win her back. He played with exaggerated emotion, he courted her with it, but felt it was futile. For the first time in his life, he was in unhappy love with her. The applause after Georg's songs was strong.

"That was your best period," Else said softly to him as she put the notes away. "Two or three years ago."

The others were also appreciative, but without distinguishing between different periods in his artistic development.

Nuernberger confessed to having been most pleasantly surprised by

Georg's songs. "I'll not conceal from you," he said, "that from the views I sometimes hear expressed of you, dear Baron, I would have imagined them considerably more unintelligible."

"Really charming," said Wilt. "All so melodious and simple, without affectation or bombast."

He's the one, thought Georg grimly, who called me a dilettante.

Willy had walked up. "Now just say again, Herr Privy Councillor, that you could whistle them from memory, and if I understand anything about physiognomy, the Baron will be sending two fellows over to see you in the morning."

"Oh no," said Georg, collecting himself and smiling. "The songs fortunately come from a long bygone time. I don't feel offended by any sort of reproach or praise."

A servant brought ice cream, the group broke up, and Anna stood alone with Georg at the piano. He asked her quickly, "What did that mean?"

"Well, I don't know," she replied, and looked at him with large eyes.

"Is everything all right now?"

"Completely," she answered.

"Is today the first time this has happened to you?" Georg asked somewhat hesitantly.

She answered: "Last night at home something similar happened. A kind of faintness. It even lasted a little longer. While we were still sitting at supper. But no one noticed it."

"Why didn't you say something to me about it?"

She shrugged her shoulders.

"Anna," he said animatedly, and a little guiltily, "I want to talk to you anyway. Give me a sign, when you want to go. I'll leave a few minutes ahead of you, and wait on Schwarzenbergplatz until you come in the wagon. Then I'll get in with you and we'll ride around a little. Is that all right?"

She nodded.

He said: "I'll see you later, treasure," and went into the smoking room. The old Ehrenberg, Nuernberger, and Wilt had sat down at a small green table to a game of tarok. The old Eissler and his son sat next to each other in two immense, green leather armchairs, and used the opportunity to finally have a proper conversation with each other. Georg took a cigar from a box, lit it, and contemplated the pictures on the wall without any particular sympathy. On a grotesquely depicted watercolor, that showed red-coated horsemen riding in a steeple chase, he saw Willy's name signed in the lower corner with pale red letters on

the green meadow. Involuntarily he turned to the young man and said:
"I had absolutely no idea."

"It's rather new," Willy remarked casually.

"A dashing picture, isn't it?" said the old Eissler.

"Oh, rather more than that," replied Georg.

"Hopefully I'll be able to offer something better soon," said Willy.

"He's going to Africa on the lion hunt," commented the old Eissler,
"with Prince Wangenheim."

"Really?" said Georg. "Felician should be part of the group too. But
he hasn't decided yet."

"Why's that?" asked Willy.

"He wants to take his diplomatic exam in the spring."

"But he could put that off," said Willy. "Lions are becoming extinct,
something which unfortunately can't be said of professors."

"I'll pay in advance for a picture, Willy," Ehrenberg called over from
the card table.

"Play Maecenus[4] later, Father Ehrenberg," said Wilt, "I've called a
three."

"One under," responded Ehrenberg, and continued: "If I may purchase something for myself, Willy, you could paint a desert landscape
for me in which Prince Wangenheim is being eaten by lions . . . but
from life if possible."

"You have the wrong person, Herr Ehrenberg," said Willy. "The
famous anti-Semite you mean is the cousin of my Wangenheim."

"As far as I'm concerned," replied Ehrenberg, "the lions could make
a mistake too; every anti-Semite doesn't have to be famous."

"You'll lose the game if you don't pay attention," Nuernberger
admonished.

"You should have bought property in Palestine," said Privy Councillor Wilt.

"God should protect me from that," replied Ehrenberg.

"Well, since he's done that in every way until now . . . ," said
Nuernberger, and played out his card.

"It appears to me, Nuernberger, that you hold it against me for not
going around selling old clothes."

"Then, at least, you would have the right to complain about anti-
Semitism," said Nuernberger. "For who feels it more in Austria than
the peddlers? . . . Unfortunately, only them, one could say."

---

4. Gaius Cilnius Maecenas, 73 B.C.–8 B.C. Roman statesman and the patron of Virgil
and Horace.

"And a few people with a sense of honor," responded Ehrenberg. "Twenty seven . . . thirty one . . . thirty eight . . . so, who won the game?"

Willy had gone back into the salon. Georg sat smoking on the arm of a chair and suddenly saw the gaze of the old Eissler directed at him in a particularly sympathetic way, and felt reminded of something, without knowing what.

"Recently," said the old man, "I spoke casually with your brother Felician, at the Schoensteins. It's striking how similar he looks to your blessed father. Especially when one knew your Papa as a very young man, like I did."

Now suddenly Georg knew what the look of the old man reminded him of: the old Doctor Stauber had rested his eyes on him at the Rosners with the same paternal expression. These old Jews! he thought derisively, but in a distant corner of his soul he was a little touched. It occurred to him that his father had often gone for morning walks in the Prater with Eissler, for whose understanding of art he had the greatest respect.

The old Eissler spoke further: "You Georg, more resemble your mother, in my opinion."

"Some people say that. It's hard to judge that for oneself."

"Your mother must have had a very lovely voice."

"Yes, in her early youth. I never really heard her sing myself. She tried it a few times. Three or four years before her death, a doctor in Merano even advised her to practice her singing. As a sort of lung exercise.—But unfortunately it wasn't very successful."

The old Eissler nodded and looked down. "You probably won't be able to remember any more that my poor wife was in Merano at the same time with your late mother."

Georg rummaged through his memory. It had escaped him.

"Once," said the old Eissler, "I rode down there in the same coach with your father. Neither of us had been able to sleep that night, and he told me a great deal about you two. About you and Felician I mean."

"Yes . . ."

"For example, that as a boy in Rome you played one of your own compositions for some sort of Italian virtuoso, and that he prophesied a great future for you."

"Great future . . . oh God! It was no virtuoso, Herr Eissler, it was a priest who had taught me to play the organ."

Eissler continued: "And in the evenings, when your mother had gone to bed, you would sometimes improvise for her for hours from the next room."

Georg nodded and silently sighed. It seemed to him that he had much more talent then than now. Work, he thought with fervor, work. . . . He looked up again. "Yes," he said, as if joking, "the problem is that prodigies so rarely ever come to anything."

"I have heard that you want to become a *Kapellmeister*, Baron."

"Yes," Georg answered with determination. "Next fall I'm going to Germany, possibly as rehearsal accompanist at first, in a small municipal theater, if it works out."

"But you wouldn't object to a court theater either?"

"Of course not. But why do you say that, Herr Eissler, if I may ask—?"

"I know quite well," said Eissler smiling, and letting his monocle fall, "that you would not ask for my assistance, but on the other hand I can imagine that it possibly would not be disagreeable to you to be able to dispense with the mediation of agents and other amenities of that sort . . . I mean apart from the consideration of the percentage."

Georg remained cool. "When one decides on a theater career, one knows all the things one has to put up with in the deal."

"Are you perhaps acquainted with Baron Malnitz?" asked Eissler, unconcerned with Georg's worldliness.

"Malnitz? Do you mean Baron Eberhard Malnitz, who had a suite performed a few years ago?"

"Yes, that's the one."

"I don't know him personally, and as far as the suite is concerned . . ."

Eissler dismissed Malnitz as a composer with a wave of the hand. "Since the beginning of the season," he then said, "he has been theater director in Detmold. That's why I asked you if you knew him. He's a good, old friend of mine. He used to live in Vienna. We've been meeting each year in Karlsbad or Ischl for the last ten or twelve years. This year at Easter we want to take a little Mediterranean trip. Would you permit me to mention your name at that opportunity, dear Baron, and to say a word about your aspirations as a *Kapellmeister*?"

Georg hesitated to answer, and smiled politely.

"Oh, please don't understand my offer as an importunity, dear Baron. If you would rather, I'll hold my tongue."

"You misunderstand my silence," replied Georg courteously, though not without pride. "But I really don't know—"

"I would suggest that a small court theater like that," Eissler continued, "is the right platform for you for a start. It also won't hurt you that you are of the nobility, not even with my friend Malnitz, although he likes to play the democrat, sometimes even the anarchist . . . with indulgence toward the bombings of course. But he's a charming fellow and really enormously musical . . . as long as he doesn't compose."

"Well," replied Georg, a little embarrassed, "if you wished to be so kind as to speak with him . . . one would be grateful for the generosity. In any case I thank you very much."

"It's nothing. Of course I can't promise success. It's just one chance among others."

Frau Oberberger and Sissy came in, accompanied by Demeter Stanzides.

"What sort of interesting conversation have we interrupted here?" asked Frau Oberberger. "The seasoned Platonist and the unseasoned libertine! We should have been here."

"Calm yourself, Katerina," said Eissler, and his voice again had that deep, tremulous ring. "One sometimes also speaks of other things than the future of the human race."

Sissy put a cigarette between her lips, took a light from Georg, and sat down in the corner of the green leather divan. "You're not paying any attention to me today," she began with that English accent which Georg so loved in her. "As if I didn't even exist any more. Oh, it's true. But I have a more faithful nature than you. Don't I?"

"You, faithful Sissy? . . ." He pushed an armchair up right next to her. They spoke of the past summer, and of the coming one.

"Last year," said Sissy, "you gave me your word that you would come out to see me. You didn't do it. But this year you must keep your word."

"Are you going to the Isle of Wight again?"

"No, this time we're going to the mountains, to the Tyrol, or Salzkammergut. I'll let you know. Will you come?"

"You'll probably have a big entourage again, I suppose?"

"I won't be interested in anyone else but you, Georg."

"Even if Willy Eissler should happen to be staying in the neighborhood?"

"Oh," she said with a wicked smile and ground out her cigarette forcefully in the glass ash tray.

They continued talking. It was one of those conversations like they had so often had over the past years. Joking and light in the beginning, and glowing in the end, with tender lies which for a moment were truth. Georg was once again enchanted with Sissy.

"What I would like best is to take a trip with you," he whispered very close to her.

She just nodded, her left arm laying on the broad back of the divan. "If only one could do what one wanted," she said with a look that dreamed of a hundred men.

He leaned over her trembling arm, went on, and became fascinated with his own words. "I'd like to be somewhere with you where no one knew us, where we wouldn't have to worry about anyone, Sissy. Many days and nights."

Sissy trembled. The word *nights* sent a shudder through her blood.

Anna appeared in the doorway, gave Georg a sign by a look, and vanished immediately. He inwardly resisted, but yet felt it was all right that he should have to take leave of Sissy just now. In the door of the salon he encountered Heinrich, who spoke to him. "When you leave, let me know. I'd like to talk to you."

"With pleasure. But I have to . . . I promised Fraulein Rosner I would accompany her home. Then I'll come right to the coffeehouse. See you there."

A few minutes later he was standing on the Schwarzenberg bridge. The sky was full of stars, the streets lay white and still. Georg turned his collar up, although it was no longer cold, and walked back and forth. Will anything come of the Detmold story? he thought. Well, if it's not Detmold, it'll be some other town. In any case, it's now in earnest. And much, very much, will lie behind me by then. He tried to reflect calmly. How will it all turn out? It's the end of December now. By March we'll have to leave—at the latest. . . . People will take us for a married couple. I'll go walking arm-in-arm with her, in Rome, on the Posilipo,[5] in Venice. . . . There are women who get very ugly in that condition . . . but she won't, no, not her. . . . She always had something maternal in her appearance. . . . In the summer she'll live in some quiet area where no one knows her . . . in the Thuringian forest maybe, or on the Rhine. . . . How strangely she said that today: the house in which the child will be born already exists. Yes! Somewhere far away, or maybe even quite near, the house is already standing—and people we've never seen are living in it. How strange. . . . When will it come? In late summer . . . around the beginning of September. By that time I'll fi-

5. Capo di Posilipo. The top of the high promontory to the south of the city of Naples; it overlooks the Gulf.

nally have to go. How will I do it? And a year from now the child will be four months old. It will grow up . . . get big. One fine day a young man will be there, my son. Or a young lady. A lovely girl of seventeen, my daughter. . . . By then I'll be forty-four. . . . I could be a grandfather by forty six . . . maybe even director of an opera company and a famous composer, in spite of Else's prophesies. But one must work for it, that's for sure. More than I have up to now. Else's right that I'm too easy on myself. That has to change. . . . And it will. I feel as if something is stirring within me. Yes—something's stirring in me too.

A wagon came from the Heugasse and someone leaned out of the window. Georg recognized Anna's face under the white shawl. He was very happy, climbed in with her, and kissed her hand. They talked cheerfully, ridiculing a little the company from which they had just come, and found it rather comical to spend an evening in such an empty fashion. He held her hands in his and was touched by her presence. He got out in front of her house, rang the bell, went back to the open carriage door, and they made a date for the next day. "I think we have a lot to talk about," said Anna. He just nodded. The house door opened, she got out of the wagon, calmly cast an intimate look at Georg, and vanished into the hallway.

Sweetheart, thought Georg with a feeling of happiness and pride. Life lay before him like something deeply mysterious, and full of challenges and wonders.

When he entered the coffeehouse, Heinrich was sitting in a window booth. Next to him was a very young, beardless, greenishly pale man in a smoking jacket with velvet lapels, but a shirtfront of dubious cleanliness, whom Georg had casually spoken to a few times. As Georg approached, the young man looked up with glowing eyes from a small notebook that he held in restless, unkempt hands.

"Oh, I'm interrupting," said Georg.

"Not at all," replied the young man with an insane laugh. "The more the merrier."

"Herr Winternitz," explained Heinrich as he extended Georg his hand, "was just reading me a poem cycle. Perhaps we'll stop for now."

Georg, moved a little by the disappointed look of the young man, suggested that he would be pleased to listen in, if that would be all right.

"It doesn't last much longer," Winternitz explained gratefully. "It's too bad that you missed the beginning. I could . . ."

"Yes, then there's a connection?" Heinrich asked surprised.

"What, you didn't see it?" cried Winternitz and laughed madly again.

"Oh, I see," said Heinrich, "it's always the same woman that your poems talk about. I thought it was always someone else."

"Of course it's always the same. It's characteristic of her that she always acts like a different person."

Herr Winternitz read softly, but urgently, as though inwardly consumed. From his cycle it followed that he had been loved like no one before him, but also betrayed like no one else, for which, in some sense, metaphysical causes were to blame rather than defects in his own personality. In the last poem however, he showed himself to be completely freed from his passion, and declared himself ready from now on to enjoy all pleasures that the world would offer him. This poem had four strophes, the last verse of each strophe began with a "Hail," and concluded with the cry: "Hail, so I go chasing through the world."

Georg had to admit that the reading had made a certain impression on him, and as Winternitz laid the notebook down in front of himself, and looked around with enlarged eyes, Georg nodded appreciatively and said: "Very good."

Winternitz looked expectantly at Heinrich, who was silent for a few seconds and finally remarked: "On the whole it's very interesting . . . but why do you say 'Hail,' if I may ask? No one will believe you."

"Why not?" cried Winternitz.

"Examine your own conscience if this 'Hail' is honestly felt. Everything else that you have read to me, I believe of you. That is, I believe it in a higher sense, though none of it is true. I believe that you seduce a fifteen year old girl, that you behave like a callous Don Juan, that you ruin the poor creature in the worst way, that with a . . . what was he now? . . ."

"A clown, of course," cried Winternitz with insane laughter.

"That she betrays you with a clown, that because of this creature you embark upon ever darker adventures, that you want to kill your beloved, even yourself, that you finally become weary of the whole story, that you travel, or rather chase, through the world, to Australia for all I care, yes, all that I believe of you; but that you are the man to cry 'Hail,' that, dear Winternitz, that's just humbug."

Winternitz defended himself. He swore that this "Hail" would come from his innermost being, at least from a certain element of his innermost being. With continued objections from Heinrich, he gradually retreated and finally declared that he hoped sometime to fight his way through to that inner freedom from which it would be possible to cry "Hail."

"This time will never come," Heinrich replied definitely. "You may perhaps come sometime to an epic or dramatic 'Hail,' but the lyrical, subjective 'Hail' remains for you, remains for all like us, my dear Winternitz, denied for all eternity."

Winternitz promised to revise the last poem, to develop himself further in general, and to work on his inner purification. He stood up, whereupon his starched shirtfront cracked and a button popped open, extended Heinrich and Georg his somewhat damp hand, and proceeded to the table for writers at the back of the room. Georg expressed himself to Heinrich with cautious appreciation about the poems he had heard.

"To me, he's still the best of the whole lot, personally anyway," said Heinrich. "At least he knows inwardly how to preserve a certain distance. Yes. You don't need to look at me as if you'd caught me in an attack of megalomania again. But I can assure you Georg," he reconnoitered the table back there with a fleeting glance, "that by now I have had quite enough of the sort of people who always have an *a soi*[6] floating on their lips."

"What floats on their lips?"

Heinrich laughed. "You know the story about the Polish Jew who sat with a stranger in a railroad car, very politely—until he realized from a remark of the other that he was a Jew too, whereupon, with a sigh of *a soi*, he immediately put his legs up on the seat across from him."

"Very good," said Georg.

"More than that," continued Heinrich forcefully. "Deep. Deep like so many Jewish anecdotes. They offer an insight into the tragicomedy of contemporary Judaism. They express the eternal truth that one Jew never really gets respect from another. Never. Just as little as prisoners in an enemy country really have respect for one another, especially the hopeless. Envy, hatred, sometimes even admiration, in the end even love can exist between them; respect never. For all emotional relationships take place in an atmosphere of familiarity, so to speak, in which respect is stifled."

"Do you know what I think," Georg remarked. "That you are a worse anti-Semite than most Christians I know."

6. A Yiddish phrase literally meaning "like that" or "that's how it is," but used here as an exclamation of surprise roughly equivalent to "Aha!" or "Oh my!"

"Do you think so?" He laughed. "Certainly not a real one. The real ones are the ones who, at bottom, resent the good qualities of the Jews, and do everything to develop their bad ones. But in a certain sense you're right. I finally permitted myself to also be anti-Arian. Every race as such is naturally repulsive. Only the individual is able sometimes, through personal strengths, to reconcile himself to the repulsiveness of his race. But that I'm particularly sensitive to the failings of the Jews, I will not at all deny. Possibly it lies in the fact that I, we all, we Jews I mean, have been systematically raised with this sensitivity. From our youth on we have been driven to see precisely Jewish characteristics as especially comical or repulsive, which is not the case with regard to the equally comical or repulsive characteristics of the others. And I won't conceal the fact that when a Jew behaves crudely or comically in my presence, sometimes such a painful feeling seizes me that I want to die, to sink into the earth. It's a sort of shame that is perhaps related some-how to the shame a brother feels if his sister undresses in front of him. Perhaps the whole thing is just egotism. It's exasperating that one is continually made responsible for the mistakes of others, that one must atone for every offense, for every crudity, for every thoughtless act that any Jew in the world makes himself guilty of. Naturally one easily be-comes unjust. But this is just nervousness, sensitivity, nothing more. One comes to one's senses again. One can't call that anti-Semitism. But there are Jews who I really hate, hate as Jews. They are those who be-have in front of others, and sometimes among themselves, as if they weren't Jews at all. Who try to appease their enemies and despisers in a cheap, cringing manner and think they can ransom themselves like this from the eternal curse, which weighs on them, or from that which they only feel as a curse. They are, by the way, almost always the kind of Jews who go around with a feeling of their own highly personal worthlessness, and consciously or unconsciously want to make their race responsible for it. Naturally it doesn't help them in the slightest. What has ever helped the Jews at all? The good and the bad. Naturally I mean," he added quickly, "those who need something like outward or inward help." And with a deliberately light tone he broke off. "Yes, my dear Georg, the matter is rather complicated, and it's quite natural that all those who do not have to deal directly with the question lack the right understanding for it."

"Well, one may not so . . ."

Heinrich interrupted him immediately. "One may indeed, dear Georg. That's the way it is. You don't understand us. Perhaps some

have an idea. But understand!? No. In any case we understand you far
better than you do us. Even if you shake your head! It's not what we
deserve. We have found it more necessary to learn to understand you
than you have us. This gift of understanding has had to develop in us
in the course of time . . . by the law of survival, if you wish. For you
see, in order to learn your way around among strangers, or as I said
earlier, in enemy country, to be prepared for all dangers and animosities
that lie in wait, it behooves everyone, above all, to learn to know his
enemies as well as possible—their strengths and their weaknesses."

"So you live among enemies? Among strangers? You wouldn't admit
that to Leo Golowski. I am not of his opinion either, by the way. Absolutely not. But what a strange contradiction that today you . . ."

Heinrich interrupted him, quite upset. "I told you that the matter is
much too complicated to be settled anyway. I feel it's almost impossible.
And certainly not with words! Yes, one would sometimes like to believe
that things weren't that bad. Sometimes one really is at home, in spite
of it all, feels so at home here, yes,—even more at home than the so-
called natives can feel. It's obviously true that through the consciousness of understanding, the feeling of strangeness can be, in a certain
sense, overcome again. Yes, it becomes, as it were, saturated with pride,
condescension, tenderness; it dissolves. To be sure, sometimes in sentimentality, which is a bad thing again." He sat there with deep wrinkles
on his forehead, and looked down.

Does he really understand me better, thought Georg, than I do him?
Or is it just megalomania again—?

Heinrich suddenly got up, as if from a dream. He looked at the clock.
"Two-thirty! And my train leaves in the morning at eight."

"So, you're leaving?"

"Yes. That's why I wanted so much to talk to you. Unfortunately I
must bid you *adieu* for some time. I'm going to Prague. I'm bringing
my father home from the asylum, to his own country."

"So he's improved?"

"No. He's just gotten to the stage where he's no longer a danger to
his surroundings. . . . Yes, it came quite quickly too."

"About when do you think you'll be back?"

Heinrich shrugged his shoulders. "That can't be predicted yet. But
however things develop, there's no way I can leave my mother and sister
alone now."

Georg felt a genuine regret to have to be without Heinrich's company
in the near future. "It's possible that you won't find me in Vienna when

you get back. I'll probably be leaving myself this spring." And he almost felt a desire to take Heinrich into his confidence.

"You're going to the south?" asked Heinrich.

"Yes, I think so. To enjoy my freedom one more time. For a couple of months. In the coming fall, life will begin in earnest. I'm going to look around Germany for a post, in some theater."

"Oh, really."

The waiter came over to the table, they paid and left. At the door they met Rapp and Gleissner. A few words of greeting were exchanged.

"What have you been up to, Herr Rapp?" Georg asked obligingly.

Rapp wiped off his pince-nez. "Just my sad old handiwork. I am occupied proving the nothingness of nothings."

"You could give yourself a change, Rapp," said Heinrich. "Try your luck once, and praise the glory of the glorious."

"For what?" said Rapp and put his pince-nez on. "That will show itself in the course of time. But the bunglers usually experience their fame and fortune, and by the time the world comes to see the swindle, they've long since fled to their graves or . . . into their supposed immortality."

They stood on the street and all turned their collars up, as it had begun to snow heavily again. Gleissner, who had just experienced his first big theatrical success a few weeks ago, explained quickly that the seventh performance of his work had been sold out tonight as well.

Rapp added some scornful remarks about the stupidity of the public. Gleissner responded with derision about the impotence of the critic against the true genius;—and so they walked along, with turned up collars, through the snow, completely enveloped in the muffled hate of their old friendship.

"Rapp has no luck," Heinrich said to Georg. "With all of his friends for whom he prophesied success ten years ago, it has all actually come true. And he'll never forgive Gleissner for not disappointing him as well."

"Do you really think he's that envious?"

"One can't necessarily say that. These things are rarely so simple that one can finish with them in one word. But just consider what kind of fate it is, to go around with the belief that one carries around, just as much as Shakespeare did, the deepest wisdom of the world, and to feel that one is not even in as good a position to express it as, for example, Herr Gleissner, although one is perhaps just as worthy—or more."

They went along for a time silently next to each other. The trees on the

Ring stood stiffly with white limbs. From the Rathaus it struck three. They crossed the empty street and took the way through the silent park. All around it shimmered almost brightly in the unremitting snow.

"I haven't explained the newest thing to you yet," Heinrich finally began, looking down and in a dry tone.

"What's that?"

"That I am receiving anonymous letters, for some time."

"Anonymous letters? Containing what?"

"Well, you can quite imagine."

"Oh, I see." It was clear to Georg that it could only have to do with the actress. Heinrich had returned from that foreign city, where he had seen his beloved in a new play, playing the role of a depraved creature with what was for him an unendurable truth to nature, in an even more bitter torment than before. Georg knew that since then letters full of tenderness and scorn, resentment and forgiveness, painfully confused and wearily consoling, had passed between them.

"These good tidings have come regularly every morning for about a week," explained Heinrich. "Not very pleasant, I assure you!"

"Oh God, what do you make of it? You know yourself anonymous letters never contain the truth."

"On the contrary, dear Georg, always."

"But!"

"Such letters contain the higher truth to some extent. The great truth of possibilities. People in general lack sufficient imagination to create out of nothingness."

"That would be a lovely concept. How would one come to it? You would make the matter too easy for slanderers of all sorts."

"Why do you say slanderers? I wouldn't say that the anonymous letters I'm getting contain slanders. Exaggerations perhaps, embellishments, inaccuracies . . ."

"Lies."

"No, it certainly wouldn't be lies. A few maybe. But how can one distinguish truth from lies in such a case?"

"But there's a very simple solution. Go there."

"I should go there?"

"Of course you should. You must get to the truth of the matter at the source."

"I suppose it would be possible."

They wandered under archways, on damp stone. Their voices and steps echoed. Georg started up again. "Instead of continuing on with these disturbing unpleasantries, I'd prefer to clarify for myself how things stand."

"Yes, that would certainly be the best."

"So, why don't you do it?"

Heinrich stood still, and with teeth clenched, forced out: "Tell me, dear Georg, shouldn't you have noticed by now that I'm cowardly."

"Oh, one doesn't call that cowardly."

"Call it what you want. Words don't tell the whole story—the more precise they try to be, the less they are. I know how I am. I'm not going out there. Ridiculous isn't it? No, no, no. . . ."

"So what will you do?"

Heinrich shrugged his shoulders, as if it had nothing to do with him.

Somewhat annoyed, Georg asked further: "If you will permit me a remark, what does the . . . principal party say?"

"The principal party, as you call her with devilish, if unconscious wit, does not know for the moment that I am receiving anonymous letters."

"Have you broken off your correspondence with her?"

"What are you thinking? We write every day, just like before; she the tenderest and most mendacious, I the most general you can imagine—as insincere, insidious, tormented as if in blood."

"Listen Heinrich, you're truly not a very noble character."

Heinrich laughed out loud. "No, noble I am not; I was obviously not born to that."

"And when one thinks, at bottom it's nothing but slander!" Georg, for his part, naturally did not doubt that the anonymous letters contained the truth. In spite of this he did honestly wish that Heinrich would go to the source, to satisfy himself, to do something, to give someone a good box on the ear, or shoot somebody. He imagined Felician in a similar trap, or Stanzides, or Willy Eissler. All would have handled themselves better, or at least differently, and certainly in a way more appealing to him. Suddenly the question went through his mind, how he would act if Anna deceived him. Anna, deceive him?! . . . Was that even possible? He thought about the darkly curious look that she cast toward Demeter Stanzides this evening. No, it didn't mean anything, that was for sure. And the old stories with Leo and the singing teacher? They were harmless, childish almost. But something else, perhaps more meaningful, occurred to him. He remembered a strange question that she had put to him as she had recently come late to meet him, and with an excuse, had to hurry home. She had asked him if he was afraid of regretting someday having made her a liar. It had sounded half like a reproach, half like a warning. And if she seemed so unsure of herself, could he continue to simply trust her? Didn't he love her— and didn't he betray her in spite of it, or was ready to at any moment, which amounted to the same thing? An hour ago in the wagon, as he held her in his arms and kissed her, had she suspected that he had another thought on his mind than her? And that at one moment, with his lips on hers, he had longed for Sissy? Why shouldn't it happen that Anna could betray him? . . . Maybe she already had . . . without him suspecting. . . . But all these thoughts were, so to speak, without weight. They floated before his mind like fantastic, almost amusing possibilities. He stood with Heinrich in front of the door in the Florianigasse and gave him his hand. "So, be well," he said, "and when we meet again, may you have recovered from your doubts."

"Would that really be a gain?" asked Heinrich. "Can one calm one's heartaches with certainties? At most with bad ones, since they are forever. But a good certainty is at best an illusion. . . . Well, so long. Hopefully we'll meet again in May. I'll be back sometime around then, whatever may happen, and then we can talk about our famous opera again."

"Yes, if I'm back in Vienna by May. It could happen that I won't be back until fall."

"And then off again immediately on your new career?"

"It wouldn't be impossible that it happen that way." And he looked Heinrich in the eyes with a sort of childishly defiant smile: "I can't tell you yet."

Heinrich seemed distant. "Listen Georg, we may be standing together for the last time in front of this door. Oh, I'm far from really entering into your confidence. Maybe this rather one-sided relationship will always remain between us. Oh well, it doesn't matter."

Georg looked down.

"May heaven protect you," said Heinrich as the door opened. "And let me hear from you occasionally."

"Certainly," Georg replied and suddenly saw Heinrich's eyes resting on him with an unexpected look of emotion. "Certainly, and you must write to me too. In any case let me know how it's going at home and what you're working on. We must remain in constant communication," he added warmly.

The concierge stood there with bristling hair and a sleepy and irritable look, in a green and brown robe, and slippers on his otherwise bare feet.

Heinrich gave Georg his hand one last time. "*Auf Wiedersehen* dear friend," he said. And then, softly, indicating toward the doorman: "I can't keep him waiting any longer. What he's calling me at this moment you can guess without difficulty from his unadulterated indigenous physiognomy. *Adieu.*"

Georg had to laugh. Heinrich vanished, and the door slammed shut.

Georg didn't feel the slightest bit sleepy, and decided to head home on foot. He was in an excited, elevated mood. He looked forward to the days to come with particular tension. He thought about tomorrow's meeting with Anna, about upcoming discussions, about their departure, about the house that already existed somewhere and which he could already picture vaguely in his imagination, as though in a toy-box, light, green, with a bright red roof and a black chimney. And his own figure appeared to him like a picture cast by a projector onto white curtains: he saw himself sitting on a balcony, in happy solitude, before a table covered with music paper; branches swayed in front of the trellis; a bright sky rested over him, and far below at his feet, in a dreamlike intense blue, lay the sea.

Fifth Chapter

Georg quietly opened the door to Anna's room. She lay in bed still sleeping, and breathed deeply and calmly. He went out of the softly dimmed room, back into his study, and closed the door. Then he walked over to the open window and looked out. Over the water floated fog, shimmering in the sunlight. The mountains stood against the brilliant sky with clearly drawn lines in the distance, while over the gardens and houses of Lugano shone the brightest blue. Georg once again had the thrill of breathing in this June morning air, which carried up to him the humid freshness of the lake and the smell of plane trees, magnolias, and roses from the hotel garden; of regarding this scene, whose spring peace had greeted him every morning for three weeks like a newfound joy. He quickly finished his tea and ran down the stairs as quickly and expectantly as when he had been a boy on his way out to play, and in the grey air of early morning shadows, he followed the familiar way along the shore. Here he thought of his solitary morning walks in Palermo and Taormina the past spring, which he had often stretched out for hours while Grace gladly lay in bed with open eyes. That time in his life, over which an imminent, though sometimes welcome farewell hung like a dark cloud, appeared gloomily in his memory. This time everything painful seemed to him to lie in the remote future, and in any case it was within his power to postpone an end, as long as it did not come from fate itself, as long as he wanted.

He had left Vienna with Anna at the beginning of March, as it was

no longer possible to conceal her condition. Georg had decided to speak
to her mother already in January. He had prepared himself to some extent, so he was able to present his news in calm and well-chosen words.
The mother listened silently, and her eyes became large and damp. Anna
sat on the divan with a shy smile and watched Georg as he spoke, with
a sort of curiosity. The plan for the coming months was outlined. Georg
wanted to stay with Anna in another country until early summer, then
a country house would be rented in the outskirts of Vienna so that, in
the most difficult time, the mother would not be far away, and the child
could be turned over to foster parents without difficulty, close to the
city. An explanation was also worked out for Anna's departure and
absence, for any uninvited curiosity. As her voice had significantly improved recently—which was almost the truth—she had gone to a famous singing teacher in Dresden to complete her training. Frau Rosner
nodded occasionally, as though she agreed with everything. But the expression on her face grew constantly sadder. Not so much that what
she heard was crushing her, as much as the realization that she had to
let it all go by helplessly above her, a poor mother of lower-middle-class
standing who sat powerless across from the noble seducer. Georg, who
noted this with regret, looked for an even gentler and kinder tone. He
moved closer to the good woman, took her hands, and held them for
some moments in his own. Anna had hardly contributed a word to the
conversation. But as Georg prepared to leave, she got up, and for the
first time in front of her mother, as though she had just announced her
engagement, offered him her lips to kiss. Georg went down the steps
in a raised mood, as though the worst were actually behind him. More
often than before he spent whole hours at the Rosners, making music
with Anna, whose voice during this time achieved a notable fullness and
strength. The mother's behavior toward Georg became friendlier, and
sometimes it appeared to him as if she actually had to ward off a growing sympathy for him. And there was an evening in the family circle
when Georg stayed for supper, after which, cigar in his mouth, he improvised for the assembled company from *Meistersinger* and *Lohengrin*, and had enjoyed rousing applause, especially from Josef's side. On
the way home he had noticed, almost shocked, that he had felt as contented as if in a newfound home.

A few days later, as he sat over a black coffee with Felician, the servant brought him a card, at receipt of which he felt himself blush
slightly. Felician acted as if he hadn't noticed his brother's embarrassment, said *adieu*, and left the room. In the door he encountered the

older Rosner, gently nodded his head in greeting, and looked away. Georg led Herr Rosner, who had entered in a winter coat with a hat and umbrella, to a seat, and offered him a cigar. The old Rosner said: "I've just smoked," which somehow reassured Georg, and took a seat, while Georg remained standing, leaning against the table. Then the old man began with his usual slowness: "Herr Baron can probably imagine why I have taken the liberty of disturbing him. I actually wanted to come this morning, but unfortunately I couldn't get out of the office."

"You wouldn't have found me at home this morning, Herr Rosner," Georg replied courteously.

"Well, all the better that I haven't come all this way for nothing. So, my wife explained to me this morning . . . what has happened." He looked at the floor.

"I see," Georg said, and chewed on his upper lip. "I actually intended myself . . . But wouldn't you like to remove your winter coat? It's very warm in the room."

"Oh, thank you, thank you, it's not at all too warm for me. Well, I was quite shocked when my wife gave me the news. Yes Herr Baron, I'd never have thought it of Anna . . . never considered it possible . . . it's just awful. . . ." He said all this in his customary monotone, only shaking his head more often than usual. Georg could see only the top of the balding head with its thin yellow-grey hair, and felt nothing but a vacant boredom. "Things are certainly not awful, Herr Rosner," he finally said. "If you knew how much I . . . how deep my attachment to Anna is, you would certainly be far from finding things awful. Your Frau wife has no doubt told you about our plans for the future,—or am I mistaken?"

"Not at all, Herr Baron, I was informed of everything this morning. But I can't conceal that for several weeks I've felt that something wasn't in order in the house. In particular it seemed to me that my wife was rather agitated, and frequently even close to tears."

"Close to tears?—There's really no ground for that, Herr Rosner; Anna herself, who's really the one most concerned, feels very well, as cheerful as ever. . . ."

"Yes, Anna is in good spirits, to be sure, and this, to tell the truth, gives me some consolation. But besides that, I cannot describe to you, Herr Baron, what a heavy blow . . . how, I want to say . . . how cut off from heaven . . . never, never would I have believed . . ." He could not continue, his voice trembled.

"I am really very troubled," said Georg, "that you regard the matter in this way, despite the fact that your Frau wife has already explained our plans to you, and the timetable that we have suggested for the future will surely meet with your approval. Of a more distant future, a hopefully not too distant future, I would rather not speak today, because phrases of that sort are rather repulsive to me. But you may be assured Herr Rosner, that I certainly will not forget what I owe to a person like Anna . . . what I owe to myself." He swallowed.

As far as he could remember, there had been no moment in his life in which he had appeared so distasteful to himself. And now, as in conversations so hopeless that nothing else seems possible, they repeated the same thing several times again, until Herr Rosner finally apologized for having disturbed him, and took leave of Georg, who accompanied him to the stairs. For several days after this visit Georg retained an unpleasant aftertaste in his heart. Now all I need is for her brother to show up, he thought irritably, and he involuntarily imagined a confrontation in the course of which the young man sought to act as the avenger of the family honor, and Georg reproved him with extraordinarily forceful words. Apart from this, Georg felt relieved after the discussions with Anna's parents were finished. And over the hours that he spent alone with the beloved in the peaceful room across from the church, lay a singular feeling of contentment and certainty. Sometimes it seemed to them both that time stood still. Happily Georg would bring guide books for the coming trip, Burckhardt's *Cicerone*, even maps along, and proposed, together with Anna, all sorts of routes to take, without really believing that all this would come true some day. But concerning the house in which the child would be born, they were both convinced of the necessity that it must be found and rented before they left Vienna. Once Anna saw in the newspaper, which she read painstakingly thereafter, an advertisement for a country house, right on the forest, not far from a train station, an hour-and-a-half's ride from Vienna. One morning they both rode to the indicated place—and took home the memory of a lonely, snow-covered, wooden house, with antlers over the door, of an old, drunken forester, of a young blond maid, of a whirlwind sleigh ride over a sunlit winter road, of an unbelievably festive lunch in the immense hall of an inn, and of a poorly lit and overheated coupe. This was the only time that Georg went together with Anna, looking for the house which already existed somewhere and waited for its destiny. . . . Usually he took the train alone, or went by tram to the nearby countryside to look around.

Once, on a spring day lost in the depths of winter, Georg went walking through a small spot quite near the city, which he particularly loved, where village-like houses, modest country homes, and elegant villas stood next to each other. He had completely forgotten, as sometimes happened to him, why he had gone there, and thought with emotion that, many years before, Beethoven and Schubert had taken the very same road as he, when he unexpectedly encountered Nuernberger. They greeted one another, praised the glorious day which had lured them so far away, and warmly regretted that they met so rarely now that Bermann had left Vienna.

"Haven't you heard from him for a while?" asked Georg.

"Since he left," said Nuernberger, "I've received only one card from him. It's to be assumed that he keeps more regular correspondence with you, than with me."

"Why is that to be assumed?" asked Georg, rather annoyed, as he sometimes was, by Nuernberger's tone.

"Well, at least you have the advantage over me of being a new acquaintance for him, and thus of offering a more stimulating problem for his psychological interests than I do."

In these resentfully derisive words, Georg detected a certain amount of hurt feelings, which he found understandable. For as a matter of fact, Heinrich had recently paid little attention to Nuernberger, with whom he had earlier had close relations, as it was his way in general to form attachments with people and then, with the greatest inconsideration, drop them, according as their personalities suited his mood or not.

"In spite of that, I'm no better off than you," said Georg. "I haven't received any news from him for several weeks either. From the last I heard, it appeared to be going very badly for his father."

"So it will soon be all over for the pitiable old man."

"Who knows. From what Bermann writes, it could also drag out for months."

Nuernberger earnestly shook his head.

"Yes," Georg said lightly, "in such cases doctors really should be allowed to . . . cut the thing short."

"You might be right," answered Nuernberger. "But who knows if our friend Heinrich, however much it disturbs him in his work or perhaps even in many other ways, seeing his father wasting away beyond help, who knows if, in spite of this, he might not be opposed to the suggestion of bringing this hopeless situation to a close through a morphine injection."

Once again Georg felt put off by Nuernberger's scornfully bitter tone. And yet, as he remembered the time when he saw Heinrich more concerned over a few ambiguous lines in a letter from a sweetheart than over the illness of his father, he couldn't escape the impression that Nuernberger had correctly judged their mutual friend. . . . "Did you know the older Bermann?" he asked.

"Not personally. But I still remember the time when his name would often be mentioned in the newspapers, and also many very staunch speeches which he delivered in the House of Deputies. But, I'm holding you up, dear Baron. Good day. In any case we'll meet again one of these days at the coffeehouse or at the Ehrenbergs."

"You're not holding me up at all," replied Georg with deliberate courtesy. "I was just out walking and took the opportunity to look around at summer places."

"So you want to stay in the Vienna countryside this year?"

"Yes, probably for a while. And besides, a family I know has asked me, if by chance I should find one on this occasion . . ." He became a little red, as he always did when he strayed from the truth.

Nuernberger noted this and said disarmingly: "I just walked past some villas that were for rent. See this white one, for example, with the wide terrace?"

"It looks quite nice. We could actually take a look at that one, if it wouldn't be too boring for you to accompany me,—then we could go back to town together."

The garden, which they entered, rose upward, long and narrow, and reminded Nuernberger of another in which he had played as a child. "Perhaps it's even the same one," he said. "We lived for years in the country in Grinzing or Heiligenstadt."

This 'we' struck Georg quite strangely. He could scarcely imagine that Nuernberger too had once been young, had lived as a son with father and mother, as a brother with sisters, and he suddenly felt the whole existence of this man as something singular and sad.

From the top of the garden, from an open arbor, there was a marvelous view of the city, which they enjoyed for some time. Then they slowly went back down, accompanied by the housekeeper's wife who carried a small child on her arm, wrapped in a grey blanket. Now they looked at the living quarters; low, musty rooms with cheap, faded carpets on the floor, narrow wooden beds, dull or broken mirrors. "In the spring it will all be refurnished," the housekeeper explained. "Then it will all look very friendly." The little child suddenly stretched its hands out toward Georg, as if it wanted to be taken onto his arm. Georg was a little touched and gave an embarrassed smile.

While he rode back to the city on the tram platform with Nuernberger, and talked to him, he had the feeling that, in their many earlier encounters, he had never gotten to know him as well as during these bright sunlit winter hours in the country. As they parted, it happened quite naturally that they agreed to another walk in a few days, and so it came about that Georg was accompanied a few times by Nuernberger on his trips into the surroundings of Vienna, looking for a house. They always preserved the fiction that Georg was looking for a place for the family he was friends with, that Nuernberger believed this, and that Georg believed that Nuernberger believed it.

On these walks Nuernberger would sometimes talk about his childhood, about his parents, whom he had lost quite early, of one of his sisters, who had died young, and of his older brother, the only one of his relatives who was still alive. He however, an aging bachelor like Edmund himself, did not live in Vienna, but was a high school teacher in a small, Lower Austrian town, where he was transferred fifteen years ago as a teaching assistant. Later he could have secured an appointment in the capital again without particular difficulty; but after a few years of embitterment, even rage, he had become so accustomed to the quiet circumstances of his little stopping place, that a return to Vienna would have seemed to him a sacrifice. And he lived now, devoted to his work, and in particular to his language studies, remote, solitary, contented, as a sort of philosopher in the little town. When Nuernberger spoke about this distant brother, it sometimes seemed to Georg as if he were talking about a dead man, so completely did he seem to have given up every possibility of a future sustained reunion. He spoke completely differently, and with an ever-present longing, about his sister, who had been dead for many years, almost like someone who could still return.

It was on a foggy February day, at a train station, while they walked together back and forth on the platform waiting for the train to Vienna, that Nuernberger related to Georg the story of this sister, who already as a child of sixteen, as if possessed by an intense passion for the theater, had left home on a childish, romantic impulse without even saying good-bye. For ten years she wandered from town to town, from stage to stage, always in lesser and lesser positions, for neither her talent nor her beauty seemed sufficient for this demanding profession; but always with the same enthusiasm, always with the same anticipation, despite the disappointments she had suffered, and the misery she saw. During vacations she would sometimes appear by the brothers, who lived together at that time, and for weeks, or sometimes only days, would tell about the music halls where she appeared as though they were great theaters; of her scanty successes like great triumphs she had won; of the miserable comedians beside whom she worked like great artists, of the petty intrigues which went on around her like mighty tragedies of passion. And instead of gradually coming to see in what a wretched world she lived as one of the most pathetic, she clung from year to year to her golden dream. It went on for a long time, until she came home once feverish and ill. She lay in bed for months, her cheeks red, raving in her delirium about fame and success, which she had never experienced. Gradually she returned to apparent health, and went out again, only to return home after a few weeks, utterly shattered, with death on her brow. Now her brother traveled with her to the south; to Arco, to Merano, to the Italian lakes. And now for the first time, in the southern gardens, reclined under blossoming trees, far from the milieu that had for years entranced and confused her, she came to the realization that her life had been an illusion, lived under a painted sky, and between paper walls,—that its whole content had been a fantasy. But also the little adventures of the day, in rented rooms and inns, on the streets of strange towns, appeared in her memory like scenes in footlights which she had played as an actress, and not like any she had really experienced. And as she neared her grave, there awakened in her an immense longing for the real life, which she had missed; the surer she became that she had lost it forever, the clearer did she recognize the fullness of the world. But the strangest thing was that in the last weeks of her life, talent, to which she had sacrificed her entire existence without really possessing it, began mysteriously and demonically to appear in her. "It still seems to me today," said Nuernberger, "that even by the greatest actresses, I have never heard verses read, or seen whole scenes acted, as by my sister in that hotel room in Cadenabbia with the view of Lake Como, a few days before she died. Of course," he added, "it's possible, even likely, that my memory deceives me."

"Why's that?" asked Georg, who liked this ending so well that he didn't want him to spoil it. And he endeavored to convince Nuernberger, who listened smiling, that he couldn't have been mistaken, and that a great actress had gone to her grave with the strange girl who lay buried in Cadenabbia. . . .

The country house for which Georg was searching was not to be found on his wanderings with Nuernberger either; from one time to the next the discovery seemed to become more and more difficult. Nuernberger would sometimes grumble about the impossible demands made by Georg, who appeared to be looking for a villa with a well-kept road in front and a garden door opening into primeval forest in back. In the end, Georg himself ceased to seriously believe that he would succeed in finding the desired house, and released himself from the obligation of finding it after the return from the trip. It seemed more important to him to come to an understanding as soon as possible with a doctor; but that too Georg put off from one day to the next. But one evening Anna informed him that she had visited Doctor Stauber after having been alarmed by a new attack of faintness, and had explained her condition to him. He had been very kind, had not expressed the slightest surprise, had reassured her in every respect, and had only expressed the desire to speak to Georg before their departure.

A few days later, Georg accepted the doctor's invitation. The interview was almost at an end. Doctor Stauber had received him with the expected friendliness, appeared to find the whole affair as unobjectionable and natural as possible, and spoke of Anna exactly like a young wife, which touched Georg strangely, but not unpleasantly. As the essential discussions closed, the doctor inquired about the destination of the journey. Georg had still not outlined an itinerary; all that had been fixed was that the spring should be spent in the south, probably in Italy. Doctor Stauber took the occasion to tell about his last stay in Rome, ten years ago. He was at the time, as once before, in personal contact with the director of excavations, and spoke to Georg, in an almost excited tone, about the latest discoveries on the Palatine, about which he had himself studied as a younger man, and had published in the *Journal of Archaeology*. Then he showed Georg, not without pride, his library, which was divided into a medical and an art-historical section, and offered him a few rare books as a loan, one from the year 1834 on the Vatican collection, and one on the history of Sicily. Georg felt most stimulated as the rich days that stood ahead appeared so vividly to him. A sort of homesickness overcame him for familiar and long yearned-for lands, and half-forgotten images emerged before him: the pyramid of Cestius stood on the horizon in sharp outline, as it had appeared to him as he rode back to the evening city as a boy with the Prince of Macedonia; the dusky church appeared, where he had seen his first love step to the altar as a bride; a small boat with singular, sulphur-yellow sails drew near under a dark sky along the coast. . . . He began talking, and spoke of the many cities and regions of the south which he had seen in his childhood and youth; he explained his yearning for these places, which often seized him like a true homesickness, and his joy to be able to see all these longed-for places, both remembered and forgotten, and many new ones, with a mature eye, and this time in the company of another being who was capable of understanding and enjoying it with him, and who was dear to him. Doctor Stauber, who was about to put a book back on the shelf, turned suddenly to Georg, looked gently at him and said: "I can accept that." As Georg returned his look a little put off, he added: "That was the first warm word about your relationship to Annerl that I've heard from you in the course of this past hour. I know, I know, it's not your way to open up to a person who's little more than a stranger, but it pleases me precisely because I couldn't really expect it. It really came from the heart, one could see that. And it would have bothered me about Annerl—excuse me, I've always called her that—if I had to think that you didn't care as much for her as she deserves."

"I really don't know," Georg answered coolly, "what caused you to doubt it, Herr Doctor."

"Did I say anything about doubt?" Stauber replied good naturedly. "But after all, it has happened before that a young man with lots of experience didn't sufficiently appreciate such a sacrifice. It remains, after all, a sacrifice, dear Baron. We can be above all prejudices—it's still no triviality when a young girl of good family does such a thing. And I won't conceal from you—I naturally said nothing of this to Annerl—it did give me a little jolt when she recently came and explained the matter to me."

"Forgive me, Herr Doctor," Georg replied annoyed, but courteously, "if it gave you a jolt, but it says something against your being above prejudice. . . ."

"You're right," said Stauber smiling. "But perhaps you'll forgive my backwardness when you think that I'm a bit older than you and come from another time. And even a relatively independently thinking person . . . which I flatter myself to be . . . cannot entirely escape the influence of his time. That's the strange thing. But believe me, there are today, even among the young people who grew up with Nietzsche and Ibsen, just as many Philistines as there were thirty years ago; only they don't let themselves be known, unless one gets into trouble, like when one seduces his sister, or when his Frau wife gets the idea into her head to do some fast living. . . . Lots of them naturally are consistent and play out their roles . . . but that's more a question of self-control than world view. But earlier again, you know, in the period I come from, when certain concepts stood more authoritatively firm, when everyone knew quite well: one must honor one's parents, or else one was a lout . . . or: a true love comes only once in one's life . . . or: it is an honor to die for the Fatherland . . . you know, in the time when every decent man held some banner high, or at least had written something on his banner . . . believe me, the so-called modern ideas already had more adherents then than people suspect. Only these adherents sometimes didn't quite realize that they didn't trust their ideas themselves, that to a certain degree they felt like degenerates or even criminals. Shall I tell you something, Herr Baron? There are no new ideas at all. New intensities of thought—that, yes. But do you honestly believe that Nietzsche invented the Superman, or Ibsen invented duplicity, or Anzengruber the truth that later it would be the parents themselves who would want love and respect from their children? Not at all. All ethnic ideas have always been like that, and one would be astonished if one knew what sort of dimwits thought up these so-called great new ideas, and perhaps even expressed them, long before the geniuses to whom we ascribe these truths, or more, who had the courage to regard these truths as true. But I have wandered pretty far, forgive me. All I really wanted to say . . . and I'm sure you'll agree . . . I know as well as you, Herr Baron, that there are many apparently innocent young ladies who are a thousand times more depraved than the so-called 'fallen' ones, and many young men who pass for respectable, who have worse things on their consciences than that they're having an affair with an innocent young girl. And yet . . . it's the curse of my generation . . ." he added smiling, "I couldn't help myself: in the first moment, as Annerl was telling me the story, certain unpleasant words, whose meaning was fixed long ago, began sounding in my old head with their old tone, ignorantly surviving words like . . . libertine . . . seduction . . . abandonment . . . and so forth. And from that—I must once again ask for forgiveness, now that I've gotten to know you better—comes the shock that a modern man really shouldn't confess to having felt. But, to be completely serious again, just think for a moment how your blessed Herr father, who didn't even know Annerl, would have felt about the matter. He was surely one of the brightest men, and the most free of prejudice, that one can think of. And despite that, don't think for a moment that it would be completely without shock even to him."

Georg involuntarily gave the doctor his hand. The unexpectedness

of this sudden reminder of the dear dead man awakened such a powerful nostalgia in him that he only wanted to allay it, and he began talking
about the departed. And the doctor too still knew of many encounters
with the late baron to relate, mostly accidental, fleeting ones on the
street, at meetings of the Academy of Sciences, or at concerts. It was
another one of those moments when Georg felt particularly guilty about
the deceased man, and he made a deep resolution to be worthy of his
memory.

"Give my greetings to Annerl," the doctor said to him as he left, "but
please don't say anything about my 'jolt.' She's a very sensitive creature,
as you know very well, and the main thing now is to spare her any disagreeable excitement. You must think, dear Baron, the primary concern
is that a healthy child is born, everything else . . . well, give her my
greetings, hopefully we'll all be well and meet again in the summer."

Georg left with a heightened awareness of his obligations to the person who had given herself to him, and to the other who, in a few
months, would awaken to existence. He thought for the first time of
making a will and having it notarized. After closer consideration however, he found it better to confide in his brother, who was closest to
him, even inwardly, of all other people. But due to that peculiar reserve
which always existed in the otherwise intimate relationship between the
brothers, he let day after day pass by until finally Felician's departure
for Africa on the safari was quite close. The night before it, on the way
home from the club, Georg told his brother that he was thinking about
a long trip in the near future.

"Really? How long will you be gone?" Felician asked.

Georg heard a certain concern in the tone of these words, and felt
the opportunity to broach the subject. "It'll be the last big trip that I'll
be able to take for years. In the fall I'll hopefully find myself with a
fixed position."

"So you've firmly decided then?"

"Yes, obviously."

"I'm very pleased, Georg, for various reasons which you can imagine, that you finally want to get going in earnest. And in general it's
better that one of us won't be going out into the world while the other
stays home alone. That would've been a little sad."

Georg knew well that next fall Felician would likely be assigned to
a foreign attaché's office, but it had never been so clear to him that in
a few months the years of brotherly association, their living together

in the old house across from the park, to a certain extent his whole youth, would be irretrievably past. And life looked serious, almost threatening to him.

"Do you have any idea," he asked "where they may send you?"

"There's some chance for Athens."

"Would you like that?"

"Why not. The staff there is supposed to be interesting. Bernburg was there for three years and didn't want to leave. Then they transferred him to London, which isn't bad either."

They walked on silently for a while, and took the path through the park as usual. There was an air of approaching spring around them, although small spots of snow still sparkled on the lawn.

"So, you're going to Italy?" asked Felician.

"Yes."

"Are you going as far south as last spring?"

"I don't know that yet."

Another short silence.

Suddenly Felician's voice came out of the darkness: "Have you heard anything from Grace since then?"

"From Grace," Georg repeated somewhat surprised, as Felician had not mentioned this name for a long time. "I haven't heard anything more from Grace. We had agreed to that between us. We said good-bye forever in Genoa. For over a year now . . ."

On a bench, completely in the dark, sat a gentleman in fur with a top hat and white gloves. Ah, Labinski, Georg thought for a moment. But then it naturally occurred to him that Labinski had shot himself. . . . It wasn't the first time that he thought he had seen him. On a bright day in the botanic garden at Palermo, there had been someone sitting under a Japanese Ash whom Georg momentarily took for Labinski. And recently, behind the closed windows of a *fiaker*, Georg thought he had recognized the face of his dead father.

Houses glimmered behind the leafless branches. One of them was where the two brothers lived.

It's about time to begin explaining the situation, Georg thought. And to start out quickly he remarked softly: "I'm not going to be alone in Italy this year either, by the way."

"Oh really," Felician said, and looked down.

At that moment Georg felt that he had not set the right tone. He was concerned that Felician could be thinking something like: oh, now he's off on another adventure with one of these dubious people. And he continued seriously: "Felician, I have something rather important to discuss with you."

"Something important?"

"Yes."

"Well Georg," said Felician softly and looked at him from the side. "What's up now, are you finally getting married?"

"Oh no," replied Georg, immediately annoyed again that he had so definitely rejected this possibility. "No, it's not a question of marriage, but actually something much more important."

Felician stood still for a moment. "You have a child?" he asked seriously.

"No, not yet. But that's it. That's why we're leaving."

"So," said Felician.

They had come out of the park. The two involuntarily looked up at the window where they lived, from which, only a year ago, their father had sometimes nodded to them in greeting. They both thought with sadness of how they had gradually drifted apart since the death of their father—and with a little dread about how much further apart life could take them.

"Let's go to my room," Georg said as they arrived upstairs. "It's the most comfortable there."

He sat down in his cozy armchair at the desk. Felician leaned in the corner of the small, green leather divan, which had been pushed up near the desk, and listened quietly. Georg told him the name of his lover, spoke highly of her in warm words, and asked Felician to care for the mother and child in case something mortal should befall him, Georg, in the near future. He had, of course, willed the available part of his inheritance to the child, with the mother having usufruct until the child reaches majority. When Georg had finished, Felician said, after a short silence, smiling: "Well, you have just as good a reason to hope to return from your trip healthy and well as I do from Africa, so our conversation really has only academic meaning."

"Naturally I hope so too. But in any case, it's reassuring to me, Felician, that you've been initiated, and that I can carry on without worry."

"Yes, of course you can." He gave his brother his hand. Then he stood up and walked back and forth in the room. Finally he asked: "You're not thinking of legitimizing the relationship?"

"Not for the moment. What the future will bring, one never knows."

Felician stood still. "Well, yes . . ."

"Do you think that I should get married?" cried Georg with astonishment.

"Not at all."

"Felician, I beg you, be honest!"

"You know, in situations like this, no one can tell you what to do,
even your brother."

"But, if I may ask you, Felician, it seems to me that there's something
about the story you don't like."

"Yes, you see Georg . . . don't misunderstand me . . . I know of
course that you're not thinking of leaving her in the lurch; on the contrary, I'm even convinced that in that respect you'll behave in a more
honorable way than many people in your position. But in the end, the
question is simply this: would you have let yourself in for this if you'd
considered the consequences from all sides?"

"Yes, of course that's difficult to answer," said Georg.

"I mean quite simply: did you have the intention . . . to have a child
with her without actually taking her for your life's partner?"

"God, who thinks about that? When one would so absolutely have
wished to avoid it—."

Felician interrupted him. "Does she know that you're not planning
to marry her?"

"Well, you don't believe that I promised to marry her."

"No, but not to just abandon her either."

"That would have been too shallow, Felician. It's come about like
things of that kind usually do; it all just happened, without a plan, right
up to today."

"Yes, that's all fine. It's just the question of whether or not one is
obligated to some extent to plan when it comes to the weightier matters
in life."

"Possibly. . . . But that was never my thing, unfortunately."

Felician stood in front of Georg, made an affectionate face, and
nodded a couple of times. "That's for sure, Georg. You're not getting
angry . . . but since we're speaking about it . . . of course I don't pre-
sume to have the right to tell you how to run your life . . ."

"Go ahead, Felician . . . really . . . it's good for me. . . ." He gently
touched his hand, which was lying on the back of the leather divan.

"Well, there's not much more to say. I just mean that with you,
everything is like that . . . such a lack of plans. You see, to bring up

another important point, for my part, I'm convinced of your talent, and so are many others. But you work so damn little, you know? And fame will not come by itself, even if one . . ."

"Of course not. But I don't work as little as you think, Felician. It's just that work for people like me is a different story. Sometimes on walks, or even in one's sleep, all sorts of things come to one. . . . And then in the fall . . ."

"Well yes, we hope; but I'm afraid that you won't be able to live at first on your salary. And how long your little money will last, with your style of living, is very much in question. I'll tell you sincerely, when you mentioned earlier to me the money you could leave the child, I really had to wince."

"Have patience, Felician. In three or five years, when I've finished my opera . . ." he said in a self-ironic tone.

"Are you really writing an opera, Georg?"

"I'm starting on it next."

"Who's doing the text for you?"

"Heinrich Bermann. Of course you're making a face again."

"Dear Georg, I've always refrained from advising you on things which are only your own business. It's quite natural that, given your intellectual direction, you will move in other circles than I do, and will associate with people for whom I have little taste. But as long as the text from Herr Bermann is good, you have my blessing . . . and Herr Bermann naturally too.

"The text isn't finished yet, only the scenario."

Felician had to laugh against his will. "So much for your opera. I hope the theater's been built that's going to hire you as conductor."

"Well," said Georg, a little hurt.

"Forgive me," replied Felician. "I really have no doubts about your future. I just wish that you'd do a little more for it yourself. I'd be . . . really, Georg, I'd be so proud if something great would come of you. And it's all up to you. Willy Eissler, who's a very musical person, just recently said to me again that he thinks more of you than most other young composers."

"On account of those few songs of mine he knows?"

"Yes, he really feels they're outstanding. The quantity isn't important."

"You're a good fellow Felician. But you really don't need to encourage me. I know what I have in me, I just need to be more diligent. And the trip will be very good for me. It's always good to get away from

one's familiar surroundings like that for a while. This year it's something completely different than last year. It's the first time, Felician,
that I have been with a person who's completely on my level, who's
more . . . who is truly a friend. And the awareness that I'm going to
have a child, and with her, despite all the attenuating circumstances, is
quite pleasing to me."

"I can well believe that," said Felician and contemplated Georg earnestly and affectionately.

The clock on the desk struck two.

"Oh, so late already," cried Felician. "And I have to pack early in
the morning. Well, tomorrow morning we can talk it all over at the
table. So, good night Georg."

"Good night, Felician. Thank you," he added warmly.

"Why do you thank me? You're funny Georg." They shook hands
and kissed each other, which had not happened for a long time. And
Georg resolved to name his child, if it should be a boy, Felician, and
relished the good portent in the happy sound of this name.

After his brother's departure Georg felt as alone as if he had never
had a single other friend. Staying in the large, lonely house, where a
similar mood seemed to weigh on him as in the time right after the death
of his father, made him almost sad.

He felt that the days which still had to pass before their departure
were a time of transition, in which nothing was really left to be done.
The hours together in the room across from the church were colorless
and dull. Anna too seemed to undergo an emotional change. She was
sometimes irritable, then taciturn again, almost melancholy, and often,
when with her, Georg was overcome with such boredom that he actually dreaded the coming months when they would be constantly in close
quarters together. Of course the trip promised sufficient variety. But
what would it be like in the last months when it would be necessary to
pass the time quietly somewhere near Vienna? He had to be mindful
of companionship for Anna. He was still hesitating to speak to Anna
about it when she came to him herself with news that was well suited
to alleviate this difficulty, and at the same time another, in the simplest
way. Recently, in particular since Anna had gradually dropped her lessons, she had again drawn closer to Therese, and confided everything
to her; and so Therese's mother was soon included in the secret. She
in turn moved closer to Anna than her own mother, who, after a brief
burst of sympathy, had become disapproving and reticent toward the
guilty daughter. Frau Golowski declared herself not only prepared to

stay with Anna in the country, but also promised to find the little house which Georg had been unable to locate, while the young couple was away. However much this willingness accommodated Georg's peace of mind, it was still a little disturbing to be obligated to this strange old woman; and that precisely they, Leo's mother and Berthold's father, were destined to play such an important role in such a momentous experience of Anna's, appeared to him, in his ill-humored moments, to be almost ridiculous.

Three days before their departure, on a lovely March afternoon, Georg paid a farewell visit to the Ehrenbergs. He had rarely been seen there since that Christmas holiday, and his conversations with Else since then had remained completely harmless. She confessed to him, like a friend who could no longer misunderstand such remarks, how she felt less and less comfortable at home. In particular, as Georg had sometimes observed for himself, the mood of the house seemed permanently disrupted by the hostile relationship between father and son. When Oskar would come through the door with his nonchalant noble demeanor, and begin to talk in his Viennese aristocratic tone, the father would turn away with scorn, or couldn't suppress insinuations that between today and tomorrow he could put an end to all this nobility through withdrawal or reduction of his so-called salary, which would be only good for pocket money. The father began, with obvious deliberation, to speak in jargon in front of people, so that Oskar would bite his lips together and be glad to leave the room. But recently it happened only seldom that father and son stayed at the same time in Vienna or in Neuhaus. They could no longer stand to be near each other.

When Georg arrived at the Ehrenbergs, the room was almost completely dark. The marble Isis shone from behind the piano, and the twilight of late afternoon fell in the alcove where mother and daughter sat across from one another. For the first time, the image of these two women had something strangely touching for Georg. A presentiment arose in him that this picture stood before his eyes for the last time, and Else's smile came to him so painfully sweetly that he thought for a moment: wouldn't there have been happiness here in the end? . . .

Now he sat down across from Else and next to Frau Ehrenberg, who continued quietly sewing, smoked a cigarette, and felt completely at home. He explained that, seduced by the enticing spring weather, he was starting the intended trip sooner than planned, and that he would possibly stretch it out until summer.

"And we want to go out to the Auhof by mid-May this time," said

Frau Ehrenberg. "But this year we're expecting to see you there for sure."

"If you're not otherwise occupied," Else added, without showing any expression.

Georg promised to come in August, for a few days at least.

Then they talked about Felician and Willy, who had left a few days before from Biskra with their party to go hunting in the jungle; about Demeter Stanzides, who would soon take his discharge from the military, and who wanted to withdraw to an estate in Hungary, and finally about Heinrich Bermann, from whom no one had received any news for weeks.

"Who knows if he will ever come back to Vienna," said Else.

"Why shouldn't he?—Where did you get that idea, Fraulein Else?"

"God, maybe he'll marry this actress and take off with her for somewhere."

Georg shrugged his shoulders. He didn't know of any actress that Heinrich was involved with, and allowed himself to express his doubts that Heinrich would ever get married, even to a princess or a circus rider.

"That would be too bad for Bermann," said Frau Ehrenberg, caring nothing for Georg's discretion. "In general it seems to me that the young people take these things either too lightly or too seriously."

Else replied: "Yes, it's strange. You're all either much smarter or much dumber in these things than in any others, although in precisely such matters of life one should remain as true as possible to oneself."

"Dear Else," said Georg casually, "if passions come into play . . ."

"Yes, *if* they come into play," intoned Frau Ehrenberg.

"Passions!" cried Else. "I think they are something very rare, like everything grand in the world."

"What do you know about it, my child?" said Frau Ehrenberg.

"At least in my circle I still haven't seen anything of the sort," explained Else.

"Who knows if you would recognize it," added Georg, "even if it did happen in your circle. Sometimes a flirtation and a genuine tragedy may have the same appearance from the outside."

"That is certainly not true," said Else. "Passion is something that absolutely must express itself."

"How is it that you know this, Else?" Frau Ehrenberg turned to her. "It is precisely passions that sometimes may be hidden deeper than any trivial little feeling, because so much more is at stake."

"I believe, dear lady," responded Georg, "that it's very individual. There are people who have everything written on their forehead, and others who are impenetrable. Impenetrability is, to a certain extent, a talent like any other."

"And one can cultivate it like any other," said Else.

The conversation faltered for a moment, as easily happens when the application behind a seemingly general remark is suddenly all too obvious.

Frau Ehrenberg started again: "Have you composed anything nice recently, Georg?" she asked.

"A couple of little pieces for piano. And my quintet is almost finished."

"The quintet is starting to look like a myth," Else said, unsatisfied.

"Else," scolded her mother.

"Well yes, but it really would be better if he were more industrious."

"Of course you're right," replied Georg.

"I think that artists worked much harder before than now."

"The great ones," Georg added.

"No, all of them," Else persisted.

"Perhaps it's good that you're taking a trip," Frau Ehrenberg said with foresight. "You'd be too distracted here."

"He'll be distracted everywhere," Else forcefully asserted. "Even in Iglau,[1] or wherever else he'll be next year."

"I never really thought that you'd be going," said Frau Ehrenberg, and shook her head. "And next year your brother will be in Sophia or Athens, and Stanzides in Hungary. . . . Sad actually, how the nicest people are scattered in every direction of the wind."

"If I were a man," said Else, "I'd scatter too."

Georg laughed. "You're dreaming of a trip around the world in a white yacht. Madeira, Ceylon, San Francisco."

"Oh no, I don't want to be without a career; but maybe I'd have become a naval officer."

"Would you be sweet enough," Frau Ehrenberg turned to Georg, "to play some of your new pieces for us?"

"Gladly." He got up from the corner by the window and walked into the darkness of the room. Else got up and turned on the overhead light. Georg opened the piano, sat down, and played his ballad. Else had taken a place in an armchair, and as she sat there with her arm on the

---

1. A small town in Bohemia where Gustav Mahler spent his boyhood.

back and her head resting on her arm, with the bearing of a grande dame and the melancholy face of a precocious child, Georg again felt strangely touched by her look. He wasn't very satisfied with his ballad today, and he was well aware that he was trying to increase its effectiveness with overly expressive playing.

Privy Councillor Wilt came quietly in and made a sign for no one to disturb themselves. Then he stood for a while, thoughtful and amicable, with his grey, short, bristling hair, leaning against the wall next to the door until Georg brought the performance to a close with excessively sonorous chords. They greeted one another. Wilt congratulated Georg for being a free man who could go on a trip to the south. "Unfortunately I can't," he added, "though meanwhile one sometimes has a dark foreboding that in Austria nothing in the slightest would change, even if one didn't go to one's office for a whole year." As always, he spoke of his career and his Fatherland with irony. Frau Ehrenberg replied to him that there was no one who loved the Fatherland more, or who took his career more seriously, than precisely himself. He granted that. But for him, Austria meant a boundlessly complex instrument that only a master could correctly handle, and for that reason so often sounded badly, as so many bunglers tried their art on it. "They will go slamming around on it," he said sadly, "until all the strings are broken and the cabinet too."

As Georg was leaving, Else accompanied him into the hallway. She had a few words yet to say to him about his ballad. She particularly liked the middle movement. It had been so deeply fervent. And besides, she wished him a good trip. He thanked her. "So," she said suddenly, as he already held his hat in his hand, "the time has come at last to say good-bye to certain dreams."

"What dreams?" he said puzzled.

"Obviously I mean the ones that can't have remained unknown to you."

Georg was shocked. She had never been so clear about it. He smiled embarrassed, and searched for an answer. "Who knows what the future will bring," he finally said softly.

She frowned. "Why won't you at least be honest with me, like I am with you? I know you're not going alone . . . and I know who's going with you. . . . I know all about it. God, what haven't I known since we've known each other."

And Georg heard pain and anger trembling behind her words. And he knew: if he ever took her for his wife, she would make him feel that she had had to wait too long for him. He looked down, silent, as though guilty and stubborn at the same time. Then Else laughed cheerfully, gave him her hand, and said: "Have a good trip."

He squeezed her hand, as if he had to apologize to her for something. She pulled away from him, turned, and went back into the room. He remained standing for a few seconds at the door, and then hurried down to the street.

That evening Georg saw Leo Golowski again in the coffeehouse for the first time in many weeks. He knew through Anna that, as a volunteer, Leo had recently gone through some unpleasant things; that in particular the "Beast in Human Form" persecuted him with malice, even with a genuine hatred. Georg was struck today by how much Leo had changed in the short time since he had last seen him. He looked positively aged.

"I'm glad to see you again in person once more before my trip," Georg said, and sat down across from him at the table. "You are glad," replied Leo, "that by accident you found me in person, but for me it was a necessity to see you again, that's the difference." His voice sounded more tender than usual. He looked Georg in the eyes, amicable, almost fatherly. At this moment Georg no longer doubted that Leo knew everything, and was embarrassed for a few seconds as though he would have to justify himself to him, was angry with himself over his embarrassment, and was grateful to Leo that he appeared not to notice. They spoke almost only about music this evening. Leo asked about the progress of Georg's work, and in the course of the conversation Georg said he would be ready tomorrow afternoon, Sunday, to play some of his newest compositions for Leo. But as they left one another, Georg had an uncomfortable feeling, as though he had just passed a theoretical exam with moderate success, but still faced the practical exam tomorrow. What did this young man, who acted so mature beyond his years, really want from him? Was Georg supposed to prove to him that his talent entitled him to be Anna's lover, or to be the father of her child? He awaited Leo's visit with deep trepidation. He even thought at one moment of not seeing him. But when Leo appeared, so harmless and sincere, as he sometimes liked to be, Georg soon was less anxious. They had tea, smoked cigarettes, Georg showed his library, the pictures that hung in the house, the antiques and weapons, and the feeling of examination disappeared. Georg sat at the piano, played a few of his earlier pieces, and the latest ones, including the ballad, much better than yesterday at the Ehrenbergs, then a few songs to which Leo added the melody, without a fine voice, but with sure musical feeling. Finally he began to play the quintet from the score, had trouble with it, so Leo took the score to the window and read it attentively. "I really can't tell yet," he said. "Some of it is like a dilettante with a lot of taste, and some like an artist without enough discipline. One feels it most in the songs . . . but what? . . . Talent? . . . I don't know. . . . In any case one feels that you have a noble nature, a musically noble nature."

"Well, that's not much."

"It may seem rather little. But since you still have worked so little, it doesn't prove anything against you. Worked little and experienced little."

"You think . . ." Georg responded, forcing a derisive smile.

"Oh, lived through a lot, perhaps, but *felt* . . . do you know what I mean Georg?"

"Yes, I can imagine. But you're quite wrong. I even feel that I have a certain inclination to sentimentality, which I have to resist."

"Yes, that's it. Sentimentality is something that stands in direct opposition to feeling, something with which one compensates for one's lack of feeling, one's inner coldness. Sentimentality is feeling that one has bought, so to speak, for the purchase price. I hate sentimentality."

"Hm, and yet I think you're not entirely free of it yourself."

"I'm Jewish. It's a national illness with us. Decent people try to turn it into anger or rage. With the Germans it's a bad habit, emotional laziness, so to speak."

"Therefore, to be excused with you, but not with us?"

"Even illnesses are not to be forgiven when one has, with full awareness of his disposition, neglected to protect oneself against infection. But we're beginning to become aphoristic, and we're coming up with only half or quarter truths along the way. Let's go back to your quintet. I liked the theme of the Adagio the best."

Georg nodded. "I heard it once in Palermo."

"What," asked Leo, "it's supposed to be a Sicilian melody?"

"No; it came to me out of the waves of the sea as I went walking alone on the shore one morning. Solitude is generally good for my output. New places too. I've promised myself a lot from my trip." He told him about Heinrich Bermann's libretto, which was very stimulating for him. When Heinrich got back, Leo should encourage him to take up work on it in earnest.

"Didn't you know yet," said Leo, "his father is dead."

"Really? When did it happen? How do you know?"

"It appeared in the newspaper this morning."

They talked about Heinrich's relationship with his late father, and Leo expressed the view that things would go better in the world if parents would learn more often from the experiences of their children, instead of insisting that the children adapt themselves to their accumulated wisdom. They went into a discussion about the relationship between fathers and sons, about genuine and false types of gratitude, about the death of loved ones, about the varieties of sadness and pain, about the dangers of remembering and the obligations of forgetting. Georg could see that Leo reflected on the most serious things, was quite alone, and understood how to live in solitude. He almost loved him as the door closed behind him at that late night hour, and the thought that he had been Anna's first infatuation felt very good to him.

The next few days went by faster than expected, with shopping, details, preparations of all sorts. And then one evening Georg and Anna went, one after the other, in two coaches, to the train station, and for fun greeted each other mutually with great courtesy in the entrance hall, like distant acquaintances who had by chance run into each other. "Oh, Fraulein, what a happy circumstance, are you by any chance traveling to Munich also?" "Yes indeed, Herr Baron." "Well, isn't that marvelous. And do you have a sleeping accommodation, my dear?" "Certainly, Herr Baron, bed number five." "No! How remarkable. I have number six!" Then they walked up and down along the platform. Georg was very well dressed, and it pleased him that, in her English dress with the narrow brimmed traveling hat and blue veil, Anna looked like an intriguing stranger. They walked the whole length of the train, up to the locomotive, which stood outside the station and blew light grey steam into the dark sky in agitated puffs. Further out along the line, in dim light, green and red lanterns were glowing. Anxious whistles came from somewhere in the distance, and slowly from out of the darkness, a train pulled into the station. A red light swung magically back and forth above the ground, looked miles away, and as it stood still, suddenly seemed quite close. And in the distance, shimmering and losing themselves in uncertainty, the tracks went their way, to near and far, into the night, into the morning, into the next day, into the inscrutable.

Anna got into the compartment. Georg remained standing outside for a while and amused himself looking at the travelers: the hurrying and stressed, the distinguished and composed, and those who pretended to be composed,—and at the diverse varieties of companions: the melancholy, the cheerful, and the indifferent.

Anna leaned out of the window. Georg talked to her as though he had no thought of leaving, and got in at the last moment. The train left. People stood on the platform—incomprehensible people who were remaining behind in Vienna, and to whom all the others, who were now departing so seriously, seemed incomprehensible. A few handkerchiefs waved, the stationmaster stood there pompously and gave the train a stern look, a porter in a blue-and-white-striped linen shirt held up a yellow bag and looked eagerly into each window. Strange, Georg thought casually, there are people who are leaving and have forgotten their yellow bag in Vienna. Everything vanished: handkerchiefs, bags, stationmaster, buildings, the brightly lit signal house, the Gloriette,[2] the flickering lights of the city, the small, empty gardens on the bank; and the train rushed deep into the night. Georg turned from the window. Anna sat in the corner and had laid her hat and veil next to her; small, delicate tears ran down her cheeks. "But," Georg said, put his arms around her, and kissed her on the eyes and mouth. "But Anna," he repeated more tenderly and kissed her again. "Why are you crying? It will be beautiful."

"It's easy for you," she said, and more tears flowed over her smiling face.

It was beautiful. First they stopped in Munich. They walked around in the lofty halls of the picture gallery, stood absorbed in front of old, darkened pictures, wandered in the sculpture gallery between marble gods, kings, and heroes; and when Anna suddenly dropped onto a divan, exhausted, she felt Georg's tender gaze on her head. They rode through the English garden, along wide boulevards, under still bare trees, snuggled close to each other, young and happy, and gladly believing that people took them for honeymooners. And they sat next to each other at the opera, and saw *Figaro*, *Meistersinger*, and *Tristan*; and it seemed as though the beloved music wove a transparent aural veil around them alone, that isolated them from all the other listeners. And they sat, unknown by anyone, at charmingly set inn tables, eating, drinking, and talking in high spirits. And they walked home through streets with the marvelous breath of strangeness, where the gentle night awaited them in their room together, and slept blissfully cheek to cheek; and when they awoke, a friendly day, which they could use in any way

2. A large baroque monument built on the hilltop of the Schoenbruenn Park in 1775 by Empress Maria Therese to commemorate a military victory.

they pleased, smiled at them through the window. They were contented with each other as never before, and belonged totally to one another at last. Then they traveled on, into the beckoning spring, through long valleys in which snow sparkled and melted away; then, as through a final, white, winter dream, through the Brenner Pass to Bozen, where they sunned themselves in bright sunshine in the noisy market square. On the weathered steps of the amphitheater in Verona, under a cool Easter evening sky, Georg found himself at last in the longed-for world, where a true love was this time granted to accompany him. From the pale-red distance, together with the eternal memories that belonged to other men, his own vanished childhood greeted him; yes, a breath of bygone days, when his mother was still alive, trembled yet, here in the air of his second homeland. Venice impressed him favorably, though familiar and without magic, as though he had just left it yesterday. In St. Mark's Square he was greeted by some casual acquaintances from Vienna, and the veiled lady at his side in the broad coat drew some curious glances. Only once, late in the evening, on a gondola ride through the narrow canals, did the staring palaces, which in daylight had gradually been degraded to the appearance of theatrical sets, appear to him in the heavy splendor of their deep, golden past.

Then came a few days in cities that he knew only scarcely or not at all, where he had spent a few hours as a boy, or had never been before. On a humid afternoon in Padua they entered a dim church and walked slowly from altar to altar, studying the simple, edifying pictures in which saints worked their miracles and martyrs met their destiny. On a dark, rain-filled day they drove a rickety, sad wagon past a red brick castle, around which stood grey-green water in a wide moat, above a marketplace where carelessly dressed villagers sat in front of the coffeehouse; in sad, silent streets where grass grew through the buckling stones; and it was hard to believe that this pitiful, vanishing town bore the resounding name of Ferrara. In Bologna, where the lively and blossoming city was not contented to be proud of a bygone splendor, they breathed freer. But as soon as Georg caught sight of the hills of Fiesole he felt greeted by another homeland. This was the city where he had ceased to be a boy, where the stream of life had begun to course through his veins. At many places, memories arose in him which he kept to himself; and in the cathedral, where that Florentine girl had sent her last look at him from under her bridal veil, he spoke to Anna only of the fall evening hour in the Altlerchenfeld church where they had first anxiously begun to talk about this trip, which had become a reality so inconceivably fast. He showed Anna the house where he had lived nine years ago. They found themselves among the same shops in which coral dealers, clock makers, and lace makers sold their wares. As the second floor was for rent, Georg could have easily seen the room in which his mother had died. But he hesitated a long time to enter the room again. Only on the day before they left, alone and without telling Anna ahead of time, as if by compulsion, did he enter the house, climb the stairs, and go into the room. The porter, who had grown old, led him around, and did not recognize him. It still had the same furniture everywhere; his mother's bedroom looked exactly as it did ten years ago, and in the same corner, in brown wood, with the dark green, silver-streaked velvet coverlet, stood that very bed. But nothing of what Georg had expected stirred in him. A tired memory, more insipid and dull than usual, passed through his soul. He lingered long in front of the bed, consciously determined to conjure the emotions which he felt obligated to experience. He whispered the word *mother*; he tried to imagine her as she had lain there, in this bed, for many days and nights. He remembered the hours in which it had gone better for her, and he read to her, or played for her on the piano in the next room; he saw the small round table standing in the corner where their father and Felician had spoken softly, as their mother had just fallen asleep; and finally, as sharp and vivid as a scene at the theater, the image arose in him of that dreadful evening on which his father and brother were gone, and he sat all alone by his mother's bed, her hand in his. . . . He saw and heard it all again: how she suddenly felt sick after a quiet day, how he had thrown open the window and how the laughter and conversation of strangers had poured into the room with the tepid March air; how she at last lay there, with open and extinguished eyes; her wavy hair, still flowing for a few seconds across her forehead and temples, now lay ruffled and dry on the pillow, while her bare left arm hung down over the bed rail with rigid, widely spread fingers. The image rose up in him with such intense lucidity that he saw his own child's face in his mind again, and heard the sound of his long vanished crying . . . but he felt no pain. It was too long ago. Ten years almost.

"The view's wonderful from this window," the porter suddenly said from behind him, and opened the window;—and suddenly, as on that bygone evening, voices came up from below. And at that moment, he heard his mother's voice in his ear, just as he had heard it then, fleeting, fading . . . "Georg . . . Georg . . . ," and from the dark corner, in the place where at that time the pillows had lain, he saw something pale shining toward him. He went to the window and confirmed: "Wonder-ful view." But a dark veil covered the beautiful vista. "Mother" he mur-mured, and once again: but *mother* meant, to his own amazement, no longer the long interred woman who had born him; the word meant that other woman who was not a mother yet, but who would be in a few months . . . the mother of a child of whom he was the father. And now the word suddenly sounded as though it intoned something never heard before, never understood, as if rung from mysteriously singing bells in the distant future. And Georg was ashamed that he had come here alone, had sneaked here, as it were. He would never dare tell Anna that he had been here.

The next morning they went to Rome. And as Georg, from day-to-day, felt more at home, more buoyant, more refreshed, Anna began to suffer more frequently from exhaustion. She often remained alone back in the hotel, while he wandered the streets, explored the Vatican, or wandered around the Forum and Palatine. She never held him back, though he felt obligated to console her before he left and would say: "Now, you save yourself for another time; hopefully we'll be back here again soon." She would then smile in her mischievous way, as though she no longer doubted that she would ever be his wife; and he himself had to admit that he no longer regarded this outcome as impossible. For that they should separate this fall, with a farewell forever, had gradually become almost inconceivable to him. But during this time they never spoke in clear terms about the distant future. He was re-luctant to, and she felt that she would do well not to disturb this reluc-tance. And precisely during these Rome days, during which he often wandered for hours alone in the strange city, he sometimes felt that it was not altogether unpleasant to have slipped away from Anna like this. One evening he walked until the onset of darkness among the ruins of the Caesars' palaces and on the heights of the Palatine hill, with the proud delight of the solitary, and watched the sun set over the Cam-pagna. Then he went for a ride along the ancient city wall on the Monte Pincio,[3] and as he reclined in the corner of his wagon, gazing back over the roofs at the view of the dome of Saint Peter's, deeply moved, he felt himself to be experiencing the most elevated moments of the whole trip. He did not get back to the hotel until late, and found Anna stand-ing at the window, pale, with red patches on her puffy cheeks from cry-

3. The hilltop park on the east side of the Piazza del Popolo; it overlooks the square. The hill extends several blocks to the southeast and connects with the top of the more familiar Spanish Steps.

ing. For two hours she had been dying of fear, and had imagined that an accident had befallen him, that he had been attacked, or murdered. He reassured her, but couldn't find words of the sincerity she required, and he felt cornered and trapped in a very undignified way. She felt his coolness, and let him know that he didn't love her enough; he responded irritably, almost desperately; she called him heartless and selfish. He bit his lips, answered nothing, and paced up and down the room. They went to the dining room unreconciled, where they ate their supper without speaking, and then went to bed without wishing each other "good night." The next days stood under the shadow of this scene. Not until the trip to Naples, alone in the carriage, under the spell of the new landscape through which they rode, did they find one another again. From now on he hardly left her for a moment; she seemed helpless to him, and a little touching. He gave up the visit to the museum, since she couldn't go with him. They went to Posilipo[4] together and went for a walk in the Villa Nazionale. On an excursion through Pompeii he walked along beside her sedan chair like a tenderly devoted husband, and while the guide gave explanations in bad French, Georg took Anna's hand, kissed it, and tried in animated words to impart to her the delight he felt again this time in the mysterious, roofless city which gradually emerged, after a two-thousand-year burial, street by street, house by house, into the changeless light of this blue sky. And as they stopped at a spot where a few workers were occupied trying to coax a broken pillar from the ashes with cautious scoops of the shovel, he pointed them out to Anna with such bright eyes that it seemed as if this sight was a present he had been saving for her for a long time, and as though, in all that had happened until now, he had only followed the purpose of bringing her at this moment to this place to show her these wonders.

On a dark blue May night they reclined in two canvas chairs on the deck of a ship which was taking them to Genoa. An old Frenchman with bright eyes who had sat across from them at dinner stood by them for a while and pointed out the stars, which hung like heavy drops of silver in the vastness. Some he called by name, charmingly and obligingly, as though he felt obligated to make the sparkling heavenly wanderers and the young couple acquainted with each other. Then he excused himself and went down to his cabin. Georg however thought

4. The town just to the north of the Capo di Posilipo mentioned in chapter 4, note 5. All this is within 10 miles of Pompeii, along the coast running northwest past Mt. Vesuvius.

of his solitary trip along the same route and under the same sky the previous spring after his farewell from Grace. He had told Anna about her, not so much from an inner need as, through the description of a certain character and naming of a certain name from his past, to free them from a mysterious strangeness in which they seemed to merge with Anna. Anna knew about Labinski's death, about Georg's conversation with Grace at Labinski's grave, about Georg's stay with her in Sicily; he had even shown her a picture of Grace. And yet he had to admit with a mild shudder how little Anna knew about this time in his life, about which he had spoken with her almost unreservedly; and he felt how impossible it was to give another person a clear conception of a time that they have not shared, of the content of so many days and nights whose every minute had been fulfilled by the present. He recognized how little the small distortions of which he was sometimes guilty in his explanations meant compared to the indestructible breath of the lie which every memory bore from itself on the short journey from the lips of one to the ears of the other. And if later Anna wanted to tell a friend, or a new lover, of the time she had spent with Georg, as honestly as she could, what in the end could he experience of it? Not much more than a story which he had read a hundred times in books: of a young creature whom a young man had loved, who had traveled with him, experienced rapture with him and sometimes boredom, who felt at one with him and yet sometimes alone; and even if she tried to give an account of every minute . . . it remained an unrecoverable past, and for the one who never himself experienced it, the past can never become real.

The stars shimmered above them. Anna's head had slowly sunk onto his chest, and he held it gently with his hands. Only the gentle rumbling in the deep reported that the ship was moving ahead. Now it steadily went on toward the morning, toward home, toward the future. Time, which had for so long rested silently over them, began to sound and to circulate. Georg felt suddenly that he no longer held his fate in his own hand. Everything took its course. And now he felt in his entire body, all the way up to his hair as it were, that the ship below his feet hurried forward inexorably.

They only stayed in Genoa for one day. They were both longing for rest, and beyond this, Georg was also eager to get to work. They only wanted to linger for a couple of weeks yet on one of the Italian lakes and then go home in the middle of June. By that time the house in which Anna would stay should be ready. Frau Golowski had discovered a half-dozen that were suitable, sent Anna precise reports, waited for a decision, and continued looking just in case. From Genoa they went to Milan, but they could no longer tolerate the noisy life of the city and went on to Lugano the next day.

They stayed here for four weeks. And morning after morning Georg went the way which took him again today along the lovely shore, out past Paradiso,[5] to the bend in the road which led to that always eagerly anticipated vista. Only a few days remained of their stay. However well Anna's condition had held up from the start, the time had come to return to Vienna, to be able to look forward calmly to the coming events. The days in Lugano seemed to Georg to be the best he had experienced since he had left Vienna. And he asked himself several times during happy moments if this weren't perhaps the best time of his entire life. Never had he felt so fulfilled, so confident in both prospect and remembrance as here, and he saw with joy that Anna too was completely happy. Expectant gentleness shown on her brow, her eyes looked happy and intelligent, like in the time when Georg was courting her at home. Without anxiety, without impatience, and with a feeling of her blossoming motherhood spread widely over the memory of prejudices at home and concern for impending confusion, she anticipated with joy the great hour when she would return the awaited being as a living soul which her womb had drunk in, in a half-unconscious moment of rapture. Georg happily saw her maturing into the companion which he had hoped to find in her from the beginning, but who had sometimes vanished from him in the course of those days. In conversations about his work, all of which she carefully examined, about the character of the songs, about general musical questions, she displayed more knowledge and sensitivity than he had previously recognized in her. Although he wrote little down, he was content, as it were, to be moving ahead inwardly. Melodies sang and harmonies sounded in him, and with deep understanding he recalled a remark of Felician's, who once had said, after he had not practiced his fencing for a whole month: his arm had gotten some good ideas during this time. So the future inspired no worries in him. He knew that serious work would begin as soon as he got back to Vienna, and the road lay in open prospect before him.

Georg stood for a long time at the bend in the road to which his steps had hastened. A short, wide peninsula, densely overgrown with low shrubs, stretched out into the lake, and a narrower path led gently,

5. A small town also on the shore of the lake, about a half-mile south of Lugano, at the point where the shoreline bends east.

in a few steps, down to a wooden bench that couldn't be seen from the road, on which Georg always liked to sit down for a while before going back to the hotel.

How many times were left! he thought today, involuntarily. Five or six maybe, and then back to Vienna. And he asked himself, what would happen if they didn't go back, if they settled somewhere in Italy or in Switzerland with the child, in the double peace of nature and remoteness, and built a new life for themselves. What would happen? . . . Nothing. Hardly anyone would even wonder about it. And no one would miss either him or her, not painfully, as if they were someone irreplaceable. This consideration made him more relieved than sad; only it annoyed him that a sort of homesickness, even of longing to see certain individuals, sometimes overcame him. And even now, while he drank in the lake air, under a strange but trusted bright blue sky, enjoying the pleasure of rapture and solitude, his heart would pound when he thought of the forests and hills around Vienna, of the Ringstrasse, the Club, of his large room with the view of the Stadtpark. And it would have been a painful feeling for him had it not been possible for his child to be born in Vienna. Suddenly it occurred to him that there would surely be another report from Frau Golowski today, as well as other news from Vienna, so he decided to detour by the post office on the way back to the hotel. For, as during the entire trip, he did not have the mail sent to the hotel, because this way he felt freer from any events he heard about from the outside. Not that anyone wrote all that much from Vienna. Usually, in spite of their brevity, there was in Heinrich's letters something, which Georg clearly felt, for which he had less to thank the writer's need to communicate than the fact that he practiced the profession that made it his job to breathe life into the written word. Felician's letters were as cool as though he had completely forgotten that last intimate conversation in Georg's room and the brotherly kiss with which they had parted. . . . He must expect, thought Georg, that his letters would also be read by Anna, and doesn't feel prepared to give this strange woman a look into his private affairs and private feelings. Nuernberger had sent a few short replies to his greeting cards, and to a letter from Rome, in which Georg warmly recalled their walks together in the early spring. Nuernberger had expressed, with ironically apologetic words, his regret for having talked so much to Georg on those walks about his family relations, in which he could not have had the slightest interest. A letter came to Naples from the elder Eissler which reported that a vacancy at the Detmold Court Theater next year could not be expected, but that Georg would be invited by Count Malnitz, as a preferred guest, to attend the rehearsals and performances, through which opportunity the way might be paved for a closer relationship in the future. Georg warmly thanked him, but was for the moment little inclined to undertake a long stay in a strange city on so vague a prospect, and determined to look around for a firm position as soon as he got back to Vienna.

Otherwise nothing personal came to him here from home. The greetings intended for him that Frau Rosner felt obligated to send, which were included in letters to her daughter, did not touch him, despite the fact that since recently they had ceased to be directed to "Herr Baron," but to "Georg." He felt that Anna's parents were simply accepting what they could not change, but that inwardly they remained depressed and lacking in the desired understanding.

As usual, Georg did not take the way back along the shore. Through narrow streets, between garden walls, under walkways, finally across a wide piazza from which one again had an open view of the lake, he arrived at the post office, whose bright yellow paint reflected the dazzling sun. A young lady, whom Georg had already noticed from a distance walking up and down along the pavement, stood still as he approached. She was dressed in white and carried an open white parasol above a wide straw hat with a red band. As Georg drew near, she smiled, and now he suddenly saw a familiar face under the white speckled lace veil. "Could this possibly be Fraulein Therese?" he cried and took the hand she extended out to him.

"Greetings Baron," she replied innocently, as if this encounter were the most natural thing in the world. "How is everything with Anna?"

"Just fine, thank you. You're going to visit her of course?"

"If that would be all right."

"But tell me, what in the world are you doing here? Are you traveling . . ." he looked with amazement over her whole appearance, "as a political agitator?"

"One really can't say that," she replied, and thrust her chin forward, only without this motion making her face ugly this time like it did before. "It's more of a vacation trip." And her face shone with inward laughter as she saw Georg's gaze directed at the gate through which Demeter Stanzides was now walking in a black-and-white striped flannel suit. He lifted his soft grey hat in greeting and gave Georg his hand. "Good morning, Baron, I'm delighted to see you again."

"I'm delighted as well, Herr Stanzides."

"No letter for me?" Therese turned to Demeter.

"No, Therese, only a couple of cards for me," and he put them in his pocket.

"How long have you been here?" Georg asked, trying to look as little surprised as possible.

"We got here last night," replied Demeter.

"Straight from Vienna?" asked Georg.

"No, from Milan. We've been traveling for a week."

"First we were in Venice, as is usual," Therese added, pulled smilingly at her veil, and took Demeter's arm.

"You've been gone much longer," said Demeter, "I saw a card from you at the Ehrenbergs a few weeks ago. Vettier House, Pompeii."

"Yes, I have a wonderful trip behind me."

"Now we want to have a look around the place," said Therese, "and don't want to hold the Baron up any longer, who in any case has letters to pick up."

"Oh, there's no hurry. And of course we'll see each other again later anyway?"

"Would you give us the pleasure, Baron," said Demeter, "of lunching with us today at the Europe, where we're staying?"

"Thank you very much, but unfortunately I can't. But . . . perhaps you could come for dinner with . . . with . . . us at the Park Hotel, yes? At six-thirty, if that's all right. I'll have a table set in the garden under a nice plane tree, where we usually eat."

"Yes, we'll accept gladly," said Therese. "Maybe I'll come an hour before to be able to talk with Anna in peace."

"Lovely," replied Georg. "She'll be delighted."

"So, *auf Wiedersehen*, Baron," said Demeter, and as he squeezed Georg's hand warmly he added, "and take my greetings home with you as well."

Therese winked happily at Georg, and then set out with Demeter on the way to the shore.

Georg looked after them. If I hadn't already known her, he thought, Demeter could have introduced her without further ado as his wife, the hereditary Princess X. How bizarre! These two! . . . Then he went into the hall, picked up his messages at the window, and looked through them cursorily. The first one to catch his eye was a card from Leo Golowski. There was nothing on it except: "Have a great time, dear Georg." Then there was a card from the Waldstein Garden in the

Prater. "We have just finished a toast to our honored fugitive. Guido Schoenstein, Ralph Skelton, and Rattenmamsell."

Georg wanted to read the letters from Felician, Frau Rosner, and Heinrich at home with Anna in peace. And he wanted to share with Anna the news of the arrival of the unlikely pair. He was not entirely without apprehension. For Anna's bourgeois instincts could sometimes be reawakened in quite unexpected ways. In any case Georg decided to present his invitation to Demeter and Therese as something completely a matter of course, but was prepared, in the event that the idea should upset or anger her or make her feel insecure, to set her concerns aside with firmness. He himself was quite happy about the coming evening after the many weeks which he had spent exclusively in Anna's company. He almost felt a little envy for Demeter, who was on so carefree a pleasure trip, like the one he had taken himself the previous year with Grace. He also thought that he liked Therese better than before. However many beautiful women he had encountered in the course of the last few months, he had never been seriously tempted, even though Anna was steadily losing her feminine charm. Today was the first time he had felt a yearning for new embraces again.

Soon he saw Anna's light blue morning dress through the latticework of the balcony. In his usual manner, Georg whistled the first measures of Beethoven's *Fifth Symphony* to announce his arrival, and the pale, gentle face of his beloved immediately appeared over the railing, and her large eyes greeted him, smiling. He held the bundle of letters in the air, she nodded with satisfaction, and he hurried quickly up to her room and out onto the balcony. She reclined in a wicker armchair in front of the little table with the green protective cover on which she had laid some handicraft, as was almost always the case when Georg came home from his morning walk. He kissed her on the forehead and on the mouth. "So, who do you suppose I ran into?" he asked immediately.

"Else Ehrenberg," answered Anna, without thinking.

"Why do you say that? How would she get here?"

"Well," said Anna slyly, "one could come here after you."

"One could, but it's not her. Guess again. You get three chances."

"Heinrich Bermann."

"Not even close. There's a letter from him here, by the way. Try again."

She thought it over. "Demeter Stanzides," she finally said.

"What, do you know something?"

"What is there to know? Is he really here?"

"My gosh, you've turned completely red, oh!" He was aware of her attraction for Demeter's melancholy cavalier handsomeness, but felt no trace of jealousy.

"So, it is Stanzides?" she asked.

"Yes, it certainly is Stanzides."

"I really don't find anything all that strange about that."

"That's not the strange part. But when you hear who he's here with . . ."

"With Sissy Wyner."

"But . . ."

"I thought, married . . . That's possible."

"No, not with Sissy, and not married, but with your friend Therese, and as unmarried as can be."

"Oh, come on . . ."

"I'm telling you, with Therese. They've been traveling for a week. What do you say to that? They were in Venice and Milan. Did you have any idea?"

"None."

"Really, none?"

"Really, none. You know that Therese has only written once, casually, and you read her letter with obvious interest yourself."

"You don't seem surprised enough to me."

"God, I've always known that she had good taste."

"Demeter too," Georg said with conviction.

"Elective affinities,"[6] Anna remarked with raised eyebrows, and continued crocheting.

"And this is now the mother of my child," Georg said with a jocular shake of the head.

She looked at him smilingly. "When is she coming to see me?"

"This evening, around six, I think. And . . . and Stanzides is coming too . . . a little later. They'll be dining with us. You don't mind do you?"

"Mind? I'm delighted," Anna replied simply. Georg was pleasantly surprised. If Anna saw Stanzides in Vienna in her condition! . . . he thought. How it liberates and purifies to get away from one's old surroundings!

6. *Wahlverwandschaften*—An allusion to the title of a novel by Goethe that has been published in English under the title *Elective Affinities,* and implying some of the determinacy of a chemical process.

"Did they tell you anything new?" asked Anna.

"We hardly stood for three minutes outside the post office. He sends his greetings, by the way."

Anna did not answer, and it seemed to Georg that her thinking was turning to bourgeois ways again.

"Have you been up for long?" he asked quickly.

"Yes, I sat for quite a while on the balcony. And I napped for a while; the air is sort of heavy today; and I dreamed too."

"What did you dream about?"

"About the baby," she said.

"Again?"

She nodded. "Just the same as last time. I'm in the dream too, sitting on the balcony, holding it in my arms, nursing it. . . ."

"What was it? A boy or a girl?"

"I don't know. Just a baby. So little and sweet. And it was a joy . . . No, I won't give it away," she said softly with her eyes closed.

He stood leaning on the railing, and felt the gentle afternoon wind blowing in his hair. "If you don't want to give it away, you don't have to," he said; and it went through his mind: wouldn't it be the easiest thing for me to marry her? . . . But something held him back from saying it. They both said nothing. He had laid the letters on the table in front of him. Now he took them and opened one. "Let's see what your mother writes first," he said.

Frau Rosner's letter contained the news that all was well at home, that everyone was glad they would soon see Anna again, and that Josef had gotten a position in the administration of the *People's Messenger* with a salary of fifty gulden a month. Further, they had received an inquiry from Frau Bittner as to when Anna would be back from Dresden, and if it was really certain that she would be there next fall, since if she wasn't, they had to start looking around for another teacher. Anna sat motionless and said nothing.

Then Georg took Heinrich's letter. He read: " 'Dear Georg, I'm overjoyed that you will soon be back, and gladly write this to you today, because once you're back here, I'll never tell you how glad I am. A few days ago, on a lonely evening bicycle excursion along the Danube, I really missed you. What an ineradicable air of loneliness those banks have. I remember having experienced it once five or six years ago, on a Sunday, as I had been sitting in what one would call genial company at the Klosterneuberg monastery, in the large garden with the view of the mountains and the meadows. How it came up from the depths of

the water, the loneliness, which obviously represented something completely different than one usually thinks. By no means the opposite of
sociability. Perhaps one only has the right to feel lonely among people.
Take that as aphoristic, an absurdly false extra editorial embellishment,
or just set it aside. But to get back to my Danube bicycle ride,—precisely
in that rather humid evening hour, all sorts of good ideas came to me,
and I hope soon to tell you many remarkable things about Aegidius, as
the sad and murderous youth is finally named, about the profound and
inscrutable prince, about the ridiculous duke Heliodor, under which
name I have the honor of introducing to you the groom of the princess,
and much besides about the princess herself, who seems to be a more
remarkable person herself, than I at first supposed.'"

"All this refers to the opera libretto?" Anna asked, and put down
her work.

"Naturally," Georg answered, and continued reading.

"'You will also soon see, dear friend, that in the last few weeks I
have completed some for the moment not particularly immortal verses
for the first act, which, awaiting further developments, that is to say
your music, wander around the world like angels without wings. The
material appeals to me in a strange way. And I'm curious myself as to
where I actually want to go with it. And there are all sorts of things I
have begun . . . sketched . . . considered. Short and sweet, it seems to
me that a new epoch was announcing itself within me. That sounds
more smug than it is. Even chimney sweeps, sausage vendors, and
sergeants have their epochs. Only people like us know it as well. What
seems very likely to me is that I will quite soon climb down or up from
the fantastic element in which I am now content, into a very real one.
What would you say, for example, if I got involved in a political satire.
And already I feel that the word doesn't quite fit the reality. It seems
to me that politics is the most fantastic element in which people can
get involved, only that they don't notice it. . . . Here perhaps we may
get to the heart of the matter. It occurred to me as I recently attended
a political gathering (well, actually these thoughts just came to me);
anyway, I was at a meeting of workers, men and women, in Brigittenau,
to which I had gone at the side of Mademoiselle Therese Golowski and
at which I was obliged to listen to seven speeches on universal suffrage.
Each of the speakers—Therese among them—spoke as if there was
nothing more personally urgent for them than the solution to this problem, and I believe that none of them suspected that in the depths of
their souls the whole question was really a matter of profound indiffer-

ence. Therese was, of course, most indignant when I suggested this to her, and explained to me that I had been contaminated by the poisonous skepticism of Nuernberger, with whom I have far too much to do. She speaks very badly of him, ever since he asked her a few weeks ago in the coffeehouse whether she would wear high coiffure or pinned-up braids to her next trial for high treason. It is true that I spend a lot of time together with Nuernberger. In hard times there is no one who brings more kindness. Only that there are sometimes hours whose difficulty he does not suspect, or does not want to know. There are all sorts of pains which I feel he underestimates, and about which I have ceased to speak with him.'"

"What does he mean?" Anna interrupted him.

"Obviously the story with the actress," Georg replied and continued reading. "'On the other hand he is inclined again to over estimate other problems, but that is probably my fault, not his. I must confess, he brought a sympathy to the loss I suffered through the death of my father which embarrassed me. But however hard it hit me, we had already grown so far apart, long before the madness overcame him, that his death seemed more like another further dreadful estrangement, rather than a new experience.'"

"Well?" asked Anna, as Georg paused.

"Something just occurred to me."

"What's that?"

"Nuernberger's sister is buried in the cemetery at Cadenabbia. I've told you about her. I want to go over there in the next few days."

Anna nodded. "Maybe I'll go with you if I'm feeling well enough. From what I've heard of him, I find Nuernberger much more sympathetic than your friend Heinrich, that awful egoist."

"You think?"

"Well listen, the way he writes about his father is almost unendurable."

"God, if people had grown as far apart as those two."

"Despite that. I'm not particularly close to my parents either. And yet . . . if I . . . no, no, I don't want to think about things like that. Do you want to go on reading?"

Georg read: "'There are more serious things than death, sadder certainly, because these other things lack the finality which elevates the sadness of death in the higher sense. There are, for example living ghosts who wander the streets in the light of day, with long dead and yet seeing eyes, ghosts that sit down and speak to you with human voices that sound more remote than from the grave. And one could say that, at times when one experiences things like that, the character of death discloses itself in a more sinister way than when one stands by as someone is lowered into the earth . . . however close they were.' "

Georg involuntarily put the letter down, and Anna said with conviction: "You can keep him, your friend Heinrich."

"Yes," Georg replied slowly, "he is a little affected sometimes. And yet . . . oh, that's the first lunch bell already, let's just go ahead and finish. 'But then I have to tell you what took place here yesterday, the most painful and ridiculous story I have heard in a long time, and unfortunately the parties involved are our good acquaintances the Ehrenbergs, father and son.' "

"Oh!" Anna cried involuntarily.

Georg read the remaining lines quickly to himself, and shook his head.

"What is it?" asked Anna.

"This is something. . . . Well, listen," and he continued reading. " 'How critical the relationship between Oskar and his father has become in the last year will not have escaped you. You already know the underlying reasons, so I can simply report the incident without elaborating on the motives. So, just think. Yesterday at noontime Oskar crossed over to St. Michael's and lifted his hat. You know that nowadays there is hardly a quality that passes for elegance like piety. And so it perhaps needs no further explanation than that, for example, as a couple of young aristocrats may have just come out of the church, Oskar would want to make a Catholic gesture. Heaven knows how often before he had been guilty of making this same sort of false impression. Only, as luck would have it yesterday, at that same moment, the older Ehrenberg was walking along the way. He saw how Oskar raised his hat at the church door, and seized by an uncontrollable rage, he wound up and struck his son on the side of the head. Struck him! Oskar, the reserve lieutenant! At noon, in the middle of the city! That the incident should have been known all over town that same evening is not surprising. Today you can read about it in the newspapers. The Jews are as silent as the dead, except for a few gossip rags, while the anti-Semites are making as much as possible of it. The best comes from the *Christian People's Messenger* which reports that both the Ehrenbergs are to be brought before a jury for religious disruption, or even blasphemy. Oskar has left for the time being, no one knows where.' "

"Nice family," said Anna, with conviction.

Georg had to laugh against his will. "Else really had nothing to do with *this* story."

The bell rang for the second time. They went to the dining room and sat down at their little table by the window, which was always set for them alone. At the long table in the middle of the hall sat barely a dozen guests, mostly British and French, as well as a no-longer-young man who had been there for two days and whom Georg believed to be an Austrian officer in civilian clothes. He was, in general, no more interested in him than in the others. Georg had brought Heinrich's letter with him. It occurred to him that he had not yet read it to the end. Over a black coffee he took it out again and skimmed it to the conclusion.

"What else does he write?" Anna asked.

"Nothing in particular," Georg answered. "About people who wouldn't interest you much. He seems to have gotten involved with his coffeehouse group again, more than he likes, and more than he admits, obviously."

"He'll fit right in," Anna said casually. Georg smiled indulgently. "In any case, they're strange people."

"What's up with them?" asked Anna.

Georg had laid the letter next to his cup, and looked down.

"That little Winternitz . . . you know . . . the one who read Heinrich and me his poem last winter . . . is going to Berlin as producer of a newly formed theater company. And Gleissner, who stared at us in the museum once . . ."

"Yes, that repulsive fellow with the monocle. . . ."

"Well, he explained that he has finally given up writing to devote himself exclusively to his sport. . . ."

"His sport?"

"A very unusual one. He plays with human souls."

"What?"

"Just listen." He read: " 'Now this clown asserted that he was occupied with the solution of the following two psychological projects at the same time, which compliment each other in the wittiest manner. First: to degrade a young and innocent creature in the most depraved way, and second, to convert a prostitute into a nun, as he expressed it. He swore not to rest until the first ended up in a brothel and the second in a convent.' "

"A nice group," Anna remarked, and stood up from the table.

"How strange all this sounds here!" Georg said, and followed her into the park. Over the tops of the trees rested a deep blue, sun-laden day. They stood for a while by the low balustrade which separated the garden from the road, and looked across the lake toward the mountains which shone through a silver-grey veil trembling in the sunlight. Then they walked deeper into the park, where the shade was cooler and darker, and while they strolled arm-in-arm over the softly crunching gravel, and along the tall brown ivy-grown wall, over which the old houses stared down at them through their tiny windows, they chatted about the news which had arrived today. And for the first time a vague anxiety arose in them at the thought that they soon had to leave the friendly safety of their stay abroad, to return home, where even the commonplace seemed filled with mysterious dangers. They sat down under the plane tree at the white lacquered table. This place was always open, as if deliberately kept free for them. Only yesterday had the newly arrived Austrian gentleman been sitting there, though he left with a courteous greeting following a disapproving look from Anna.

Georg hurried back to the room and got a couple of books for Anna, and a volume of Goethe's poems and the manuscript of his quintet for himself. Now they sat there beside one another, reading, working, looking up occasionally, smiling at each other, speaking a few words, going back to their books, looking over the balustrade into the open, feeling peace in their souls and summer in the air. They listened as the fountain behind the bushes gurgled and its tiny drops fell on the surface of the water. Sometimes the wheels of a wagon would rattle past on the far side of the tall wall, or one could hear the thin, distant whistles from the lake, or more rarely, human voices could be heard coming from the shore into the garden. The sun-drenched day weighed down on the tree tops. Later, more noise and voices came along with the gentle wind which blew in every afternoon from the lake. The waves struck audibly along the beach, the calls of boatmen could be heard, and from beyond the wall came the songs of young people. Tiny droplets could be felt from the spray of the fountain. The breath of the coming night reawakened people, land, and water.

Steps could be heard on the gravel. Therese, thin and white, came hurrying along the path. Georg stood up, went toward her a few steps, and reached out his hand. Anna wanted to get up too, but Therese wouldn't let her, gave her a hug and a kiss on the cheek, and sat down with her. "It's so lovely here!" she cried. "But maybe I've come too early."

"What are you thinking, I'm delighted," replied Anna.

Therese regarded her with a questioning smile, and took both her hands.

"Well, your appearance is reassuring," she said.

"I'm really quite well," responded Anna. "And it seems you are no less so," she added with friendly scorn.

Georg's eyes rested on Therese, who was again dressed in white like this morning, only more elegant this time, in embroidered English linen, and wearing a string of light rose coral around an open neck. While the two ladies talked about the remarkable accident of their seeing each other, Georg got up and went off to place the order for dinner. When he got back to the garden, the other two were no longer there. He saw Therese on the balcony, her back leaning on the banister, speaking with Anna, who was somewhere inside the room and could not be seen. He walked up and down the path in high spirits, with melodies singing in him, feeling young and fortunate, casting an occasional glance up to the balcony or over the balustrade to the road, and finally saw Demeter Stanzides coming. He went to meet him. "A hearty welcome!" he said in greeting at the garden gate. "The ladies are upstairs in the room, but they'll be down soon. Would you like to see the park in the meantime?"

"Sure."

They walked along together.

"Are you planning to stay longer in Lugano?" Georg asked.

"No, we're going to Bellaggio tomorrow, and from there to Lago Maggiore, Isola Bella. This splendid season won't last much longer. We have to be home again in two weeks."

"Such a short vacation?"

"Well, it's not on my account. Therese has to go back. I'm as free as the breeze. I already have my discharge in my pocket."

"So, you'd like to withdraw to your estate?"

"My estate?"

"Yes, I've heard something of the sort, at the Ehrenbergs."

"But I don't have that estate yet. I am in negotiations though."

"Where are you thinking of buying, if I may ask?"

"Where the foxes say good night. At least it'll seem that way to you. On the Hungarian-Croatian border. Rather lonely and remote, but quite striking. I have a certain sympathy for the region. Memories of youth. Three years as a lieutenant. Obviously I imagine I'll become young there again. Well, who knows."

"A nice estate?"

"Not bad. I saw it again two months ago. I recognized it from before. It belonged to Count Jaczewicz then. Finally to some industrialist. His wife has died. Now he feels lonely down there and wants to get rid of it."

"I don't know," said Georg, "but I picture the region as being a little melancholy."

"Melancholy? Well, it seems to me that in a certain period of life any region can get a melancholy appearance." And he looked around himself, as though to find a new demonstration of the truth of his words.

"In what period?"

"Well, when one begins to get old."

Georg smiled. Demeter appeared so handsome to him, and despite the grey hair at his temples, still young. "How old are you, Herr Stanzides, if I may ask?"

"Thirty-seven. Not being old, I'd say, but becoming old. Most people don't speak about growing old until it's long since happened."

At the end of the garden, where it ran into the wall, they sat down on a bench. From here they had a view of the hotel and the large garden terrace. The upper floors with the balconies were hidden from them by the treetops. Georg offered Demeter a cigarette and took one himself. And both were silent for a while.

"I have heard you may be leaving Vienna yourself," said Demeter.

"Yes, that's quite possible. . . . That is if I can find a position with some opera company. And if it's not this year, then it's next year."

Demeter sat with crossed legs, holding one at the ankle with his hand, and nodded. "Yes, yes," he said, and slowly blew a narrow stream of smoke through his lips. "It's really wonderful to have a talent. It must make the periods of life somehow different. Actually, it's the only thing I can envy in a man."

"There's no reason to. In general, people with talent are not to be envied at all. At most people with genius. And I probably envy them more than you do. But I find that talents like yours are something more absolute, something more secure, so to speak. One is occasionally not in form, good . . . but as long as one can work at all one can still get something done, even something quite considerable, whereas someone like me, when he's not in good form, is a complete beggar."

Demeter laughed. "Yes, but it *lasts* longer, such an artistic talent, and it even grows greater with the years. For example with Beethoven. The *Ninth Symphony* is the greatest, isn't it? Well, and the second part of

Faust! . . . While we unquestionably decline with the years, and nothing can help it. Even Beethoven among us. And it starts so soon. Apart from the rarest exceptions. I, for example, was at my height at twenty-five. I have never regained what I had in me at twenty-five. Yes, dear Baron, those were the days!"

"Well, I remember having seen you win a race two years ago against Buzgo, who was the favorite then. . . . I even bet on him . . ."

"Dear Baron," Stanzides interrupted him, "believe me, I know why I stopped. Such a thing one can only feel for oneself. And nobody knows when growing old begins as well as an athlete. No amount of additional training will help. It becomes just an artificial matter. And if anyone tries to tell you otherwise, then he's simply . . . but here come our ladies."

They both stood up. Therese and Anna came up, arm-in-arm, the one all in white, the other in a black dress which, falling in broad folds to the ground, completely hid her figure. The pairs met at the fountain. Demeter kissed Anna's hand.

"Quite a lovely patch of earth on which I have the good fortune of greeting you again, my dear lady."

"It's a pleasant surprise for me too," replied Anna, "quite apart from the region."

"Did you know," Georg said to Anna, "that they were leaving in the morning?"

"Yes, Therese told me."

"But we'd still like to see as much as possible," Demeter explained. "And as I recall, the other upper Italian lakes are even grander than the one here."

"I don't know about the other ones," said Anna. "We haven't been away from here yet."

"Well, perhaps you'll take the opportunity," said Demeter, "to join us for a little getaway. Bellaggio, Pallanza, Isola Bella."

Anna shook her head. "It would be lovely, but unfortunately I can't get around well enough any more. Actually, I'm incredibly lazy. There are whole days when I never leave the park. But if Georg would like to get away from me for a day or two, I don't mind."

"I have no wish to get away from you," said Georg. He cast a quick glance at Therese, whose eyes were shining and laughing. They all strolled slowly through the garden while it gradually grew dark, and chatted about the places they had seen recently. When they came back to the table under the plane tree, it had been set, and the garden lights were burning in their glass flutes. Then the waiter brought a bucket with Asti. Anna sat down on the bench, which was leaning against the trunk of the plane tree, with Therese sitting across from her; Georg and Demeter were at the ladies sides.

Dinner was served and the wine poured. Georg asked about their acquaintances in Vienna. Demeter explained that Willy Eissler had brought some brilliant caricatures back from the trip, both of the hunters and the animals. The older Ehrenberg had bought the pictures.

"Have you already heard," said Georg, "the story about Oskar?"

"What story?"

"Well, the incident with his father in front of St. Michael's." He remembered that he had wanted to tell the story to Demeter earlier, before the ladies had appeared, but that he had found it better to keep still. Now the wine loosened his tongue against his better judgment. He reported in brief what Heinrich had written to him.

"That's a really sad story," said Demeter, quite disconcerted, so that suddenly all the others felt themselves becoming more serious too.

"Why a sad story?" asked Therese, "I think it's a riot."

"Dear Therese, you're not thinking of the consequences it could have for the young man."

"God, I know quite well, it'll be impossible for him in certain circles. Hopefully it will give him an insight as to what a stupid imbecile he's been until now."

"Well," said Georg, "if Oskar is one of those people who get insights . . . I really don't know."

"Apart from that, dear Therese," Demeter added, "what you call insight might not be at all the real thing. All groups of people have their prejudices, even you are not free from them."

"What kind of prejudices do we have, I'd like to know," cried Therese. And she angrily drank down her wine. "We want only to clean out certain prejudices, especially the one that there are privileged classes, that their special honor . . ."

"Please, Therese dear, you're not at a meeting here. And it is to be feared that the applause at the end of your speech will be less than you're accustomed to."

"So, you see," Therese said turning to Anna, "that's the sort of discussion you get from a cavalry officer."

"Excuse me," said Georg, "but the whole thing has hardly anything to do with prejudices. To be struck on the open street by your own father ... I think it doesn't matter if you're a reserve officer or a student ..."

"This blow," said Therese, "has something positively liberating about it for me. It gives a worthy conclusion to a ridiculous and superfluous existence."

"We won't hope for a conclusion," said Demeter.

"I've been told," remarked Georg, "that Oskar has left, nobody knows where."

"If anything bothers me about it," said Therese, "it's that in any case it's only that good-hearted old man who might already regret the difficulties he has caused for that snobbish son of his."

"Good-hearted!" Demeter cried out, "a millionaire! a factory owner! ... But Therese ..."

"Yes, it happens. He happens to be one of those who are with us in the depths of their souls. And on the evening, Demeter, when you had the pleasure of meeting me for the first time, do you know why I had been at the Ehrenbergs? ... And do you know for what purpose he gave me a thousand gulden at the time? For ...," she bit her lips, "I can't say; it was the condition."

Suddenly Demeter stood up and gave a bow to someone who walked by. It was the Austrian gentleman who had arrived yesterday. He lifted his hat and disappeared into the darkness of the garden.

"Do you know that man?" Georg asked after a few seconds. "It seems to me that I know him too; who is he?"

"Prince von Guastalla," said Demeter.

"Really?" Therese cried involuntarily, and her eyes drilled into the darkness.

"What are you looking at," said Demeter. "A man like any other."

"He's supposed to be banished from the court," said Georg, "isn't that right?"

"I don't know about that," replied Demeter, "but in any case he's not liked. He recently published a pamphlet about certain conditions in the army, in particular about the life of officers in the provinces, which was held very much against him, although there wasn't really anything bad in it."

"He should have asked me," said Therese, "I'd have told him a thing or two about it."

"Dear child," Demeter said defensively, "what you're probably referring to again is an exception that one cannot generalize from."

"I'm not generalizing, but one such case shows that the whole system . . ."

"No *speeches*, Therese. . . ."

"I'm talking about Leo," Therese said, turning to Georg. "What he's gone through this year is really atrocious."

Georg suddenly remembered the completely forgotten and most extraordinary fact that Therese was Leo's sister. Did he know she was here, and with whom?

Demeter chewed rather nervously on his lips.

"There's an anti-Semitic first lieutenant," said Therese, "who persecutes him in a particularly despicable way, because he feels how Leo despises him."

Georg nodded. He knew about it.

"Dear child," said Demeter, "as I've already said several times, something's wrong with this story. I happen to know Lieutenant Sefranek, and I assure you, one can get along with him. He's not particularly bright, and it may be true enough that he has no fondness for the Israelites, but after all, one must say that there are so-called anti-Semitic slurs that have hardly any meaning at all, and which in my experience can be used by Jews just as well as by Christians. And your Herr brother certainly suffers here from a sick sort of sensitivity."

"Sensitivity is not a sickness," countered Therese. "Only insensitivity is a sickness, and to be sure, the most repulsive one I know. It's well known that I'm in as little agreement with my brother as is possible in my political views; you know this better than anyone Georg; to me Jewish bankers are just as repulsive as the feudal estate owners, and orthodox rabbis just as repulsive as catholic priests. But when someone feels superior to me because I have a different belief, or belong to another race, and in the consciousness of his advantage makes me feel this superiority, I would . . . I don't know what I would do to such a person. But in any case I'd understand if Leo flew in the face of this Herr Sefranek at the next provocation."

"My dear child," said Demeter, "if you have any influence over your brother at all, then you should try to prevent such an attack at any cost. In my opinion, it remains the best in such a case to follow orderly, which is to say prescribed, procedures. It is not true that nothing will necessarily come of it; the upper ranks are usually calm, in any case the right people, and . . ."

"But Leo did that a long time ago . . . last February. He went to the colonel; the colonel was even quite nice to him and has, from various indications, spoken quite seriously to the lieutenant; only unfortunately it has been of absolutely no use, on the contrary. At the next opportunity the first lieutenant started up his maliciousness again, and went about it with refined consistency. I assure you, Baron, from day to day I fear that something terrible is going to happen."

Demeter shook his head. "We live in a crazy time. I assure you," he turned to Georg, "First Lieutenant Sefranek is no more anti-Semitic than you or me. He's a guest in Jewish homes; I even know that he's been quite intimate with a Jewish regiment doctor for years. It's really as if people were going crazy."

"You could be right," said Therese.

"Well, Leo is so reasonable," said Georg, "so smart, for all his temperament, that I'm convinced he won't let himself do anything stupid. And besides, he knows that in a couple of months it will all be over, as long as he can get through it."

"By the way, you know, Baron," said Therese, as she followed the lead of the gentlemen and took a cigarette from a box the waiter had brought, "you know that Leo was very delighted by your compositions?"

"Well, delighted," Georg said as he gave Therese a light, "I really hadn't noticed that."

"Well, some pleased him enough," Therese qualified, "that it's almost as much as if someone else were delighted."

"Have you done any composing on your trip?" Demeter asked courteously.

"Nothing except a couple of songs."

"We'd love to get to hear them in the fall," said Demeter.

"Oh God, let's not talk about the fall," said Therese. "By then we could all be dead, or in prison."

"Well, the latter could be avoided by a little good will," cried Demeter.

Therese shrugged her shoulders. Georg sat quite close to her and thought he could feel the warmth of her body. Lights were shining from the windows of the hotel, and a long red streak shone all the way to the table where the two couples sat.

"I suggest that we take advantage of the lovely evening and go for a walk along the shore."

"Or go for a boat ride!" cried Therese.

All were agreed. Georg hurried back to the room to get wraps. When he came back down, he found the others ready to go, standing at the gate of the park. He helped Anna into her light grey coat, hung his own long overcoat around Therese's shoulders, and laid a dark green blanket over his arm. They walked slowly along the avenue to the place where boats were anchored. Two boatmen took the group from the darkness of the shore into the black glimmering water with quick strokes of the oars. The mountains rose up to the sky with unnatural immensity. The stars were not particularly numerous. Small blue-grey clouds hung in the air. The oarsmen sat on two cross planks; the two couples sat across from each other in the middle of the boat on two small benches: Georg and Anna, Demeter and Therese. Everyone was completely silent at first. After a few minutes Georg was the first to break the stillness. He named the mountain which met the lake to the south, and pointed out a village which rested at the foot of a cliff as though an infinite distance away, but which could be reached in a quarter of an hour; he recognized the white, lit-up house on the heights over Lugano as the hotel where Demeter and Therese were staying, and talked about a walk he had recently taken between two sunlit, vine-covered mountains further inland.

While he spoke, Anna held his hand tightly underneath the blanket. Demeter and Therese sat serious and proper next to each other, not at all like lovers who had only recently discovered one another. Only now did Georg gradually recover his attraction for Therese, which had almost vanished during her loud heavy speeches.

How long will this relationship with Demeter last? he thought. Will it be over by the fall, or will it last as long or longer than mine with Anna? Will this trip on the dark lake also become a memory of something completely vanished, just like the trip on the Veldeser See with that peasant girl, who now occurs to me for the first time in years . . . like the sea trip with Grace? How strange. Anna is holding my hand, I squeeze it, and who knows if she is not at this moment feeling something with regard to Demeter similar to what I feel about Therese? No, no chance. . . . She's carrying a child beneath her heart, that already is moving . . . on account of which . . . oh God . . . it's *my* child too. . . . Now our child is on a boat ride on Lake Lugano. . . . Will I tell him someday that before he was born he rode on Lake Lugano? . . . How will it all turn out? In a few days we'll be in Vienna again. Does Vienna even exist? It slowly arises again as we return . . . yes, that's it. . . . As soon as I'm home again there'll be serious work. I'll live quietly in my Vienna home, and just visit Anna rather than

live with her in the country . . . maybe just before the final days. . . .
And in the fall . . . to Detmold? And where will Anna be? And the
child? . . . With strange people somewhere in the country? How unlikely all this seems. . . . But a year ago it was highly unlikely that I
would be riding on Lake Lugano with Fraulein Anna Rosner, and Stanzides with Therese Golowski . . . and now it's the most natural thing
in the world. Suddenly he heard Demeter's voice next to him, quite
abruptly, as if he had just awakened. "What time does our boat leave
in the morning?"

"At nine A.M." answered Therese.

"She's the boss on this trip," Demeter said, "I don't need to worry
about anything at all."

Now the moon suddenly came out over the lake.

It was as if it had waited behind the mountains, and now came out
to bid them farewell. Now that infinitely remote village at the foot of
the mountains suddenly looked completely white and near at hand. The
boat landed. Therese got up and, surrounded by darkness, looked strikingly large. Georg jumped out of the boat and helped her get out. He
felt her cool fingers, which were not trembling, but which moved as
though deliberately in his hand, and felt the breath of her lips come
near. After her Demeter got out, then came Anna, clumsy and tired.
The boatmen thanked them for their generous tip, and the two couples
headed toward home. The prince sat on a bench by the shoreline path,
in a long, dark coat, smoking a cigar, appeared to be looking out over
the dark lake, and turned his head, obviously in order to avoid being
greeted.

"A fellow like that could tell us a lot," Therese said to Georg, with
whom she was lingering ever further behind, while Demeter and Anna
walked ahead.

"You're going back to Vienna so soon?" asked Georg.

"In two weeks, do you think that's soon? In any case, you'll be home
before we will, won't you?"

"Yes, we're leaving in a couple of days. We can't put it off any
longer. And we'll have to stop several times. Anna can't handle the
traveling."

"Did you know that I found the villa for Anna just before I left?"
said Therese.

"Really? You? You were looking for it too?"

"Yes, I went into the country with my mother a couple of times. It's a small, rather old house in Salmansdorf,[7] with a beautiful garden which leads straight into the meadows and forest, and the front garden is completely overgrown. . . . Anna will tell you more. I think it's the last house in the place; then there's an inn, but rather far away."

"Could I have overlooked this house on my expeditions last spring?"

"Obviously, otherwise you would have rented it. There's a little clay figure in a grassy yard near the garden fence."

"I can't remember it. But you know, Therese, it was very nice of you to trouble yourself for us. More than nice." Along with your activities as an agitator, he wanted to add, but he repressed it.

"Why are you surprised?" asked Therese. "I like Anna very much."

"Do you know what I once heard said of you?" Georg remarked after a short pause.

"No, what?"

"That you'll end up either on the scaffold, or as a princess."

"That's one of Doctor Berthold Stauber's expressions; he said that to me once. He's very proud of it, but it's crazy."

"I think the chances are more on the side of the princess."

"Who told you that? The princess dream is about to come to an end."

"Dream?"

"Yes, I'm beginning to wake up. It's rather like when the morning air blows into the bedroom."

"And the other dream begins?"

"Why the other dream?"

"I'll explain it to you. When you appear again in public, give speeches, make sacrifices for something, it seems to you at some moments rather like a dream, doesn't it? And you think to yourself, real life is something different."

"What you say isn't really so dumb."

At this moment Demeter and Anna, who were already at the garden gate, turned around to the other two, and then took the wide path to the entrance of the hotel. Georg and Therese went on, unseen, outside the fence, in the darkness of the cast shadows. Suddenly Georg took the hand of his companion. She turned toward him, as if startled, and the two stood face to face, wrapped in darkness, and closer than they realized. They didn't know how . . . they scarcely willed it, and their

7. A village five miles northwest of the center of Vienna. Running east and west along the southern side of the village is a one-mile-long road called Sommerhaidenweg, on the south side of which is the Neustifter Friedhof cemetery.

lips rested on each other for a brief moment which was filled more with the painful joy of deception than anything else. Then they continued on, silent, unsatisfied, desiring, and walked through the garden gate.

In front of the hotel the other two turned and came to meet them. Quickly Therese said to Georg: "Obviously you're not going with us." Georg nodded gently. Now they all stood in the wide, quiet light of the arc-lamps.

"It was a marvelous evening," Demeter said and kissed Anna's hand.

"So, until we meet again in Vienna," Therese said and gave Anna a hug.

Demeter turned to Georg. "Hopefully we'll see each other tomorrow morning on the ship."

"It's possible, but I won't promise."

"*Adieu*," Therese said and gave Georg her hand.

Then she turned to go with Demeter.

"Would you like to go with them?" Anna asked as they went through the door into the hall, where men and women sat smoking, drinking, and chatting.

"What are you thinking of," replied Georg, "I wasn't even considering it."

"Herr Baron," someone called out behind him. It was the porter, who held a telegram in his hand.

"What is it?" asked Georg, somewhat startled, and opened it quickly. "Oh!" he cried out, "how awful."

"What is it?" asked Anna.

He read aloud, while the two of them looked at the page. "'Oskar Ehrenberg attempted suicide this morning in the forest near Neuhaus. Shot in the temple, little hope to save his life. Heinrich.'" Anna shook her head. Silently they climbed the stairs to the room Anna stayed in. The balcony door was wide open. Georg walked out into the open. A heavy scent of magnolias and roses came out of the darkness. Nothing could be seen of the lake. The mountains rose as if growing out of a pit. Anna came up to Georg. He put his arm on her shoulder and loved her intensely. It was as if the disastrous event of which he had just received news had forced the feeling of her true meaning into his own experience. He realized again that nothing in the world was more important for him than the happiness of this dear woman who stood with him on the balcony and would bear him a child.

Sixth Chapter

As Georg came out of the cool public restaurant in which he had been having lunch for the last few weeks and walked onto the summer-heated pavement, taking the way toward Heinrich's house, he made the decision to take the trip to the mountains in the next few days. Anna was prepared for it, and had even suggested herself that he get away for a few days, since she could sense that he was becoming bored by the monotonous life they had been leading lately and was beginning to get restless.

They had come back to Vienna on a tepid, rainy evening six weeks ago, and Georg had brought Anna straight from the train to the villa where, in a large but rather empty room with tired yellow wallpaper and the dim light of a hanging lamp, Anna's mother and Frau Golowski had waited for two hours for the late arrivals. The door to the garden veranda stood open; outside the rain fell noisily on the wooden floor, and the heavy smell of wet leaves and grass blew in. By the light of a candle that Frau Golowski had brought, Georg inspected the spacious-ness of the house, while Anna leaned exhausted in the corner of the large sofa with the floral cotton cover and gave feeble answers to her mother's questions. Soon Georg had taken a tender and gentle leave of Anna, had gotten into the wagon which waited outside with her mother, and related to the shy woman the unimportant experiences of the last few days of the trip with forced attentiveness as they rode over the rain soaked streets to the city. He was home an hour after midnight, decided against waking Felician, who was already asleep, and stretched out in his own, long awaited bed to the soothing sleep of home with unexpected delight after so many nights away.

Since then he had gone out to the country to see Anna almost every day. When he didn't take any little detours around the resorts of the area, he could easily get there in an hour by bicycle. More often he took the horse-drawn wagons and then walked through the little villages to the low, green painted picket fence behind which stood, in the small, gently rising garden, the modest country house with the three-cornered wooden gable. Often he chose a way which took him above the village and led between the gardens and meadows, and then went down the green slope to a bench at the edge of the forest where a view of the little village, set in a long narrow valley, spread out before him. From here he could see straight over to the roof under which Anna lived, deliberately allow his longing for the beloved, who was so near, to well up, until he would hurry down, open the little gate, and cross the gravel through the garden to the house. Often, in the humid afternoon hours, if Anna was still sleeping, he would sit on the covered wooden veranda which ran along the back side of the house, on a comfortable floral cotton-covered recliner, take a book he had brought with him out of his pocket, and read. Then, in a simple, clean, dark dress, Frau Golowski would come out of the darkening inner room, and with a soft, somewhat sorrowful voice and an expression of motherly kindness on her face, give a report of Anna's condition, in particular if she had eaten well, or had diligently taken her walk in the garden. When she ended, she always had something important to tend to in the kitchen or house, and vanished. Then, while Georg continued reading, a pregnant St. Bernard who belonged to people in the neighborhood would come by, greet Georg with tearful, serious eyes, let him stroke her short fur, and stretch out gratefully at his feet. Later, when a certain strong whistle that was familiar to the animal would blow, it would get up with the heaviness of its condition, appear to excuse itself with a sorrowful glance, that it could not stay any longer, and slink away. In the garden next door children laughed and played, occasionally throwing a rubber ball over, whereupon a pale nanny would appear at the low hedge and ask shyly if he would throw it back again. Finally, when it had gotten cooler, Anna's face would appear at the window that opened onto the veranda, greeting Georg with her quiet blue eyes, and soon she would come out in a light, bright housedress. They would walk up and down in the garden along the lilac bushes that had passed their bloom, and the sprouting currant bushes, usually on the left side which bordered the open meadow, and then rest on the white bench near the upper end of the garden under the pear tree. Frau Golowski would only appear again when supper was served, shyly take her place at the table, and talk about her own family matters; about Therese, who had joined the editorial staff of a socialist paper, about Leo, who was less occupied with the service than before and was seriously applying himself to the study of mathematics, about her husband, for whom new hopes of earning a regular living were always opening up and then closing again while he sat with devotion watching the tireless chess players in a smoky corner of a coffeehouse. Only rarely did Frau Rosner come for a visit, and would usually leave almost as soon as Georg would appear. Once, on a Sunday afternoon, the father had been here too, and had a conversation with Georg about the weather and the scenery, as though they had just encountered each other while visiting a sick friend. Anna only stayed completely inside the villa for the sake of her parents. For she had matured with complete unaffectedness, and felt that she was nothing less than Georg's wedded wife, and had, to Georg's pleasant surprise, agreed without further ado when he, bored with the monotonous evenings, asked for permission to bring Heinrich over.

Heinrich was the only one of Georg's close acquaintances who still remained in the city during those oppressive July days. Felician, who seemed to have joined in a newly awakened youthful friendship with his returned brother, had been staying with Ralph Skelton on the North Sea since passing the Diplomatic Examination. Else Ehrenberg, whom Georg spoke to in the sanitarium at the bedside of her brother shortly after his return, was finally at the Auhof by the lake with her mother again. Oskar, whose unfortunate attempt at suicide had cost him his right eye, had escaped the lieutenant's charge, so it seemed, and had left Vienna with a black patch over his blind eye. Demeter Stanzides, Willy Eissler, Guido Schoenstein, and Breitner had all left; and even Nuernberger, who had so ceremoniously explained that he didn't intend to leave the city this year, had suddenly vanished.

After his return, Georg had visited him before all the others, to bring him flowers from the grave of his sister in Cadenabbia. On the trip, he finally read Nuernberger's novel, which took place in a now half-vanished time, the same time, it seemed to Georg, as the one the old Doctor Stauber had spoken to him about. Over that hypocritical world in which grown-up people passed for mature, old people passed for experienced, those who violated no written law passed for upright, in which the love of freedom, humanity, and patriotism mattered only as abstract virtues, especially when they had sprung up on the putrid soil of ingratitude or cowardice, Nuernberger had lit some grimly illuminating lights; for the hero of his book he had chosen a vigorous and courageous man who, repelled by the cheap phrases of the time, achieved a higher comprehension and insight, and seized by horror at the recognition of his own corrupt rise from obscurity, fell back into the nothingness from which he came. That someone who had written this powerful and still resounding work should have later taken to making nothing more than indolent, scornful, marginal remarks with the passage of time surprised Georg very much, and now a saying of Heinrich's helped him understand why Nuernberger's work was finished forever: It is given to anger, not disgust, to bear fruit.—The lonely, deep blue, late afternoon hour at the cemetery in Cadenabbia had impressed Georg unusually deeply, as if he had himself known, been intimate with, the person at whose grave he was standing. It had moved him that the golden letters on the grey stone had grown faint, and the borders along the grass has become overgrown with weeds; and after he had picked a few yellow and blue Pansies for his friend, he left with a heavy heart. Outside the cemetery gate he looked through the open window of the mausoleum and saw a woman laid out in the dimness between two tall lighted candles, with a black veil draped over her lips, and over whose small wax face the light of the candles and the day mixed together. Nuernberger had not remained untouched by Georg's sympathetic attention, and they spoke together that day more trustingly than they ever had before.

The house where Nuernberger lived stood in a dark, narrow street which wandered out of the inner city toward the Danube; it was ancient, narrow, and tall. Nuernberger's apartment was on the fifth,[1] top floor, which one got to by means of a complex, winding staircase. In the low but spacious room which Georg entered from a dark anteroom, stood old but well kept furniture, and from the alcove at the back, in front of which hung a faded green drape, came the smell of camphor and lavender. Childhood pictures of Nuernberger's parents hung on the wall along with brownish prints of landscapes by Dutch masters. On the chest, in carved wood frames, stood all sorts of old photographs; and from a desk drawer, from under yellowed letters, Nuernberger

---

1. Readers in the United States are reminded that what we call the "first floor" is called the "ground floor" in Europe, with the first floor being the one above that. Nuernberger lives on the floor reached by five flights of stairs.

brought out a picture of the dead sister, which showed an eighteen year old girl in a charming historical local costume, a ball in her hand, standing in front of a fence, with a craggy landscape rising up behind her. Nuernberger introduced all these unknown, remote and deceased people to his friend today in pictures, and spoke of them in a tone that seemed to increase and deepen the expanse of time between then and now.

Sometimes Georg's gaze would roam outside along the narrow street to the grey stonework of the ancient houses. He saw small, dusty panes with all sorts of furniture behind them; on one window ledge stood flowerpots with pathetic plants in them; in a gutter between two houses were pieces of broken bottles and clay vases, shreds of paper, rotten vegetables. A rusty pipe ran through all this junk and disappeared behind a chimney. Other chimneys appeared to the right and left, the back side of a yellowish stone gable was visible, steeples rose up to a pale blue sky and, unexpectedly close by, in light grey, with an openwork stone spire, was one which Georg knew very well. Involuntarily his eyes sought the direction where he expected the house over whose entry the two stone giants carried the crest of a vanished family on their powerful arms, and in which his child, who would be born in a few weeks, had been conceived. Georg told about his trip, and in the mood of the hour would have appeared petty to himself if he had settled for half truths. But Nuernberger had known about the whole thing for a long time, and as Georg looked somewhat surprised by this, he smiled scornfully. "Don't you remember," he asked, "that morning in Grinzing when we were looking at a summer place?"

"Certainly."

"And do you also remember how a woman with a child on her arm showed us around the house and garden?"

"Yes."

"Before we left the child stretched its arms out to you, and you regarded it with a rather tender look."

"And from that you concluded that I . . ."

"You're not the kind of man to be made sentimental by the sight of small, not to mention rather dirty, children unless there are associations of a personal kind."

"One has to be careful with you," Georg said jokingly, but not without a certain discomfort.

The mild annoyance that he always felt at Nuernberger's superiority did not hold him back from associating with him. Sometimes he would pick him up at home to go walking around the streets and gardens, and he felt it with satisfaction, even as a personal triumph, when he succeeded in drawing him out of the arid regions of bitter wisdom into the gentle pastures of warm conversation. Georg had grown so pleasantly accustomed to these walks with him that he felt a real loss when one morning he found Nuernberger's apartment locked up. A few days later an apologetic farewell card came from Salzburg, also signed by a married couple, a factory owner and his wife, kind and cheerful people which Georg had met casually through Nuernberger on the Graben[2] once. From Heinrich's caustic account, their mutual friend had been dragged down the stairs by the couple, after a vain resistance of course, stuffed into a wagon, and carried off to the train station, a virtual prisoner. As Heinrich put it, Nuernberger had a few acquaintances of this harmless sort, who felt the need to let the famous derider squeeze a few drops of rancor into the tasty drink of their existence, just as Nuernberger, for his part, liked to escape from his tiring acquaintances in literary and psychological circles into their more genial company.

The reunion with Heinrich had meant a disappointment for Georg. After the first words of greeting, the writer, as usual, had spoken only of himself, and to be sure, in tones of the utmost self-contempt. He had finally decided that he really had no talent, only intellect, though this in enormous amounts. But what he condemned most in himself were the inconsistencies of his character, because of which, he well knew, not only he himself, but anyone around him suffered. He was heartless and sentimental, careless and melancholic, sensitive and inconsiderate, quarrelsome and yet dependent on people . . . at least sometimes. A person with these qualities could only prove his right to exist by a great achievement, and if the masterpiece he was obligated to produce did not soon, very soon, appear, he was obligated as a decent man to shoot himself. But he was no decent man . . . that was the problem. Georg thought: of course you're not going to shoot yourself, mainly because you're too cowardly. Naturally he didn't say this, but was much more generous, and spoke of the moods which any artist is subject to, and asked, like a friend, about the external circumstances of Heinrich's life. Soon it became plain that things were really not so bad for him. It seemed to Georg that he led an even more carefree life than before. A

---

2. Literally "The Ditch." A large pedestrian square near St. Stephen's Cathedral in the center of the old town, in the middle of which is an ornate baroque monument called the *Pestsaeule,* or Column of the Plague, built between 1682 and 1694 to commemorate the end of the plague of 1679.

small inheritance had secured the existence of his mother and sister for the next few years; despite all the animosities that were working against him, his reputation grew from day to day; the regrettable episode with the actress seemed finally to be over, and a completely new and desirably light relationship with a young lady even brought some cheerfulness into his life. Even his work was progressing well. The first act of the opera libretto was as good as finished, and a lot was written down for the political satire. He had the intention of visiting some sessions of Parliament next year, going to meetings, and was toying with the admittedly childish and fantastic plan of posing as a fellow Social-Democrat to try to gain acceptance by the leadership, and if it's possible, even to become an active member in some organization, just to know what really goes on in the machinery of a party. Ah, when he spoke with a person once, even for just five minutes, he understood him completely. Some word, which someone else would never notice, tore away the veil from his soul for him like a storm wind. It was his dream to show the world, as a master of the fantastic in opera and through the portrayal of realistic moments in satire, that he was equally at home in heaven and on earth. At a later meeting Georg was read what was finished of the first act of the opera. He found the verses quite singable, and asked permission to take the manuscript to Anna. She was not able to find what Georg read to her of it much to her liking; but he asserted, without real conviction, that she actually felt the longing of these verses to be set to music, which she necessarily perceived as a defect.

When Georg came to Heinrich's apartment today, he was sitting at the large table in the middle of the room, which was covered with pages and letters. Handwritten papers of all kinds lay on the piano and divan as well. Heinrich was still holding a yellowed page in his hand when he stood up and greeted Georg with the words: "Well, how's it going in the country?" This was the way in which he always inquired about Anna's condition and which Georg always found too familiar. "Just fine, thank you," he replied. "I came to ask if you'd like to come out for a visit today."

"Oh, very much. It's just that I'm busy straightening out all these papers. I couldn't come until evening, around seven. Is that all right with you?"

"Certainly," said Georg. "But I see I'm disturbing you," he added, while he looked over the paper-strewn table.

"Not at all," responded Heinrich, "I was just putting things in order, as I just said. It's the papers my father left behind. Those are letters to him. And these are daily records, mainly from his time in Parliament. Moving, I'll tell you. How much this man loved his country! And how they thanked him for it! You have no idea of the refined ways in which they drove him out of his party. A convoluted intrigue of malice, narrow-mindedness, brutality . . . truly German, in a word."

Georg was repelled. And he dares, he thought, to find fault with anti-Semitism? Is he any better? More just? Has he forgotten that I am a German . . . ?

Heinrich continued. "But I will build a monument to this man. . . . He, and no other will be the hero of my political drama. He is the genuine tragicomic central figure I have been missing until now."

Georg's inner revulsion was growing. He was taken by a great desire to defend the older Bermann against his son. "Tragicomic figure?" he repeated, almost with animosity.

"Yes," replied Heinrich definitely. "A Jew who loves his country . . . I mean like my father did, with feelings of solidarity, with enthusiasm for the dynasty, is absolutely a tragicomic figure. That is . . . he was, in that liberalized period of the seventies and eighties, since even clever men are under the influence of the verbal delirium of the times. Now-adays such a man would be exclusively comic. Yes, even if he hung him-self on the first good nail, I couldn't see his fate any differently."

"It's a mania with you," replied Georg. "One really has the impres-sion sometimes that you're no longer able to see anything else in the world except the Jewish question. If I were as rude as sometimes ap-pears the case with you, I'd say you had a . . . you'll forgive me, perse-cution mania."

"Persecution mania . . ." Heinrich repeated tonelessly, and looked at the wall. "So, you call that persecution mania. . . . Well!" And suddenly he continued heavily, with his teeth clenched: "I'd like to ask you some-thing Georg, of your conscience."

"I'm listening."

He positioned himself directly in front of Georg and drilled his eyes into Georg's forehead. "Do you believe that there is one Christian on earth, be he the noblest, the justest, the truest, a single one who never once took out his resentment, ill humor, anger, even against his best friend, against his sweetheart, or his wife, if they happened to be Jewish, or of Jewish descent, for their Jewishness, at least inwardly?" And with-out waiting for Georg's answer: "There's no one, I assure you. You can make another test, by the way. Read, for example, the letters of any famous, or otherwise intelligent and outstanding person, and pay attention to the passages with hostile and ironic remarks about contemporaries. Ninety-nine times it concerns an individual without consideration of his heritage or faith; in the hundredth case, where the reviled fellow has the misfortune to be a Jew, the writer will never fail to mention this fact. It's just the way it is, I can't help it. What you like to call persecution mania, dear Georg, is in reality nothing other than an uninterrupted, conscious, and highly intense awareness of a condition in which we Jews find ourselves; and one could speak even more about a mania for safety, for being left in peace, than of persecution mania, of a mania for security, which is perhaps a less dramatic one, but for those concerned, represents a much more dangerous form of illness. My father suffered from it, and many others of his generation. He became so thoroughly cured of it that he went crazy over it."

Deep wrinkles appeared on Heinrich's forehead, and he looked at the wall again, over Georg, who had sat down on the hard, black leather divan.

"If that's your feeling," replied Georg,—"then logically you should join Leo Golowski . . ."

"And emigrate with him to Palestine—you think? Politico-symbolically or in reality—how?" He laughed. "Have I ever said that I wanted to leave here? That I would rather live somewhere else than here? In particular, that I would like to live only among Jews? For me at least, that would be a purely extraneous solution to a highly internal problem."

"Actually, I think so too. And, to tell the truth, I understand less and less what you want in that regard, Heinrich. Last year, at the Sophienalpe,[3] when you argued with Golowski, I had the impression that you were more optimistic about the matter."

"Optimistic?" Heinrich repeated, offended.

"Yes. One had to think that you believed in the possibility of a general assimilation."

Heinrich twitched the corner of his mouth contemptuously. "Assimilation . . . A word . . . Yes, it will come, someday . . . in a very, very long time. It will not come like many of them wish, nor like many of them fear . . . and it won't exactly be assimilation . . . but perhaps something that lies concealed in the heart of this word, so to speak. Do you know what might come of it in the end? That we, we Jews I mean, will have become a distillation of humanity—yes, that could happen in

3. In the hills, seven and one-half miles west-northwest of Vienna.

maybe a thousand or two thousand years. A consolation, you're thinking to yourself!" He laughed again.

"Who knows," Georg said indulgently, "if in a thousand years you'll
be right. But what about until then?"

"Yes, before that, dear Georg, there'll be no solution to the problem.
There'll be no solution in our time, that's for sure. Nothing general at
least. Instead there will be a hundred-thousand individual solutions. Because it's a predicament from which, until something happens, everyone
must extricate himself as best he can. Everyone must discover for himself how to escape from his anger, or his despair, or his disgust, to somewhere where he can breathe free again. Maybe there really are people
who have to move to Jerusalem to do it. . . . I'm just afraid that many
who arrive at their imagined goal would only find themselves more lost
than before. I don't believe at all that such journeys to freedom can even
be undertaken together, since the roads to our destination do not run
through the outside world, but lie within ourselves. It's up to each person to find his own inner way. To do it, of course, it is necessary to
look as clearly as possible into oneself, to shine a light into one's most
hidden corners! To have the courage of your own convictions. You
must be perseverant. Yes, this must be the daily prayer of every decent
person: perseverance!"

Georg thought: So where is he now? In his own way he's just as sick
as his father was. Yet one can't say because of that that he has personally had difficult experiences. And he once said that he has never felt a
relationship to anyone! It's not true. He feels related to every Jew, and
closer to the least of them than he does to me. While these thoughts
were going through his head his glance fell on a large envelope which
lay on the table, and he read the words written on it in large Roman
letters: "Do not forget, never forget this."

Heinrich sensed Georg's look, took the envelope in his hand, on the
backside of which three enormous grey seals appeared, threw it down
on the table again, dropped his lower lip disparagingly, and said: "I
put these things in order today too. There are these days when we really
clean house. Other people would have burned the stuff. Why? Maybe
I'll enjoy reading it again sometime. In this envelope are the anonymous
letters I once told you about."

Georg was silent. Until now Heinrich had divulged nothing of the
circumstances under which the relationship with the actress had ended;
only a single passage in the letter to Lugano had indicated that he had
seen his former sweetheart again, though not without an inner shudder.

Almost against his will, the words came to Georg's lips: "Do you know the story of Nuernberger's sister, who is buried in Cadenabbia?"

Heinrich nodded. "What made you think of that?"

"I visited her grave a few days before I left." He hesitated. Heinrich looked at him fixedly, with a heavily questioning look that forced him to continue. "And you know, it's strange, since then these two people, one of whom I've never met, and the other only cursorily at the theater, as you know, are constantly becoming confused in my memory— Nuernberger's dead sister, and . . . this actress."

Heinrich grew pale all the way to his lips. "Are you superstitious?" he asked scornfully, though it sounded like he was asking himself.

"Not at all," Georg answered. "What does this have to do with superstition?"

"I will only say that everything that has to do with mysticism is repulsive to me to the bottom of my soul. To talk about things of which one can know nothing, whose nature it is that one can never know anything about them, that seems to me to be, of all the kinds of twaddle that pass for science on earth, to be the most unendurable."

Could this actress be dead? thought Georg.

Suddenly Heinrich picked up the envelope again, and in the dry tone that he usually struck precisely when he was the most deeply troubled, he said: "That I wrote these words here is just childishness—or affectation, whichever you like. I could have also written, like Daudet[4] to Sapho: For my sons, when they are twenty years old. Stupid. As if a person could do anything at all with someone else's experiences! The experiences of one may sometimes be amusing to someone else, or more often confusing, but never instructive. . . . And do you know how it has come about that you confuse these two figures in your mind? I'll tell you. Simply because I chose the expression 'ghost' to refer to my former sweetheart in one of my letters. That explains this mysterious confusion."

"That's not impossible," replied Georg.

From somewhere, indistinctly, came the sound of bad piano playing. Georg looked outside. The sun shone on the yellow wall across the way. Many windows were open. At one sat a young boy, his arms resting on the window ledge, reading. From another two girls were looking down into the courtyard. The clatter of dishes could be heard. Georg

4. Alphonse Daudet (1840–1897). French novelist and dramatist of the Naturalist School. His long and stormy relationship with the beautiful model Marie Rieu provided the basis of his novel *Sapho,* published in 1884.

longed for fresh air, for his bench by the woods. Before he turned to go, something occurred to him: "The other thing I wanted to say, Heinrich, is that Anna liked your verses very much too. Have you gotten any further?"

"Not much."

"It would be nice if you'd bring whatever else you've finished of the text with you tonight and read it to us." He stood at the piano and struck a few chords.

"What's that," asked Heinrich.

"A theme," replied Georg, "that occurred to me for the second act. It will accompany the moment when the mysterious stranger appears on the ship."

Heinrich closed the window, Georg sat down and continued to play. There was a knock at the door, and Heinrich involuntarily called out: "Come in."

A young lady came in, in a light cloth skirt, with a red silk blouse, and a white velvet ribbon with a small gold cross around her neck. A wide brimmed Florentine hat, decorated with roses, shaded the small pale face from which looked two large black eyes.

"Good afternoon," said the strange lady with a dark voice, that sounded at once defiant and embarrassed. "Excuse me, Herr Bermann, I didn't know that you had a visitor." She looked curiously at Georg, whom she recognized at once.

Heinrich was pale and had wrinkles on his forehead. "I really wasn't expecting . . ." he began, made introductions, and said to the lady: "Won't you have a seat?"

"Thank you," she replied irritably, and remained standing. "Perhaps I'll come back later."

"Oh, please," Georg interjected. "I was just about to go." He saw how the actress's gaze scanned the room and felt a strange compassion for her, like one sometimes feels for the dead in a dream where they don't know that they have died. Then he saw again how Heinrich looked at this pale, small face with such inconceivable hardness, and left. He remembered very clearly how he had seen her on the stage, with the reddish-blond hair which fell onto her forehead, and those wandering eyes. He thought, people who intend to belong to *one person* don't look like that. And Heinrich never noticed this, he, who is so proud of his character judgment? What does he really want from her? It was vanity that burned in his soul, nothing but vanity.

Georg walked through the street as though through dry embers. The

walls of the houses threw the summer heat that they had drunk in back
into the air. Georg took the horse-carriage line out to the hills and
forests, and breathed freer as he got out into the country. He walked
on slowly between the gardens and villas, then, past the cemetery, he
took a slowly rising white street which was called by the pleasantly
charming name Sommerhaidenweg, and which, at this sunny, late afternoon hour had hardly any people on it. There was still no shade from
the forested hills to the left, only a gentle breath of breeze which had
been sleeping in the leaves. The green hill sloped down to the right toward the long expanse of the valley, where rooftops peeked out from
between branches and treetops. Further, behind garden fences, wine
slopes and fields rose up toward meadows and stone quarries over
which hung glimmering foliage and underbrush. The path, which on
other days Georg sometimes liked to follow, ran like a narrow line often
lost in the terrain, and his eyes sought the place on the edge of the forest
where his special bench stood. Meadows and forested hills blocked the
view at the far end of the valley, and in the play of the evening air, new
valleys and hills could be sensed beyond in the dusky distance.

This landscape was wonderfully dear to Georg, and the thought that
fame and fortune was calling him away cast a feeling of farewell over
his solitary walks these days, which were naturally heavier with nostalgia than sadness. At the same time though, there arose in him a pre-
monition of a richer life. It seemed to him that much was preparing itself in his soul which he should not disturb with anxious thoughts, and
that in the depths of his soul, where it was not yet given to him to hear,
the melodies of days to come were stirring. He had not remained idle
in drawing out the contours of his future clearly. He had written an
obliging letter to Detmold in which, with reservations, he placed himself
at the disposal of the theater manager for the coming fall; he also
looked up old professor Viebiger, explained his plans to him, and asked
him to remember his former student in case of any opportunities. But
even if, contrary to expectations, no position could be found by fall,
he was still determined to leave Vienna and withdraw for a while to a
small town or to the country and continue working on his own in peace.
He could give no clear account of how his relationship with Anna
would develop under these circumstances; he only knew that it wasn't
going to end. He imagined that he and Anna would visit each other and
take trips together at opportune times; later she would move to the
place where he lived and worked. But it appeared unnecessary to him

to ponder all this deeply before the moment arrived which would decide his fate, at least for the course of the next few years.

Sommerhaidenweg ran into the forest, and Georg took the wide Villenweg which turned down at this point and crossed the valley. In a few minutes he was on the street where, at the end near the forest, next to a group of yellow one-floor cottages, the little villa stood where Anna lived, raised above the others only by a mansard attic room with a balcony covered by a three-cornered wooden gable. He crossed the front garden where, in the middle of the grass between the flower patches, the small, blue, clay angel greeted him from its square pedestal, and then went through the narrow hallway next to the kitchen, the bare central room on whose floor lines of sunlight from the dilapidated green Venetian blinds were playing, and out to the veranda. He turned to the left and looked in the open window of Anna's room, which he found empty. Then he walked up in the garden along the lilac bushes and currants and soon he saw Anna at the far end, sitting on the white bench under the pear tree, in her full, blue dress. She didn't see him coming and looked lost in thought. He approached slowly. She still didn't look up. He loved her very much in such moments, when she didn't know she was being watched, and the kindness and tranquility of her character rested peacefully on her untroubled brow. Sunbeams danced on the gravel at her feet. Across from her, on the grass, the neighbor's St. Bernard lay sleeping. It was the animal which, as it woke up, first noticed Georg's arrival. It got up and heavily toddled over to Georg. Anna finally looked up and a happy smile floated over her face. Why aren't I here more often, passed through Georg's mind. Why don't I live out here and work up on the balcony under the gable, where one has the lovely view of Sommerhaidenweg. The late afternoon sun was still burning so hot that his forehead had become wet.

He stood in front of Anna, kissed her on the eyes and mouth, and sat down next to her. The animal had crept up by him and stretched out at his feet.

"How are you, treasure?" he asked as he put his arm around her neck.

Everything was fine, as usual, and today had been a particularly lovely day. She had been completely alone since this morning, since Frau Golowski had gone into the city again to visit her family. It really wasn't bad to be so totally alone sometimes. One can sink completely into one's dreams, undisturbed. Of course they were always the same, but they were so dear to her that she never became tired of them. She had dreamed about her child. How much she loved it already, even before it was born. She had never imagined it was possible. Could Georg understand it too? . . . and as he nodded, lost in thought, she shook her head. No, no . . . a man can't understand, even the best, not even the kindest. She could already feel the tiny being moving, sensed the beating of its delicate heart, felt its new and intangible soul breathing within her, just as she felt the new young body within her bloom and awaken. Georg looked down, as if ashamed that she anticipated with so much more purity of soul than he did the arrival of the one who was so soon to come. For here, conceived by him, there would be another creature like him, a being who was, like himself, destined to bestow life again; in the pregnant body of this woman, which he had long ceased to desire, according to eternal laws, a life grew which only a year ago was still lost in an insentient, volitionless, and boundless indeterminacy, and was yet as if destined from prehistory to press forward toward the light;— and he knew that he himself was held fast, as it were, inescapably clasped by both hands, in the continuous chain from ancestor to offspring, . . . but he did not feel himself summoned by this wonder as strongly as it required.

They spoke today more seriously than they usually did about what would happen once the child was born. For the first few weeks Anna would naturally keep it herself; then, of course, she would have to give it to other people; in any case it should live nearby so Anna could see it at any time without difficulty.

"And you," she suddenly said softly, "will you be coming sometimes to visit us?"

He looked in her mischievously smiling face, took both her hands, and kissed her. "Darling, what should I do, tell me yourself? You can imagine how hard it will be for me. But what else can I do? There has to be a start made. Did I tell you," he quickly added, as if this cut off all retreat, "we've given notice on the apartment. Felician is probably going to Athens. Of course it would be lovely if I could take you with me! But unfortunately it's not possible; there has to be some security there first. I mean at least the security that I'll be staying in one place for a while. . . ."

She had listened calmly and seriously. Then she began earnestly to speak about her newest idea. He should not think that she intended to place the whole burden on him. She had decided, as soon as it was possible, to open a music school. Here in Vienna if he left her here for a while, or there where they were living if he came to get her right away. And when she was able to stand on her own two feet, then she wanted to retrieve her child, whether she was his wife or not. She was not at all ashamed, as he well knew. She was proud . . . yes, proud that she would be a mother!

He took her hands between his own and stroked them. "So it shall be," he said, a little depressed. Suddenly he saw himself in a very bourgeois home, under the modest light of a hanging lamp, sitting at supper between wife and child. And from this imaginary family scene a breath of deep, careworn boredom blew toward him. Oh, it was too soon for this; he was still too young. How would it all turn out? Was it possible that she could be the last woman he would ever have? Maybe in a few years, even a few months . . . but not yet. He shrank back from the thought of bringing deception and lies into a well ordered home. Yet the thought of escaping from her into the arms of others he desired, knowing he could return again to find Anna as he had left her, was enticing and comforting at the same time.

The familiar whistle sounded from the other yard. The dog got up, let Georg stroke its yellow flecked back once more, and crept sadly on its way.

"Oh God," said Georg, "I almost forgot. Heinrich could be here any minute." He told Anna about his visit, and did not neglect to tell her that he had encountered the faithless actress on the way out.

"Did she succeed?" cried Anna, who had no fondness for women with wandering eyes.

"I don't think," said Georg, "that she succeeded in anything. Heinrich was even rather annoyed at her appearance, it seemed to me."

"Well, maybe he'll bring her with him," Anna said derisively, "and you'll have someone to flirt with again, like the little regicide in Lugano."

"Oh God," Georg said innocently, and casually continued, "What's with Therese anyway; why doesn't she come to see you more often? Demeter isn't in Vienna any more. She certainly has plenty of time."

"She was just here a couple of days ago. I told you about it, don't pretend I didn't."

"I really had forgotten about it," replied Georg quite honestly. "What did she have to say?"

"All sorts of things. The affair with Demeter is over. Her heart now beats only for the poor and suffering again—until further notice." And under a vow of the strictest secrecy Anna confided Therese's winter plans to him. She wanted to visit the warming houses, soup- and tea-kitchens, work-houses, and shelters for the homeless, dressed as a poor woman, to shed some light on the so-called golden hearts of Vienna in the most hidden corners. She seemed determined, and hoped by this, perhaps, to expose some monstrous social ills.

Georg looked down. He remembered the elegant lady in the white dress who had stood in the sunlight in front of the post office in Lugano, far from all the misery of the world. Strange creature, he thought. "Naturally she wants to make a book out of it," said Anna. "Just be sure that you don't tell a soul, including your friend Bermann."

"I wouldn't think of it. But say Anna, don't you need to get ready for this evening?"

She nodded. "Come with me. I'll see what we have and talk it over with Marie . . . as much as that's possible."

They stood up. The shadows were long. The children were playing in the garden next door. Anna took the arm of her sweetheart and slowly walked back with him. She related the latest examples of the legendary stupidity of the maid. Me, a husband, thought Georg, and listened in-dulgently. By the house he expressed his intention of going to meet Hein-rich, left Anna, and went out onto the road. A one-horse carriage rolled up; Heinrich jumped out and released the driver. "Greetings," he said to Georg, "have you been waiting long? It's not that late yet."

"Not at all, you're quite punctual. If you'd like, we could go for a little walk."

"Sure."

They walked on, past the yellow inn with the red terraces, to the forest.

"It's wonderful here," said Heinrich. "And your villa looks quite nice too. Why don't you live out here?"

"Yes, it's crazy," granted Georg without any further explanation. Then they were quiet for a while.

Heinrich was wearing a light grey summer suit, and carried his coat over his arm, which was dragging along a little. "Did you recognize her?" he suddenly asked without looking up.

"Yes," replied Georg.

"She's only here for one day, from her summer engagement. She's going back again tonight. A sneak attack, so to speak. But it didn't work." He laughed.

"Why are you so hard?" Georg asked, and thought about the giant envelope with the grey seals and the silly inscription. "You really have no reason. It's only by chance that she didn't get anonymous letters too, just like you, Heinrich. And who knows, if you hadn't left her alone, God knows for what reasons . . ."

Heinrich shook his head and looked at Georg almost sympathetically. "Maybe you think it's my intention to quarrel or take revenge? Or do you think that I'm one of those fools who become disillusioned with the world because something has happened to them that they know has happened to thousands before them and will happen to thousands after them? Do you think that I have contempt for the betrayer, or that I hate her? It wouldn't even occur to me. Which is not to say that I don't sometimes take on the gestures of hatred or contempt, naturally just to get better results from her. But in reality, I understand everything that has happened, much too well for me to . . ." He shrugged his shoulders.

"Well, if you understand it . . ."

"But dear friend, understanding helps nothing. Understanding is a sport like any other. A very noble sport, and a very expensive one. One can squander his whole soul on it and be left a beggar. But understanding has nothing in the slightest to do with our feelings—almost as little as with our actions. It won't save us from sadness, from disgust, or from annihilation. It leads to nothing. It's a blind alley, so to speak. Understanding only means an end."

On a steeply inclining side path, slowly and silently, each with his own thoughts, they came out of the forest into an open meadow with a clear view of the valley. They looked out over the town and beyond to the misty distance, through which the river ran glimmering, toward distant mountains with a thin haze spreading in front of them. Then, in the peaceful evening sun, they walked on to Georg's favorite bench at the edge of the forest. The sun went down. Georg looked beyond the valley along the forested hills that bordered Sommerhaidenweg, pale and cooled. Then he looked down and knew that in the garden at his feet stood a pear tree, under which only a short time ago he had sat with a deeply loved woman who carried his child beneath her heart, and he was moved. For the women who perhaps awaited him elsewhere he felt a mild contempt, although his longing for them was not necessarily quenched by this. Below, on the path between the gardens and meadows, summer visitors strolled. A young girl looked up, and whispered something to another one. "You're a popular personality in this place," Heinrich remarked with a sarcastic twitch of his mouth.

"Not that I know of."

"The pretty girls have found you quite interesting. Someone's being unmarried will always be a constant source of stimulation for people. In any case, these summer folk down there take you for some sort of Don Juan and . . . and your lady friend a girl you carried off and seduced. Don't you think?"

"I don't know," Georg said, avoiding the conversation.

"And what did the theater folk in that other little town make of me?" Heinrich continued unconcerned. "Obviously the betrayed lover, therefore an exclusively comic figure. And her? Well, one can easily imagine. These things appear immensely simple to the unconcerned. Every story looks completely different close up. But mightn't they show their truer face from the distance? Mightn't one persuade oneself of all sorts of things when one has a role to play in the comedy oneself?"

He should have stayed home, Georg thought. But since he couldn't send him back, and at least had to try a different conversation, he quickly asked: "Have you heard from the Ehrenbergs?"

"A couple of days ago," replied Heinrich, "I had a rather melancholy letter from Fraulein Else."

"You keep in correspondence with her?"

"No, I don't keep in correspondence with her; at least I haven't answered her yet."

"She took the matter with Oskar," said Georg, "more seriously than she wants to admit. I talked to her once at the sanitarium. We stood for quite a while on the walk in front of the white lacquered door to poor Oskar's room. At that time they were worried about the other eye too. It's really a tragic story."

"Tragicomic," Heinrich corrected sternly.

"You see something tragicomic everywhere. And I'll tell you why. Because you're a little heartless. But in this case there's nothing comic."

"You're mistaken," replied Heinrich. "The blow from the old Ehrenberg was a brutality; Oskar's attempted suicide was foolishness; that he hurt himself so badly was ineptitude. Nothing tragic can result from such things. It's a rather revolting affair, that's all."

Georg shook his head angrily. Since this misfortune he had developed a real sympathy for Oskar. And he felt pity for the old Ehrenberg too, who had lived out in Neuhaus since then, caring only for his work and not wanting to see anyone any more. They had both punished each other harder than they deserved. Couldn't Heinrich see and feel that just as well as he? Sometimes they really made one nervous, these over-clever, pitiless, Jewish examiners of human nature like Bermann

and Nuernberger. That they should never appear surprised by anything, that was the most important thing for them. But kindness, that's
what was lacking in them. Only when they had become older did a certain mellowness come over them. Georg thought of the old Doctor
Stauber, Frau Golowski, and the elder Eissler. But as long as they were
young . . . they always held to living *qui vive.*[5] Just so as not to look
stupid! What a disagreeable group. A longing for Felician and Skelton,
who were certainly quite clever enough too, rose in him;—even for
Guido Schoenstein.

"Aside from the melancholy," Heinrich said after a time, "Fraulein
Else seems to be enjoying herself tolerably. There are already visitors
again at the Auhof. The Wyners were recently there, Sissy and James.
James got his doctorate from Cambridge. Noble, don't you think?"

Sissy's name stabbed at Georg's heart like a glittering dagger. Suddenly he realized that in a few days he would be near her again. His
longing swelled so powerfully in him that he could scarcely believe it.

Evening descended. Georg and Heinrich got up, went down through
the meadow, and entered the garden. There they saw Anna coming toward them down the middle path, accompanied by a man.

"The old Doctor Stauber," said Georg. "Do you know him?"

They all greeted each other. "I'm very glad," Anna said to Heinrich,
"that you've finally come to see us."

To see us, Georg repeated to himself, with a certain annoyance,
which he immediately repressed. He walked in front with Doctor
Stauber. Heinrich and Anna followed slowly.

"Are you satisfied with Anna?" Georg asked the doctor.

"It couldn't be going better," replied Stauber. "Only she should be
more conscientious about getting regular exercise."

It occurred to Georg that he had not returned to the doctor, whom
he was seeing for the first time since his return, the books he had loaned
him, and made an apology.

"There's plenty of time," replied Stauber. "I hope they proved useful
to you." And he asked about the impressions he brought back from
Rome with him.

Georg told about his walks through the old Caesars' palaces, of
rides on the Campagna in the evening splendor, of a stormy hour in
Hadrian's garden. Doctor Stauber asked him to stop, lest he leave all
his patients in the lurch and run off to the beloved city. Then Georg

5. Literally "Who goes there?" in French; on the alert, suspicious.

inquired obligingly after Doctor Berthold. Was it based on fact that the
next winter would find him politically active again?

Doctor Stauber shrugged his shoulders. "He's coming back in September. For the moment that's the only thing for certain. He's been very
busy at the Pasteur, and will be taking up very important work on a
serum again here at the Pathology Institute, which he began in Paris.
If he listened to me he would stay with that. What he's doing there is
surely more important for humanity than the loveliest revolution, in my
unauthoritative opinion. Of course, his talents are diverse, and I certainly have nothing against opportune revolutions. But, between us, my
son's talents lay more on the scientific side. In the other direction he's
driven more by temperament . . . possibly exclusively by rancor. Well,
we'll see. But how do things stand with your plans for the fall?" he suddenly added and looked at Georg with his benevolent, paternal gaze.
"Where will you be swinging the baton?"

"Yes, if I only knew myself," replied Georg. And as he explained his
efforts and prospects with emphasized seriousness to the doctor, who
went aside with him with half-closed lids and a cigar in his mouth, he
believed he could feel how everything he said would only sound to Doctor Stauber like a justification for his delay in marrying Anna. A mild
irritation against her arose in him as she came along behind them,
perhaps silently happy that Doctor Stauber would give him a good talking to. He deliberately struck an increasingly lighter tone, as if his personal plans for the future had nothing whatever to do with Anna, and
finally said optimistically: "Yes, who knows where I'll be next year at
this time, maybe in America."

"That wouldn't be the worst thing," replied Doctor Stauber calmly.
"I have a cousin who is a violinist in Boston, a certain Schwarz, who
earns at least six times as much there as he got here at the opera."

Georg did not care at all to be compared with violinists named
Schwarz and firmly asserted that, in the beginning at least, it was not
a question of earning money, which sounded a little excessive, even to
himself. Suddenly, without knowing where the idea came from, the
thought went through his mind: What if Anna died! If the child were
her death! He was horrified to the depths, as if by this thought he had
laid some guilt upon himself. And in his mind he saw Anna laid out,
the veil pulled over her chin, and the mixture of daylight and candlelight
running over her waxen face. Almost in dread he turned around, as if
to reassure himself that she was there and still alive. The expressions
on her face were lost in the darkness, which made him shudder. He

stood still with the doctor, until Anna and Heinrich caught up. He was glad to have her so close. "But you must be getting tired by now," he said to her in the tenderest tone.

"Well I've honestly absolved myself of my duty for today," she replied. "By the way," and she indicated toward the veranda, where the lamp with the green paper shade was burning on the set table, "supper will be ready by now. It would be lovely, Herr Doctor, if you would stay with us, yes?"

"Unfortunately my dear, it's not possible. I should already be back in the city. Give my greetings to Frau Golowski. *Auf Wiedersehen. Adieu* Herr Bermann. Well," he added, "will we have something nice to hear or read from you soon?"

Heinrich shrugged his shoulders, smiled affably and said nothing. Why, he thought, are even the most well-bred men usually tactless when they are around people like me? Do I ask him about his affairs?

The doctor said a few more words to Heinrich to express his condolences on the death of the elder Bermann. He recalled the now famous speech against the introduction of the Czech legal terminology in certain Bohemian districts. At that time it hung by a thread if the Jewish provincial attorney would be made Justice Minister. Yes, the times have changed.

Heinrich paid attention. This could be of use in his political satire.

Doctor Stauber took his leave; Georg accompanied him to the wagon, which was waiting outside, and used the opportunity to ask the doctor a few questions of a medical nature. The doctor reassured him in every respect. "It's only a shame," he concluded, "that circumstances don't permit her nursing the child herself."

Georg stood thoughtfully. But it couldn't hurt anything? . . . Especially the child. Or her either? . . . he asked the doctor.

"What's there to talk about when it can't happen, dear Baron. Well, don't worry about anything," he added with his foot already on the wagon step. "There's nothing to fear from a child of you two."

Georg looked him firmly in the eyes and said: "In any case, I'll worry that it spends its first year of life in healthy air."

"That's very nice," Doctor Stauber said gently. "But there's no healthier air in the world for children than in the home of their parents." He shook hands with Georg, and the wagon rolled away.

Georg stood still for a moment, felt an intense annoyance at the doctor, and promised himself never again to get into conversations with him that gave him an excuse, so to speak, for giving unasked-for advice or to make veiled reproaches. What did the old man know? What did he understand of the matter anyway? Georg grew angrier. I'll marry her when it suits me, he said to himself. Can't she keep the child anyway? Didn't she say herself that she was proud to have a child? I won't disavow it. And I'll do everything in my power. And later, later sometime. . . . But it would be an injustice to myself, to her, to the child, if I committed myself to something today that's premature at best.

Slowly he passed the narrow side of the house and walked into the garden. He saw Anna and Heinrich sitting on the veranda. Just then Marie came out of the house, very red in the face, and sat a warm bowl on the table from which steam was rising. How peacefully Anna sits there, Georg thought, and stood still in the dark. How good-natured, how carefree, as though she could trust me completely. As if there were no such thing as death, poverty, and betrayal. As if I loved her as much as she deserves! And he was again horrified. Do I not love her enough? Should she not trust me? When I was sitting on the bench at the edge of the forest, so much tenderness would sometimes well up in me I thought I'd die. Why do I feel so little of it now? He stood only a few steps away, and watched how she served; and how she stared into the darkness from which he would emerge, and how her eyes began to brighten as he suddenly walked into the light. My only love! he thought. As he sat with the others Anna said: "That was quite a conference you had with the doctor."

"No conference, just a chat. He was just telling me about his son, who's about to come back."

Heinrich asked about Berthold. The young man interested him, and he hoped very much to get to know him next winter. The speeches last year about the Therese Golowski case, and the open letter to his constituents in which he explained the reason for his resignation, those had been matters of a high order . . . yes, and more than that—documents of the time.

A gentle, almost proud smile crossed Anna's face. She looked down at her plate, and then quickly up at Georg. Georg smiled too. He felt no trace of jealousy. Did Berthold know? Certainly. Did it hurt him? Possibly. Could he forgive Anna? One would have to forgive. How stupid.

A dish of mushrooms was served, at whose appearance Heinrich could not suppress the question as to whether they might not be poisonous. Georg laughed.

"There's no need to make fun of me," said Heinrich. "If I wanted to kill myself, I wouldn't use either poisonous mushrooms or spoiled sausage, but a quick and effective poison. One is sometimes tired of life, but one is never tired of health, even for the last quarter-hour of one's existence. And besides, anxiety is a perfectly legitimate, if often shamefully maligned, daughter of the understanding. For what is anxiety? Taking into consideration every possibility that could result from an action, the bad as well as the good. And what is courage? Naturally I mean the real thing, which is much more rare than one thinks. Since affected, or feigned, or implied courage counts for nothing. True courage is often nothing other than the expression of a metaphysical conviction, so to speak, of our own superfluousness."

You Jew, Georg thought without animosity, and then: perhaps he's not so wrong.

The beer, which Anna did not drink, tasted so good that Marie was sent to the inn for a second pitcher. Everyone was in high spirits. Georg talked about the trip again: of the sun-drenched days in Lugano, of the trip through the snow-covered Brenner, of the walk through the roofless city that emerged into the light after a two-thousand-year night; he conjured up the moment again in which they, he and Anna, had been present while workers cautiously and painstakingly dug a column out of the ashes. Heinrich had not yet seen Italy. He wanted to go there next spring. He explained that he often pined in longing, if not precisely for Italy, yet for the strange, distant world. Sometimes, when he heard talk of travel, his heart would pound like a child's on the day before his birthday. He doubted that he was destined to finish his life in his homeland. But perhaps he would return, after many years of wandering, to a small house in the country, to find the peace of his late maturity. Who knew, there were stranger accidents, if he were not destined to end his existence precisely in this house in which he was now a guest and felt better than he had in a long time. Anna felt as though she were mistress of the house, not only here in the villa, but throughout this whole, still, evening world. A gentle light began to come from the darkness of the garden. A warm, damp smell came from the grass and flowers. The wide meadow, which came up to the fence, rose up in the moonlight, and the white bench under the pear tree shimmered forth as though from a great distance. Anna spoke amicably to Heinrich about the verses from the opera libretto which Georg had recently read to her.

"That's right," Georg remarked, with his legs comfortably crossed and smoking a cigar, "have you brought anything new with you?"

Heinrich shook his head. "No, nothing."

"Too bad," Anna said, and made the suggestion that Heinrich should explain the course of the action in an orderly and detailed manner. She had wanted this for a long time. No clear picture could be formed from Georg's descriptions.

They looked at each other. The dark, sweet hour appeared to them in which they had lain breast to breast in a dark room, where, beyond the windows and behind a fluttering veil of snow, a grey church stood in the twilight as the muffled tones of the organ surrounded them. Yes, now they knew where the house stood in which the child would be born. And perhaps another one already stands somewhere, Georg thought, in which the child, who is not even born yet, will end his life— as a man—perhaps an old man—or—oh, such thoughts . . . away, away.

Heinrich declared himself ready to satisfy Anna's wish, and stood up. "It may be useful to me too," he said, as though by way of excuse. "It might clarify some things."

"But be careful not to stray off into your political satire," Georg remarked. And turning to Anna: "He's writing a play with a German art student as hero, who poisons himself with mushrooms, from despair over the emancipation of the Jews."

Heinrich winced. "One less glass of beer and you wouldn't have made that joke."

"Jealous," responded Georg. He felt in exceptionally good spirits, particularly because he had firmly decided to leave the day after tomorrow. He sat very close to Anna, held her hand in his, and listened as melodies of later days stirred in the depths of his soul.

Suddenly Heinrich stood in the garden off the veranda, reached over the railing, took his coat from the chair and threw it romantically over his shoulders. "To begin." he said. "First Act."

"First, overture in D-minor," Georg interrupted him. He whistled a solemn melody, just a few notes, and concluded with "and so forth."

"The curtain rises," said Heinrich. "Celebration in the royal garden. Night. The princess is to be married to Duke Heliodor the next day. For the moment I call him Heliodor; he may possibly have another name. The king adores his daughter and cannot tolerate Heliodor, who seems to be a kind of megalomaniac coxcomb. To this festival, which the king has arranged primarily to anger Heliodor, not only the nobility of the land has been invited, but the youth of all classes, so long as they have won the right through their handsomeness. And the princess is to dance that evening with everyone she fancies. There is one in particular,

Aegidius by name, to whom she seems quite attracted. And no one is happier about this than the king. Jealousy from Heliodor. Growing satisfaction on the part of the king. Argument between Heliodor and the king. Derision, animosity. Now something most unexpected happens. Aegidius draws his dagger on the king and intends to kill him. This murder attempt must be very carefully composed, dear Georg, if you would be kind enough to set the whole thing to music. It will be sufficient to indicate that the youth is an enemy of tyranny, a member of a secret society, or perhaps a fool or a hero on his own responsibility. I don't yet know myself. The attempt fails. Aegidius is taken prisoner. The king wishes to be alone with him. Duet. The youth is proud, resolute, grand, the king superior, cruel, inscrutable. I imagine him something like this: he has already sent many to their deaths, seen many die, but to him, in his condition of immense suspiciousness, all other men seem to live in a state of half-consciousness, so that their departure from life meant, to a certain extent, nothing more than a step from twilight into darkness. Such a fate seemed to him, in this case, too mild or too banal. He would hurl this youth from a day such as no mortal had ever enjoyed into the most dreadful night. Yes, such are his thoughts. How much of this he expresses or sings, naturally I don't know yet. Aegidius, as one condemned, from all appearances, to a speedy death, is sent off, and to be sure, on the same ship which is to take Heliodor and the princess on their journey the following night. The curtain falls. The second act takes place on the deck of the ship. The ship is fully underway. Chorus. Individual figures rise and fall. Their meaning will come to light later. Daybreak. Aegidius is brought up from below. As he naturally believes, to his death. But something else happens. His chains are loosened, all bow before him. He is greeted as a prince. The sun comes up. Aegidius has occasion to remark that he finds himself in the best of company. Beautiful women. Noblemen. A wise man, a singer, and a fool are destined to play major roles. Standing out from the women's chorus is none other than the princess, who now belongs to Aegidius, like everything on the ship."

"A splendid lord and king," said Georg.

"For a brilliant idea, no price is too high for him," explained Heinrich, "that is his nature. A noble duet follows between Aegidius and the princess, then all sit down to dinner. After dinner, dancing. High spirits. Aegidius must naturally consider himself saved. But he did not wonder excessively, for his hatred of the king had always been mingled with admiration. Evening falls. Suddenly there is a stranger at the side of Aegidius. Perhaps he's been there for a long time. One among many, unnoticed, silent. He has something to tell Aegidius. Merriment and dancing continue all around. Aegidius and the stranger. All this is yours, says the stranger. You may rule as you please, seize estates, kill, completely as you wish. But tomorrow . . . or in two, or seven days, or in a year, or in ten, or even later, this ship will approach an island where, on a cliff above the shore, a marble hall stands. And there death awaits you. Death. Your murderer is with you on the ship. But only the one who is destined to be your murderer knows it himself. No one else knows him. In fact, no one else on this ship knows that you are a doomed man. And the secret must stay with you! For should you ever let it be known that your fate is known to you, in that very hour, death will befall you."

Heinrich spoke these words with affected pathos, as though to conceal his embarrassment. He continued more simply. "The stranger disappears. Perhaps I'll have him put ashore, by two silent men who accompany him. Aegidius remains behind, among hundreds, men and women, one of whom is his murderer. Who? The wise man? The fool? The astrologer over there? One of those cowering in the dark? Those creeping along by the rail? One of the dancers? The princess herself? She comes up to him again, is very tender, even passionate. Hypocrite? Murderess? Lover? Knower? In any case, his. All this shall be so today. Night over the sea. Dread. Bliss. The ship moves slowly on, toward that shore which lies hours or years away, wrapped in mist. The princess rests at his feet. Aegidius stares into the night and waits." Heinrich paused, as though himself moved. Georg could hear it all. He heard the music to the scene where the stranger vanished, accompanied by the two silent men, and then gradually the celebration going on in the foreground of the stage returned. He could hear not only the melody, but the full orchestration. Weren't the flute, oboe, and clarinet playing? Were the cello and violin not singing? Could the low rolling of the drum not be heard from the corner of the orchestra? Involuntarily he raised his right arm, as though he held the baton in his hand.

"And the third act?" Anna asked, as Heinrich continued to remain silent.

"The third act," repeated Heinrich, and his voice sounded oppressed, "the third will take place in that hall on the cliff—don't you think? It must begin, I believe, with a conversation between the king and the stranger. Or with a chorus? No, there is no chorus on an uninhabited island. But in any case the king is there, and the ship is in sight. Why does the island have to be uninhabited anyway?" He paused.

"Well?" Georg asked impatiently.

Heinrich laid both arms on the railing of the veranda. "Shall I tell you something?—it's not an opera . . ."

"How do you mean that?"

"There's a good reason why I haven't been able to get past this point. It's a tragedy, obviously. And I just don't have the courage to write it. You know what would be described there? The inward transformation of Aegidius would be described. That is obviously the most difficult and beautiful part of the material, in other words, the part I don't dare to write. The idea for the opera is an escape, and I don't know if I can allow myself to do this kind of thing." He fell silent.

"But in any case," said Anna, "you must explain the end to us, whatever you have in mind for the opera. I can hardly conceal that I'm very curious."

Heinrich shrugged his shoulders and answered wearily: "So, the ship lands. Aegidius comes ashore, and is to be thrown into the sea."

"By whom?" asked Anna.

"I don't really know yet," Heinrich replied painfully. "From this point on I don't know much else."

"I thought it would be the princess who . . ." Anna said and made a gesture in the air signifying death.

Heinrich smiled softly. "Naturally I thought of that too, but . . ." He interrupted himself and suddenly looked intently up at the night sky.

"In the first outline," Georg remarked irritably, "it was supposed to end with a sort of reprieve. But something like that's only good enough for an opera. Now, as a tragic hero, he naturally will have to be cast into the sea, your Aegidius."

Heinrich raised his index finger mysteriously upward, and his expression became more animated again. "I think something just came to me. But let's not talk about it for the moment, if I may ask. Perhaps it's good that I've explained the beginning."

"But if you think I'm going to write the intermezzo for you," Georg said without much force, "you're fooling yourself."

Heinrich smiled with guilty indifference, and the high spirits evaporated. Anna felt with disappointment that the whole story had fizzled. Georg was unsure if he should be angry that his hopes had begun to falter, or glad that he had been freed from a sort of obligation. But to Heinrich it seemed that his own characters had deserted him in a shadowy confusion, scornfully, without a farewell, and without a promise to return. He found himself alone, lost, in a sad garden, in the company of an amiable good acquaintance, and a young lady who asked nothing of him. He suddenly thought of a creature who rode at this moment with red, teary eyes, in a poorly lit coach, hopelessly toward dark mountains, worried if she would arrive tomorrow morning in time for rehearsal. Now he felt it again: since that had come to an end, he had gone steadily downhill. Now he had nothing and no one. The sadness over that lamented and painfully hated person was his only possession. And who knows, maybe tomorrow she will smile at someone else with those red, teary eyes, still with pain and longing in her soul, and yet a new lust for life flowing in her blood.

Frau Golowski appeared on the veranda, somewhat late and in a hurry, still holding her hat and umbrella. She brought greetings from town from Therese, who wanted to pay Anna a visit again in the next few days. Georg, who was leaning against one of the wooden posts of the veranda, turned to Frau Golowski with that deliberate courteousness that he always used with her for appearances. "Would you ask Fraulein Therese in our name if she would not care to stay out here for a few days? The mansard room is completely at her disposal. I'm going to the mountains for a short time," he added, as if he otherwise lived regularly in the little room up there.

Frau Golowski thanked him. She would mention it to Therese. Georg looked at the clock and found that it was time to be heading home. Then he left with Heinrich. Anna accompanied them as far as the garden gate, remained standing there for a while watching after them, until they were on the hill where Sommerhaidenweg began.

The little village in the valley flowed downward in the moonlight. The hills stood pale, like thin walls. The forest breathed darkness. A thousand lights glimmered from the summer night haze of the city. Heinrich and Georg walked toward it together silently, and distance rose up between them. Georg remembered that walk through the Prater last fall, when their first, almost intimate conversation had brought them closer. How much had happened since then! But wasn't it all as if blown into the air? Even yet today Georg was unable to walk silently through the night with Heinrich as he had before sometimes with Guido, with Labinski too, without inwardly losing touch with him. The silence grew oppressive. He began talking, because it was the first thing to come to him, about the older Doctor Stauber, and praised his dependability and diversity. Heinrich was not so taken by him, found him a little intoxicated with his own goodness, wisdom, and ability. That was another sort of Jew he could not quite abide: the ones who agreed with themselves. They began to talk about the younger Stauber, whose wavering between politics and science seemed to hold something quite appealing for Heinrich. From there they went on to a conversation about the session of Parliament, about the conflict between the Germans and the Czechs, about the clerics' attack on the Education Minister. They argued with that rigorous assiduousness that one uses only when speaking of things that one is, in the bottom of one's soul, completely indifferent to. Finally they debated whether or not the minister should remain in office after the dubious role he had played in the civil marriage question; in the end they no longer clearly knew which of the two of them had spoken for, which against, the resignation. They walked past the cemetery. Crosses and gravestones rose over the wall and hovered in the moonlight. The way ran downward to the road. They both hurried in order to catch the last horse coach, and once on the platform, rolled toward the city through the humid, hazy, night air. Georg explained that he was thinking about taking the first leg of his trip on bicycle. And, following a sudden impulse, he asked Heinrich if he would not like to join the party. Heinrich accepted, and after a few minutes, became excited. They got off at the Schottentor,[6] found a cafe nearby, and, with the help of special maps they found in an encyclopedia, identified every possible route in a detailed conversation. When they said good night, the plan was still not yet firmly set, but they knew that early on the morning after next they would leave Vienna together and get on their bicycles at Lambach.

Georg stood for quite a while yet, looking out of the open window of his bedroom, wide awake. He thought of Anna, from whom he would be gone for just a few days, and saw her before him as she must be at this hour, sleeping in her bed in the country, in the pale evening light between moon and morning. But it was a dim experience, as though this apparition did not stand together with his own destiny, but rather somehow with that of some stranger, who himself knew nothing of it.—And that in that slumbering creature another slept, more deeply and mysteriously, and that this other was to be his child—this he was

6. Literally the Scottish Gate, which was the name of one of the monumental gates into the city through the old city walls. It was torn down when the walls were destroyed to make room for the Ringstrasse, but the intersection at this point, on the northwest corner of the Ring and across from the Votive Church, is still known by this name.

unable to grasp. Now, as the dullness of early morning crept almost painfully through his senses, the whole experience seemed distant and unreal as never before. Ever-brighter light spread itself over the roofs and towers, but the city was still far from awakening. The air lay completely motionless. No breeze came from the trees outside in the park, no scent from the bushes, which were past their bloom. And Georg stood at the window without happiness or understanding.

Seventh Chapter

Slowly Georg came up from the room below deck, on narrow carpeted stairs, between elongated crooked mirrors; and, wrapped in a long dark green blanket which dragged after him, he walked up and down beneath the starry sky on the vacant deck of the ship. At the helm, motionless as always, stood Labinski, who turned the wheel and had his gaze directed out to the open sea. What a career! thought Georg. First a dead man, then minister, then a little boy with a muff, and now a helmsman. If he knew that I was on this ship he'd certainly call to me. "Watch out," the two girls dressed in blue whom he knew from shore called out from behind him; but then he fell down, tangled himself up in his blanket, and heard the wings of white sea gulls flapping over his head. Right after that he sat below, in the salon, at the table which was so long that the people at the other end actually looked quite small. A man who sat next to him, and who resembled the old Grillparzer, remarked angrily: "This ship is always late; we should already be in Boston." Now Georg grew alarmed; for if he could not produce the three scores in the green binding when they disembarked, he would certainly be arrested for high treason. Sometimes the prince, who rode up and down the deck on a bicycle all day, would look at him from an odd side angle. And to increase suspicions, he had to sit at the table in his shirt-sleeves, while the rest of the men, as always aboard ship, wore general's uniforms, and all the ladies wore red velvet. "We arrive soon in America," said a hoarse steward who was serving asparagus, "just one more sta-

tion." The others can remain sitting quietly, thought Georg, they don't
have anything to do, but I have to swim right over to the theater. And
in the large mirror across from him he saw the coast: mere houses without roofs which rose up in terraces; and all the way at the top, in a
white kiosk with an openwork stone spire, the orchestra was waiting
impatiently. The bell on deck rang, and Georg stumbled with his green
blanket and two handbags up the stairs to the garden. But they had been
brought to the wrong place; it was the Stadtpark; on a bench sat
Felician with an old woman in a coat next to him. He put his fingers
to his lips, whistled very loud, and said, in an unusually deep voice:
"Kemmelbach—Ybs."[1] No, thought Georg, Felician would never say
something like that . . . rubbed his eyes, and woke up.

The train started moving again. Two red lanterns lit up outside the
closed coach window. Then the night ran by, silent and black. Georg
pulled his traveling blanket tighter around him and stared at the green
lamp hanging from the ceiling. I'm glad I'm alone in the coach, he
thought; at least I got four or five hours of good sleep. What kind of
weird confused dream was that? The white sea gulls were the first thing
to come back to him. Did they mean anything? Then he thought of the
old woman in the coat, who actually was none other that Frau Oberberger. She wouldn't feel particularly flattered. But hadn't she actually
looked like a really old woman when he saw her a few days ago at the
side of her brilliant husband in the box of the little red and white resort
theater? And Labinski had been in the dream too, as the helmsman, of
all things. And the girls in the blue dresses, who had looked from the
hotel garden into the piano room as soon as they had heard him play.
But what had been the most ghostly thing in this dream?

Not the girls in blue, and not Labinski either, and not Prince von
Guastalla who had raced over the deck on bicycle. No, it was his own
figure, which had appeared so ghostly to him as he had seen it reflected
on both sides and multiplied a hundred-fold in the elongated, crooked
mirrors.

He began to feel cold. Cool night air was blowing into the coach
through the vent above. The deep black sky outside was gradually turning to heavy grey, and suddenly Georg heard words in his ear which
he had first heard a few hours ago, in a dark female voice, sounding
whispered and sad: How soon will you have forgotten me. . . . He did
not wish to hear these words. He wished they had been true already,

1. The names of two small Austrian towns.

and, as if desperate, he threw himself back into the memory of his dream. It was clear that the steamer, on which he had undertaken his concert tour of America, really had meant the ship on which Aegidius approached his gloomy fate. And the kiosk with the orchestra had been the hall where death awaited Aegidius. The starry sky had spread wonderfully over the sea. The sky had never been as blue, the stars as silver, when he was awake, not even the night when he had traveled with Grace from Palermo to Naples. Suddenly again, whispered and sad, the voice of the beloved woman sounded through the darkness: How soon will you have forgotten me. . . . And now he saw her before him, as he had just seen her only a few hours ago, pale and naked, her dark hair flowing over the pillow. He didn't want to think about it, and conjured up other images from the depths of his memory, and drove them willfully before his mind. He saw himself walking in the cemetery in the melting February snow with Grace; he saw himself riding on a white highway with Marianne toward the wintry forest; he saw himself walking with his father around the Ringstrasse in the late evening hours; and finally a carrousel turned rapidly before him, Sissy with laughing lips and eyes rocking on a wooden, brown horse, Else, charming and lady-like, sitting in a red wagon, and Anna on an Arabian, gently holding the reins in her hand. Anna! How young and lovely she looked! Was it really the same person he would see again in a few hours;—and had he only been away from her for ten days? And would he again see everything he had left behind ten days ago: the blue clay angel between the flower beds, the balcony with the wooden gable, the quiet garden with the currant bushes and lilacs? It all appeared incomprehensible to him. She'll be waiting for me on the white bench under the pear tree, he thought. And I'll kiss her hands as if nothing had happened. "How are you, Georg," she will ask me, "have you been true to me?" No . . . it's not her way to ask me. But without her asking, and without my answering, she'll sense that I've returned different than I left. What if she does sense it? Will I be spared from lying? But haven't I done it already? And he thought of the letters he had written to her from the lake shore, letters full of tenderness and longing, that had already been lies. And he thought how he had waited at night with pounding heart, his ear against the door, until the inn had grown still, how he had crept down the corridor to that other one, who lay there pale and naked, with dark open eyes, anointed with perfume, and with a blue luster to her hair. And he thought how, half drunk in the night with lust and boldness, they had gone out on the balcony, beneath which the water

sounded seductively. Had anyone been out on the lake in the depths of
the darkness at that hour, they'd surely have seen the white bodies shining through the night. Georg shuddered at the memory. We weren't in
our right senses, he thought. How easily it could have happened that
I'd be lying six feet under right now, with a bullet through my heart.
It could still happen. They know everything. Else knew it first, even
though she hardly ever came down to the place from the Auhof. James
Wyner surely told her that he saw me standing at night with the stranger
on the landing pier. Will Else marry him? I can understand how she
would like him. He is handsome. That chiseled face, those cold grey
eyes that look intelligently and directly into the world. A young En-
glishman. Who knows if he wouldn't have become a sort of Oskar
Ehrenberg in Vienna? And what Else had told Georg about her brother
occurred to him. On his sick bed in the sanitarium he had seemed so
composed, almost mature to Georg. And yet in Ostend[2] he's supposed
to be living such a dissolute life, gambling and going about in the worst
company, as if he absolutely wished to destroy himself. Did Heinrich
still find the matter so tragicomic? Frau Ehrenberg had grown completely white from worry, and one morning up in the park Else had
broken down with Georg and cried. Was she only crying over Oskar?

The greyness outside the coach window brightened slowly. Georg
watched as the telegraph lines floated and sped past in hurried waves,
and he thought how yesterday afternoon his deceitful words had passed
along one of these lines to Anna: Tomorrow morning I'll be back with
you, with longing, your Georg. . . . Straight from the telegraph office
he had hurried back to a fervent and despairing farewell from that
other. And he could not grasp that in this hour, while he had already
been gone from her for a whole eternity, she lay sleeping and dreaming
in that same room with the shutters closed tight. And tonight she will
be at home with husband and children—at home, like him. He knew
it was true, and he could not understand it. For the first time in his life
he had been near to doing something that people might have called
stupid. Just one word from her—and he would have gone off with her,
would have thrown away everything, friends, sweetheart, and his unborn child. And wasn't he still ready to do it? If she called him, would
he not come? And if he did, wouldn't he be right? Wasn't he made for
adventure of this kind, rather than for the quiet, dutiful existence that
he had chosen? Had it not been his destiny to go his way boldly and

2. A seaport and summer resort in northwest Belgium on the North Sea.

unhesitatingly through the world, rather than sit tight somewhere with wife and child, with the cares of the daily bread, for his career, and at most a small morsel of fame? In these days from which he had just come, he had felt alive, perhaps for the first time. Every moment had been so rich and full, not only those in her arms. He had suddenly become young again. The landscape had blossomed forth more fertile, the sky opened wider, the air which he drank had more spice and power. And melodies had stirred in him as never before. Had he ever composed a more beautiful song than that lilting one without words, "To Sing on the Water?" And strangely, from his own unperceived depths, the *Fantasy* arose one hour by the lake shore, after he had first seen the wonderful woman. Now Herr Privy Councillor Wilt could no longer regard him as a dilettante. But why should he think of him? Did the others know any better who he was? Didn't it sometimes seem to him as though even Heinrich, who had wanted to write an opera libretto for him, judged him no better? And he again heard the words that the writer had spoken to him that morning when they rode through the dew-damp forest from Lambach to Gmunden. "You do not need to create in order to be what you are—! You do not need work:—only the atmosphere of your art. . . ." Then he remembered the evening in the forester's house on the Almsee, where a thirty-seven year old hunter had sung lusty songs and Heinrich had wondered that a man of this age was still so lusty, when one must already feel the closeness of death. Then they had gone to bed in an enormous room where their words echoed and, kept awake by conversation, they philosophized a long while about life and death, and then suddenly fell asleep. The next morning, under the cool mountain sun, they parted from one another.

Georg still lay stretched out motionless, wrapped in his blanket, and considered if he should tell about his encounter with Heinrich's actress friend. How pale she became when she suddenly saw him! She had listened with wandering eyes to his report of their bicycle tour together; then, without any transition, she began to talk about her mother and small brother, who could draw so wonderfully. And her colleagues had stared at them from the theater door, especially one with a loden hat with a chamois tail stuck in it. And on the same evening Georg had seen her act in a French farce and asked himself if this attractive person who performed so uninhibitedly down there on the stage of the little summer theater could, in reality, be as despairing as Heinrich imagined her. James and Sissy enjoyed it too, not only himself. What a marvelous evening that had been! And the dinner after the theater with James,

Sissy, Frau Wyner, and Willy Eissler! And next morning the ride in old
Baron Loewenstein's four-horse carriage, which the baron drove himself! In less than an hour they had been at the lake. A boat floated near
by the shore in the early sunlight, and on the rowing plank sat the beloved woman, a green satin shawl around her shoulders. How did it
happen that even Sissy immediately sensed the relationship between
them? And then the cheerful meal up at the Auhof with the Ehrenbergs!
Georg sat between Else and Sissy, and Willy told one comical story after
another. And that afternoon, without having planned it, while the
others all rested, Georg and Sissy found themselves in the dark green
dampness of the park, in the warm smell of moss and firs, for a wonderful hour which was without promises of faithfulness or fear of fulfillment, and that floated through the day like a dream. How I will
remember and savor, moment by moment, these golden days. I can see
the two of us, Sissy and me, as we walked across the meadow, hand-in-
hand, to the tennis court. I think I played better than I ever did before.—
And I can see Sissy again, reclining in a wicker chair, a cigarette between
her lips, the old Baron Loewenstein beside her, and her gaze sparkling
at Willy. Where did I fit in for her at that moment? And the evening!
How we went out swimming in the lake at dusk, James, Willy and I,
and the warm water had caressed me so deliciously! What a joy that
was too! And then the night. . . . The night. . . . The train stopped
again. It had grown completely light outside, but Georg remained lying
motionless, like before. He heard the name of the station called out,
voices of porters, conductors, travelers, heard steps on the platform,
train signals of all sorts, and he knew that in an hour he would be in
Vienna.—Would Anna have heard reports about him, like Heinrich had
about his beloved last winter? He could not imagine that Anna would
be terribly upset over such a thing, even if she believed it. Maybe she'd
cry, but certainly only quietly, in private. He firmly decided to pretend
that nothing was wrong. Wasn't that precisely his duty? What else mattered? The only important thing was that Anna spend the final weeks
quietly and without excitement, and that a healthy child be brought into
the world. That alone. How long had it been since he had heard these
words from Doctor Stauber? The child . . . ! How near was the hour!
The child . . . he thought again; but he was not able to conceive anything but the word. Finally he tried to imagine an energetic little creature. But as if in mockery, the only things that appeared to him were
figures of little children like those in a picture book, in burlesque costumes with gaudy colors. Where would it spend its first year? he

thought. With peasants in the country, in a house with a small garden. One day we will go to get it and bring it home with us. Other things could happen. . . . One could receive a letter: Most honored sir: permit me to inform you that the child is grievously ill . . . or even . . . Why think such things? It could get sick and die even if we kept it with us.

In any case, one must give it to very reliable people. I'll take care of that myself.—It seemed to him that he faced new duties that he had never properly considered before and that he was inwardly not prepared for. The whole matter seemed, as it were, to begin all over for him. He had returned from a world in which all these things had not concerned him, where other laws governed than in this one to which he must now adapt himself again. And hadn't it seemed as if the others also felt that he didn't belong to them, as if they had all been filled with a certain respect, as if they felt a certain reverence for the power and sanctity of a great passion which they saw ruling near them? He remembered one evening when, one after the other, the hotel guests had vanished from the piano room, as if they had been aware of their duty to leave him alone with her. He had sat down at the piano and begun to improvise. She had stayed in her dim corner, in a large armchair. At first he could still see her smile, then only the dark shining of her eyes, then only the outline of her form, and finally nothing at all; but he always knew: she is there. Outside on the other shore, lights sparkled. The two girls in the blue dresses had looked in through the window and had vanished at once. Finally he stopped playing and remained sitting silently at the piano. She came slowly out of her corner like a shadow and laid her hands on his head. How unspeakably beautiful it had been! And it all came back to him. How they had rested in the boat, in the middle of the lake, with the oars pulled in, his head in her lap; and how they had walked on the shore, along the forest path, to the bench under the oak tree. It was there that he had told her everything. Everything, like a friend. And she had understood him, like no one else ever had. Was she not the one he had always searched for, she, who was lover and companion at the same time, worldly at first glance, but created for every madness and every blessedness. And the farewell yesterday . . . the dark gaze of her eyes, the blue-black stream of her undone hair, the smell of her pale naked body . . . was it possible that it was over forever, that all this should never, never return . . . ?

Georg crumpled the blanket between his fingers in impotent longing and closed his eyes. He no longer saw the gently flowing line of forest hills which was passing by outside in the morning light, and he dreamed of the dark joy of that hour of farewell as though of a final happiness. Against his will he was overcome by weariness after the rumbling night on the train, and was driven by self-evoked images through irregular dreams, over which he had no control. He walked along the Sommer-haidenweg, in a strange twilight which filled him with deep sadness. Was it morning? Was it evening? Or a dreary day? Or was it the mysterious light of a star above the world which shone for no one else but him? Suddenly he stood in a large open meadow, where Heinrich Bermann ran back and forth and asked him: are you looking for the castle of the queen too? I've been expecting you for a long time. They climbed a spiral staircase. Heinrich was in front, so that all Georg could see was the hem of his overcoat, as it dragged behind. Above, on an enormous terrace from which one could see the city and the lake, the whole group had assembled. Leo, who had begun his lecture on minor chords, stopped as Georg arrived, came down from the rostrum, and led Georg himself to an open chair which stood in the first row next to Anna. Anna smiled happily when Georg appeared. She was young and radiant, in a splendid, low-necked evening dress. Right behind her sat a small boy with blond hair, in a sailor suit with a broad white collar, and Anna said: "That's him." Georg made a sign to be quiet, since it was supposed to be a secret. Meanwhile up front, Leo played the Chopin C minor Nocturne in demonstration of his theory, and behind him, the old Boesendorfer leaned against the wall, tall, thin, and kindly, in a yellow overcoat. Everyone left the concert hall in great throngs. Georg put Anna's theater coat around her shoulders and looked directly at the people all around. Then he sat with her in the wagon, kissed her, found great pleasure in it, and thought: if it could only be like this always! Suddenly they pulled up in front of the house in Mariahilf. Many students were waiting at the window upstairs, and waived. Anna got out, took leave of Georg with a sprightly face, and vanished behind the house door, which noisily slammed shut.

"Excuse me, just ten minutes," someone said. Georg looked up. The conductor stood in the door and repeated: "In ten minutes we'll be in Vienna."

"Thank you," Georg said and stood up with a somewhat cloudy head. He opened the window and was glad that the weather outside was nice. The fresh morning air awakened him completely. Yellow walls, signaling stations, gardens, telegraph poles, streets flew past, and finally the train stood in the station. A few minutes later Georg rode

in an open *fiaker* to his house, saw workers, shop girls, and office workers walking to their daily tasks, and heard the rattle of roll-shutters
overhead; and in the midst of all this clatter that was awaiting him, in
all the yearning which called him elsewhere, he experienced the profound comfort of coming home. As he entered his room, he felt safe.
The old writing table with the green cloth pulled over it, the malachite
paper weight, the glass ashtray with the etched-in horseman, the thin
lamp with the wide, green, milk-glass shade, the pictures of father and
mother in the small mahogany frames, the round, marble table in the
corner with the silver cigar case, on the wall a copy of the Prince of
the Palatinate by van Dyck, the tall bookcase with the olive colored
drapes;—everything greeted him warmly. And even the view, fine and
familiar, over the tree tops of the park to the towers and roofs, how
good it felt! Everything he saw shined forth with unexpected joy, and
it fell heavily on his heart that all this would be lost to him in but a
few weeks. And how long would it be until he had a home again, a
real home? He would gladly have tarried in his beloved room for a few
hours, but he had no time. He had to be in the country before noon.

He had thrown off his clothes and washed himself with delight in
the warm water of his white tub. In order not to fall asleep in the bath
he used a method which had often served him in the past. He thought
through a Bach fugue, note by note. He thought of his piano playing,
which had to be diligently practiced again. And scores to be read. Might
it not be the wisest thing to devote one more year to study? Not to
negotiate for, much less accept, a position which one might not be able
to fulfill? Better to stay here and work. Stay here? Where? They were
giving up the apartment. For a moment the thought went through his
mind to rent in the old house across from the grey church where he
had spent such blissful hours with Anna; and it seemed to him that he
remembered a long forgotten story, a youthful adventure, happy and a
little mysterious, from long ago—.

Refreshed and dressed in a brand new suit, the first light one he had
worn since the death of his father, he went back into his room. A letter
lay on the writing table, which the morning post had just brought. From
Anna. He read. It was only a few words: "You have returned, my darling! My greetings. I miss you. Don't keep me waiting too long. Your
Anna." . . .

Georg looked up. He didn't know himself what it was about this
short letter that struck him so strangely. Anna's letters had always, for

all their tenderness, contained something measured, almost conventional, and sometimes he had called her "The Decree" in jest. This one was written in a tone that reminded him of the passionate girl of former times, of the love he had almost forgotten; and a strangely unexpected uneasiness gripped his heart. He hurried down the steps, sat down in the nearest *fiaker*, and rode to the country. Soon he felt pleasantly distracted by the sight of the people on the street, who meant nothing to him; and later, as he approached the forest, the charm of the blue, summer day reassured him. Suddenly, sooner than Georg expected, the wagon stopped in front of the country house. Georg first looked involuntarily up to the balcony under the gable. A small table stood there, with a white cloth and a small basket on it. Oh yes, Therese stayed here for a few days. Only now did it reoccur to him. Therese . . . ! Where was that! He got out, released the wagon, and entered the front garden where, on a modest pedestal, between the beds of withered flowers, the blue angel stood. He entered the house. In the large central room Marie was just setting the table.

"The good lady is up in the garden," she said.

The door to the veranda stood open. The planks of the floor creaked under Georg's feet. The garden, with its scent and dampness, received him. It was the old garden. It had remained there silently for all those days that Georg had been away, just as it was at this moment; in the morning light, in the glare of the sun, in the evening shadows, in the darkness of the night; always the same. . . . The gravel path cut straight up through the meadow. There were children's voices from beyond the shrubs, on which red berries hung. And there, on the white bench, her arm on the back, very pale, in a flowing blue morning dress, was Anna. Yes, it was really her. Now she saw him. She wanted to get up. He saw this and realized at once that it would be hard for her. But why? Was the excitement straining her? Or was the great hour so near? He motioned her with his hand to remain seated. She really did sit back down, and had only her arms gently spread open toward him. Her eyes lit up happily. Georg walked very quickly, his soft grey hat in his hand, and now he was beside her.

"Finally," she said, and it was a voice that sounded as distant as those words in her letter this morning. He took her hands, shook them in a strangely awkward way, felt something rising in his throat, was unable to say anything, only nodded and smiled. And suddenly he knelt in front of her on the gravel, her hands in his, his head in her lap, felt how she gently pulled her hands back and laid them on his head;—and then he heard himself crying very softly. And it seemed to him like a vague and sweet dream, as if he lay as a boy at the feet of his mother, and this moment was already a memory, remote and painful, as he was experiencing it.

Eighth Chapter

Frau Golowski came out of the house. Georg watched her walk out onto the veranda from the upper end of the garden. Excited, he hurried toward her, but as if fending him off from a distance, she shook her head.

"Not yet?" Georg asked.

"The professor thinks," replied Frau Golowski, "before it gets dark."

"Before it gets dark," said Georg, and looked at the clock. "And now it's only three."

She reached her hand out sympathetically toward him, and Georg looked into her kindly, rather glazed eyes. The sheer white curtains of Anna's window had just been gently pulled back. The old Doctor Stauber appeared in the window opening, cast Georg a friendly reassuring glance, vanished again, and the curtains fell together. Frau Rosner sat at the round table in the large central room. From the veranda Georg could only make out the outline of her figure; her face was entirely in shadows. Again a whimper, then a loud groan came from the room where Anna was lying. Georg stared at the window, waited a while; then he turned away and went, for the hundredth time today, up the path to the upper end of the garden. Obviously she's already too weak to scream, he thought; and his heart ached. Two whole days and two whole nights she has lain in labor; and the third is drawing to a close,— and now it will go on until evening comes! Already on the evening of

216

the first day Doctor Stauber had brought another professor with him, who had been there twice yesterday and since noon today. While Anna had slept for a few minutes and the attendant watched at her bed, he had walked up and down in the garden with Georg and tried to explain the case to him in all its peculiarity. For the moment there was no cause for concern; one could still hear the heartbeat of the child completely clearly. The professor was still a rather young man, with a long blond beard, and his words trickled soft and kind, like drops of anesthetic. He spoke to the patient as to a child, stroked her forehead and hair, rubbed her hands, and gave her flattering nicknames. Georg had learned from the attendant that this young doctor was filled with the same devotion and patience at every sickbed. What a career, thought Georg, who, even during these three awful days, had gotten away to Vienna for a few hours, and who had managed, even last night, to get a full six hours of deep and dreamless sleep upstairs in the attic room while Anna writhed in pain.

He walked along the lilacs, which were past blooming, tore off some leaves, crushed them in his hand, and threw them down. In the garden on the other side of the low bushes, a lady in a black and white striped morning dress was walking. She looked earnestly and as though sympathetically at Georg. Oh yes, thought Georg, naturally she heard Anna's crying too, the day before yesterday, yesterday, and today. The whole place knew what was going on here; including the young girls from the ugly Gothic villa who once regarded him as a fascinating seducer; and it was altogether too funny that a strange man with a pointed red beard who lived two houses away had suddenly greeted him yesterday with understanding and esteem in the village.

Strange how one can make oneself popular with people, Georg thought. Only Frau Rosner's glances suggested that, if she didn't regard Georg as the sole culprit for all this trouble, in any case she thought him rather insensitive. He didn't hold it against the good and depressed woman. Naturally she couldn't suspect how much he loved Anna. It had not been that long that he knew it himself.

On the morning of his arrival, when he lifted his head from her lap after a long silent cry, she never questioned him, but he read in her painfully astonished eyes that she suspected the truth. And he thought he understood why she didn't ask. She must have felt how completely she had him back now, how from now on he belonged to her more than ever before. And over the next hours and days, as he told her about the time he had spent away from her, when he would casually and ingenuously mention that one woman's name which, among all the others, sounded new and portentous to her, she would smile in her light and mischievous way; but hardly differently than when he spoke of Else or Sissy, or of the girls in the blue dresses who looked into the piano room while he played.

He had been living in the villa for two weeks, felt well, and was in good spirits and ready for serious work. On the little table where not long before Therese's sewing basket had lain, each morning he spread out scores, works on music theory, music paper, and occupied himself with exercises in the principles of harmony and counterpoint. Sometimes he would lie in a meadow at the edge of the forest, read from a favorite book, allowing melodies to sing in him, daydreamed, and was delighted by the rustle of the trees and the sunshine. In the afternoons, while Anna was resting, he would read to her or they would talk. Often they would speak with tenderness and forethought about the little being who was soon to come into the world, but never about their own near or distant future. But when he sat by her bed, or walked arm-in-arm with her up and down in the garden, or sat at her side on the white bench under the pear tree, where the shining stillness of the late summer days rested over them, he knew that now they had come together firmly for all time, and that even the temporary separation that stood before them no longer had any power over this secure feeling of togetherness.

Only since the pain overtook her did she seem taken from him, to someplace where he could not follow her. He had sat for hours by her bed yesterday, and had held her hands in his. She had been patient as always, had asked with concern if everything was in order at home, had bid him to work, go walking like before, since he couldn't help her in any case, and assured him that she only loved him more now that she was in pain. And yet Georg sensed that she was not the same in these days as she had been. Especially when she cried out—like this morning in the worst pain—, then her soul was so far from him that he shuddered.

He was close to the house again. From Anna's room, in front of whose window the curtains were gently moving, came no sound. Old Doctor Stauber came out onto the veranda. Georg hurried over to him with a dry throat. "What's going on?" he asked hastily.

Doctor Stauber laid his hand on his shoulder: "Everything's going fine." A groan came from inside, grew louder, and became a wild, wrenching scream. Georg wiped his damp forehead and said to the doctor, with a bitter smile: "You call that going fine?"

Stauber shrugged his shoulders: "It stands written: with suffering shall you . . ."

Something inside of Georg rebelled. He had never believed in the God of childish piety, who would reveal himself as the fulfiller of the prayers of the poor, as avenger and forgiver of the sins of wretched humanity. Prayers and blasphemies could not seem anything but meager words from the mouths of men to the unnameable presence which he felt beyond his senses and above all understanding. Not when his mother died in a senseless, tormenting suffering, nor when his father died what was, to his understanding at least, a painless death, had he presumed to believe that his misfortune meant any more in the course of the world than the falling of leaves. He had never bowed in cowardly deference before any inscrutable decree, or foolishly grumbled against an ungracious fate hanging over him. Today was the first time that it seemed to him that somewhere in the clouds his affairs were being played out in some incomprehensible game. The scream inside had died away, and only groaning was audible.

"And the heartbeats?" asked Georg.

Doctor Stauber looked past Georg. "Ten minutes ago they were still clear."

Georg fended off a dreadful thought that came stalking out of the depths of his soul. He was healthy; she was healthy; two strong young people . . . could something like that be possible? Doctor Stauber put his hand on his shoulder again. "Go for a walk," he said, "we'll call you as soon as it's time." And he turned away.

Georg remained standing on the veranda for a moment. In the main room, which was beginning to grow dark in the late afternoon twilight, he saw Frau Rosner, completely withdrawn into herself, sitting on the sofa against the wall. He went off, walked around the house and then went up the wooden stairs to his attic room. He threw himself on the bed and closed his eyes; after a few minutes he stood up, walked back and forth in the room, but gave that up as the floor creaked. He walked onto the balcony. The score of *Tristan* lay thrown open on the table. Georg looked at the notes. It was the prelude to the third act. The sounds rang in his ear. Ocean waves broke with a muffled roar on a rocky shore, and from the sorrowful distance came the melody on the English horn. He looked over the pages into the silver-white splendor of the day. The sun rested over everything, over roofs, roads, gardens, hills, and forests. Dark blue, the sky stretched away, and the smell of the harvest came out of the distance. What was I doing a year ago?

thought Georg. I was in Vienna, completely alone. I suspected nothing.
I had sent her a song . . . "Your look to comfort me . . ." But I hardly
thought of her. And now she lies downstairs dying. . . . He was utterly
horrified. He had intended to think . . . she lies in pain, and instead it
had come to his lips as: she is dying. But why be so shocked. How childish. As if there were premonitions like that! And if there was really a
danger, and the doctors had to make a decision, of course they would
save the mother. Doctor Stauber had explained that to him a few days
ago. What is a child who has not even lived yet? Nothing. He had conceived it in a moment, without having wished it, without having even
thought of the possibility that he could become a father. Did he know
that he had not, a few weeks ago, in that dark hour of rapture, behind
closed shutters . . . become a father again, without having wished it,
without having even thought of the possibility; and perhaps, if it happened, without ever even knowing it?

He heard voices and looked below; the professor's driver held a servant girl by the arm, who resisted only slightly. Here too the ground
would perhaps be laid for a new human life, Georg thought, and turned
away in disgust. Then he went back into his room, filled his cigarette
case carefully from the box which sat on the table, and suddenly his
agitation seemed unfounded to him, even childish. And it occurred to
him: just as Anna is lying today, so my own mother was lying before
I was born. Did my father walk around worried like this? What if he
were here today, if he were still alive? Would I have told him all about
it? Would all this have happened if he were still alive? He thought of
beautiful carefree summer days on the Veldeser See. His comfortable
room in his father's villa floated through his memory, and in a vague,
almost dreamlike way, the bare attic room with the creaky floor in
which he now found himself became an image of his whole present existence, compared to the carefree and burdenless life of before. He remembered a serious conversation about the future that he had a few
days ago with Felician. Right after that, the discussion with a woman
from the country who had responded to the proposal for taking care
of the child came into his mind. She and her husband owned a small
farm near the railroad, only an hour from Vienna, and last year their
own daughter had died. She had promised that the child would be well
cared for with them, just as well as if it were not with strangers. And
as Georg thought about it, it suddenly seemed to him like his heart
stood still. Before it's dark, it will be here . . . the child. His child, for

which strangers were already waiting to take it away. He was so tired from the excitement of the last few days that his knees hurt. He remembered similar bodily experiences from before, on the night after his final exams, and in the hour when he learned about Labinski's suicide. Three days ago, when the pain started, how different, how happy and expectant he had been! Now he felt nothing but an unequalled disappointment, and the musty air of the attic room became more and more disagreeable to him. He lit a cigarette and went back out onto the balcony. The warm still air did him good. The sun still shone on Sommerhaidenweg, and over the wall of the cemetery could be seen a gilded cross.

He heard sounds below him. Steps? Yes, steps, and voices too. He left the balcony and room, and ran down the creaky wooden stairs. A door opened; hurried footsteps were in the hallway. The next moment he stood on the bottom-most step facing Frau Golowski. His heart stood still. He opened his mouth without asking. "Yes," she said, "a boy."

He took both her hands, felt like he was laughing across his whole face, and a rush of joy, hotter and more forceful than he ever expected, ran through his soul. Suddenly he noticed that the eyes of Frau Golowski were not shining as brightly as they should have. The rush of joy in him dammed up. Something tied up his throat. "Well?" he asked. And almost threateningly: "Is it alive?" "It took a breath . . . the professor hopes . . ." Georg pushed the woman aside; with three large steps he was in the large central room, and stood still as if spellbound. The professor, in a long, white, linen smock, held a tiny being in his arms and was moving it quickly back and forth. Georg remained fixed. The professor nodded to him and continued. He observed the tiny being he was holding with penetrating eyes. He laid it down on the table, over which a white cloth had been spread, and made vigorous movements with the child's limbs, rubbed its chest and face, then raised it several times in the air; and each time Georg saw how the child's head fell heavily onto its chest. Then the doctor laid the child down on the linen, listened at its chest, stood up, laid a hand on the tiny body, and motioned with the other for Georg to come over.

Georg, involuntarily holding his breath, walked up quite close to him. He looked first at the doctor, and then at the tiny being that lay on the white linen. Its eyes were wide open, unusually large, blue eyes, that had come from Anna. The face looked different than Georg had expected, not wrinkled and ugly like that of an old dwarf, no; it was really a human face, a beautiful, quiet, child's face; and Georg knew that these features were the image of his own.

The professor said softly: "I haven't heard heartbeats for an hour now."

Georg nodded. Then he asked hoarsely: "How is *she*?" "Quite well. But you shouldn't go in yet, Herr Baron."

"No," replied Georg, and shook his head. He stared at the shining, blue, motionless, tiny body, and knew that he stood before the corpse of his child. Still, he turned to the doctor and asked: "Nothing more to be done?"

The doctor shrugged his shoulders.

Georg breathed deeply and looked at the closed bedroom door. "Does she know yet—?" he asked the doctor.

"Not yet. Let's be satisfied for the moment that it's over. She's suffered a lot, the poor thing. I only regret that in the end it was all for nothing."

"You were expecting this, Herr Professor?"

"I've been afraid of this since this morning."

"But why . . . why?"

Softly and gently, the doctor replied: "A very unusual case, as I've already told you."

"You told me? . . ."

"Yes, I tried to explain to you that this possibility . . . It got strangled by the umbilical cord. Scarcely one or two percent of all births turn out like this." He fell silent. Georg stared at the child. It was true; the professor had prepared him; he just hadn't taken it seriously. Frau Rosner stood next to him with helpless eyes. Georg took her hand and they looked at each other, like the sorely tried, whom misfortune has made into companions. Then Frau Rosner dropped into a chair against the wall.

The professor said to Georg: "I want to look in on the mother now."

"Mother," Georg repeated and looked at him.

The doctor looked away.

"You want to tell her?" asked Georg.

"No, not yet. In any case she'll take it calmly. She asked several times in the course of the day if it was still alive. It won't upset her as badly as you imagine, Herr Baron . . . at least not during the first hours and days. You mustn't forget what she's gone through."

He squeezed Georg's limply hanging hand and went. Georg stood

there motionless, staring constantly at the tiny being, and it appeared
to him like an image of unexpected loveliness. He touched cheeks,
shoulders, arms, hands, fingers. How mysteriously complete it all was.
And now it lay there dead, without ever having lived, destined to travel
from one darkness, through a mindless nothingness, into another. There
lay this sweet, tiny body, which was ready for existence, and which now
could not move. There shone large, blue eyes, as if in longing to drink
in the light of the sky, blind as death before they had ever seen a single
ray. There opened, as if thirsty, a tiny, round mouth, which would never
be permitted to drink from the breast of a mother. There stared this
pale child's face, with fully formed human features, that would never
receive and experience the kiss of mother or father. How he loved this
child! How he loved it, now that it was too late. A bound up feeling
of desperation rose in his throat. He could not cry. He looked around.
No one was in the room, and in the next one all was still. He had no
wish to go into that other room, but no fear either; he only felt that it
would have made no sense. His eyes went back to the dead child, and
suddenly the trembling question went through him if it had to be true?
Couldn't they all be mistaken? The doctor as well as the inexperienced.
He held his flattened hand over the open lips of the child, and it seemed
to him that something cool wafted toward him. Then he held both
hands on the child's chest, and again it seemed to him that air moved
in the tiny body. But he soon realized: it was not the breath of life that
had blown on him. He bent down and his lips touched the child's cool
forehead. Something strange that he had never experienced before rip-
pled through his body all the way down to his toes. Now he knew: the
game up there was over for him; his child was dead. He raised his head
slowly and turned away. The light of the garden beckoned him outside.
He went onto the veranda and saw Doctor Stauber and Frau Rosner
sitting on the bench against the wall. Both silent. They looked at him.
He turned away, as if he didn't know them, and went into the garden.
The shadow of the house fell obliquely across the grass; further on, the
sun was still up, but feeble, as if lacking the strength to shine through
the air. What did this light want to remind him of, this light which was
the sun, but did not shine, this blue in the sky, which was the heavens,
but gave no blessing? Of what the silence of this garden, which should
be trusted and consoling to him, but which today received him like
something strange and inhospitable? Gradually it occurred to him that
a short while ago a heavy and unfamiliar twilight glow had come upon
him in a dream, and had filled his soul with a sadness he could not

understand. What now? he said to himself, looked for no answer, and knew only that something unforeseen and irrevocable had happened that must change for all time his view of the world. He thought of the day his father died. A wild pain had seized him then; but he had been able to cry, and the world had not, in a moment, grown dark and empty. His father had lived, had been young once, had worked, loved, had children, experienced joy and pain. And the mother who had born him had not suffered for nothing. And if he himself had to die today, however prematurely, he still had a life behind him, filled with light and sounds, happiness and sorrow, hope and fear, filled with all the substance of the world. And if Anna had died today, in the hour when she had given life to a new being, she would have fulfilled her destiny and her end would have had a horrible, but profound meaning. But this that had happened to his child was senseless, repulsive, a mockery from somewhere where one could not question or get an answer. Why, why all this? What had all these past months meant, with all their dreams, cares, and hopes? Then he suddenly knew that the expectation of the wonderful moment when his child would be born had always been, on every day, even the most commonplace, empty, and careless, in the depths of his soul; and he felt ashamed, impoverished, miserable.

He stood at the garden fence and looked up toward the edge of the forest, to his bench, on which he had often rested, and it seemed to him as if before, the forest, meadow, and bench had been his possessions, and that he must now give them up also, like so much else. In a corner of the garden stood a dark-grey and neglected summer house with three small window openings and a narrow doorway. He had never liked it and had only been in it once for a few moments. Today it beckoned him in. He sat down on the cracked bench and felt suddenly safe and calmed, as if everything that had happened were less true, or in some inconceivable way, repairable. But this illusion soon vanished again, and he left the inhospitable room and went out into the open. I have to go back into the house, he thought wearily, and did not entirely understand that in the dark room which he saw from here behind the veranda, as if in the bottomless sky, the corpse of his child would be lying. Slowly he went down. Anna's mother was standing on the veranda with a man. Georg recognized the old Rosner. He stood there in an overcoat, having laid his hat on the table in front of him, wiped his handkerchief across his head, and his red-ringed eyes twitched. He walked toward Georg and extended his hand.

"It has turned out differently," he said, "than we had all expected or hoped."

Georg nodded. Then he remembered that in recent weeks the old man had been having some problems with his heart, and inquired about his condition.

"Thank you for asking Herr Baron, I'm a little better; just climbing stairs gives me some problems."

Georg noticed that the glass door to the central room was closed. "Excuse me," he said to the old Rosner, walked directly over to the door, opened it, and then closed it quickly behind him. Frau Golowski and Doctor Stauber stood by the table and spoke to one another. He walked up to them and they suddenly fell silent.

"Well?" he then asked.

Doctor Stauber said: "We were talking about . . . the formalities. Frau Golowski will be kind enough to take care of all that."

"Thank you," replied Georg, and gave Frau Golowski his hand. "All that," he thought. A casket, a burial, a report to the municipal office: a son born to the unmarried Anna Rosner, died the same day. Nothing of the father, naturally. Yes, his role was finished. Only now? Had it not been over from that very second when he by chance had become a father?

He looked down at the table. The linen had been pulled over the tiny body. Oh, how soon, he thought bitterly. Shall I never be allowed to see it again? It will be permitted one more time. He pulled the cloth back a little from the body and held it up. He saw a pale child's face that was well known to him, except that the eyes had been closed by someone since before. The old floor clock in the corner ticked. Six o'clock. It hadn't even been an hour since his child had been born and had died; and already the fact stood with such irrevocable finality as if it could never have been otherwise.

He felt something gently touching his shoulder.

"She took it calmly," said Doctor Stauber, who was standing behind him.

Georg let the linen fall over the face of the child, and turned his head to the side. "She knows already? . . ."

Doctor Stauber nodded. Frau Golowski had turned away.

"Who told her?" asked Georg.

"No one had to tell her," replied Doctor Stauber. "Isn't that right," he turned to Frau Golowski.

She reported: "When I went in to her, she just looked at me, and then I saw that she already knew."

"And what did she say?"

"Nothing. Nothing at all. She had her eyes turned toward the window and was completely quiet. She asked me where you had gone, Herr Baron, and what you were doing."

Georg breathed deeply. The door to Anna's room opened. The professor, in a black coat, came out. "She's quite calm," he said to Georg. "You can go in and see her now."

"Did she talk to you about it?" asked Georg.

The professor shook his head. Then he said: "Unfortunately I have to go back to town. You'll forgive me, won't you? I hope things will be all right now. In any case I'll be back early in the morning. Good luck, dear Herr Baron." He squeezed his hand sympathetically. "You're going back with me, aren't you, Doctor Stauber?"

"Yes," said Doctor Stauber. "I just want to say *adieu* to Anna." He went.

Georg turned to the professor. "May I ask you something?"

"Of course."

"I would really like to know, Herr Professor, if it might only be an illusion. But it seems to me"—and he lifted the cloth again away from the little body—"as if this child did not look like a newborn at all. More beautiful to some extent. I thought that the faces of newborns were more wrinkled, more ugly. I don't know any more if I saw one myself once, or if I just read about it."

"You're not mistaken," answered the professor, "precisely in cases of this sort, and in more happy outcomes, the features of the children are not distorted, yes, sometimes even beautiful." He regarded the tiny face with objective sympathy, nodded a couple of times, "too bad, too bad . . . ," put the cloth back again, and Georg knew that he had seen the face of his child for the last time. What would it have been named? Felician. . . . Farewell, little Felician.

Doctor Stauber came out of the next room and softly closed the door. "Anna is waiting for you," he said to Georg. Georg shook hands with him, and once more with the professor, nodded to Frau Golowski, and went into the next room.

The attendant got up from Anna's side and left the room. Across from the door hung a mirror in which Georg saw a young, elegant man, who was pale and smiling. Anna lay in her bed, which stood out in the middle of the room, with large clear eyes that looked toward Georg. How can I stand here in front of her, he thought. He pushed the armchair up close to her bed with a certain formality, sat down, took her hand, lifted it to his face, and kissed her fingers long and almost ardently.

Anna spoke first. "You were in the garden?" she asked.

"Yes, I was in the garden."

"I saw you coming down from up there a while ago."

"You shouldn't talk, Anna. Doesn't it tire you?"

"A few words, oh no. But you could just talk to me. . . ."

He continued to hold her hand in his, and looked at her fingers. Then he said: "Did you know that there was a little summer house at the upper end of the garden? Yes, of course you knew. . . . I just mean, we never really paid attention to it."

"I was in it a few times during the first few days," Anna said. "It isn't very nice."

"No, that's for sure."

"Did you get any work done this morning?" she then asked.

"How could I, Anna?"

She shook her head gently. "And it was going so well for you these last few days."

"Yes, that's really true, Anna; you've been very inconsiderate." He smiled; she remained serious.

"You were in the city yesterday?" she asked.

"You knew that."

"Did you get any letters? I mean important ones?"

"You really shouldn't talk so much, Anna; I'll tell you all about it. So: I found no letters of any importance. Nothing from Detmold either. By the way, I'm going to see Professor Viebiger again while I'm here. But we could really talk about these things another time, don't you think? And as far as work is concerned . . . I studied *Tristan* a little more this morning. I really know it down to the smallest detail. I could trust myself to conduct it today, if I had to."

She was silent and looked at him.

He remembered the evening he had sat with her at the Munich Opera, as though enveloped in a transparent veil of beloved sounds. But he didn't bring it up.

It grew dark. He began to lose sight of Anna's features.

"Are you still going back to the city tonight?" she asked.

He hadn't even thought of it. But now it seemed to him that a sort of deliverance winked at him. Yes, he wanted to. What could he still do out here anyway? But he didn't answer right away.

Anna began again. "I imagine you'll probably want to talk to your brother."

"Yes, I really want to do that. And you'll be asleep soon?"

"I hope so."

"How tired you must be," he said, as he rubbed her hand.

"No, it's really strange. I'm so awake . . . I can hardly tell you how awake I am. It's like I've never been so wide awake in my whole life. And at the same time I know that I'll sleep deeper than I ever have before . . . as soon as I close my eyes."

"Of course you will. But can I stay with you for a while yet? What I'd like most is to sit with you until you've fallen asleep."

"No Georg, as long as you're here I can't fall asleep. But stay a little while yet. It's good."

He continued to hold her hand and looked out into the garden, which now lay completely in evening shadows.

"You didn't go up to the Auhof very often this year?" Anna asked casually, as if just to talk about something.

"Oh yes, almost every day. Didn't I tell you?—I think Else is going to marry James Wyner and go to England with him."

He knew that she wasn't thinking of Else, but of someone entirely different. And he asked himself: does she think—that's to blame?

A mild breeze blew in from outside. Children's voices could be heard. Georg looked out. He saw the white bench shining under the pear tree and thought of how Anna had waited up there for him in a flowing dress, the fruit-laden branches above her, overflowing with the gentle wonder of her motherhood. And he asked himself: was it already decided then that it would end like this? Or was it determined in the moment that we first embraced each other? The professor's remark went through his mind, that one to two percent of all births ended like this. Therefore, as long as people have been born it has been so: that of every hundred, one or two must die in this senseless way, in the same moment that they emerged into the light! And so-and-so many must die in the first year, and so many in the flower of youth, and so many as men, and again a certain number end their own lives, like Labinski, and with so-and-so many the attempt will fail, like with Oskar Ehrenberg. Why look for reasons? Some law governs it all, beyond understanding, relentless, against which we men may not protest. Who can say: why does this happen to me? If it didn't happen to him, it would happen to someone else. Innocent or guilty, like him. It happens to one or two percent; that is the divine law. The children who are laughing in the garden over there, they were permitted to live. Permitted? No, they *had* to live, just like his had to die after its first breath, destined to travel from one darkness, through a mindless nothingness, into another.

Outside it was dusk, and inside it was almost night already. Anna lay silent and motionless. Her hand was not moving in Georg's. But as Georg got up he saw that her eyes were open. He bent down, hesitated a moment, then put his arm around her neck and kissed her on the lips, which were hot and dry and did not respond to his touch. Then he left. In the next room the hanging lamp was burning over the table on which earlier the dead child had lain. Now the green tablecloth was spread out, as though nothing had happened. The door to the room in which Frau Golowski lived was open. The light of a candle shined from it, and Georg knew that his child slept its first and last sleep.

Frau Golowski and Frau Rosner sat next to each other on the sofa next to the wall, silent, as if cowering together. Georg went over to them. "Your Herr husband has gone?" he turned to Frau Rosner.

"Yes, he went back to the city with the Herr Doctors," she replied, and looked at him as if questioningly.

"She's calm," Georg answered her look. "I think she will be asleep soon."

"Wouldn't you like to have something to eat," asked Frau Golowski. "Since one o'clock you haven't . . ."

"Thank you, no. I'm going to the city now. I want to talk to my brother. And I'm expecting important letters. I'll be back early tomorrow morning." He excused himself, went to his room, brought the score of *Tristan* in from the balcony, took his overcoat and cane, lit a cigarette, and left the house. He felt freer as soon as he was on the street. A tremendous episode lay behind him. It was over in an unfortunate way, but over all the same. And for Anna things would go fine now. Of course there was always the ominous law of percentages. But it was clear that now the possibility of a bad outcome was, precisely by the law of probability, much smaller than if the child had survived.[1]

He crossed the sprawling village with hasty steps, wanting to think about nothing, and regarded each individual house that he passed with deliberate attentiveness. They were all low, and for the most part rather sad and poor. Behind them, in the evening haze, tiny gardens led up to vineyards, fields, and meadows. At an oblong table in an inn garden almost empty of people, a little group of musicians sat playing a sorrowful waltz on a violin, guitar, and harmonica. Later he encountered some imposing country houses, and he looked through open windows into

1. In 1894, Schnitzler began a prolonged relationship with a young singer named Marie Reinhard. They did not marry, but lived together for several years. In 1897 a child was born to them, a boy, but dead. Marie died suddenly in 1899 of a ruptured appendix.

respectable, well-lit rooms in which set tables were standing. He finally sat down in a friendly inn garden, as far as possible from the other not very numerous guests, had supper, and soon an agreeable weariness came over him. He nearly dozed off in his corner of the horse-drawn wagon. Only when the wagon rode through the bustling streets did he come to himself again, and he contemplated what had happened with painful, but dry clarity. He got out and walked home through the oppressive humidity of the Stadtpark. Felician was not home. He found a telegram lying on the writing table. It was from Detmold and read: "We respectfully inquire if it would be possible for you to appear here in the next three days. Of course this invitation shall be regarded, for the moment, as being without further obligation for either party. In any case, travel expenses will be reimbursed. Most respectfully, Court Theater Management." Next to it lay the red blank form for the reply.

Georg was exhausted. How should he respond? The telegram obviously indicated that a *Kapellmeister's* position had opened. Should he try to get a postponement? He could certainly go for a meeting in a week, and then come right back again. It tired him to think about it. At least the matter could wait until morning. And if that was too late, then it wouldn't have changed anything substantial anyway. He was welcome as a guest in any case; he already knew that. Perhaps it would be better not to tie himself down . . . to work somewhere without obligations or responsibilities, and then, to be prepared for the following year. But what sort of trivial considerations were these compared to the tremendous event that had occurred in his life today? He took the malachite and put it on the telegram. What now? . . . he asked himself. Go to the club to find Felician? But that was not the place to tell him what had happened. It would be best to stay at home and wait for him. It was even a little tempting to get undressed and lie down for a rest. But he wouldn't be able to sleep yet. So he hit on the idea of finally bringing a little order to his papers again. He opened a desk drawer, pulled out bills and letters, and entered remarks in his notebook. The noise from the street came in through the open window as if from a long way off. He thought back of how, in the previous summer, after his father's death, he had read the letters of his dead parents at this same spot, and how this same noise of the city and this same smell of the park had streamed in to him as today. The year which had gone by since then stretched out in his tired mind into an eternity, shrank again into a short span of time, and something whispered in his soul: for what . . . for what. His child was dead. It will be buried out there in the cemetery by the Sommerhaidenweg; there it will rest in consecrated ground from the tiring path it was destined to travel from one darkness, through a mindless nothingness, into another. It would lie beneath a tiny cross, as if it had lived and suffered through a human fate. . . . As if it had lived? It really had lived, from the moment its heart had begun to beat inside the womb of its mother. No, before that. . . . It had belonged to the land of the living from the moment that its mother's womb had received it. And Georg thought of how many children were destined to perish even sooner than his own, how many, wanted and unwanted, die in the first days of their lives, without even their own mothers suspecting. And while he mused at his writing table, with closed eyes, between sleeping and waking, he saw little shimmering crosses rising on tiny hills, as if in a cemetery on a game board, with a reddish-yellow doll's sun shining over it. Suddenly this picture became the cemetery at Cadenabbia. Georg sat like a little boy on the stone enclosing wall and turned suddenly to look down toward the sea. There, a woman, whose face he tried almost painfully and in vain to recognize, rode in a narrow, very long boat with sulphur-yellow sails, sitting motionless on the rowing plank, with a green shawl around her shoulders.

The bell rang. Georg jumped up. What was that? Oh yes, there was no one there to answer. The servant had recently been let go, and the porter woman who was still with his brother wasn't home at the moment. Georg went to the entry way and opened. Heinrich Bermann stood in the hall. "I saw light in your room from below," he said. "It was a good thing for me to come by the house first. Actually I was on my way to see you in the country."

Was he really speaking so excitedly, Georg thought, or does it just sound that way to me? He invited him in and offered him a chair.

"Thank you, thank you, but I'd rather walk around. No, don't light the overhead light, the desk lamp is enough.—By the way, how are things going with you out there?"

"The child was born this afternoon," he replied calmly. "But unfortunately it was dead."

"Stillborn?"

"I don't know if one could call it that," responded Georg with a bitter smile, "since the doctor said that it was supposed to have taken a breath. The labor lasted for three days. It was awful. Now it's over."

"Dead. I'm really sorry, believe me." He gave Georg his hand.

"It was a boy," Georg said, "and strange to say, very beautiful, not like newborns normally look." Then he explained how he had stopped

for a while in the inhospitable garden house that he had never been in
before, and how strangely the lighting of the landscape had changed
suddenly. "It was a light," he said, "like regions sometimes have in
dreams, completely undetermined, . . . dusky, . . . but rather sad." As
he spoke, he knew that he would explain the whole thing differently to
Felician.

Heinrich sat in the corner of the divan and let Georg talk. Then he
began: "It's strange, all this stirs me very much, of course, and yet . . . it
relieves me at the same time."

"Relieves you?"

"Yes. Like when certain things that I have to be afraid of now suddenly seem less likely."

"What kinds of things?"

Without listening to him, Heinrich continued talking, with clenched
teeth. "Or is it only because I'm confronting someone else's pain? Or
just because I'm somewhere else, in a strange house? That would be
possible. Haven't you noticed that even one's own death seems something highly unlikely when one is, for example, on a trip; sometimes
just on a walk? People are always subject to such incomprehensible self-
deceptions." He had gotten up, gone to the window, and turned his face
away. Georg, leaning on the writing table, waited expectantly for what
he would hear. After a few seconds, as if he had regained his composure, Heinrich turned back to him, remained standing at the window,
with both hands turned backward propped on the sill, and said, short
and hard: "It's possible that the young lady you recently became acquainted with through me has committed suicide. Please don't make
such a shocked face. You know that it could be inferred from many of
her letters that she wanted to do it."

"Well, so," said Georg.

Heinrich put his hand up defensively. "I never took it seriously
either. But a letter came this morning that, how shall I put it, had an
uncanny ring of truth about it. Actually there was nothing in it that
she hadn't already written me ten or twenty times, but the tone . . . the
tone . . . short and sweet, I am as good as convinced that this time it
has happened. That perhaps at this very moment . . . ," he paused and
looked down.

"No Heinrich." Georg went over to him and put his hand on his
shoulder. "No," he continued more firmly, "I absolutely don't believe
it. I spoke to her, only a couple of weeks ago. You know that. And
I absolutely did not have the impression that . . . I saw her in a com-

edy . . . if you had seen her acting, in this satirical farce, you wouldn't believe it either, Heinrich! She just wants to get even with you for your cruelty. Maybe without knowing it. Maybe she's sometimes convinced herself that she can't go on living, but since she's held out until now . . . Yes, if she'd done it right away . . . "

Heinrich shook his head impatiently. "Listen Georg, I telegraphed the summer theater. I asked if she was still there, rather like it concerned a role for her, rehearsal arrangements for a new piece of mine, or something like that. I waited at home—until now . . . but there's still no answer. If nothing comes, or nothing satisfactory, then I'm going there."

"Well, why didn't you simply ask if she . . ."

"If she had killed herself? One doesn't like to make a fool of oneself, Georg! I could have asked that about every third day. . . . Of course that wouldn't have been without a certain grotesque humor."

"Now look, you don't believe it yourself."

"I want to go home now and see if there's a telegram. *Adieu* Georg. Forgive me. I just couldn't stand it at home any more. . . . I'm really sorry that I've burdened you with my own affairs at a time like this. Again, forgive me. . . . "

"You didn't know. . . . And even if you had known . . . With me it's . . . a finished story, so too speak. In my case there's unfortunately absolutely nothing more to be done." He looked tensely out of the window over the tops of the trees, at the dark towers and roofs which rose through the faint red glow of the evening city. Then he said: "I'll go with you, Heinrich. I can't start anything here at home. I mean—if my company isn't disagreeable to you."

"Disagreeable? . . . Georg! . . . " He squeezed his hand.

They left. At first they walked along the park and were silent. Georg remembered a walk with Heinrich along the avenue of the Prater last fall, and right after that the May evening when Anna Rosner appeared in the Waldstein Garden later than the others came to his mind, and Frau Ehrenberg had whispered to him: "I invited her for you." Yes, for him! Had that evening not taken place, Anna would never have become his lover, and none of this that weighed on him today would ever have happened. Or was some sort of law at work here too? Certainly! So-and-so many children must be born every year, and a certain number of them out of wedlock. And the good Frau Ehrenberg had imagined that it was within her discretion to invite Fraulein Anna Rosner for the Baron von Wergenthin!

"Anna is out of danger now?" asked Heinrich.

"I hope so," answered Georg. Then he talked about the pain she suffered, about her patience, and her goodness. He had a need to portray her as a complete angel; as though he could thereby atone for some of the guilt he felt toward her.

Heinrich nodded. "She seems to be one of the few women who's really suited for motherhood. It isn't true that there are a lot of that sort. To make children—they're all here for that,—but to be a mother! And precisely she had to go through this! It never entered my mind that something like this could happen."

Georg shrugged his shoulders. Then he said: "I had expected to see you out there one more time. I think you promised something of the kind when you had supper with us a week ago with Therese."

"Oh yes, what a quarrel we had, Therese and I. On the way home it got even worse. Comical. We went on foot all the way to the city. We had such a brawl that the people who passed us must for sure have taken us for a pair of lovers."

"And who turned out right in the end?"

"Right? Does it ever happen that one is right? One talks only to convince oneself, not the other one. Just think if in the end Therese had realized that a reasonable man could never join a party! Or if I had to agree with her that my lack of membership in a party meant a lack of world-view, as she asserted! We could have both shot each other on the spot. What do you say anyway about this talk of a world-view? As if a world-view were something other than the will and ability to really see the world, that is, to observe without being confused by a preconceived notion, without the compulsion to derive a new law from an experience, or to adapt it to an existing one. But world-view doesn't mean anything to people but a higher kind of resoluteness—resoluteness in the face of the eternal, so to speak. Or they talk about gloomy or cheerful world-views, even about the hues in which the world appears by virtue of their temperaments and in chance personal experiences. People with open minds have a world-view, and those with restricted ones don't. That's the way it is. One certainly doesn't have to be a philosopher to have a world-view. . . . Perhaps one even can't be one. In any case, philosophy has nothing in the slightest to do with world-view. Of the philosophers, they have all known that they represent nothing else but a sort of poet. Kant believed in the thing-in-itself, Schopenhauer in the world as will and representation, like Shakespeare in *Hamlet* and Beethoven in the *Ninth*. They knew that now another work of art was in the world, but they surely never imagined that they had discovered a final 'Truth.' Every philosophical system, if it has rhythm and depth, is one more possession in this world. But what would that change in the relationship between the world and a man who is blessed with an open mind." He continued talking, more and more excitedly, and worked himself, so it seemed to Georg, into a state of feverish confusion. Georg remembered how Heinrich had once dreamed of a carrousel which wound in spirals higher and higher above the ground to finally arrive at the top of a tower.

They took the way through sparsely populated and modestly lit suburban streets. Georg felt as if he were walking in a strange city. Suddenly a house looked strangely familiar to him, and he only then realized that they were going by the Rosners' house. There was light in the dining room. Probably the old man was sitting there alone, or in the company of his son. Is it possible, Georg thought, that Anna will be sitting there again in a few weeks, at the same table with father, mother, and brother, as if nothing had happened? That she would again sleep, night after night, behind that window with the now closed blinds, go to her poor lessons day after day from this house—that she would take up this whole wretched life again as if nothing, absolutely nothing, had changed? No! She must not go back to her family; that would be senseless. She must come with him, live together with him, to whom she belonged. The telegram from Detmold! He had almost forgotten about it. He had to talk to her about it. Here was hope and prospect! In a little town like that life was inexpensive. And Georg's personal legacy would not be used up so quickly. One could risk it. Besides, the position there was only a beginning. Perhaps a better one would soon come along, in a different, larger city; overnight, unexpected, like such things always happen, a success would be there, one would have a name, not only as a conductor, but as a composer, and it would scarcely be two or three years before they could get the child back. . . . The child! . . . How the thought stormed through his mind. . . . Could one forget even that for a moment?

Heinrich went on talking; it was quite obvious that he wanted to distract himself. He continued to annihilate the philosophers. He went so far as to degrade them from poets into playactors. Every system—every philosophy and every morality—was word play. A flight from the turbulent fullness of appearances to the puppet stare of the categories. But that was just what people wanted. That was the source of all philosophy, all religion, all the laws of custom! They were constantly engaged in this flight. A few, only a few, were given the immense inner capacity to perceive each experience as new and individual—the strength to endure that in each moment they stood, as it were, in a new world. And yet: only to those who overcome the cowardly impulse to reduce every experience to words, only to them does life—the diverse unity—the wondrous, appear in its true form.

Georg had the feeling that Heinrich was only trying to achieve one thing with all his talking: to shake off any responsibility for himself toward a higher law, by recognizing none. And he felt, as though in a growing opposition to Heinrich's astonishingly drivelling behavior, how in his own soul the picture of the world, which had threatened to crumble to pieces for him a few hours ago, began gradually to come together again. Until now he had rebelled against the senselessness of the fate that had struck him today, but now he began vaguely to suspect that even that which seemed to him a tragic accident, had not descended on his head from out of nowhere, but that it had come to him from a predetermined, but dark path, like something remotely visible that approached him from far down the road, and which he was accustomed to calling necessity.

They were in front of the house in which Heinrich lived. The concierge stood in the doorway and informed them that he had just put a telegram in Heinrich's room.

"Oh?" Heinrich said casually and went slowly up the steps. Georg followed. Heinrich lit a candle in the anteroom. The telegram lay on a tiny table. Heinrich opened it, held it up to the flickering light, read for himself, and then turned to Georg. "She was expected this morning for a rehearsal, and did not appear." He took the candlestick in his hand and went into the next room, followed by Georg, put the light on the writing table, and walked back and forth in the room. Georg heard piano playing across the dark courtyard through the open window. "There's nothing else in the telegram?" he asked.

"No. But obviously she didn't only fail to appear at the rehearsal, but wasn't in her room either. Otherwise they would have telegraphed that she was sick, or at least a word of explanation. Yes, dear Georg,"— he breathed deeply—"this time it has happened."

"Why? There's no proof of that, hardly a clue."

Heinrich cut off the comments of his friend with one of his short waves of the hand. Then he looked at the clock and said: "There isn't another train today. . . . Yes . . . how should one—how should one begin?" He paused, stood still, and suddenly said: "I'll go to her mother. Yes. That's the best. . . . Maybe, maybe . . ."

They left the house. They took a wagon at the next corner.

"Did her mother know anything?" asked Georg.

"Oh God," said Heinrich. "Only what mothers care to know. It's unbelievable how little people think about what goes on next to them unless it's brought to their attention by some extraneous cause. And most people never even suspect what they all know in the depths of their souls, without admitting it. The good woman will be rather surprised when I turn up so suddenly. . . . I haven't seen her for a long time."

"What will you say to her?"

"Yes, what will I say to her?" repeated Heinrich, and chewed his cigar. "Listen, I have a great idea. You come with me, Georg, and I'll introduce you as a director, yes? You're just traveling through here and have to leave tonight at eleven on a special train to Petersburg, have heard somewhere that the lady was staying in Vienna, and that I, as an old acquaintance of the house, have been so kind as to offer an introduction."

"Are you inclined to put on an act like that?" asked Georg.

"Oh, excuse me Georg! All this isn't necessary at all. I could simply ask the old lady if she's heard a report . . . what do you say . . . on what the humidity is tonight?"

They rode along the Ring, past the resounding palace court, through the streets of the city. Georg was strangely tense. What if the actress was really sitting calmly at home with her mother, he thought. He felt that it would mean a sort of disappointment for him. Then he was ashamed of this emotion. Is this whole story then nothing but a distraction for me, he thought. What happens to other people . . . is rarely more, Nuernberger would say. . . . A singular way of distracting oneself, to forget about the death of the child. . . . But what could one do? I can't change any more. I'll be leaving in a few days. Thank God.

The wagon stopped in front of a house near the Prater intersection. A train was just rumbling over the viaduct across the way, under which the avenue to the Prater lay in darkness. Heinrich sent the wagon away. "Thanks a lot," he said to Georg. "Good night."

"I'll wait here for you."

"Will you really? Well, I really appreciate it."

He vanished through the house door. Georg walked up and down. Despite the late hour it was still rather busy on the street. The sound of a military band carried toward him from the Prater. A man and a woman walked past him. The man carried a sleeping child on his arm, which had wrapped its arms around its father's neck. Georg thought

about the garden in Grinzing, about the dirty little thing that had
stretched its hands out to him from his mother's arms. Had he really
been touched at the time, like Nuernberger said? No, he wasn't really
touched. Something else perhaps. The vague consciousness of standing
in the continuous chain that stretched from ancestor to offspring, held
fast by both hands, to have a part in the universal human destiny. Now
he suddenly stood detached again, alone . . . as if scorned by a wonder
whose call he had heard without devotion. It struck ten o'clock from
a nearby church tower. Five hours ago, Georg thought. And how distant it all was. Now he would be able to go into the world freely again,
like before. . . . Could he really?

Heinrich came out of the house. The door closed behind him. "Nothing," he said. "Her mother doesn't suspect anything. I asked for her
address as if I had something important to tell her. I had just come from
the Prater, and it occurred to me . . . well, and so on. A nice old woman.
Her brother sat at the table with a drawing board and was drawing a
knight's castle with countless towers from an illustrated magazine."

"Now be sincere for once," said Georg. "If you could save her by
forgiving her, wouldn't you be able to do it?"

"Yes Georg, haven't you noticed yet that it's not a matter of whether
or not I want to forgive her? But just think, if I had simply ceased to
love her, which can sometimes happen, without one's having been betrayed. Think, if a woman whom you loved were to pursue you, a
woman whose contact you were afraid of for some reason, and were
to swear to you that she would kill herself if you scorned her. Would
you be obligated to give in to her? Could you reproach yourself in the
slightest if she were really to go to her death for unrequited love, so to
speak? Would you feel yourself to be her murderer? That's just crazi-
ness, isn't it? So if you think that it's my so-called conscience that
bothers me, you're mistaken. It's simply concern for the fate of a person
who was once close to me, and to a certain extent still is. The uncertainty . . ." Suddenly he stared fixedly in one direction.

"What is it?" asked Georg.

"Don't you see. A telegraph messenger. He just went up to the house
door." Before the man could ring, Heinrich was next to him and said
a few words that Georg could not make out. The messenger appeared
to make objections, Heinrich replied, and Georg, who had gone closer,
could now hear. "I've been waiting here by the door for you, because
the doctor urgently asked me to. This telegram contains . . . perhaps . . .
sad news . . . and it could be the death of my mother. . . . Well, if you

don't believe me, just ring, I'll go in the house with you." But he already had the dispatch in his hand, opened it hastily, and read by the light of a street lamp. His face remained completely motionless. Then he folded the dispatch up again, handed it to the messenger, put a few silver coins in his hand and said: "You'll have to deliver it yourself."

The messenger was put off, but softened by the drink money. Heinrich rang the bell and turned away. "Let's go," he said to Georg. They went silently down the street. After a couple of minutes Heinrich said: "It's happened."

Georg was more shocked than he expected. "Is it possible . . ." he cried out.

"Yes," said Heinrich. "She drowned herself in the lake. In the lake where you stayed a few days this summer," he added, in a tone as if Georg now, in some way, carried some part of the responsibility for what had happened too.

"What was in the telegram?" Georg asked.

"It's from the director. He had just received news that an accident had befallen her on a boat trip. He requested further instructions from the mother." He spoke coolly, hard, as if he were reading a notice in a newspaper.

"The poor woman! But Heinrich, shouldn't you . . ."

"What? . . . To her? What could I do for her?"

"Who besides you can stand by her now . . . and should?"

"Who besides me?" He stood still. "You think, because it has happened on account of me, so to speak? I fervently declare to you herewith that I feel myself totally unresponsible. The boat from which she drowned herself, and the waves that received her couldn't feel less guilty than I do. I'll hold to that.—But that I should go to her mother . . . yes, you're completely right." And he turned again in the direction of the house. "If you want," said Georg, "I could stay with you." "What are you thinking, Georg. Go on home. What more could I ask of you. And give my greetings to Anna and tell her how sorry I am . . . well, you know. . . . Here we are. Just give me a few seconds, before I . . ." He remained standing there silently. Then he began again, and his features grew distorted: "I want to tell you something Georg. The following: It is a great good fortune that in certain moments one doesn't know what has really happened to one. If one so clearly understood the dreadfulness of such moments all at once, like one will experience it later in one's memory, or like one has felt it in expectation—one would go crazy. You too Georg, yes you too. And some people really do go crazy.

Those are probably the people who have the gift of being able to experience clearly immediately.—My sweetheart has drowned herself, do you
hear? There's nothing else to say. Has anything like this ever really happened before? Oh no. You surely believe that you have read or heard
something similar. It isn't true. Today is the first time . . . the first time
since the world began, that such a thing has happened."

The door opened and closed again. Georg stood alone on the street.
His head spun; his heart was oppressed. He walked a few steps, then
took a wagon and went home. He saw the dead girl before him just as
she had stood in front of the theater door on that bright summer day,
in a red blouse and a short white skirt, with those wandering eyes beneath her reddish hair. At that time he would have sworn that she was
having an affair with the actor who looked like Guido. Maybe it was
true. That could have been *one* kind of love, and what she felt for Heinrich, another. There really weren't enough words. For one kind one
goes to one's death, for the other one goes to bed,—perhaps the night
before one drowns oneself for the other. And what does a suicide prove
in the end? Perhaps only that at one moment one didn't really understand death properly. How few ever try it again if they failed at it once.
The conversation with Grace by Labinski's grave came to him, coldly
glowing, on that sunny February day in the melting snow. At that hour
she had confessed to him that she had felt no horror when she found
Labinski shot in front of her house door. And when many years ago
her little sister had died, she had sat awake an entire night at the death-
bed without feeling a trace of what other people call horror. But she
explained to Georg that she had come to know something which must
be similar in the embraces of men. At first it had been a puzzle to even
herself; later she believed she understood it. She was, by the diagnosis
of doctors, destined to be barren, and thus it happened that the moment
of highest rapture, rendered meaningless as it were through this fate,
immersed her in a foreboding anxiety. At the time this seemed to Georg
to be an affected conversation, but today, for the first time, he felt a
breath of truth in it. She had been a remarkable creature. Would he
ever encounter such a person again? Why not? Maybe even soon. Now
a new period of his life was beginning, and somewhere perhaps the
next adventure was waiting. Adventure? . . . Could he still think about
that? . . . Didn't he have more serious obligations from now on than before? Didn't he love Anna now more than ever before? . . . The child
was dead. . . . But the next one would live! . . . Heinrich was right,

Anna was meant to be a mother. Mother . . . But, he thought feeling chilled, is she therefore meant to be the mother of *my* children? . . . The wagon stopped. Georg got out and went up the two flights of stairs to his apartment. Felician was still not back yet. Who knew when he would come? Georg thought. I can't wait for him, I'm too tired. He undressed quickly, sank into bed, and was overcome by deep sleep.

When he awoke, his eyes searched through the window, as he had done for days now, for a white line between the forest and meadows: the Sommerhaidenweg. But he saw only an empty blue sky pierced by a spire, and suddenly he realized that he was at home, and everything he had experienced yesterday came back to him. Yet his body and spirit felt refreshed, and it seemed to him that, besides the tragedy that had occurred, he had something positive to remember. Oh yes, the telegram from Detmold. . . . Was that something so positive? He hadn't thought so yesterday evening.

There was a knock at his door. Felician came into the room, his hat and stick in his hand. "I didn't realize that you slept at home last night," he said. "Good morning. So what's the news from out there?"

Georg had propped his arm on the pillow and looked up at his brother. "It's over," he said. "A boy, but dead." And he looked down.

"Oh, no," Felician said with emotion, walked over to him, and involuntarily laid his hand on his brother's head. Then he put his hat and stick aside, sat down on the bed with him, and Georg thought of morning hours in his childhood when he had seen his father sitting on the bed rail like that when he woke up. He explained to Felician how everything had happened, spoke in particular about Anna's patience and gentleness, but he felt with a certain discomfort that he had to force himself a little to preserve in his report the tone of gravity and sadness that seemed appropriate to him. Felician listened with sympathy, then got up and walked back and forth in the room. Meanwhile Georg rose, began to clean up, and reported to his brother how strangely the rest of the evening had evolved; he told about the walk and ride with Heinrich Bermann, and of the peculiar way in which they finally learned of the suicide of the actress.

"Oh, that's the one," Felician said. "It's already in the newspapers."

"So, how did it happen?" Georg asked curiously.

"She went out on the lake and jumped into the water from the boat. . . . Well, you'll read about it. . . . Are you going back out to the country again?" he added.

"Of course," replied Georg. "But I still have something to tell you, Felician, that should interest you." And he told his brother about the telegram from Detmold.

Felician looked surprised. "That's important," he cried.

"Yes, that's important," repeated Georg.

"You haven't answered yet?"

"No, how could I?"

"What do you plan to do?"

"To be honest, I don't really know. You realize that I can't go there immediately, especially under these circumstances."

Felician looked pensive. Then he said: "Nothing will be lost by a short postponement."

"That's what I think too. First I have to know how it's going out there. And of course I want to talk it over with Anna."

"Where do you have the telegram; can I read it?"

"It's lying in there on the writing table," said Georg, who was occupied at the moment with tying his shoes.

Felician went into the next room, took the dispatch in hand, and read.

"This is much more urgent," he remarked, "than I thought."

"It appears to me, Felician, that it still seems strange to you that I'm going to have a real career soon."

Felician stood beside his brother again, stroked his hair, and said: "Perhaps it's a happy coincidence that this dispatch came precisely yesterday."

"Happy? In what way?"

"I mean, after such a sad experience, the prospect of practical activity will be doubly good for you. . . . But unfortunately I have to leave. I still have a whole mass of things to do; farewell calls, among other things."

"When are you leaving, Felician?"

"A week from today. Say Georg, are you coming back again from the country today?"

"If everything's in order out there, for sure."

"We could get together again tonight?"

"I'd really like that, Felician."

"So, if it's all right with you—I'll be home at seven o'clock. Perhaps we could have supper together, but alone, not at the club."

"Yes, gladly."

"And I'd like to ask you something," Felician began again, after a short silence. "Take a greeting out there from me, a warm one . . . and tell her of my heartfelt sympathy."

"Thank you, Felician, I'll tell her."

"Really Georg, I can hardly tell you how sorry I am," Felician continued with warmth. "I only hope she recovers quickly . . . and you too."

Georg nodded. "Do you know," he said softly, "what it would have been named? Felician!"

Felician looked into his brother's eyes, very earnestly, then squeezed his hand. "Next time," he said with a warm smile. He squeezed his brother's hand once again and left. Georg looked after him, with conflicting emotions. But it's still not completely disagreeable to him, he thought, that it turned out this way.—He quickly finished getting ready and decided to ride out to the country on bicycle again today.

He felt himself again as soon as he was out on the bustling streets. The sky had grown a little overcast, and a cool wind blew toward Georg from the hills, like the greeting of autumn. He didn't want to meet anyone in the little village where the events of yesterday would in any case already be known, and took the upper road between the meadows and gardens to the rear entrance. The nearer the moment came when he would see Anna again, the heavier his heart grew. At the fence he got down from his bicycle and hesitated a while. The garden was empty; below lay the house, sunk in silence. Georg breathed deeply and painfully. How different it could have been! he thought, walked down, and heard the gravel crunching beneath his feet. He stepped onto the veranda, leaned the bicycle against the railing, and looked into the room through the open window. Anna was lying with open eyes.

"Good morning," he called out as cheerfully as possible.

Frau Golowski, who was sitting on Anna's bed, got up and explained at once: "We slept fine, sound and well."

"Well, that's good," said Georg, who swung himself over the sill into the room.

"You're certainly lively today," Anna said with her mischievous smile, which Georg remembered from times long ago. Frau Golowski told him that the professor had been there early in the morning, had appeared completely satisfied, and had taken Frau Rosner back to the city with him in his coach. Then she left with a friendly look.

Georg bent down to Anna, kissed her tenderly on the eyes and mouth, pulled the chair closer, sat down and said: "My brother—greets you warmly."

Her lips twitched imperceptibly. "Thanks," she said softly and then remarked: "You rode out here on your bicycle?"

"Yes," he replied. "That way one has to pay attention along the way, which sometimes is good for one." Then he reported to her the events of last evening, related the whole thing like an engrossing story, and only at the end, as was appropriate, did Anna learn how Heinrich's sweetheart had ended. He expected to see her moved, but she had a strangely hard expression on her mouth.

"It's really awful," said Georg. "Don't you think?"

"Yes," replied Anna tersely, and Georg felt that her compassion completely broke down at this point. He saw the disgust flowing from her soul, not mildly from one person to another, but strong and deep, like a stream of hate from one world to another. He changed the subject and began again: "Now the most important thing, my dear." He smiled, but his heart pounded a little.

"Well?" she asked anxiously.

He took the telegram from Detmold out of his breast pocket and read it to her. "What do you say to that?" he asked her with pretended pride.

"And what did you answer?"

"Nothing yet," he replied casually, as though he were not inclined to take the matter especially seriously. "Naturally I wanted to talk it over with you first."

"So, what do you think?" she asked without moving.

"I'll . . . decline, of course. I'll telegram that I . . . simply can't come in the near future." And he explained to her earnestly that nothing would be lost by a postponement, that he was welcome as a guest in any case, and that this urgent proposal was only due to chance anyway, which one hadn't had the right to hope for.

She let him talk for a while, and then she said: "You're being irresponsible again. Above all, I think you should answer immediately. And . . . "

"Well, and? . . . Perhaps then go out there early this afternoon, instead of coming to see you—well?" he joked.

She remained serious. "Why not?" she said. And after he threw back his head in disagreement: "I'm doing very well Georg, thank God; and even if it wasn't so good with me, you couldn't help, so . . . "

"Yes dear," he interrupted her, "it seems to me you don't really understand what's involved! Going there is naturally a rather simple thing—but—staying there! Staying there at least until Easter! That's how long the season lasts."

"Well, that you wouldn't go without saying good-bye to me, Georg, that I find quite in order. But look, you have to go anyway, isn't that true? Even if we haven't spoken about it recently, we both knew. So, if you were to leave in four weeks, or the day after tomorrow—or today . . ."

Now Georg began to earnestly object. It was absolutely not the same, if he left in four weeks or today. One could really firm up one's ideas in the course of four weeks—and talk it over frankly—as far as the future is concerned.

"How much is there to talk about," she answered wearily. "In four weeks you take . . . you can't take me with you any more than you can today. I even think that any—serious discussion between us can only be meaningful after you come back. A lot will have been clarified by then. . . . At least with regard to your prospects." She looked out of the window into the garden. Georg showed a mild irritation at the cold objectivity which did not fail her, even at such moments. "Yes, absolutely!" he said, "When one thinks about what it means—that you stay here and I . . ."

She looked at him. "I know what it means," she said.

He involuntarily avoided her glance, took her hands, kissed them, and was inwardly disconcerted. When he looked up again, he saw her eyes resting motherly on him. And she spoke to him like a mother. She explained to him that precisely for the sake of the future—and this word hovered almost like the gentle breath of her own hope—such an opportunity must not be missed. In two or three weeks he would be able to come back from Detmold to Vienna for a few days. For the people there would certainly understand that he had to get his affairs here in order. But above all it was important to give them some sign of his good intentions. And if he put any stock in *her* advice, there was only one way: to leave tonight. He need have no concerns about her, she felt that she was completely out of danger; she was quite sure of this. Of course he would have daily reports, twice if he wanted, morning and evening. He did not give in right away, but replied that the unexpectedness of this separation would weigh heavily on him. She answered that such a sudden farewell was much better than the prospect of another four weeks of uneasiness, agitation, and waiting to say good-bye. And the most important thing always remained: that it was only a matter of not much more than a half year. Then one would have the other half for oneself, and if everything went well, there would be no more periods of separation to face.

Now he began again: "And what will you do in this half year while I'm gone? It's . . ."

She interrupted him: "For the time being things will continue just like they have for the past year. But I thought about a lot of things early this morning."

"The singing school?"

"That too. Although that's not so easy or so simple—and besides," she added with her mischievous face, "it would be a shame if one had to close it up again so soon. But we'll talk about this later. Now go and telegraph."

"But what?" he cried so desperately that she had to laugh. Then she said, "Very simple. Will have the honor to be in your office tomorrow afternoon. Your most humble, or most devoted . . . or most proud . . ."

He looked at her. Then he kissed her hand and said: "You are certainly the smarter of the two of us." His tone indicated: also the colder, but one look from her—gentle, tender, and somewhat teasing—refuted this additional feeling.

"I'll be back in ten minutes." He left her with a cheerful expression, went into the next room, and closed the door. Across the room, behind the other door, he now realized powerfully,—his dead child lay in a casket . . . as the "necessities," as Doctor Stauber put it yesterday, had already been taken care of. His heart ached in a woeful longing. Frau Golowski came from the anteroom. She walked up to him, and spoke with admiration of Anna's devotion and composure. Georg listened somewhat distractedly. His glance kept slipping over to that door, and finally he said softly: "I want to see it one more time."

She looked at him, a little startled at first, and then sympathetically.

"Already nailed up?" he asked anxiously.

"Already gone," replied Frau Golowski slowly.

"Gone?!" His face suddenly contracted so painfully that the old woman laid her hand consolingly on his arm. "I made the announcement early this morning," she said, "and the rest happened very quickly. They took it to the mortuary an hour ago."

To the mortuary . . . Georg trembled. And he stood there silently for a long time, disordered, as if he had just learned of some totally unexpected horrible news. When he came to himself again, he felt the friendly hand of Frau Golowski still on his arm, and saw her look resting on his face from her kind and weary eyes.

"So, finished," he said with a defiant look upward, as if he had maliciously been robbed of his last hope. Then he gave Frau Golowski his hand. "And you have taken all this upon yourself, dear, gracious lady. . . . Truly I don't know . . . how I ever will . . ."

A motion from the old woman fended off any further thanks.

Georg left the house, cast a contemptuous glance at the little blue angel who looked down anxiously at the withered flower beds, and entered the street. On the way to the telegraph office he carefully considered the wording of the telegram that should announce his arrival in the place of the new profession and the new promise.

Ninth Chapter

The old Doctor Stauber and his son sat over a black coffee. The elder held a page from a newspaper in his hand and appeared to be looking for something. "The date for the opening of the case," he said, "isn't firm yet."

"Well," replied Berthold, "Leo Golowski thinks it will start in mid-November, or about three weeks. Therese visited her brother in jail a couple of days ago. He's supposed to be completely calm, even in good spirits."

"Well, who knows, maybe he'll be acquitted," said the old man.

"That's quite unlikely, Father. He should be glad that he hasn't ended up charged with first degree murder. In any case, the attempt was certainly made."

"You can't call that a serious attempt, Berthold. You see that the State's Attorney's Office paid no attention to the ridiculous calumny you are alluding to."

"But if they had judged it to be calumny," Berthold responded sharply, "then they would be obligated to bring the perpetrator to justice. Besides, it's well known that we live in a country where a Jew is not safe from being condemned to death for a ritual killing; why should the authorities shy away from the official assumption that by pistol duels with Christians—perhaps on religious grounds—Jews know how to secure a criminal advantage? That the authorities have not lacked the goodwill to do the ruling party a service this time as well can be seen from the fact that they would not release him from custody, even with the admittedly high bail."

"I don't believe the story about the bail," said the old doctor. "Where would Leo Golowski get fifty-thousand gulden?"

"It wasn't fifty—it was a hundred-thousand, and even today Leo Golowski knows absolutely nothing about it. I can tell you in confidence, Father, that Salomon Ehrenberg put up the money."

"Really? Then I'll also tell you something in confidence, Berthold."

"Well?"

"It's possible that it will never go to trial. Golowski's attorney has petitioned for a dismissal."

Berthold laughed out loud. "Because of that! And you think that that could have the slightest prospect of a favorable ruling, Father? Sure, if Leo had died and the first lieutenant were still alive . . . maybe then."

The old man shook his head impatiently. "You have to give the opposition speech at any price, my son."

"Excuse me, Father," Berthold said with twitching brows, "but everyone does not have the enviable gift of being able to simply look away from certain events in public life because they don't involve them personally."

"Is that perhaps my custom?" responded the old man heavily, and the half-closed eyes glared from beneath the high forehead, almost incensed. "You, Berthold, are the one, far more than I, who closes his eyes where he doesn't wish to see. I think you are beginning to become stubborn about your ideas. It's getting to be a sickness with you. I had hoped that the stay in another city, in another country, would cure you of certain narrow-minded and petty views. But instead it's gotten worse. I've noticed it. That someone strikes out like Leo Golowski did, I can still understand, however little I may approve of it. But to just stand there, with a clenched fist in one's pocket, so to speak, what's the purpose of that? Think about yourself! Personality and leadership always succeed in the end. What evil could befall you? That you obtain a professorship a few years later than someone else. I don't find the misfortune so great in this. No one will be able to destroy your work, if it has merit. . . ."

"It isn't only a matter of myself!" Berthold objected.

"But it's usually about matters of secondary importance. And to come back to our earlier theme, if an Ehrenberg, or an Ehrenmann with

a hundred-thousand gulden would have been found for the first lieutenant if he had shot Leo Golowski, that is very much the question. So,
now you're free to consider me an anti-Semite too, if it would be fun
for you, although at this moment I happen to be going to Rembrandtstrasse to see the old Golowski. So, have a nice day, and try to be sen-
sible." He gave his son his hand. He accepted it, noncommittally. The
old man turned to go. At the door he said: "We'll see each other at the
Medical Society tonight?"

Berthold shook his head. "No, Father, I'm spending the evening in
less cultivated company, at the Silver Grape, where a meeting of the
Social-Political Union is being held."

"Which you can't miss?"

"Impossible."

"Well, tell me now honestly. Are you running for the Provincial
Diet?"

"I . . . will be nominated."

"So! Do you think that you'll be able now to stand the unpleasant-
ness of sacrificing your forehead, which made you take to your heals
last year?"

Berthold looked out of the window, into the fall rain. "You know,
Father," he said with twitching brows, "that I didn't have the right attitude at that time. Now I feel strong and forearmed . . . despite your
earlier remarks, which don't prove anything. And most importantly: I
know exactly what I want."

The old man shrugged his shoulders. "I just don't really understand
how someone can give up constructive work . . . yes, you will have to
give it up, for one cannot serve two masters . . . how one can throw
all this down to . . . to give speeches to people whose business it is, so
to speak, to hold preconceived opinions—to espouse convictions that
for the most part they don't believe themselves, but only pretend to
represent."

Berthold shook his head. "This time I assure you, Father, it is no
oratorical or dialectical ambition that attracts me. This time I have
chosen an area where hopefully it will be possible for me to do just as
much positive work as in the laboratory. It is my intention, to be
specific, to concern myself entirely with the question of the public health
service. For this kind of political activity, perhaps I can even count on
your blessing, Father."

"On mine . . . yes. But what about your own?"

"How do you mean that?"

"On the blessing that one can call something like an inner calling."

"You have doubts about it?" answered Berthold, taken aback.

The servant walked in and gave the old doctor a calling card. He read it. "I'm at his disposal." The servant left.

Berthold, somewhat agitated, continued speaking: "I can certainly say that my education, my knowledge . . ."

The father, playing with the card, interrupted him.

"I have no doubts about your knowledge, your energy, your industry. But it seems to me, that to do anything significant in the field of public health, besides these excellent qualities, one requires one more which you have very little of: kindness, Berthold, love of humanity."

Berthold shook his head vigorously. "The kind of love for humanity you mean, Father, I consider quite superfluous, even harmful. Compassion—and what else can be meant by love for people whom one does not know personally—necessarily leads to sentimentality, to weakness. And precisely if one wants to help whole groups of people, one must be able occasionally to be hard against the individual, one must even be prepared to sacrifice him when the general good requires it. You need only think, Father, that the most honest and consistent social hygiene must lead directly to the annihilation of the sick, or at least their exclusion from every enjoyment of life. And I won't deny that I have all sorts of ideas in this direction which could appear cruel at first glance. But ideas which, I believe, belong to the future. You need not fear, Father, that I will begin immediately to preach the death of the burdensome and the superfluous. But philosophically my program leads roughly in that direction. By the way, do you know with whom I recently had a very interesting conversation on this subject?"

"What sort of subject do you mean?"

"Precisely expressed: a conversation on the right to kill. With Heinrich Bermann, the writer, the son of the late deputy of Parliament."

"Where did you have the opportunity to see him?"

"At a meeting recently. Therese Golowski brought him with her. You know him too, don't you, Father?"

"Yes," replied the old man, "for quite a while."

And he added: "I spoke with him again this summer, by Anna Rosner."

Berthold's brows twitched strongly again. Then he said, as though derisively: "I thought something of the sort. Bermann mentioned that he had seen you a while ago, but didn't care to remember exactly where. I concluded from this that it was a matter of some sort of discreet affair. Yes. So it pleased the Herr Baron to bring his friends to see her!"

"Your tone, dear Berthold, leads one to suspect that certain things have not been put as far behind you as you have previously indicated."

Berthold shrugged his shoulders. "I have never denied that I find the Baron Wergenthin uncongenial. That's why this whole story has been so painful for me from the beginning."

"Because of that?"

"Yes."

"And yet I think, Berthold, you would feel differently about the matter, if you were to encounter Anna Rosner again somewhere as a widow—even in the case where the late husband had been someone even more uncongenial to you than the Baron von Wergenthin."

"That's possible. One could then assume that she had been loved— or at least respected, not simply taken and—discarded, as soon as the fun was over. To me that's . . . well, I don't care to express myself any more precisely."

The old man looked at his son and shook his head. "It really seems that all the progressive views of you young people fall by the wayside as soon as your passions and conceits come into play."

"I'm not aware of being guilty of any progressive opinions with regard to questions of cleanliness or purity, Father. And I think that you would not be particularly thrilled if I should feel the urge to be the successor of a more or less deceased Baron von Wergenthin."

"Certainly not, Berthold. Especially for *her* sake, since you'd torment her to death."

"Be assured," replied Berthold. "Anna is in no danger from my side. It's over."

"That's a good reason. But happily there's a better one. The Baron Wergenthin is neither dead nor out of the picture. . . ."

"That doesn't mean anything will come of it."

"As you know, he has a position as *Kapellmeister* in Germany. . . ."

"That was a lucky stroke. In general he's had a lot of good luck in the whole business. Not to even have to care for a child!"

"You have two failings, Berthold. First, you're really an unkind person, and second, you don't let someone else talk. What I want to say is that it does not appear to be over between Anna and the Baron Wergenthin. Just the day before yesterday she sent me a greeting from him."

Berthold shrugged his shoulders as though the matter was closed for him. "How is it going with the old Rosner?" he then asked.

"This time he'll pull through," replied the old man. "I also hope, Berthold, that you preserve the necessary objectivity to know that it was not grief over the undutiful daughter that was to blame for this attack, but an unfortunately rather well-progressed arteriosclerosis."

"Is Anna giving her lessons again?" Berthold asked after some hesitation.

"Yes," replied the old man, "but possibly not for much longer." And he showed his son the visiting card that he was still holding in his hand.

Berthold contracted the corner of his mouth. "You think," he asked scornfully, "he's come back here to get married, Father?"

"I'll soon find out," answered the old man. "In any case, I'm delighted to see him again—for I assure you, that he's one of the most congenial young men that I have ever come to know."

"Remarkable," said Berthold. "An unequalled conqueror of hearts. Even Therese is infatuated with him. And recently Heinrich Bermann; he was almost comical. . . . Well yes, a handsome, slender, blond young man; Baron, German, Christian,—what Jew could resist this magic. . . . *Adieu*, Father!"

"Berthold!"

"What now?" He bit his lip.

"Think about yourself! Know who you are."

"I . . . know that."

"No. You don't know. Otherwise you couldn't forget so often who the others are."

Berthold raised his head, as if questioning.

"You should go to the Rosner's sometime. It's not worthy of you to show your disapproval to Anna in such a—childish way.—*Auf Wiedersehen*. . . . And have a nice meeting at the Silver Grape." He gave his son his hand, and then went into the consulting room. He opened the door to the waiting salon and invited Georg von Wergenthin, who was leafing through an album, to join him with a friendly nod of the head.

"First of all Herr Doctor," said Georg, after he had taken a seat, "I have to offer my apologies. My departure came so suddenly . . . I unfortunately had no chance to come to see you to say good-bye, to personally thank you for all the . . . "

Doctor Stauber demurred. "I'm delighted to see you again," he then said. "You're here in Vienna on a leave?"

"Naturally," answered Georg. "But it's only for three days. They need me there very badly," he added with a modest smile.

Doctor Stauber sat across from him in the desk chair and regarded him warmly. "You feel quite satisfied with your new position, from what Anna tells me."

"Oh yes. Naturally there are always difficulties when one takes up a new position so suddenly. But in general it's all gone more smoothly than I expected."

"That's what I hear. And you're supposed to have had a successful introduction to the court."

Georg smiled. "Anna makes it sound more important than it really was. I played once for the Prince Heir; and a woman member of the theater sang two of my songs; that's all. More important is that I have the prospect of being named *Kapellmeister* yet this season."

"I thought you were already."

"No, Herr Doctor, not yet officially. To be sure, I have already conducted a few times, as a substitute, in *Freischutz* and *Undine*; but for the moment I'm only rehearsal accompanist."

In response to further questions from the doctor, he related more about his activities at the Detmold Opera, then stood up and began to take his leave.

"Perhaps I could take you part way in my coach," said the doctor, "I'm going to Rembrandtstrasse, to the Golowskis."

"Thanks very much, Herr Doctor, but that's not in my direction. I do, by the way, intend to visit Frau Golowski during the day tomorrow. She's not sick?"

"No. Of course the exertions of the last few weeks didn't fail to leave their mark on her."

Georg mentioned that he had written a few words to her, and to Leo too, right after the duel. "When one thinks that it could have turned out differently . . ." he added.

Doctor Stauber looked down. "To have children is a pleasure," he said, "for which one pays in installments . . . and one never knows if the One above is satisfied."

At the door Georg began somewhat hesitantly: "And I want . . . to inquire from you, Herr Doctor, how it really is going with Herr Rosner. . . . I must say that I found him looking better than I expected from Anna's letters."

"I hope he'll recover," answered Stauber. "But one must always consider . . . he's an old man. Even older than he has to be from his years."

"But it's not necessarily that serious?"

"Old age is, in itself, a serious matter," responded Doctor Stauber, "especially when everything that has happened before, youth and adulthood, was not particularly happy either."

Georg's eyes had been wandering about the room, and he suddenly cried: "It just occurred to me, Herr Doctor, I never sent back the books you were so kind to lend me last spring. And now all our things are with the movers; the books as well as our silver, furniture, pictures. So I'll have to ask you, Herr Doctor, to be patient until spring."

"When you have no more urgent concerns, dear Baron. . . ."

They went down the stairs together, and Doctor Stauber inquired after Felician.

"He's in Athens," replied Georg, "I've only heard from him twice, but not in much detail. . . . It's really odd, Herr Doctor, to return as a stranger to a city in which one was so at home only a short time ago, and to live in a hotel, as a gentleman from Detmold. . . ."

Doctor Stauber got into the wagon. Georg sent his greetings to Frau Golowski.

"I'll tell her. And you, dear Baron, I wish much further good luck. *Auf Wiedersehen!*"

By the clock on St. Stephen's it was five P.M. Georg had an empty hour in front of him. He decided to go strolling in the light, mild, autumn rain in the outer city, which would also be a way to relax. He had spent an almost sleepless night in the railroad car, and he had been at the Rosner's within two hours of his arrival. Anna herself had come to open the door, and welcomed him with a tender kiss, but led him right into the room where her parents greeted him more courteously than warmly. The mother, shy and a little sensitive, said little as usual; the father, sitting in the corner of the divan, a leather-colored lap blanket over his knees, felt obligated to inquire about social and musical conditions at the small Court Residence from which Georg had come. Then he was left alone with Anna for a while; first in an all-too-hasty exchange of questions and answers, later in faintly self-conscious tendernesses, both as if perplexed at not feeling the joy of seeing each other again quite as their yearning had promised. Soon, one of Anna's students appeared; Georg excused himself, and in the anteroom he and his sweetheart hastily agreed on a rendezvous for that evening; he wanted to pick her up from the Bittners and go with her to the opera to a performance of *Tristan*, on the new production of which his manager had asked him to report. Then he took his early meal at a large window of a Ringstrasse restaurant, made some purchases and orders at his purveyor, looked for Heinrich, who was not at home, and decided to follow the sudden idea of paying his thank-you visit to Doctor Stauber.

He continued walking along, through the streets which were so familiar to him, and yet which already held the breath of strangeness; and he thought of the city from which he had come and in which he was beginning to feel at home more quickly than he had expected. Count Malnitz treated him from the very first with great cordiality; he was himself occupied with a plan to reform the opera in the modern spirit, and was hoping in Georg, so it seemed to him, to attract a collaborator and friend for his long-term plans. For the first *Kapellmeister* was certainly a capable musician, but by this time had become more of a court official than an artist. He had been called there as a twenty-five-year-old, and had stayed for thirty years now in the little city, a paterfamilias with six children, respected, contented, and without ambition. Soon after his arrival, at a concert, Georg had heard some songs sung which, many years ago, had carried the fame of the young *Kapellmeister* almost throughout the entire world; Georg found this long faded popularity difficult to understand, although he expressed himself with great warmth to the composer out of a certain sympathy for the old man, in whose eyes the distant light of a rich and promising past seemed to glow. Georg sometimes asked himself if the old *Kapellmeister* ever thought about the fact that he had once been regarded as someone called to the highest goals? Or if for him, like so many others among the established, the little city seemed like the center from which the rays of their success and reputation would extend far into the world? Georg had found only a few with a longing for greater and broader circumstances; sometimes it seemed to him that they treated him much more with a sort of good natured compassion, because he came from a large city, and in particular because he came from Vienna. For when these people heard the name of this city, Georg noted their satisfied and rather derisive attitude, which, as predictably as the overtones above a bass note, immediately brought forth certain other words as though in sympathetic vibration, without their ever having been expressed: waltz . . . coffeehouse . . . sweet ladies . . . roast chicken . . . *fiaker* . . . parliamentary scandal. It sometimes made Georg angry, and he became determined to do his utmost to improve the reputation of his countrymen in Detmold. They had called him because the third *Kapellmeister*, still a quite young man, had suddenly died, and so Georg had to sit down at the piano in the small rehearsal room on his very first day and accompany the singing. It went splendidly; he rejoiced in his gifts, which were more secure and strong than he had expected, and upon reflection, it seemed to him that even Anna had underestimated his talent. Beyond this, he was more seriously engaged in his composing than before. He was working on an overture, which had developed from themes for Bermann's opera, had begun a violin sonata; and the quintet, that Else had called mythical, was very nearly complete. It was to be performed this winter in one of the chamber soirees led by the concertmaster of the Detmold orchestra, a gifted young man, the only person in Georg's new place of residence to whom he had grown personally close, and with whom he liked to have meals at the Elephant. Georg rented a lovely room in this hotel, with a view out on the large linden-lined plaza, and he continued to delay from one day to the next renting a regular apartment. It was as yet uncertain if he would still be in Detmold next year, and beyond this he had the feeling that it might hurt Anna's feelings if he set himself up domestically as a bachelor, as though for a long stay. However, in his letters to her he had not written a word about the many possibilities for the future, just as she refrained from asking him impatient or suspicious questions. They informed each other almost only of factual matters: she wrote about her gradual return to her old activities; he about all the new conditions he had to get used to. But although there had been as good as nothing that he had to conceal from her, he skimmed over, with deliberate casualness, much that could easily have led to misunderstandings. How could one fix in words the peculiar atmosphere that floated in the half-darkened auditorium, in the mornings, at rehearsals, when the smell of make-up, perfume, costumes, gas, old wood, and fresh stain from the stage came down to the stalls;—when figures one couldn't recognize immediately scurried up and down the aisles, in costume or every day dress, or when someone's breath blew across one's neck, heavy and scented? Or how could one describe a glance, which came down from the eyes of a young lady singer when one just looked up at her from the keyboard? . . . Or when one accompanied this young singer in the light of midday across the theater square and the Konigsstrasse to her house door, and on this occasion spoke not only about the part of Micaela,[1] which one had just been studying with her, but about all sorts of other, if totally harmless things; could one write about this to a sweetheart in Vienna, without

1. Don Jose's ever-faithful, but jilted, sweetheart in Bizet's *Carmen*.

her looking for something suspicious between the lines? And even if one had emphasized that Micaela was engaged to a young doctor from Berlin, who adored her, as she did him, it would hardly have been better; for it would only appear as if one felt it necessary to divert and reassure her.

How strange, thought Georg, that *she* would really be singing Micaela, which I had studied with her, precisely tonight, and that I am walking this same way here, out to Mariahilf, like I did a year ago so often and so happily. And he thought about a particular evening when he had picked Anna up from there and had gone walking with her around the silent streets, looked at amusing photographs under a house door, and finally strolled across the cool stone floor slabs of an old church in a soft, but presentient discussion about an unknown future. . . . Now it had all turned out differently than he had dreamed. Differently . . . why did it seem that way to him? . . . What had he expected then? . . . Hadn't this year which had just passed been wonderfully rich and beautiful, with its joys and sorrows? And didn't he love Anna today better and deeper than ever? And in that new city, had he not sometimes longed for her as heatedly as for a woman who had never belonged to him? Their reunion early this morning, in the gloomy mood of a grey day, with its faintly embarrassed tenderness, should not confuse him. . . .

He was at his destination. As he looked up to the bright window behind which Anna was giving her lesson, a gentle emotion came over him. And as she came out of the door the next moment, in a simple English dress, the grey felt hat over her thick, dark blond hair, a book in her hand, just like a year ago, there suddenly streamed through him an unexpected feeling of happiness. She didn't see him right away, as he was standing in the shadow of a house, opened her umbrella and walked to the corner where he used to wait for her last year. He watched her for a while and enjoyed how noble and honest she looked. Then he went quickly after her and in a few steps had taken hold of her.

First she had to tell him that she couldn't go to the opera with him tonight; her father hadn't been feeling at all well this afternoon.

Georg was very disappointed. "Won't you at least come with me for the first act?"

She shook her head. "No, I really don't want to. It'll be better for you to give the seat to a friend. Pick up Nuernberger or Bermann."

"No," he replied. "If you don't come with me, I'd rather go alone. I was looking forward to it so much. I don't care that much about the production myself. I'd rather stay with you . . . as far as I'm concerned, together with all of you upstairs; but I have to go; I have to—make a report."

"Of course you have to go," confirmed Anna; and she added: "I wouldn't really enjoy bringing you up for an evening with us anyway, it's really not very cheerful."

He had taken the umbrella from her hand, held it over her, and she clung to his arm.

"Anna," he said, "I want to propose something to you." He was surprised that he was searching for an introduction, and he began hesitantly: "My few days in Vienna are naturally a little hectic, disconnected—and now this oppressive mood has settled on all of you. . . . We really don't have enough time for ourselves, don't you think?"

She nodded, without looking at him.

"So, wouldn't you like to come with me for a while, Anna, when I head back."

She looked at him from the side in her mischievous way and did not answer.

He continued talking: "I could get one more day of leave quite easily if I telegraphed the theater. It would be really wonderful if we could get away for a few hours alone together."

She granted that, warmly, but without enthusiasm, and made the decision dependent on the condition of her father. Then she asked him how he had spent the day. He explained thoroughly, and related his plan for tomorrow. "So we won't be able to see each other until tomorrow night," he concluded. "I'll come up to see you, if that's all right. And then we can talk about the rest."

"Yes," said Anna, and looked down at the damp brownish-grey street.

He tried again to persuade her to come to the opera with him; but in vain. Then he inquired about her singing lessons and began to talk about his own activities as if he had to convince her that in the end things weren't much better for him than for her. And he alluded to his letters, in which he had written to her about everything in detail.

"As for that," she suddenly said quite hard . . . and as he involuntarily threw his head back from being struck by her tone: "how much do letters tell, however detailed they are?"

He knew what she was thinking, which she expressed openly today as little as she ever had,—and something heavy lay on his heart. Was not everything she was repressing concealed in the very persistence of this silence: questions, reproaches, anger? He had already felt it this morning, and now he felt again, that something positively hostile to him was emerging in her, against which she herself seemed to struggle in vain. Since only this morning? . . . Hadn't it been there longer than that? Perhaps always? From the very moment when they first belonged to each other, and even in the moments of highest bliss? Had this animosity not been there as they lay behind the dark draperies, with the sound of organ music, her breast against his; as she waited in the hotel room in Rome, with reddened eyes, while he enjoyed the most wonderful hour of the entire trip alone, watching with delight as the sun set on the Campagna from Monte Pincio? Had it not been there on that hot morning when he walked over to her on the gravel path, sank at her feet, and wept in her bosom, like in the bosom of a mother;—and as he had sat by her bed and looked out into the sunset garden, while inside a dead child that she had born an hour before lay on the white linen; was it not there again, darker than ever and difficult to bear, as if one should not have resigned oneself after all this time, like with so many other deficiencies, to so many sorrows that arise in the deepest human relationships. And now, how painfully he felt it, as he walked arm-in-arm with her over the damp pavement, carefully holding the umbrella over her, as it appeared again; threatening and familiar. The words she had spoken still echoed in his ear: How much do letters tell, however detailed they are? . . . But he heard even more serious ones at the same time: What in the end does even the most fervent kiss mean, in which body and soul seem to mingle? What in the end does it mean that we traveled for months through strange countries together? What does it mean that I had a child with you? What does it mean that you cried in my lap over your affair? What does all that mean, since you still have left me alone . . . alone even in the moment when my body drank in the seed of life, which I carried in me for nine months, and which was destined, as our child, to live with strangers, and did not wish to remain in the world.

But while all this sank heavily into his soul, he told her in gentle words, that she really was not altogether wrong, and that letters—even if they were twenty pages long—couldn't actually tell very much; and while a painful sympathy for her welled up in him, he softly expressed the hope of a time when they would both no longer be dependent on letters. And then he found more tender words, told about his lonely walks in the surroundings of the strange city, where he would think of her; of the hours in that bland hotel room with the view onto the linden-lined square, and of his longing for her, which was always present, whether he sat alone over his work, accompanied singers on the piano, or talked with new acquaintances. But as he stood with her in front of the house door, with her hand in his, and looked in her eyes with a cheerful "*Auf Wiedersehen*," he saw with surprise a tired, no longer painful disappointment glimmer in them. And he knew: all the words he had spoken to her had meant nothing, less than nothing to her, compared to the one that scarcely was expected any more, yet always hoped for, and never said.

A quarter-hour later Georg sat in his main floor seat at the opera, at first a little sullen and tired; soon however the joy of revival streamed through his blood. And as Brangaene threw the queen's mantle around the shoulders of her mistress, Kurwenal announced the approach of the king, and as the people on ship rejoiced under the shining sky at reaching land, Georg no longer remembered anything about a dismal night in a train car, boring appointments, a forced conversation with an old Jewish Doctor, or about a walk over damp paving stones in which the light of street lamps sparkled, at the side of a young lady who looked honest, noble, and somewhat depressed. And as the curtain fell for the first time and light streamed through the immense reddish-gold auditorium, he did not feel disenchanted in any disagreeable way, but rather it seemed more to him as if his head had emerged from one dream into another; and a reality filled with all sorts of serious and regrettable things floated by powerlessly somewhere outside. It seemed to him that the atmosphere of this building had never delighted him so much as it did today; never had his feeling been so clear that during the time when they were there, all people, in some mysterious way, were immune from all the pain and baseness of life. He stood in front of his corner seat in the center aisle, saw many satisfied looks directed at him, and was aware of appearing handsome, elegant, and even a little unusual. And besides that—this too he felt with satisfaction—he was a man with a career, a position, even here at the theater, with a commission and responsibility to some extent as a representative of a German court theater. He looked around with his opera glasses. From the back stalls Gleissner greeted him with a somewhat too endearing nod and appeared to be explaining who Georg was to the young lady sitting next to him. Who might she be? Was she the prostitute who the spiritually experimenting writer wanted to turn into a saint, or the saint he wanted to turn into a prostitute? Difficult to decide, Georg thought. Halfway through the process they would both look about the same. Georg felt the lenses of an opera glass burning through his skull. He looked up. It was Else, who was looking down at him from a first level loge. Frau Ehrenberg sat near her, and between them a tall young man leaned out over the railing who was none other than James Wyner. Georg bowed, and two minutes later walked into the loge, greeted with friendliness but by no means with surprise. Else, dressed in a low cut, black velvet dress, a small string of pearls around her neck, and an unusual but interesting hairdo, extended her hand to him. "What are you doing here? Vacation? Dismissal? Flight?"

Georg explained, briefly and good naturedly.

"By the way, it was nice," said Frau Ehrenberg, "that you wrote a few lines to us from Detmold."

"Shouldn't he have done that?" Else remarked. "One might have thought that he had taken off with someone to America."

James stood in the middle of the loge, tall, thin, with chiseled features and his dark, smooth hair combed to the side. "So tell us Georg, how do you feel in Detmold?"

Else looked up at him with lowered lashes. She seemed delighted by his way of always speaking German as though he had to translate it from English. Nevertheless, she used the opportunity to make a joke and said: "How Georg feels in Detmold? I fear, James, that your question is indiscreet." Then she turned to Georg and said: "We're engaged."

"We still haven't sent out any notices yet," Frau Ehrenberg added.

Georg offered his best wishes.

"Why don't you have breakfast with us tomorrow morning," said Frau Ehrenberg. "You'll only encounter a few people, all of whom will certainly be very glad to see you. Sissy, Frau Oberberger, Willy Eissler."

Georg excused himself. He couldn't commit himself for any definite time, but he would try to come by in the course of the afternoon if at all possible.

"Well yes," said Else, without looking at him, and with one arm in a long white glove laying on the railing. "You must be spending noontime in your family circle."

Georg acted as if he heard nothing and began praising tonight's performance. James replied that he loved *Tristan* more than any other Wagner opera, *Meistersinger* included.

Else observed simply: "It's certainly marvelous, but actually I'm against love potions and such stories."

Georg explained that here the love potion must be understood as a symbol, whereupon Else declared herself to be also against symbols. The first signal for the second act was given. Georg took his leave, hurried down, and had just enough time to get to his seat before the curtain went up. He remembered again the semi-official status with which he sat in the theater tonight, and resolved not to further express his impressions without criticism. He soon succeeded in discovering that the love scene could be presented quite differently than was done here; and he was not at all satisfied that Melot, by whose hand Tristan must die, was portrayed by a singer of the second rank, though this was usually the case. After the second fall of the curtain he got up with a certain increase in self-respect, remained standing by his seat, and looked sometimes up to the first level loge from which Frau Ehrenberg nodded to him benevolently while Else talked with James, who stood motionless behind her with crossed arms. It occurred to Georg that he would see James's sister again tomorrow. Did she still think sometimes about that wonderful afternoon hour in the park, in the dark green dampness, with the warm smell of moss and pines? How distant it was! Then he remembered a fleeting kiss in the evening shadow of the garden wall in Lugano. How remote this too was! He thought of the evening under the plane tree, and the conversation about Leo came back to him. Actually one could have seen it all coming then. Truly a remarkable person, Leo! How he concealed his plans inside of him!—Naturally he must have formed them long before. And obviously Leo had waited for the day when he could lay aside his uniform to carry them out. No answer had ever come to the letter that Georg wrote to him right after he received the news of the duel. He resolved to visit Leo in jail if that were possible.

A man greeted him from the first row. It was Ralph Skelton. Georg agreed with him through gestures that they would meet after the finish of the performance.

The lights went down and the prelude to the third act began. Georg heard tired waves breaking on a dreary shore, and the moaning sighs of a mortally wounded hero blowing in thin bluish air. Where was it that he last heard this? Had it not been in Munich? . . . No, it couldn't have been that long ago. And suddenly he remembered the hour on the balcony under the wooden gable when the pages of the *Tristan* score had lain open in front of him. Across the way a sunlit road had led between forest and meadow to the cemetery, and a gilded cross had glimmered; below in the house a beloved woman had groaned in pain, and his heart had ached. And yet, even this memory had its melancholy sweetness, like everything that was completely past. The balcony, the little blue angel between the flower beds, the white bench under the pear tree . . . where was it all now! He had to see the house again, one more time before he left Vienna.

The curtain raised. The shawm sounded mournfully under a pale and indifferently receding sky; the wounded hero slept in the shade of a linden tree, and by his head, Kurwenal, the faithful, was watching. The shawm fell silent, the questioning shepherd bent over the wall, and Kurwenal answered. Truly, this was a voice of remarkable quality. If only we had a baritone like this, Georg thought. And a lot of other things we need! He felt called upon to make the modest theater in which he worked, over the course of time, into a stage of the first rank, if only he would be given the necessary power. He dreamed of model performances to which people would stream from every direction; he no longer sat there as a delegate, but as one who might be destined in the not-too-distant future to be a leader himself. His hopes grew broader and higher. Perhaps only a few years would pass—and inevitable harmonies would ring through a wide ceremonial hall; and the audience would listen entranced, like here tonight, while somewhere outside an insipid reality drifted by powerlessly. Powerlessly? That was the question! . . . Did he know then if it was given to him to stir men through his art like the master who expressed himself here tonight? To be victorious over the dubious, lamentable, miserable, the commonplace? Impatience and doubt wanted to rise from within him; but will and insight quickly barred them, and now he again felt the pure delight that he always did when he listened to beautiful music, without thinking that he himself often wished to work and be accepted as a creator himself. At such moments, of all his relationships to this beloved art, only one remained: to be able to penetrate it with deeper understanding than any other person. And he felt that Heinrich had spoken the truth as they walked through the morning dew-damp forest together: it was not creative work—but the atmosphere of his art alone that was necessary for him to exist; but he was not condemned to failure like Heinrich, who was always driven to grapple, to shape, to defend, and for whom the world always fell to pieces and slipped through his creative grasp.

Isolde had fallen dead in Brangaene's arms over Tristan's body, the last notes died away, and the curtain fell. Georg cast a glance up to the loge on the first level. Else stood at the railing, her eyes directed at him, while James put her dark red coat around her shoulders, and only now, after a nod of the head—as quick as if no one should notice it—she turned to the exit. Strange, Georg thought; from a distance her de-

meanor, many of her gestures, had something . . . melancholy and
dramatic about them. She reminds me most of the gypsy girl from Nice,
or the strange young creature with whom I stood in front of Titian's
Venus in Florence. . . . Did she ever love me? No. And she doesn't love
her James either. Who then? . . . Maybe . . . it was the crazy drawing
teacher in Florence? Or no one. Or even Heinrich?

He met Skelton in the foyer. "So, you've come back again?" Skelton
asked.

"Only for a few days," Georg answered. It became clear that Skelton
had not really known what all had happened to Georg, and thought
that he was on some sort of musical studying trip through the German
cities. Now he was rather surprised to hear that Georg was here on a
leave and was reviewing the new production of *Tristan* on assignment,
so to speak, from the theater management.

"If you'd care to join us," said Skelton, "I'm meeting Breitner at the
Imperial, the white hall."

"Terrific," replied Georg. "I'm staying there."

Doctor von Breitner was smoking one of his famous giant cigars
when the two gentlemen appeared at his table. "What a surprise," he
cried, as Georg greeted him. He was aware that Georg was working as
Kapellmeister in Duesseldorf.

"Detmold," Georg said, and he thought: These people don't have
that much to do with me. . . . What's the deal?

Skelton told about the *Tristan* performance, and Georg mentioned
that he had spoken with the Ehrenbergs.

"Did you know that Oskar Ehrenberg was on his way to India or
Ceylon?" asked Doctor von Breitner.

"Really?"

"And who do you think he's going with?"

"Probably in female company."

"Yes, of course; I've even heard that they have five or seven women
with them."

"Who do you mean—them?"

"Oskar Ehrenberg . . . and—take one guess. . . . Well, Prince von
Guastalla."

"That's impossible!"

"Strange, isn't it? They became great friends at Ostend, at a spa.
Cherchez and all that. Just as there are women for whose sake one
fights, so there are apparently others over whom one, so to speak, joins
hands. They all left Europe together. Maybe they'll found a kingdom
on some island, and Oskar Ehrenberg will become a minister."

Willy Eissler appeared, pale yellow in the face, bleary-eyed, and hoarse. "Greetings, Herr Baron; forgive me for not being surprised, but I had already heard that you were here. Someone saw you on Kaerntnerstrasse."

Georg asked Willy to take greetings from Count Malnitz to his father—he unfortunately had no time himself to look up the old man to whom—as he observed with modest ingratiation—he owed his position in Detmold.

"As far as your future is concerned, dear Baron," said Willy, "I have never had any concerns, especially since last year—or has it already been longer than that—when I heard your songs sung by Fraulein Bellini. But it was a good idea for you to have decided to leave Vienna. People here would have regarded you as a dilettante for a decade. That's the way it is in Vienna. I know that. When people know that someone is from a good family, with a sense for a nice necktie, good cigarettes, and the other amenities of life, they won't believe he can be an artist too. Without a certificate from somewhere else you'll never be taken seriously here . . . so bring back a stunning one soon, Baron."

"I'll certainly try," said Georg.

"By the way, have the gentlemen heard the latest," Willy began again. "Leo Golowski, you know, the one-year-man who shot First Lieutenant Sefranek, is free."

"Released from custody?" asked Georg.

"No, he's completely free. His attorney petitioned the Kaiser for a dismissal, which was graciously granted today."

"Unbelievable," cried Breitner.

"Why are you so surprised, Breitner?" responded Willy. "Something reasonable can happen once, even in Austria."

"Duels are never reasonable," said Skelton, "and a pardon resulting from a duel cannot be either."

"Duels may be either much worse or much better than reasonable," replied Willy. Either a monstrous stupidity or an inevitable necessity. Either a crime or a redeeming act. It's not reasonable, and doesn't need to be. In the case of exceptions, one can't do anything with reason. And that in a case like the one about which we were just speaking, the duel was unavoidable, you will have to grant that too, Skelton."

"Absolutely," said Breitner.

"I can think of a country," remarked Skelton, "in which even differences like that would be worked out within the law."

"Differences like that within the law! Come on! . . . Do you really think, Skelton, that in a case where it isn't a matter of property or privilege, but one where people face each other with immense hatred, do you really believe that the threat of fines or imprisonment could bring a settlement? There's a deeper meaning here, gentlemen—that declining a duel in such cases will be regarded, by everyone who has temperament, honor, and uprightness within them, as cowardice. Among Jews at least," he added. "With Catholics it's always considered piety that keeps them from fighting."

"That certainly happens," said Breitner simply.

Georg wanted to know how it had all come about between Leo Golowski and the first lieutenant.

"Oh yes," said Willy, "you're a newcomer. Well, this first lieutenant brutally persecuted Leo through the whole year and . . ."

"I know the preliminaries," Georg interrupted him, "in part right from the source."

"Oh, all right. So on the first of October, the preliminaries, to stay with this expression, were over; that is, Leo had his year as a volunteer behind him. And on the morning of the second he waited calmly outside the barracks until the first lieutenant came out of the door. At this moment he walked up to him, the lieutenant reached for his sabre, Leo Golowski grabbed him by the hand and would not let go, held his other fist in front of his face—pretty much like that. It was also said, by the way, that Leo flung the following words in the first lieutenant's face. . . . I don't know if it's true."

"What words?" Georg asked curiously.

"Yesterday, Herr First Lieutenant, you were more than I, now for the moment, we are once again equal—but tomorrow at this time one of us will again be more than the other."

"Somewhat Talmudish," observed Breitner.

"You would be the best judge of that, Breitner," responded Willy, who continued with the story: "So the duel took place on the next morning, in the meadows by the Danube. Three shots apiece. Twenty paces, no advance. If no result, sabres until disabled. . . . The first shot from both sides missed, and after the second . . . after the second Golowski really was literally more than the first lieutenant—who was nothing, less than nothing; a dead man."

"Poor devil," said Breitner.

Willy shrugged his shoulders. "He just came up against the wrong man. I feel sorry for him too. But one has to say, things would be different in Austria if all Jews would know how to act, in appropriate cases, just like Leo Golowski. Unfortunately . . ."

Skelton smiled. "You know Willy, one cannot say anything against the Jews in front of me, I love them. And it would make me very sad if one decided to settle the Jewish question through a series of duels, because in that case, not a single male example would remain of this splendid race."

By the end of the conversation Skelton had to grant that the duel would not be abolished in Austria in the immediate future. But he allowed himself the question if that did not speak more badly of Austria than of the duel, as there were many other countries, he didn't care to name any out of modesty, where the duel had not been known for decades. He may have gone too far when he declared Austria, in which he had felt truly at home for six years, the land of social injustice. Here, like nowhere else, there were vulgar disputes without a trace of hatred, and a sort of tender love without the obligation to be faithful. Between political opponents there existed or developed ridiculous personal sympathies; party members, on the other hand, insulted, disavowed, betrayed one another. Only with a few does one find views expressed about things or people, and even these few are all too ready to make restrictions, to allow exceptions. One has precisely the impression here that in the political struggle, while the angriest words fly back and forth between apparently the bitterest of enemies, they are winking with their eyes at each other: "I don't really mean it the way it sounds."

"What do you think, Skelton," asked Willy, "do they wink when the bullets fly back and forth too?"

"They'd be glad to do that too, Willy, if death wasn't standing behind them. But this fact only changes their behavior, not their convictions, that's what I think."

They sat for a long time and continued talking. Georg heard all kinds of news. He learned, among other things, that Demeter Stanzides had concluded his purchase of the estate on the Hungarian-Croatian border, and that Rattenmamsell was expecting a joyous event. Willy Eissler was anxious about the result of this intermixing of races, and entertained himself in the meantime by thinking up names for the expected child like Israel Pius or Rebecca Portiuncula.[2]

Later the whole group moved to a nearby coffeehouse, and Georg played a game of billiards with Breitner; then he went up to his room. In bed, he jotted down an itinerary for the next day and finally sank into a deep and refreshing sleep.

---

2. *Portiuncula*: Literally "Little Portion." The affectionate nickname given by the Friars to the tiny chapel near Assisi that was assigned to them when the First Order of St. Francis was founded in the year 1210.

In the morning with tea he was brought the paper from the night before and a telegram. The theater manager asked him to report on a singer. It was, to Georg's satisfaction, the same one he had heard yesterday as Kurwenal. Further, he was given an additional three days beyond the stipulated leave, "to put his affairs in order," since a change in performance plans had made this possible. That's really nice, Georg thought. It occurred to him that he had completely forgotten about telegraphing his own request for an extension of his leave. Now I have even more time for Anna than I believed, he thought. Maybe we could go to the mountains. The fall is lovely and mild. Besides, we'd be mostly alone and undisturbed. But, what if we made another mistake! Made—another—mistake! This was exactly how the words went through his mind. He bit his lip. Was this how the matter suddenly looked to him now? A mistake? Where was the time when he had felt, almost with pride, like a link in the continuous chain which stretched from ancestor to offspring? And for a few moments he felt like one disillusioned with love, with many doubts and regrets.

He skimmed through the newspaper. The investigation against Leo Golowski had been halted by imperial clemency, and last night he had been released from jail. Georg was delighted and decided to visit Leo today. Then he drew up a telegram to the count and reported on yesterday's performance with articulate detail. By the time he got out onto the street it was almost eleven. The air was autumnal, cool, and clear. Georg felt well rested, fresh, and in good spirits. The day lay hopefully before him and promised to be stimulating. But something disturbed him, without his really knowing what it was. Oh yes, . . . the visit to Paulanergasse, the sad rooms, the sick father, the irritable mother. I'll just pick Anna up, he thought, go for a walk with her, and have lunch with her somewhere. He came across a flower shop, bought some wonderful dark red roses, and along with a card on which he wrote: "A thousand morning greetings, *auf Wiedersehen,*" he had them sent to Anna. After he had done this, he felt better. Then he set off down the streets of the inner city to the house where Nuernberger lived. He climbed up the five flights of stairs. A scurrying old maid with a dark scarf on her head let him in to her master's room. Nuernberger stood at the window with head slightly lowered, in the brown, fully buttoned-up jacket that he liked to wear at home. He was not alone. Heinrich had just gotten up from an old armchair by the writing table, a manuscript in his hands. Georg was warmly received.

"Could your arrival in Vienna be connected to the crisis in direction at the opera?" asked Nuernberger. He let this remark pass as a joke without further ado. "I must say," he said, "if little boys who can only demonstrate their connection to German literature by having regularly attended a literary coffeehouse for a short time recently, can be called to Berlin as producers, then I see no cause for surprise if the Baron Wergenthin should be brought in triumph to the Vienna Opera after a strenuous six-week career as *Kapellmeister* at a German court theater."

Georg clarified that the truth was that he had only a short leave, to get his affairs here in order, and did not neglect to mention that he had seen the new production of *Tristan* yesterday, to some extent as representative of his theater management; though he smiled at this with self-irony. Then he made a short and rather humorous digression into his current experiences at the little Residence. He reported his concert at court derisively too, as if he were far from ascribing any special importance to his position, his success up till now, matters of the theater, or to life in general. This, above all, was how he wished to portray his position to Nuernberger. Then the conversation turned to the release of Leo Golowski. Nuernberger was delighted with this unexpected outcome, but refused to be surprised, since in this world, and most especially in Austria, the most unlikely things were constantly happening. He was not inclined to put much stock in the rumor about Oskar Ehrenberg's yacht trip with the prince, which Georg put forward as a new proof of Nuernberger's views. But in the end he granted the possibility, since, as he had long been aware, the truth was often stranger than fiction.

Heinrich looked at the clock. It was time for him to go.

"Did I disturb you?" asked Georg. "I think you were reading something when I came in, Heinrich."

"I had just finished," Heinrich answered.

"You can read the last act for me tomorrow, Heinrich," said Nuernberger.

"I don't think so," replied Heinrich laughing. "If the first two acts fell through in the theater like they did today with you, dear Nuernberger, one couldn't finish it there either. We'll assume that you got up indignantly from your seat and walked out. I'll spare you the house key and the rotten eggs."

"My goodness!" cried Georg.

"You're exaggerating again, Heinrich," said Nuernberger. "I only permitted myself to raise a few objections," he said, turning to Georg, "that's all. But he is an author!"

"It's all a matter of interpretation," said Heinrich. "It's a rather effective objection; in the end it's nothing less than an objection against the life of a fellow man, when one knocks in his skull with a pickaxe." He indicated his manuscript and turned to Georg. "Do you know what this is? My political tragicomedy. Please send no flowers."

Nuernberger laughed. "I assure you, Heinrich, there's a lot in the play that can be made into something really splendid. You can retain almost the whole scene structure and a number of the characters. You just have to make a decision, when you start up with it again, to be less just."

"But it's really very good," said Georg, "that he's just."

Nuernberger shook his head. "In general that may be true—only not in drama." And, turning again to Heinrich: "In a piece like this, that deals with a question of the times, or with several, as was your intention, you will achieve nothing through objectivity. The public in the theater demands that the theme the writer takes up also be concluded, or at least that an illusion of this sort be provided. Of course there's never a real conclusion. And even apparent conclusions can only be reached by those who have the courage, or naiveté, or temperament to take sides. You'll soon learn, dear Heinrich, that justice doesn't work in drama."

"You know, Nuernberger," said Heinrich, "maybe it works with justice too. I think I may just not have the right kind. In reality I have no desire to be just at all. I even fancy that it's marvelous to be unjust. I think it would be the healthiest possible mental gymnastics that one could engage in. It would be really good for men whose views people attack to be able to really hate. It certainly saves one a lot of inner energy that one can make better use of in the struggle. Yes, if one still had justice in his heart . . . But I only have it here," and he pointed to his forehead. "I'm not above taking sides, but rather to some extent I'm for all of them or against all of them. I don't have the divine justice, but rather the dialectical. And therefore . . ." and he held his manuscript in the air, "only boring and fruitless twaddle comes of it."

"Woe to the man," said Nuernberger, "who ventures to write such a thing about you."

"Well, yes," replied Heinrich smiling. "If someone else says it, one cannot suppress the suspicion that he might be right. But now I really do have to go. Good-day, Georg. I'm really sorry that you missed me yesterday. When do you go back?"

"Tomorrow."

"Couldn't we see each other once more before you leave? I'll be home all afternoon and evening; come by if you can. You'll find a man who has turned with determination from the problems of the times back to the eternal problems: Death and Love. . . . By the way, do you believe in Death, Nuernberger? I won't ask about Love."

"This joke, which is a bit too cheap for your standards," said Nuernberger, "leads me to suspect that, despite your dignified behavior, my criticism . . ."

"No, Nuernberger, I swear to you, I'm not offended. I even have an agreeable feeling that the matter is quite settled."

"Settled? Why's that? It's possible that I've made a mistake, and that precisely this piece, which I regarded as less than perfect, would be destined in the theater for great success, and make you into a millionaire. I'd be heartbroken if perhaps through my unauthoritative criticism . . ."

"Certainly, certainly, Nuernberger; we must all accept sometime, and in every single case, that we may have made a mistake. Next I'm going to write a piece which, to be sure, will have the following title: No one pulls the wool over my eyes, and myself least of all . . . and you, Nuernberger, will be the hero."

Nuernberger smiled. "Me? That means that you'd take a person whom you imagine you know, attempt to depict that one side of his character that suits you for that specific purpose, suppress the others that you don't know what to do with, and in the end . . ."

"In the end," Heinrich interrupted him, "it would be a portrait, made from a distorted photograph, taken through a defective apparatus, during a quake, and an eclipse. Agreed, or is something missing?"

"The characterization is exhaustive," said Nuernberger.

Heinrich took his leave with exaggerated joviality, and left with his rolled up manuscript.

When he was gone, Georg remarked: "His mood seemed a little artificial to me."

"Do you think? I've found him recently to be in strikingly good spirits."

"Really in good spirits? Do you seriously believe that? After what he's been through?"

"Why not? People who are so much, almost exclusively, occupied with themselves like he is, overcome emotional upsets astonishingly well. On such people, though to be sure not only on them, the most trivial physical discomfort weighs much more heavily than any heartache, even the betrayal or death of loved ones. That's because emotional pains somehow flatter our vanity, which one cannot say about typhus or a stomach ache. And for an artist it's also true that nothing can be gotten from a stomach ache . . . at least that was true a short time ago . . . but from emotional pain comes whatever one wants, from lyrical poems to philosophical treatises."

"There are emotional pains of very different sorts," Georg answered. "And it's a very different matter if one is deceived or deserted by a loved one . . . or even when they die a natural death, than when they kill themselves on our account."

"Do you know for certain," Nuernberger asked, "that Heinrich's sweetheart killed herself over him?"

"Hasn't Heinrich told you about it? . . ."

"To be sure. But that doesn't prove much. With regard to things that concern ourselves, we are always fools, even the smartest of us."

Such remarks from Nuernberger's mouth had something strangely disturbing for Georg. They were of the kind that Nuernberger never tired of making and which, as Heinrich once said, actually annulled the meaning of personal interaction, indeed of all human relationships.

Nuernberger continued talking: "We only know two facts. One, that our friend once had a relationship with a young lady, and the other, that this young lady threw herself in the water. The rest, which lies in between, means as good as nothing to either of us, and possibly not much more to Heinrich. Why she killed herself we can never know, and perhaps the poor girl didn't know herself."

Georg looked out the window and saw roofs, chimneys, rusty pipes, and rather close by, the light grey steeple with the openwork spire. The sky above it was pale and empty. It suddenly occurred to Georg that Nuernberger still had not asked a single word about Anna. What did he expect? That Georg had left her in the end, and that she would already have taken comfort with another lover? Why did I come to Vienna, he thought briefly,—as if his trip had had no other purpose than to receive lectures on existence from Nuernberger, which indeed turned out unpleasantly enough. It struck twelve. Georg said good-bye. Nuernberger accompanied him to the door and thanked him for the visit. He inquired with warmth, as though the earlier inquiry was purely a formality, about Georg's activities in his new place of residence, his work, his new acquaintances, and only now learned to what circumstances Georg owed the chance of his sudden call to the little town.

"That's what I always say," he then remarked, "it is not *we* who make our destiny, but usually it's done by some circumstance that is beyond us, which we are in no position to influence, which we can't even include in the circle of our calculations. Was it really . . . with all due respect for your talents, I can well say—was it the result of your own efforts, or those of the older Eissler, whose work on your behalf you once explained to me, that you were called to Detmold by telegram and so quickly found a circle of activity there? No. An innocent person, someone completely unknown to you, had to die a sudden death in order for you to find his place free. And how many other things, over which you likewise had no control and which you could not foresee, had to happen for you to leave Vienna with a light heart, yes, to even allow you to go at all?!"

"How do you mean, with a light heart?" Georg asked, put off.

"I mean, a lighter heart, than under other circumstances. If the little creature had remained alive, who knows if you . . ."

"You may be assured that I would have gone in that case too. And Anna would have found it just as natural as she does now. You don't believe that? Perhaps I would have left with an even lighter heart if the matter had turned out differently. It was Anna who advised me to accept. I was not at all decided on it. You really have no idea what a fine and intelligent person Anna is."

"Oh, I have no doubts about that. After all that you have told me on occasion about her, she evidently acquitted herself with more dignity than young ladies from her circles normally do in such circumstances."

"Dear Herr Nuernberger, the situation was really not all that bad."

"Ah, don't say that. If she was comforted by your nobility and considerateness, you may be convinced that the Fraulein also felt the irregularity of her situation even more often. There is not one single woman, however bold and superior, who would not rather wear a ring on her finger in such a predicament. And it speaks again for the wisdom and nobility of your friend that she never let you know it, and that she accepted the bitter disappointment at the end of these not entirely sweet nine months with understanding and composure."

"Disappointment is a mild word. Pain would perhaps be a better one."

"It surely was both. But as is usual, in this case too the burning wound of pain will heal faster than the tormenting, piercing wound of disappointment."

"I don't really understand you."

"Well dear Georg, you don't doubt that you would quite soon, probably by this time, have been married if the little one had survived."

"And you think that now, because we don't have a child . . . you are apparently of the opinion that . . . that . . . it's all over? Well you are mistaken dear friend, utterly mistaken."

"Dear Georg," Nuernberger responded, "we would both do well not to talk of the future. Neither you nor I know where at this moment the thread of our destiny is being spun. At the moment when the other *Kapellmeister* was being hit by the stroke, you felt nothing in the slightest. And when I wish you good luck in your continuing career, I have no idea on whom I may be calling down death by my well wishes."

They said farewell in the hallway. On the stairs Nuernberger called after Georg: "Let me hear from you once in a while."

Georg turned around once more: "And you do the same! . . ." He saw only the defensive, resigned wave of Nuernberger's hand, smiled involuntarily, and hurried down. At the next corner he took a wagon. On the way to the Golowski's he thought about Nuernberger and Bermann. What a strange relationship it was between them! An image appeared to Georg that looked like something he thought he had seen in a dream once. The two sat across from each other; each held up to the other a mirror in which they saw themselves with a mirror in their hand, and in that mirror they saw the other with a mirror in his hand, and on and on into infinity. Did the one really know the other there, did they really know themselves? Georg felt dizzy. Then he thought of Anna. Could Nuernberger be right again? Was it really over? Could it ever end? Ever? . . . Life is long! But weren't the next few months risky? Micaela perhaps. . . . No. That was not to be taken seriously, whatever happened. And by Easter he would be back in Vienna; then came summer; they would be together. And then? What then? Marriage? Herr and Frau Rosner's son-in-law, Josef's brother-in-law! Oh, what did he care about the family. It was Anna who would be his wife, that kind, gentle, intelligent creature.

The wagon stopped in front of a rather new, ugly, yellow painted house in a wide monotonous street. Georg asked the coachman to wait and went in the door. Inside, the house looked badly neglected; plaster was crumbling from the walls in many places, and the stairs were dirty. The smell of rancid fat came from a kitchen window. In the first floor corridor two fat Jewish women were talking in what was to Georg an unendurable jargon, and one of them said to a boy, "Moritz, let the gentleman pass." Why did she say that, Georg thought. There's plenty of room. She obviously wants something from me. As if I could be of some harm or use to her. And a phrase of Heinrich's from a past conversation occurred to him: "enemy country."

A servant girl let him into a room which he at once recognized as Leo's. Books and papers lay on the writing table, the piano was open, and an open travel bag, which was not yet fully unpacked, sat on the divan. The next minute the door opened; Leo walked in, threw his arms around his guest, and kissed him on both cheeks so quickly that the recipient of this hearty greeting had no time to be embarrassed. "This is very kind of you," said Leo and shook Georg's hand with both of his.

"You can hardly imagine how delighted I am . . ." Georg began.

"I believe you . . . but come in here with me. We were still eating—but we're almost finished."

He led him into the next room. The family was assembled at the table. "I believe you do not know my father yet," Leo remarked, and introduced them to each other. The older Golowski stood up, laid down his napkin, which he had tied around his neck, and gave Georg his hand.

Georg was surprised that the old man looked completely different than he had imagined; not patriarchal, grey-bearded, and venerable, but smooth-shaven, and with wide, crafty features, he looked at best like an aging provincial actor. "I'm very pleased to make your acquaintance, Herr Baron," he said, and in his astute eyes could be read: "I know everything."

Therese quickly asked Georg the customary questions: when he had arrived, how long he was staying, how things were going; he answered patiently and politely, and she looked into his face with lively curiosity. Then he asked Leo about his plans for the near future.

"First of all I have to do some serious piano practicing, so as not to disgrace myself in front of my students. The people were very nice to me. I've had books, as many as I wanted. But they have obviously not put a piano at my disposal." He turned to Therese: "You should really whip this up in one of your next speeches. Such cruel treatment of a prisoner has to be exposed."

"Yesterday at this time," said the old Golowski, "he wasn't able to laugh about it yet."

"If you perhaps think," Therese said, "that the stroke of luck you have had will change my views, you're seriously mistaken. Quite the contrary." And turning to Georg, she continued: "Theoretically I'm ab-

solutely opposed to their having released him." Speaking again to Leo
she continued: "If you had simply shot the rat to death, as was very
well your right, without this disgusting dueling act, you would not have
been released; you'd have sat for five or ten years for sure. But because
you engaged in this grizzly, state-condoned gamble of life and death,
because you bowed before the military world-view, you have been par-
doned. Am I not right?" she said, turning again to Georg.

He only nodded and thought of the poor young man whom Leo had
shot, and who actually had no more against the Jews than that they
had been as unappealing to him as they were to most other people—and
whose guilt at bottom had consisted only in that he had come up against
the wrong man. Leo stroked his sister's hair and said: "Look, if you
would express publicly what you have just said within the confines of
these four walls, then you would impress me."

"And you would impress me," Therese replied, "if you would buy
a ticket to Jerusalem with the old Ehrenberg tomorrow."

They stood up from the table. Leo invited Georg to follow him into
his room.

"Would I be disturbing you?" asked Therese. "I'd like to have some
time with him too."

The three of them sat in Leo's room and talked. Leo appeared to be
enjoying his newly regained freedom without hesitation or regrets,
which affected Georg strangely. Therese sat on the divan in a dark,
close-fitting dress and looked again today for the first time like the
young lady who had sat under the plane tree in Lugano as the
sweetheart of a cavalry officer, drank Asti, and afterward had kissed
someone else. She asked Georg to play the piano. She hadn't ever heard
him yet. He sat down, played some music from *Tristan*, and then improvised with considerable inspiration. Leo expressed his appreciation.

"What a shame he's not staying here," Therese said, leaning against
the wall and crossing her hands behind her high coiffure.

"I'm coming back for Easter," Georg replied and looked at her.

"But only to disappear again," said Therese.

"That's true," responded Georg, and it suddenly fell upon his soul
that this was not his home any more, that now he no longer even had
one, perhaps for a long time.

"How would it be," said Leo, "if we went hiking together this summer? You, Bermann, and I. I promise we won't bore you with theoretical discussions like we did last fall . . . do you still remember?"

"Ah," Therese said and straightened up, "as good as nothing will
come of that. Deeds, gentlemen!"

"And what will come of deeds?" asked Leo. "They are at most private solutions for the moment."

"Yes, deeds that one commits for oneself," said Therese. "Only what one is capable of doing for others, without vindictiveness, without vanity of a personal nature, anonymously if possible, only this do I call a deed."

Georg finally had to go. How much he still had to do!

"I'll go with you for a while," Therese said to him.

Leo hugged him once more and said: "This was really nice of you."

Therese left to get her hat and jacket. Georg went into the next room; old Frau Golowski seemed to have been waiting for him. She walked up to him with a strangely anxious look on her face and handed him an envelope.

"What's this?"

"The certificate, Herr Baron, I didn't want to give it to Anna . . . it might have upset her too much."

"Oh yes. . . ." He put the envelope away, and found that it felt different than others. . . .

Therese appeared in a small Spanish hat, ready to go. "Here I am. *Auf Wiedersehen*, Mama. I won't be home for supper."

She went down the stairs with Georg and looked at him with pleasure from the side.

"Where can I take you?" asked Georg.

"Just take me with you, I can get out anywhere."

They got in; the wagon pulled away. She asked him about all the things he had already answered about at home, as though she assumed that now, with her alone, he would give more candid answers than he did in front of the others. She learned nothing more than that he felt well in his new circumstances, and that his work gave him satisfaction. Had his appearance here been a big surprise for Anna? No, it wasn't; he had informed her about it. And was it really true that he was coming back at Easter? That was definitely his plan. . . .

She seemed amazed. "You know, I really had imagined . . ."

"What?"

"We would never see you again."

Somewhat taken aback, he did not answer. Then the thought went through his mind: Wouldn't that have been smarter? . . . He sat quite close to Therese, and felt the warmth of her body, just like before, in Lugano. In which of her dreams would she like to live now? In the dark delusion of the fulfillment of mankind, or the happy and lighthearted one of a new romantic adventure? She was looking earnestly out of the window. He took her hand, which she did not pull back, and lifted it to his lips. Suddenly she turned to him and said innocently: "So, why don't you stop here, it's the best place for me to get out."

He let go of her hand and looked at Therese.

"Yes, dear Georg, where does one turn," she said, "if one doesn't . . ." She made a derisive expression with her mouth, "have anything to offer to humanity? Do you know what I sometimes think? Maybe it's all just to get away from myself."

"Why . . . why are you trying to get away?"

"Farewell Georg." The wagon stopped. Therese got out and a young man stood still and stared at her; she vanished in the crowd. I don't think she'll end up on the scaffold, Georg thought. He went back to his hotel, ate lunch, had a cigarette, changed clothes, and went to the Ehrenbergs.

James, Sissy, Willy Eissler, and Frau Oberberger were assembled in the dining room with the ladies of the house, over black coffee. Georg took a seat between Else and Sissy, drank a glass of Benedictine, and answered all the questions concerning his new work patiently and with humor. Soon they all went into the salon, and first he sat for a while in the raised alcove with Frau Oberberger who looked very young again today and wanted, above all, to hear more about Georg's personal experiences in Detmold. She did not believe him that he had not been having affairs with the various woman singers, since she viewed theater life in general as an occasion and excuse for gallant adventures; in any case she suspected that all sorts of wickedness went on behind the scenes, in the wardrobes, and in the director's office. As Georg could not avoid disappointing her through his reports of the respectable, bourgeois, almost rigid lifestyle of the theater members, or through the description of a singular, work-filled existence, she began visibly to transform, and soon he sat across from an old woman in whom he recognized the same person that he had seen this past summer, first in a box in a little red and white theater, and later in an almost forgotten dream. Then he stood with Sissy by the marble Isis, and during the innocent conversation, each searched in the eyes of the other for the memory of a radiant hour in the deep afternoon shadows of a dark green park. But today it seemed to both of them as if sunk in inaccessible depths. Finally he sat with Else at the little table on which photographs and books were lying. At first she asked casual questions, like the others.

But suddenly, completely unexpected, and in a rather soft voice, she asked: "How's your child doing?"

"My child? . . ." He hesitated. "Tell me, Else, why do you really ask me that? . . . It's just curiosity."

"You're wrong, Georg," she responded calmly and earnestly, "just like you usually are about me. You regard me as quite shallow, or God knows what. Well, there's no point in talking about it any more. But in any case it's not so hard to understand why I'd ask about the child. I'd like very much to see it some time."

"You'd like to see it?" He was touched.

"Yes. I even have another idea . . . that you'll possibly find totally crazy."

"What is it, Else?"

"I was thinking that we could take it ourselves."

"Who is we?"

"James and I."

"To England?"

"Who told you we were going to England? We're staying here. We've already rented a place, a country cottage outside of town. Nobody has to know that it's your child."

"What a extraordinary idea."

"God, why extraordinary? Anna can't keep it herself, and you certainly can't either. Where would you put it during rehearsals? In the prompter's box?"

Georg smiled. "You're very kind, Else."

"But I'm not kind at all. I'm only thinking, why should an innocent little creature pay, or suffer, for the fact that . . . well yes, I mean, it's not the child's fault . . . finally. . . . Is it a boy?"

"It was a boy." He made a pause. Then he said softly: "It's dead." And he looked down.

"What? Oh, well, you just want to . . . protect yourself from my importunity."

"Else, how could you . . . No, Else. People don't lie about things like that."

"So, it's true? How did it . . ."

"It died at birth."

She looked at the floor. "No, how horrible!" She shook her head. "How horrible! . . . Now she has nothing left."

Georg recoiled slightly, but was not able to respond. How definitely it appeared to everyone that the story with Anna was over. And Else didn't feel sorry for him at all. She didn't even suspect how deeply the child's death had affected him. And how could she know! What did she know about the hour when the garden lost its colors, and the sky lost its light for him, because his beautiful child lay dead inside the house.

Frau Ehrenberg had walked up. She expressed her particular satisfaction to Georg. She had never doubted that he would be able to stand on his own as soon as he had found a career. And she was quite convinced that in three to five years they would have him here, in Vienna, as *Kapellmeister*. Georg demurred. For the time being he was not even thinking of returning to Vienna. He felt that one worked more, and more seriously, in Germany. Here one was always in danger of losing oneself.

Frau Ehrenberg agreed, and took the occasion to complain about Heinrich Bermann, who seemed to have given up writing and never came around any more.

Georg defended him, and felt obligated to firmly assert that he was working harder than ever. But Frau Ehrenberg had further examples of the destructive effect of the Viennese air. Nuernberger above all, who seemed to have totally retired from the world. And what had happened to Oskar . . . Could that have happened in any other city than Vienna? Did Georg know that Oskar was traveling with Prince von Guastalla? She acted as if she found nothing strange about it, and Georg observed, that she was a little proud of it, and somehow cherished the feeling that everything had finally turned out for the best with Oskar.

While Georg was talking to Frau Ehrenberg, he sometimes saw the gaze of Else, who had withdrawn into the alcove with James, directed at him,—a knowing, melancholy gaze, which almost looked right through him. He soon took his leave, felt an incomprehensibly strange handshake from Else, indifferently cordial ones from the others, and left.

How strange it is, he thought in the wagon that was taking him to Heinrich's. These people knew everything before he did himself. They knew about his relationship with Anna before it had even started—and now they knew before he did again that it was over. He had no vengeful desire to prove that they were all wrong. Of course, in matters like these one should not be guided by resentment. It was good that a few months were coming up in which he could collect himself again, and reconsider everything maturely. It would be good for Anna too; for her perhaps most especially. Yesterday's walk with her in the rain on the damp, brownish streets came back to him and seemed to him like something unspeakably sad. Oh, those hours in the vaulted room where the sound of the organ came in through the fluttering veil of snow! Where were they! These, and so many other wonderful hours, where had they gone! He saw himself and Anna in his mind again, a young couple on their honeymoon, walking through streets that held the marvelous breath of strangeness; banal hotel rooms in which he had stayed with her for but a few short days suddenly emerged before him, and were consecrated with the air of memory. . . . Then the beloved appeared to him on a white bench beneath fruit-laden branches, her lofty forehead flowed over by the illusionary anticipation of gentle motherhood—and finally she stood there with a sheet of music in her hand, and white curtains moved gently in the breeze. And when he realized that this was the same room in which she was now waiting for him—and that barely more than a year had gone by since that late summer evening hour when she, with his accompaniment, sang his song for him for the first time—he breathed deeply and almost with anguish in the corner of his wagon.

As he stood a few minutes later in Heinrich's room, he asked him not to consider this as a visit. He just had time for a handshake—tomorrow morning, if it was all right with him, he would pick him up for a walk . . . yes—it occurred to him while they were talking—for a sort of farewell walk in the forest at Salmansdorf.

Heinrich agreed, and asked him to stay for just a few minutes. Georg asked him jokingly if he had recovered from his flop this morning.

Heinrich indicated toward the writing table, where loose pages were lying, scribbled over with large agitated notes. "Do you know what that is? I've taken up the *Aegidius* again. A rather plausible ending came to me just before you arrived. If you're interested, I'll tell you more about it tomorrow."

"Certainly. I'm very excited. It's really good that you've been able to get right back to work."

"Yes, dear Georg, I really don't like to be completely alone. I have to find some company for myself as soon as possible, of my own choice. . . . Otherwise anyone comes who wants to, and one does not wish to be available to every ghost."

Georg explained that he had been to see Leo, and had found him in better spirits than he had ever expected.

Heinrich leaned against the writing table, both hands stuffed in his pants pockets, with a gently lowered head; the shaded lamp cast vague shadows on his face from below. "Why didn't you expect to find him happy? We . . . I at least would probably react the same way."

Georg sat on the arm of a black leather chair, his legs thrown over each other, hat and stick in his hand. "Maybe you're right," he said, "but I can't hide from you that, despite that, it was strange to think, as I looked into his cheerful face, that he had a human life on his conscience."

"That means," said Heinrich, who began to walk back and forth in the room, "it's one of those cases where the relation between cause and effect is so evident that one can calmly say: 'he killed,' without it almost seeming like wordplay. . . . On the whole, Georg, don't you think we see these things a little superficially. We have to see a dagger flash, or hear a bullet whistle, to understand that a murder's been committed. As if someone who simply let someone else die was often any different from a murderer through anything more than a higher level of indifference and cowardice. . . ."

"Are you reproaching yourself, Heinrich? If you'd known that it would turn out like this—you wouldn't have—let her die?"

"Maybe. I don't know. But I can tell you one thing, Georg; if she were still alive, that is, if I'd have forgiven her, as you liked to say on occasion, I'd have ended up more guilty than I am today. Yes, yes, that's the way it is. I won't hide from you, Georg, there was a night . . . a few nights, when I almost died of pain, of desperation, of . . . well, others would have taken it for remorse. But it was nothing of the sort. For in the very midst of my pain, in my desperation, I knew that this death meant something final, something conciliating, something pure. If I'd been weak, or less vain . . . as you'll well understand . . . had we become lovers again, something much worse than this death would've happened, for her too: disgust and torment, rage and hatred would've crept into our bed . . . Our memories would've been ruined piece-by-piece, yes, our love would've rotted alive. It wouldn't have worked. It would've been a crime to drag out this sick-to-death relationship, just like it's a crime—and in the future will come to be so regarded—to prolong the life of a person who is doomed to have a painful death. Any reasonable doctor will tell you that. And for that reason I'm far from reproaching myself. I won't try to justify myself to you or to anyone else in the world, but it's true just the same: I *can't* feel guilty. Sometimes it sickens me, but it has nothing in the slightest to do with feelings of guilt."

"Did you go there then?" asked Georg.

"Yes, I went there. I was even standing there when they lowered the casket into the ground. Yes. I went there with her mother." He stood at the window, completely in the dark, and shook himself. "No, I'll never forget it. Besides, it's just a lie that people find each other in a common sorrow. People never find each other if they don't already belong to each other. They only grow farther apart in difficult times. What a trip! When I think back about it! I read almost the whole time. It was just unendurable to talk with that ignorant old person. One hates no one more than someone unimportant who demands sympathy from you. And we stood together at the grave, her mother and I. Myself, the mother and a few actors from the little theater. . . . And later, I was sitting at an inn alone with her, after the funeral. A funeral dinner for two. A hopeless story, I tell you. And by the way, do you know where she's buried? At your lake, Georg. Yes. I thought about you a lot. You know where the cemetery is. Not a hundred paces from the Auhof. One has a delightful view of our lake, Georg; if one is alive, of course."

Georg experienced a vague dread. He stood up. "Unfortunately I have to go, Heinrich. I'm expected. Forgive me."

Heinrich stepped out of the darkness by the window toward him. "Thanks very much for your visit. Tomorrow then, right? You're going to see Anna now? Please give her my greetings. I hear she's doing fine. Therese told me."

"Yes, she looks excellent. She's completely recovered."

"I'm glad. So, until tomorrow, right? I'm glad I'll be able to see you once more before you leave. You'll have to tell me about everything. Once again I've done nothing but talk about myself."

Georg smiled. As if he wasn't used to that from Heinrich! "*Auf Wiedersehen,*" he said, and left.

A lot of what Heinrich said continued to reverberate in Georg as he sat in the wagon again. "We have to see a dagger flash to understand that a murder has been committed." Georg felt that a so to speak subterranean, but long suspected connection ran from the meaning of these words to a vague anxiety he sometimes felt in his soul. He remembered a moment when it had seemed to him that a game was being played somewhere in the clouds over his unborn son, and it suddenly appeared strange to him that Anna had not yet spoken a single word to him about the death of their child, that even in her letters she had completely avoided any mention, not only of the unfortunate outcome, but of the whole expanse of time in which she carried the child within her. The wagon neared its goal. Why is my heart pounding, thought Georg. Joy? . . . Bad conscience? So suddenly today! She surely can't blame me? . . . What nonsense. I'm anxious and agitated at the same time, that's all. I shouldn't have come here. Why did I see all these people again? Wouldn't I have been a thousand times happier, in spite of my longing, to have stayed in the little town where a new life has begun for me? . . . I could have gotten together with Anna somewhere else. Maybe she'll go with me. . . . Then everything could still be straightened out. But is something wrong then? . . . Is our relationship finally sick too, and is it a crime to drag it out? . . . That could be just a convenient excuse.

As he entered the Rosners, the mother sat alone at the table, looked up from a book, and closed it. The light from a gently swaying lamp shone down from above, evenly on all sides of the table. Josef got up from a corner of the divan. Anna came out of her room, arranged her high-combed, wavy hair with both hands, greeted Georg with a light nod of the head, and looked to him at this moment more like an apparition than a real figure. Georg shook hands with everyone and inquired about the condition of Herr Rosner.

"It's not going too bad for him," said Frau Rosner. "But it's difficult for him to get up."

Josef apologized for having been caught sleeping on the divan. He had to use his Sundays to rest up. He held a position with a newspaper that kept him sometimes until three in the morning.

"He's very ambitious now," his mother confirmed.

"Yes," Josef said modestly, "when one has a circle of influence . . ." He further remarked that the *Christian People's Messenger* enjoyed an ever-increasing circulation, even in Germany. Then he asked Georg a few questions about his new place of residence, and showed a lively interest in population numbers, the condition of the roads, the extent of cycling sports, and the countryside.

Frau Rosner asked politely about the repertoire schedule, Georg gave the particulars, and soon a conversation was under way in which Anna too took part; and Georg suddenly found himself visiting a middle-class family with polite manners, in which the daughter of the house was musical. Finally the conversation led to a point where Georg found himself induced to express the wish to hear the young lady sing again—and he had to remember at the same time that it was his Anna whose voice he had asked to hear.

Josef excused himself; a rendezvous at a coffeehouse with club members called him away. . . ."Can you still remember . . . the happy group out at the Sophienalpe?"

"Sure," said Georg, smiling. And he quoted: "The Lord Who Makes Iron . . ."

"Wants No Bondsmen," Josef continued. "But we haven't sung that for a long time. It's too related to *Watch on the Rhine*; and we don't want people to say that we're squinting over the border any more. It led to some big fights for us on the committee. One man even resigned. He's an attorney in the office of Doctor Fuchs, the German national deputy. It's all politics." He winked. One should not think that he still took this humbug seriously, now that he himself had some insight into the machinery of public life. With the hardly surprising remark that he could really tell some stories, he excused himself. Frau Rosner decided it was time to check up on her husband.

Georg sat across from Anna, alone at the round table over which the light of the hanging lamp shone.

"Thank you for the lovely roses," said Anna, "I have them in there in my room." She got up and Georg followed her. He had completely forgotten that he had sent her flowers. They stood in a tall glass in front of the mirror, deep red, and reflected back colorlessly dark. The piano was open, music was out, and two candles burned at the sides. Otherwise there was only as much light as came in from the other room through the opening in the door.

"Have you been playing, Anna?" He walked further in. "The countess's aria?[3] And singing?"

"Yes. I tried."

"How did it go?"

"It's a start . . . it seems to me. Well, we'll see. But first tell me what you've been doing all day."

"In a minute. But we haven't greeted each other yet today." He put his arms around her and kissed her.

"It's been quite a while," she said, looking past him with a smile.

"So," he asked cheerfully, "will you come with me?"

Anna hesitated. "What actually are you planning, Georg?"

---

3. No doubt *Dove sono* from Act III of Mozart's *The Marriage of Figaro,* where Countess Almaviva sings her lost love for the Count:

> Where are they, those beautiful moments
> Of sweetness and delight;
> Where have they gone, the vows
> Of your deceitful lips?

"Very simple. We could leave tomorrow afternoon. Choice of destination is up to you. Reichenau, Semmering, Bruehl, wherever you want. . . . And early the day after tomorrow I'll come back with you." Something kept him from mentioning the telegram that had put a full three days at his disposal.

Anna looked down. "That would be nice," she said without tone, "but it's just not possible, Georg."

"Because of your father?"

She nodded.

"Isn't he getting better?"

"No, he's not well at all. He's so weak. Of course they wouldn't directly criticize me. But I . . . just *can't* leave my mother alone now to take a little holiday."

He shrugged his shoulders, a little hurt about the expression she had chosen.

"And tell me honestly," she said as if teasing, "is it really all that important to you?"

He shook his head, almost painfully. But he felt that this gesture too lacked sincerity. "I don't understand you, Anna," he said more weakly than he had wished. "That a few weeks of being apart, that the . . . well, I really don't know what to call it. . . . It's like we've lost ourselves. But it's *me*, Anna, it's *me*. . . ." he repeated heavily but wearily. He sat down in the armchair in front of the piano. He took her hands, and lifted them to his lips, distracted and a little stirred.

"How was it at *Tristan*?" she asked.

He reported assiduously on the performance, did not omit his visit to the Ehrenbergs' box, told her about all the other people he had seen, and delivered the greetings from Heinrich Bermann. Then he pulled her down onto his knees and kissed her. As his face pulled back from hers, he saw tears streaming down her cheeks. He pretended that he didn't understand. "What's wrong, darling? . . . What is it, why . . ."

She got up, went to the window, her face turned away from him. Now he stood up, somewhat impatient, walked back and forth across the room a few times, finally walked up to her, drew close, and began again suddenly, hastily, "Anna! Reconsider if you couldn't come with me. It will all be so different than here. One could speak out. We have such important things to talk about. And I need your advice—about my decision for next year. I wrote to you about it, didn't I? It's very possible that in the next few days they will offer me a three-year contract."

"What should one advise you?" she said. "You're the one who knows best if you like it there or not."

He began to explain about the cordial and talented director, who obviously wanted to attract him there as a colleague, about the old *Kapellmeister* for whom he felt such sympathy, and who had once been so famous, about an extremely short stagehand that they called Alexander the Great, about a young lady that he had studied Micaela with and who was engaged to a Berlin doctor, about a tenor who had worked twenty-seven years at the theater and who utterly hated Wagner. Then he began to talk about his personal prospects in both artistic and material respects. Without a doubt he could achieve a secure and profitable position at the little court theater very quickly. On the other hand, it had to be considered that it could be risky to tie oneself down for too long; a career like that of the old *Kapellmeister* was not to his liking. Of course . . . their temperaments were different; he, for his part, believed himself immune to such a fate.

Anna just looked at him the whole time, and in an indulgently derisive tone, as if she were speaking to a child, she finally said: "Aw, how he exerts himself."

He was stunned. "In what way am I exerting myself."

"Look, Georg, you don't owe me any explanations."

"Explanations? You're really . . . I wasn't giving you any explanations, Anna. I was simply describing for you how I live, and what sort of people I work with . . . because I flatter myself that these things interest you;—just like I told you where I had been today and yesterday."

She fell silent. And Georg felt again that she didn't believe him, that she had a right not to believe him—even when it happened to be the truth on his lips. All sorts of words poured at him, words of irritation, of anger, of gentle consolation—and all struck him as worthless and empty. He answered nothing, sat down at the piano and struck some soft notes and chords. Now it seemed to him again that he loved her deeply and just couldn't tell her, and as if this hour of reunion had turned out quite differently than if they had enjoyed it somewhere else. Not in this room, not in this city; the best would be in a place that neither of them knew, in strange, new, surroundings. Yes, then perhaps everything would be like it used to be again. Then they would be able to hold each other in their arms—like once before, in yearning, in bliss—and in peace. The thought went through his mind: If only I said to her: Anna! Three days and three nights belong to us! If I asked her . . . with the right words . . . implored her at her feet . . . come with me! come . . . she wouldn't resist long! Surely she'd follow me. . . . He knew it. Why didn't he say the right words? Why didn't he implore her? Why did he say nothing, and sit at the piano with his back turned, playing soft notes and chords? . . . Why? . . . Then he felt her soft hands on his head. His fingers lay heavily on the keys, while a chord continued ringing. He didn't dare to turn around. He felt: she knows it too. What does she know? . . . Is it true then? . . . Yes . . . it's true. And he thought of the hour after the birth of his dead child—when he had sat beside her bed and she had lain there silently, looking into the dusky garden. . . . At that moment she knew it already—before he did—that everything was over. He lifted his hands from the piano, took hers, which were still lying on his head, put them against his cheeks, pulled her toward him until she was very close again, and she slowly sank down onto his knees. And he began shyly again: "Anna . . . possibly . . . couldn't you still decide . . . Maybe it would be possible for me too, if I telegraphed, to get a few more days of leave. Anna . . . listen . . . it would be so wonderful. . . ." A plan came from deep inside him. What if he really did go away with her for a few days. And he took this opportunity to honestly say to her: It's over Anna! But the end of our love should be beautiful, like the beginning was. Not tired and sad like these hours in your parents home. . . . If I said this to her honestly—somewhere in the country . . . wouldn't it be more worthy of us—and our vanished happiness? . . . And he felt more urgent about this plan, bolder, passionate almost . . . and his words sounded again like they did long, long ago.

Sitting on his knees, her arms around his neck, she softly replied: "I'm not going through this again, Georg."

He already had words on his lips to divert her concerns. But he held back. For, once expressed, it would only have indicated that he was just thinking about enjoying a few more hours of pleasure with her, but that he was not inclined to take on any sort of obligations. He felt it: in order not to hurt her he had only to say: You belong to me forever! You shall have my child! By Christmas, or Easter at the latest, I will come for you—and we will never be separated again. He felt that these words were awaited with a last hope—with a hope whose fulfillment she no longer expected. But he said nothing. If he had said what she longed for, he would have tied himself down again, and—now he realized, deeper than he ever had before—that he wanted to be free.

She was still sitting on his knees, her cheek pressed against his; they were silent for a long time, and knew that this was farewell.

Finally Georg said resolutely: "If you don't want to come with me, Anna, I'm going back right away—tomorrow. And we won't see each other again until spring. Until then it will be only letters again. It could be, that at Christmas, if it's possible . . ."

She had gotten up and leaned against the piano. "You're being thoughtless again," she said. "Wouldn't it be even better if we didn't see each other again until Easter?"

"Why better?"

"By then—everything will be clearer."

He didn't wish to understand her. "You mean, the contract? Yes . . . I have to decide about that in the next few weeks. They will want to know where they stand. On the other hand, even if I sign for the three years, and other opportunities came along, they wouldn't hold me there against my will. But so far it looks like the position in the little town is very useful for me. I've never been able to work so intensively as there. Haven't I written how sometimes I've sat at my desk after the theater until three in the morning? And was done sleeping and feeling fresh by eight?"

She continued to look at him with a look that was painful and in-dulgent at the same time, that struck him as a look of despair. Had she never believed in him? Had she never trustingly and tenderly said to him, in a half-darkened church: "I will pray to heaven that you will become a great artist." Again it seemed to him that she did not think as much of him any more as she did before. He felt disturbed, and asked her hesitantly: "Is it still all right if I send you my violin sonata as soon as it's finished? You know there's no one whose judgment I trust as much as yours." And he thought: if I could still keep her as a friend . . . or win her back again . . . as a friend . . . Would it be possible?

She said: "You also wrote to me about a couple of fantasies, for piano solo."

"That's true. They aren't quite finished yet. But there's another one that I . . . that I . . ."—he felt foolish that he hesitated—"composed this summer, by the lake where that poor girl drowned, Heinrich's girl-friend, a piece you don't know about yet. Couldn't I . . . I could play it for you softly, if you wanted."

She nodded and closed the door. She stood there behind him, mo-tionless, as he began.

And he played. He played the little, passionate, melancholy piece that he had composed by his lake, while Anna and the child were com-pletely forgotten to him. It relieved him immensely to be able to play it for her. She would have to understand what these tones said to her. It was quite impossible that she would not understand. He heard himself speaking, as it were from these tones; it even seemed to him as if he only now fully understood himself. Farewell, my darling, farewell. It was beautiful. And now it is over. . . . Farewell, darling. . . . We have lived as we have both chosen. And what ever happens now, for you and for me, we will always be something unforgettable to each other. Now my life goes another way. . . . And yours too. It must come to an end . . . . I loved you. I kiss your eyes . . . and I thank you, you kind, gentle, silent creature. Farewell, my darling, farewell. . . . The tones died away. He had not looked up from the keys while he played; now he slowly turned toward her. She stood earnestly, with gently trembling lips, behind him. He took her hands and kissed them. "Anna, Anna . . . !" he cried out. His heart wanted to burst.

"Don't forget me completely," she said softly.

"I'll write as soon as I'm back."

She nodded.

"And you write back to me, Anna. . . . And everything . . . everything . . . you understand me."

She nodded again.

"And . . . and early tomorrow I'll see you one more time."

She shook her head. He wanted to respond as if surprised—as if it were self-evident that he had to see her once more before his departure. She gently raised her hand, as though asking him to be quiet. He stood up, pulled her to him, kissed her mouth, which was cool and did not answer his kiss, and left the room. She remained behind, standing with limp arms, her eyes closed. He hurried down the stairs. Below, on the street, it seemed to him that he had to go back—to say to her: "It isn't true. That was not farewell. I love you. I belong to you. It can't be over. . . ."

But he felt that he couldn't. Not now. Tomorrow perhaps. She wouldn't slip away from him between tonight and tomorrow morning. . . . And he hurried along, without a plan, through empty streets, as though in a mild frenzy of pain and freedom. He was glad that he had made no plans with anyone, and could be alone. He had supper far in the outskirts, in a quiet corner of a low, old, smokey inn where people from another world sat at the other tables, and he seemed to be in a strange city: alone; a little proud of his solitude, and a little shocked by his pride.

The next day at noon Georg walked with Heinrich along the avenues of Dornbacher Park. An air which was heavy with thin fog surrounded them; damp foliage crackled and glittered under their feet, and through the bushes glimmered the road which had taken them into the red and yellow hills exactly one year ago. The branches spread out motionlessly, as though the distant oppressiveness of the overcast sun weighed them down.

Heinrich was about to explain the conclusion of his drama that had occurred to him yesterday. Aegidius had landed on the island, determined, after his seven-day funeral journey, to meet the fate which had been foretold for him. The prince offered him his life, but he refused and threw himself down from the cliff into the sea.

Georg was not satisfied. "Why does Aegidius have to die?" He was not convinced of this.

Heinrich did not understand why this should have to be explained. "How can he go on living?" he cried. "He was condemned to death. Always in the light of the end, as the limitless master on the ship, lover of the princess, friend of wise men, singers, astrologers, but always in the light of the end, he lived the noblest days that ever a man was given. This whole richness would have lost its meaning, so to speak; the whole majestic and lofty expectation of the final moment would be degraded in Aegidius's memory to a ridiculously foolish fear of death if this funeral journey ended up as an insipid joke. That's why he has to die."

"And you really believe that?" Georg asked, with even stronger skepticism than before. "I can't help it, I don't."

"That doesn't matter," answered Heinrich. "If it seemed true to you so soon, it would have been too easy for me. But when the last syllable of my piece is written, it will have become true. Or . . ." He didn't finish. They came to a meadow, and soon the familiar valley spread out before their feet. To the right, along the slopes of the hills, glimmered Sommerhaidenweg; on the other side, right on the edge of the forest, could be seen the yellow painted inn with the red wooden terrace, and not far from that, the little house with the dark grey gable. The city could be made out through the uncertain fog; further off, the plains rose up faintly, while a low drawn line of mountains faded off into the far distance. Now they had to cross a wide highway, and finally a walking path led downward across meadows and fields. Set far back from the path, the forest rested on both sides.

Georg felt a presentiment of the longing he would feel in years to come, perhaps even by tomorrow, when remembering this landscape, which had now ceased to be his homeland.

Finally they stood in front of the little house with the gable, which Georg had wanted to see for the last time. The doors and windows were boarded up; it stood there decaying, as though old before its time, and wished to know nothing of the world outside.

"Well, it's time to say good-bye," Georg said in a soft tone. His eyes fell on the clay figure in the middle of the faded flower beds. "Funny," he said to Heinrich, "I always took that blue boy for an angel. I mean, that's what I called him, but I always knew what he looked like, and that he really was a mischievous little boy, barefoot, in a belted coat."

"And a year from now," said Heinrich, "you'll be swearing that the blue boy had wings."

Georg cast a glance up at the mansard room. It seemed to him that the possibility existed for somebody to suddenly come walking out onto the balcony. Labinski perhaps, who had not reported in since that last dream? Or he himself, a Georg von Wergenthin from an earlier time? The Georg from this summer, who had lived up there? Silly ideas. The balcony remained empty, the house was silent, and the garden slept deeply. Disappointed, Georg turned around. "Come on," he said to Heinrich. They left and took the road to Sommerhaidenweg.

"It's really gotten warm," Heinrich said, took off his coat, and threw it over his shoulder in his customary way.

A bleak and rather dry memory came to Georg. He turned to Heinrich. "I want to tell you something. The story is over."

Heinrich quickly looked at him from the side, then he nodded, not particularly surprised.

"But," Georg added in a feeble attempt at a joke, "you are earnestly requested not to think about the angel boy."

Heinrich shook his head earnestly. "Thanks. You can dedicate the story about the blue angel to Nuernberger."

"He was right again," said Georg.

"He's always right, dear Georg. One can never be deceived when one mistrusts everything on earth, even one's own mistrust. Even if you had married Anna, he would've been right . . . or at least it would've seemed that way to you. But in any case I think . . . permit me to speak openly . . . it's good the way it turned out."

"Good? For me, sure," Georg answered with deliberate sharpness, as though he had absolutely no intention of glossing over his own handling of the situation. "In your sense Heinrich, it was perhaps even a duty to myself to bring it to an end."

"In that case it was also your duty toward Anna," Heinrich said.

"That remains to be seen. Who knows if I haven't deflected her from her path."

"From her path?"

"Do you still remember how Leo Golowski once said of her that she was destined to end up middle class?"

"Do you think, Georg, that a marriage with you would've become something middle class? Anna might have been made to be your lover—not your wife. Who knows if the one that she finally marries may not have every reason to thank you, if men weren't so blasted stupid. People only have pure memories of something after they have experienced it. Women as well as us."

They continued walking down Sommerhaidenweg, in the direction of the city, which rose out of the grey fog, and approached the cemetery.

"Does it really make any sense," Georg asked hesitantly, "to visit the grave of someone who never lived?"

"Your child is buried in there?"

Georg nodded. His child! How strange it still sounded! They walked along the brown, wooden fence over which tombstones and crosses rose, up to a low, brick wall to the entrance. An attendant whom they asked showed them the way along the broad, willow-lined middle road. In an open field, right next to the fence, on low, randomly strewn hills, little oval plots arranged themselves, each with two small stakes driven into the ground. The hill Georg was looking for lay in the middle of the field. Dark red roses lay on it. Georg recognized them. His heart stood still. How good it is that we did not meet here. Could she have been hoping for that?

"The one with the roses on it?" asked Heinrich.

Georg nodded.

They stood for a while, silently. "Apparently," asked Heinrich, "you never thought during the whole time of the possibility that it could end up like this?"

"Never? I don't know about that. All sorts of possibilities go through one's mind. But of course I never took them seriously. Why should one?" He explained to Heinrich, not for the first time, how the professor had explained the child's death at the time. It had been an unfortunate accident, whereby only one or two percent of newborns die. Of course, why this accident had occurred precisely *here*, the professor was unable to say. But wasn't accident just a word? Didn't this accident too finally have to have its cause? . . .

Heinrich shrugged his shoulders. "Of course . . . one cause after the other, and the last cause at the beginning of everything. We could certainly prevent a lot of these so-called accidents if we just had more insight, more understanding, and more power. Who knows if even the death of your child might not have been prevented at some point."

"And possibly it was even within my power," Georg said slowly.

"I don't understand. Were there some sort of indications, or . . ."

Georg stood there, his gaze fixed on the little mound. "I want to ask you something, Heinrich, but don't laugh at me. Do you think it's possible that an unborn child could die because one didn't want it as much as one should: from too little love, so to speak?"

Heinrich put his hand on his shoulder. "Georg, how did someone who is otherwise such a reasonable person, get this sort of metaphysical idea?"

"Call it whatever you want, metaphysical or stupid: I haven't been able to get the idea out of my head for a while now, that to some extent I bear the guilt for the way it turned out."

"You?"

"When I said before that I didn't want it enough, I didn't express it very well. The truth is: that I had frankly forgotten about this little creature who should have come into the world. And particularly in the last few weeks before its birth, I had completely forgotten. I can't say it any differently. Of course I always knew what was coming, but it didn't concern me, so to speak. I just went on living, without thinking about it. Not always, but often, and especially during the summer, at the lake, by my lake as you call it . . . I was . . . I simply didn't realize that I was going to have a child."

"People told me all sorts of things," Heinrich said, looking past him.

Georg looked at him. "Then you know what I mean. Not only from the child, who wasn't born yet, but I was removed from the mother too, in such an uncanny way that I can't describe it to you for the life of me. I can hardly grasp it myself. And there are moments when I just can't help thinking that there must be some connection between my forgetting and the death of my child. Do you think that something of that kind is totally impossible?"

Heinrich had deep wrinkles on his forehead. "One really can't say totally impossible. The roots are often so deeply entangled that we can't see all the way down. Yes, perhaps there are even connections of that kind. But if there are . . . not for you, Georg! These connections don't have any validity for you, even if they exist."

"No validity for me?"

"The whole idea that you just expressed doesn't strike me as like you. It didn't originate in your own mind. Absolutely not. Nothing like that would ever have occurred to you in your life, if you hadn't been associating with a character like me, and if it weren't sometimes your way, not to think your own thoughts, but rather those of someone else who was stronger—or weaker than yourself. And I assure you, whatever you may have done out there by your . . . by our lake . . . you didn't lay any so-called guilt on yourself by it. For someone else it might have been guilt. But with you, who are by nature—forgive me—rather frivolous and a little amoral, it certainly isn't guilt. Shall I tell you something? You don't feel at all guilty with regard to the child, but the discomfort that you feel comes only from the obligation you believe you have to feel guilty. You see, if I had gone through some kind of adventure like yours, I would possibly have become guilty, because I might have felt guilty."

"You would have felt guilty in my situation, Heinrich?"

"Maybe not. How can I know. You're probably thinking that I recently sent someone directly to her death, and that despite that I still feel myself free of guilt, so to speak?"

"Yes, I was thinking that. So I don't understand . . ."

Heinrich shrugged his shoulders. "Yes, I have felt free of guilt. Somewhere in my mind. And somewhere else, deeper perhaps, I have felt guilty . . . and still deeper, innocent again. It's always only a matter of how deeply we look inside ourselves. And if the lights on all floors are turned on, all of us are, at the same time: guilty and innocent, cowards and heroes, fools and wise men. 'We'—maybe that's too general an expression. With you, for example, Georg, all these things may be more simple, at least when you're not being influenced by the atmosphere that I sometimes spread around you. That's why you're better off than me. Much better. I look a mess inside. Haven't you noticed that? What good does it do me that the lights are burning on all the floors? What good does my knowledge of people and my superior understanding do me? None. . . . Less than none. At bottom I'd like nothing better, George, than that all this awful business had been no more than a bad dream. I swear, Georg, I'd give my whole future, and God knows what else, if only I could undo it all. And if it were undone . . . I might be just as miserable as I am now."

His face contorted as if he wanted to cry out. But he just stood there, stiff, motionless, pale, as if extinguished. And he said: "Believe me Georg, there are moments when I envy the people with a so-called world-view. If I ever want to have a well-ordered world, I'm going to have to develop one for myself first. It's tiring for anyone who's not God himself."

He sighed heavily. Georg gave up replying to him. He walked beneath the willows with him to the gate. He knew that this person could not be helped. At some time he was surely destined to throw himself from a tower he had ascended in winding spirals; and that would be his end. But Georg was well, and quite satisfied. He made the decision to use the three days that remained to him as intelligently as possible. The best thing would be to spend them alone somewhere in a beautiful, quiet landscape, to rest up and collect himself for new work. He had brought the manuscript of the violin sonata with him to Vienna. He wanted to finish this before anything else.

They went through the gate and stood out on the street. Georg turned around, but the cemetery wall blocked his view. In a few steps he again had an open view of the valley. Now he could only guess where the little house with the grey gable stood; it was no longer visible from here. Over the red and yellow hills which enclosed the scene the sky descended in a faint autumn glow. In Georg's soul there was a soft farewell to many joys and pains, which he could hear, as it were, dying away in the valley he has now leaving; and at the same time, a greeting from unknown days which sounded toward his youth from the far-off expanses of the world.

Designer: UC Press Staff
Compositor: Prestige Typography
Text: 10/13 Sabon
Display: Sabon
Printer: Malloy Lithographing, Inc.
Binder: John H. Dekker & Sons